WARHAWK

Other Novels and Novellas

*Many of these titles are also available as abridged and unabridged audiobooks.
Order the full range of Horus Heresy novels and audiobooks from
blacklibrary.com*

Download the full range of Horus Heresy audio dramas from
blacklibrary.com

THE HORUS HERESY®
SIEGE OF **TERRA**

WARHAWK

Chris Wraight

BLACK LIBRARY

A BLACK LIBRARY PUBLICATION

First published in 2021.
This edition published in Great Britain in 2023 by
Black Library, Games Workshop Ltd.,
Willow Road, Nottingham, NG7 2WS, UK.

Represented by: Games Workshop Limited – Irish branch,
Unit 3, Lower Liffey Street, Dublin 1,
D01 K199, Ireland.

10 9 8 7 6 5 4 3 2

Produced by Games Workshop in Nottingham.
Cover illustration by Neil Roberts.

A CIP record for this book is available from the British Library.

ISBN 13: 978-1-78999-387-5

See Black Library on the internet at

blacklibrary.com

Find out more about Games Workshop
and the worlds of Warhammer at

games-workshop.com

Printed and bound by CPI Group (UK) Ltd, Croydon, CR0 4YY

To Hannah, with love.

THE HORUS HERESY
SIEGE OF TERRA

It is a time of legend.

The galaxy is in flames. The Emperor's glorious vision for humanity is in ruins. His favoured son, Horus, has turned from his father's light and embraced Chaos.

His armies, the mighty and redoubtable Space Marines, are locked in a brutal civil war. Once, these ultimate warriors fought side by side as brothers, protecting the galaxy and bringing mankind back into the Emperor's light. Now they are divided.

Some remain loyal to the Emperor, whilst others have sided with the Warmaster. Pre-eminent amongst them, the leaders of their thousands-strong Legions, are the primarchs. Magnificent, superhuman beings, they are the crowning achievement of the Emperor's genetic science. Thrust into battle against one another, victory is uncertain for either side.

Worlds are burning. At Isstvan V, Horus dealt a vicious blow and three loyal Legions were all but destroyed. War was begun, a conflict that will engulf all mankind in fire. Treachery and betrayal have usurped honour and nobility. Assassins lurk in every shadow. Armies are gathering. All must choose a side or die.

Horus musters his armada, Terra itself the object of his wrath. Seated upon the Golden Throne, the Emperor waits for his wayward son to return. But his true enemy is Chaos, a primordial force that seeks to enslave mankind to its capricious whims.

The screams of the innocent, the pleas of the righteous resound to the cruel laughter of Dark Gods. Suffering and damnation await all should the Emperor fail and the war be lost.

The end is here. The skies darken, colossal armies gather. For the fate of the Throneworld, for the fate of mankind itself... The Siege of Terra has begun.

DRAMATIS PERSONAE

The Primarchs

JAGHATAI KHAN	'The Warhawk', Primarch of the V Legion
MORTARION	'The Pale King', Primarch of the XIV Legion
ROGAL DORN	Praetorian of Terra, Primarch of the VII Legion
SANGUINIUS	'The Great Angel', Primarch of the IX Legion

The V Legion 'White Scars'

SHIBAN KHAN	Called 'Tachseer', Brotherhood of the Storm
YIMAN	Brotherhood of the Storm
CHAKAJA	Brotherhood of the Storm
QIN FAI	Noyan-khan
GANZORIG	Noyan-khan
JANGSAI KHAN	Brotherhood of the Iron Axe
NARANBAATAR	Chief of Stormseers
NAMAHI	Master of the Keshig
ILYA RAVALLION	Called 'the Sage', Counsellor to the Legion
SOJUK KHAN	Ilya's adjutant

The VII Legion 'Imperial Fists'

SIGISMUND	First Captain, Master of Templars
FAFNIR RANN	Captain, First Assault Cadre
ARCHAMUS	Master of the Huscarls

The XII Legion 'World Eaters'

KHÂRN — Captain, Eighth Assault Company
SKARR-HEI — Berserker

The XIV Legion 'Death Guard'

TYPHUS — First Captain
CAIPHA MORARG — Equerry to the Primarch
ZADAL CROSIUS — Apothecary
GREMUS KALGARO — Siegemaster, Master of Ordnance
GURGANA DHUKH — Sergeant

The XVI Legion 'Sons of Horus'

AZELAS BARAXA — Captain, Second Company
INDRAS ARCHETA — Captain, Third Company
XHOFAR BERUDDIN — Captain, Fifth Company

Talons of the Emperor

CONSTANTIN VALDOR — Captain-general of the Legio Custodes
DIOCLETIAN — Tribune, Legio Custodes
AMON TAUROMACHIAN — Custodian

Crew, 'Aika 73'

TALVET KASKA — Commander
ADRIA VOSCH — Main Gunner
ERIA JANDEV — Front Gunner
HELWA DRESI — Driver
GURT MERCK — Loader

Imperial Army

BRAN KOBA	Sergeant, 13th Astranian Void-Jackals
JERA TALMADA	Colonel, Departmento Munitorum
AYO NUTA	Major-general, Terran Orbital Command
KATSUHIRO	Trooper

In the Ruins of the Palace

BASILIO FO	Former Blackstone inmate
EUPHRATI KEELER	Former Remembrancer
GARVIEL LOKEN	'The Lone Wolf', Chosen of Malcador

The Neverborn

THE REMNANT	A Daemon

Others

ERDA	Perpetual
LEETU	Her Legionary
ACTAE	Sorceress
ALPHARIUS	Her Companion
JOHN GRAMMATICUS	Logokine
OLL PERSSON	Perpetual
DOGENT KRANK	
BALE RANE	
GRAFT	
HEBET ZYBES	
KATT	

MALCADOR THE SIGILLITE	Regent of the Imperium
KHALID HASSAN	Chosen of the Sigillite
EREBUS	The Hand of Destiny

PART ONE

ONE

The blade
Handing over
New blood

It begins under stone.

Hidden, folded up in darkness, cold as the breath of winter dawn. The people of Ong-Hashin come for it, as they have done for as long as songs have been sung in their high valley, lodged between the Takal Shoulder and the eastern fringe of the Great Borai Plain. They climb the narrow ways, leather-bound feet slipping against the rock, hauling their own picks and baskets.

The ways down are hand-cut, supported with timber frames. The lintels of those frames are scraped with angular glyphs, made with the same blunt knives they use for prising stones from their mounts' hooves. These are not high calligraphic marks, but the marks of a hard people, used to rockfalls and landslips. They wish to delve for it, to find it, then return. They do not love the deep places, the cool sweat of the narrow tunnels, for they are Chogorian after all, and like the open wind on their faces.

When they hack it out, it is brittle. Blacksand, they call it. It

crumbles in your hand, if you treat it roughly, once out of the
earth. A few moments later, though, and it is hard, so much
so that you can toss it into a basket and start to work at the
lode again. If you hold it up – a chunk the size of a man's
fist – you can see the sparkling fragments within, catching the
light of subterranean candles.

Once done, they take it all back down the track, picking
their way carefully. It rains often, as the Takal Peaks capture the
moisture rolling across the open lands, and the rocks are greasy
with moss. This party returns to a settlement deep in Hashin
country, perched between pine stands, frigid and mist-clouded.
They take the blacksand pieces and haggle with the blademakers. This takes a long time, and is a bad-tempered affair.
Those who have laboured to obtain it are weary and need to
sleep. Those who wish to take it are anxious to get to work.
And the sun is low, by then. No bargains are well made at
dusk, the sages say.

The following dawn, and the labour begins. In Hashin,
blademakers always come in pairs – a man, a woman. They
need to know one another very well. Sometimes they are
siblings; more often, bonded couples. The charcoal furnaces
are stoked until the flames spit. The blacksand chunks are
turned and assessed again, then placed in long-handled pliers.
At this stage, the man works the fire, the woman handles
the pliers. Both wear thin cotton shirts, despite the chill of the
air outside. Inside the forge, it is already punishingly hot, and
their exposed flesh glistens.

Once hot enough, the chunks are withdrawn from the fires
and beaten. The man takes up a hammer, striking hard. The
woman directs him, shifting the red metal over the anvil's
blunt surface. Impurities are beaten out. It is gruelling work, a
process that jars bones. The process is repeated, over and over,
until the steel starts to purify. The beaten flakes are broken up,

doused in cold water, then re-melted and re-struck. Plates are created, stacked on top of one another, then gently placed back into the flames, melted, compacted, re-melted. Both parties scrutinise, checking for flaws.

Neither speaks. If they need to make their feelings known to one another, they tap with a hammer in a certain way, but this is rarely necessary – they are masters of the craft, working by intuition and observation. The steel is folded, again and again, each time refining the metal, hardening it, purifying it. Soon it begins to lengthen, to thin, to extend out into the long curve of a true blade. The hammering is remorseless, clanging out of the forge's open doorway, keeping the rest of the village awake.

Finishing the blade's face is done by the woman. She mixes a clay jacket for the cutting edge, using her thinner fingers to press the spatula into the slurry. By then, both workers are weary, having been at the forge for days. When the clay is broken off after more time in the coals, the pattern on the steel is visible. Every blademaker has a different mark – for some, solak blossom; for others, tiger's claws. The most prestigious, and hardest to achieve, is the lightning spread, forking from tip to scabbard-edge. This one bears such a mark.

Then it is filed, marked, polished, washed. If all is perfect, the blade is wrapped in straw and fabric, and placed in a heavy cart drawn by *aduun*. A red pennant is tied to a long pole, marking the cart as sacred cargo – it will not be attacked on its journey, even if it passes through tribal lands at war. The blademakers rest at last, their hands calloused, their skin blistered. They will never see their creation again, and receive no payment for their work. The entire village supports them, and they occupy positions of reverence. All know where the swords are destined to find service.

The cart then travels west, descending rapidly before reaching

the open country. After many months of trekking across the
grassland, eventually the drivers spy the Khum Kharta on
the horizon, pale against the whisper of the long grass. They
pull up, and prepare the cairn. Stones are piled up, draped with
prayer-fragments and incense bowls, crowned with the pennant.
The blade, still wrapped, is placed at the top. Then the drivers
withdraw, beginning the long journey home.

The following night, it is taken up into the fortress by Legion
menials. Once inside the shadowy halls of Quan Zhou, each
prayer-fragment is studied, interpreted, then placed in the
librarium. From these scraps, the masters of Chogoris learn
much of the shifting patterns of the endless grass, and where
to draw aspirants from, and how the health of the thousand realms ebbs and flows. The blade – still without its hilt,
scabbard or guard – is unwrapped and carried into the forges.
None of the painstaking marks made by the Hashin blademakers are removed. None of the tiny flaws – few as they
ever are – are removed. This is a product of the people of
Jaghatai, not of a machine intelligence. When polished to
a mirror sheen, it reflects the authors' faces in every flash of
light from its surface.

A powered grip is added, meticulously crafted onto the steel,
bound into it, worked at by hand until the gold chasing cuts
smartly into the metal's surface. The disruptor field is blended,
harmonising with the structure of the underlying blade. It will
be tested, over and again, returned to the forges many times
by the sparring-tutors until the balance cannot be improved
upon. The flare of the energy field is bonded to the marks
made in its first forging, augmenting them, giving the sword
its signature. Thus the labour of Hashin will be witnessed
across the known galaxy, as vivid as the lightning it mimics.

Only when all is done can it be passed up to the blademasters
of the ordu for final scrutiny. They keep the weapon in their

temple vaults, surrounded by ritual guardians, unused, unlit, until an aspirant is inducted into the Legion with a suitable character for the blade.

This one is given to the warrior named Morbun Xa. Morbun Xa is famed, not just for his prowess, but also for his restraint. He is a model of the Path of Heaven, they say. The blade suits him. He takes it with him on the void-ship *Korghaz* with the Brotherhood of the Night's Star. It is first drawn against an enemy on the world of Egetha IX, where the ordu is victorious.

During the long years of the Crusade, it changes hands twice, as its bearers meet their end in battle. The great treachery nears its endgame, and now it is borne by Ajak Khan, of the Brotherhood of the Amber Eagle. He stands on the walls of the Palace as they crumble beneath his boots, and calls out curses on those who assail him. He grips the hilt loosely, making the steel dance around him. The skies are black, like calligrapher's ink. The air is ringing with noise – from the infantry yelling, from the god-machines that have all but penetrated the last solid line of defence, from the thunder of the fixed guns.

Ajak Khan spies his enemy, a captain of Angron's tragic berserkers, debased fighters he pities as much as he hates, clambering through ruins towards him, followed by a dozen more. In their wake come the hordes, still languishing in no-man's-land, exposed to the pounding of the guns. Ajak Khan runs, accompanied by his battle-brothers, racing into the close combat he loves. The blade whirls, trailing forks of lightning. It bites, it cleaves, and Ajak Khan cries aloud in pleasure.

Under the stone, on another world, by candlelight, the rock-cutters of Ong-Hashin pause. The flames have shuddered briefly, though there is no wisp of a breeze in the deep places.

It happens, sometimes. They know what it means.

Diligently, they take up their picks, and return to work.

* * *

'Why tell me this?' asked Jangsai Khan, though he felt that, in truth, he already knew.

Naranbaatar's face was in shadow, half-lit from below by a cracked sodium tube. The rest of the bunker was dark, hot from confinement, stinking of sweat and mould. The Stormseer's skin was dark too, scarred from ritual marks and newer wounds, creased with age. The crystals of his armour's hood glinted, and animal skull totems twisted gently from their fixings on lengths of twine. 'You should know its history,' he said.

Jangsai took up the sword. It was a fine piece – a mid-length blade, slightly curved, though less so than the tulwars used by the mounted units. He switched it to the horizontal, looking down it, feeling for balance. Faint lightning patterns were visible on the steel, part of the structure of the cutting-face. He slipped his thumb over the disruptor trigger, already speculating on how the blaze of energy would take its key from those marks.

'Its bearer–'

'Died well,' said Naranbaatar. 'Much was recovered, including this. Now it is yours.'

Jangsai nodded. No use in wasting it. Powerful, fully functional powerblades were valuable now. Everything was running out, on its last legs. 'I knew him,' he said. 'Ajak.'

That was less of a claim than it would once have been. Almost the entire Legion was clustered together now, their numbers winnowed cruelly, hemmed in behind walls and pressed up against the faces of the enemy. Once-sundered brotherhoods fought next to one another, mingling as their casualties mounted up. At times it felt that there was not a warrior of the ordu still alive that Jangsai didn't know the name of, or hadn't witnessed fighting, or whose unit's history he wasn't acquainted with.

'His brotherhood no longer fights,' said Naranbaatar. 'The

survivors have been distributed. But the deeds have been recorded, and will be taken to the halls of Quan Zhou when all this is over.'

That was one of the hallmarks of Naranbaatar. Jangsai had never heard him boast, but time and again the Stormseer had spoken of plans for the future, nonchalantly, with the certainty of success underpinning it all, and hence the need to move on to the next task. It was all so matter-of-fact – this thing here must be done, and then we must return to what we were doing before. Everything shall be put in order again, everything recorded. It was amusing, sometimes, to listen to it all, as the world around them sunk further into desecration.

'Then they are inside the inner wall,' Jangsai said.

'Within the hour, we think.'

'You wish me to take over Ajak's position?'

'No, that has been assigned to another. I wish you to leave your station – you have new orders.'

'From you?'

'From the Khagan himself.'

Jangsai hesitated. 'We are hard-pressed here, *zadyin arga*.' That was as close as he would ever come to pushing back. He had to register something, though – his warriors were dying, and would continue to die, and his place was with them. The unspoken undertone was understood by them both. *Why now?*

'We need you to speak to someone,' Naranbaatar told him. 'He is not a native of Terra. As we learned recently, he comes from the same world that you did. So that is the reason. I know you wish to fight on here, but, believe me, you will not be deprived of chances to do so again soon.'

Once again, a fractional pause before replying. 'This is the end, then,' he said.

'The beginning of it.'

'What can you tell me?'

'Enough for you to perform this task. After that, it depends. We do not know what will be possible yet. Maybe nothing. Maybe everything.'

It could still take you aback, that essential calmness. Jangsai knew that Chogorians got angry. He'd seen it many times in combat, and they were terrifying when they really, truly lost their composure, but for the most part they maintained an equanimity that could be as infuriating as it was impressive.

Jangsai looked down at the blade again. Ajak would have been holding it, just a matter of hours ago, maybe. They would have been a seamless pairing, both products of the same background, parts of a harmonious whole.

'Tell me where I need to go,' he said.

The world was called Ar Rija.

It had suffered greatly during the terrors of Old Night, and so when the Emperor's armies arrived during the first few decades of the Crusade, they had been welcomed enthusiastically. Its old industrial base was rebuilt quickly, and within a generation it was contributing handsomely to the war effort. Many regiments were raised for the Imperial Army, a number of which went on to earn widespread fame. By the time of the Triumph at Ullanor, Ar Rija was considered a linchpin planet – one upon which the security of an entire subsector depended, sited at the strategic junction of many established warp lanes, a settled, substantial place.

The Legiones Astartes, the Imperial Fists in particular, had begun to take aspirants from Ar Rija from the second century of the Crusade Age onwards. It had never been a major recruiting world, being generally considered too civilised to produce the optimally brutal Space Marine candidate, but the demands of the all-encompassing conquest meant that every avenue was explored. Only when the civil war broke

out in earnest did that situation change. As the scale of Horus'
treachery became apparent, Imperial strategos began a frantic
programme of asset-withdrawal, pulling everything they could
out of the reach of the oncoming enemy. Ar Rija, for a time,
was considered a safe haven. Its Naval yards were reinforced,
its regiments boosted, its defences resupplied. Recruiters for a
number of Legions turned their eyes towards it, already seeing
how desperate things were likely to become, and suddenly
needing to make use of every possible means of increasing
the supply of aspirants.

It was always a tenuous hope. The process of turning a
mortal child into a Legion warrior was a delicate art, honed
over many years and conducted in secure surroundings. It
could be speeded up, if necessary, and its programmes moved
to different locations, but both actions brought risks with
them. Even once a number of scattered Legion facilities had
been evacuated to Ar Rija, increased aspirant deaths meant
that recruitment rates failed to rise as swiftly as hoped. More
subjects were sought from the native population, fast-tracked
through the usual screening and placed onto accelerated ascension protocols.

Tuyo had known nothing of this at the time, of course. He
had been too young. His ambitions, such as he had had any
back then, had been to serve in the Army one day – to take
ship as part of one of the prestigious regiments and sail into
the void in pursuit of the Emperor's designs. When the officials had come to his parents' cramped hab-unit, with their
strange expressions and odd uniforms, he had thought little
of it. Only later, when his mother had burst into tears and
his father's face had lost all its colour, had he begun to realise
that something was very wrong.

Those were his last memories of them. It was hard even to
remember their faces, now. So much had changed – in himself,

in the Imperium. For a while, he'd been determined to hang on to those final childhood images, thinking it important that he had some kind of tether to his old life. As the training programme had commenced, however, and he had undergone the first rounds of mental conditioning, that had become hard. After a few months, he had stopped trying. Everything had been consumed by the changes raging through his pre-pubescent body – the agonising hormone treatments, the psycho-honing, the relentless physical improvements.

He had had four years of that. Far too short a time, he learned later, to be sure of success. More than half of those he started the programme with died early on. Others fell by the wayside after the first wave of implants. His memories of that phase of his life were hazy now, filled with the impressions of faces he had no names for and places that he could no longer locate. He had been angry, so angry, all the time. They had made him that way, he assumed – pumping him with chems that fuelled his rage. Those had got him through the pain, made him work harder – just for the sake of spite, it felt like sometimes.

But he had learned a great deal. He had learned that the Imperium he had assumed was ever-expanding and secure was in fact on the brink of destruction. He had learned of the Enemy and its ruthlessness. He had learned of the history of the Eighteen Legions and the role each one had played in the entire affair, including the traitors, because you had to know an enemy before you could be sure of killing him.

In other circumstances, he would have completed his training on Ar Rija. Near the end, though, everything had changed again. The war reached his home world, just as it had always been destined to. He was not permitted to fight for it. None of the aspirants were. They were herded into transports and sent hurtling away from the wave of destruction.

Now Ar Rija was far behind enemy lines, presumably destroyed or occupied. He hoped the former, with what lingering human attachment he had for the place – you did not want to live under the rule of Horus, not if you had been a loyal world.

So it was that he had seen Terra at last, the centre of all things, heart of the Imperium, and yet already threatened with attack, already vulnerable. The entire place was filled with soldiers, teeming with them, spilling out of every lander and onto every viaduct and marshalling yard, all tense, all terrified.

This was where he would fight. It was where he had been made to fight. He would know no other battlefield, not unless they were victorious here. Those final few months had been the hardest of all – the last implants had had to take, his accelerated training had had to be completed. He had needed to prove himself to the instructors, and then to his Legion, neither of whom could afford, even now, to let a substandard product enter the ranks of the Emperor's Finest.

He was a newblood. A hurriedly created product of a desperate empire on its uppers. A warrior rushed through both creation and training, given none of the immersion and cultivation that the Imperium had once lavished on its paramount living weapons. If things had not been so desperate, he would never have been changed on Ar Rija. He would never have been transported from station to station, his development interrupted, overseen by instructors drawn from a dozen worlds. Everyone knew it was suboptimal. A few even counselled against the process entirely, acutely aware of the consequences when a Space Marine entered service with a flawed background.

For all that, he had still been proud. He had burned to fight, to demonstrate what he could do, both to himself and to the established members of his Legion. He was neither Terran nor Chogorian, but he was still a warrior, a battle-brother of one of the three Blessed Legions, the honoured trinity tasked with the last defence of Terra. The soul of the primarch smouldered within his own blood. The sacred scar ran down his cheek, zigzagged like lightning.

They had left it a long time to perform the final rite of ascension. When the moment had come at last, he had stood in long lines with many others, all of them mongrels like him, plucked from obscure backwaters and outposts, painfully undertrained, painfully eager. Their armour was bone-white, immaculate, fresh from the forge. The lord commander had arrived by shuttle, making the dust on the open parade ground billow and skitter. He had clanged down the ramp, flanked by ivory-armoured giants in battle-tarnished plate. The skies were blustery and rain-blown above them, yet to be darkened by the downdraught of a million landers.

Tuyo had waited patiently, arms by his sides, tensing his muscles one by one. Spires and defence towers rose up around them, casting deep, cold shadows over the gravel. You could hear the noise of military preparations in all directions – the grind of machine-tools, the grumble of engines, the tramp of marching boots. Everything was on the edge, there. Everything had been poised, ready to explode into violence.

Eventually, the lord commander had reached Tuyo's place in the line. His name was Ganzorig, a noyan-khan in the Legion's own reckoning. He was a Chogorian, one who had been fighting against the traitors for seven terrible, arduous years. He had been a seasoned warrior for decades before that. That left its mark on him, like a scent. He looked unbreakable.

Tuyo had looked him in the eye. Ganzorig had looked back, coolly, lingering, as if appraising a steed for purchase.

'Tuyo,' the noyan-khan had said eventually. 'You are of the ordu of Jaghatai now. Your old life is no more. What name do you take to mark your ascension?'

'Jangsai,' he had said, without hesitation.

Ganzorig had nodded, satisfied. It didn't matter to them, where you came from – only what name you took, and whether you gave honour to it. 'You are one with the ordu, Jangsai.'

Jangsai had waited. One final thing remained to be done – to assign him to his *minghan*, his brotherhood. So straitened were the times, and so mauled had the Legion been on its return to the Throneworld, that reconstruction was still ongoing, and recruitment was a matter of considerable fluidity.

Ganzorig had given it much thought, as he had with every newblood warrior he'd inducted that day. Hundreds of warriors had been standing there, but the noyan-khan had known everything about all of them – their training records, their confidential instructors' reports. Jangsai waited in silence.

'You are of the Brotherhood of the Iron Axe,' Ganzorig had said, at last. 'You will not leave it except in death – may it be long in coming, and may glory accompany your deeds until that day.'

Jangsai had bowed. Now he was complete. Now, at last, he was a White Scar.

'*Hai Chogoris!*' he had said. 'Glory to the Khagan.' Then, with even more feeling, 'And a thousand deaths to his enemies.'

TWO

Death in life
Apothecary
The Pale King

But he had already died so many times he could no longer count them. Over and over, he had felt his hearts stop, with a jolt so painful that he would have screamed if he could have somehow hauled the breath in.

That was what it had been like, in the void, for that period of time that had felt longer than eternity. Perhaps it had been longer. Perhaps a part of him was still out there even now, dying and then living and then dying again. At times he'd not been able to tell the states apart – they had merged together, just one long stretch of agony. And now it was over, in a manner of speaking, but he was still somehow stuck in that halfway state, as if his soul had never truly escaped the Destroyer, caught in its vice and gently crushed into pliant mush.

In other respects, though, he had gone back to being something that he recognised. He could carry a weapon again, trudge towards a horizon, kill for his primarch. He could follow an order, give an order. He was a soldier, just as he had been ever since his youth on Barbarus. A fighter against tyranny.

So Caipha Morarg was utterly transformed, and also utterly unchanged. The externals were all rearranged, but his mind was much as it ever had been. He could no longer remove his encrusted armour, true, and he could no longer breathe without wheezing, nor blink without leaving lines of mucus across his eyeballs, but he remained himself, loyal equerry to the primarch, servant of the Legion, observer of deeds for the histories that would one day need to be written.

He lifted his heavy head, feeling the servos in his decaying battleplate catch and snick. Everything was dusty. The ruins roiled with it, running in tear-lines from mortar wounds, silting up across the foundations of half-toppled buildings in grey-black dunes. You couldn't see far, in all that. A mortal might peer out for a few dozen metres. He himself could see a bit further, all through the film of green that coloured everything for him now. He could make out the ruins of Corbenic Gard in the far distance, a slumped heap of masonry, still hot from all the munitions that had been hurled at it. Closer in, a few kilometres off, the walls of the Colossi Gate stood, blackened, damaged, but stubbornly there. In between those peaks were the blasted lands, the flattened carcasses of old dwellings and factories, a maze of low-lying rubble heaps.

Even as he watched, something shimmered in the half-light, gauzy and translucent. A face emerged from the dust clouds, briefly elongating, slipping over itself, solidifying into a distended, slack-jawed creature that popped and wobbled its way into full being. It shuddered, slipping in and out of reality, before slithering off into the shadows, looking for something to gorge on.

Morarg still hadn't got used to them. The daemons. Once, he would have been repelled by even a sniff of such horrors, but now they were everywhere, sliding across the open doorways, capering down bombed-out streets. They rose up from the soil, and squirmed down from empty window frames. Some were silent, some whispered all the time. Some took the form of animals, so that you could never be quite sure what was real and what was not, until you got close enough to sniff the wrongness. Others were gigantic and repellent, lurching and shifting through the dust clouds, towering over the troops below. They all had trouble, still. The closer they got to the great wards, the worse it was for them. Even now, even after so much pain had been piled onto the Emperor's psychic barricades, they couldn't quite cross the final threshold. They still needed flesh and blood for some things.

But that wouldn't take long, now. Every wall of the long Inner Palace perimeter was under attack. The bombardment never ceased. The pressure never slackened. What paltry territory remained in the hands of the enemy was being compressed, wrung out, tighter and tighter, until it would burst apart like rotten fruit. Then the daemons would truly go to work. Then they would run amok, unfettered, feasting on whatever living souls remained in the debris.

On some days, when Morarg thought about that, he became morose and sluggish, remembering when his purpose had been to hunt down monsters rather than enable them. And on other days, when combat roused the cold coals of his soul's furnace, he wished for nothing more than to see it, to relish it, to grin in a stupor as the lesser children of the god did their holy work. Typhus – they had to call him Typhus now – preached that doctrine endlessly, telling them all that *this* was what they were always destined to become, and never to regret the sacrifice, for even when they had been waifs and wretches on Barbarus, the god had always had them in his mind, and had always known they could be something greater.

Morarg smiled at the memory. Greater? In some ways, they were. So few things truly hurt him, now. Bolt-shells would punch through his armour, blades would bite deep into his addled flesh, and he would recover from it all so quickly, just as it had been in the warp – death to life, life to death. And yet, how could he ignore the visible price of all that power – the way his skin hung slack from wasted muscle, the way his pores oozed black gunge, the way everything he touched seemed to thicken up with corrosion and start to fester? If this was a gift, then it was a strange one. If it was a reward, then its taste was bitter.

In the distance, he heard the pounding rhythm of guns. He felt the earth under his feet tremble. The god-machines were still walking. They were at the wall, he knew. Now. This was a moment, a point of change. Once the first incision was made, all else would follow from it. He wished he was there, far away, out on the Katabatic Plain to witness the Legio Mortis demolish the last physical barrier. As the dust clouds in the north-eastern horizon kept on growing, rising up to form seething pillars between earth and sky, he imagined the panic they were causing, and started to chuckle.

That made his phlegmy throat catch, and he coughed himself to a halt. He couldn't even take pleasure in a chortle now without his body betraying him. Some bargain. Some contract. But then, it hadn't been his to make. The primarch had done it for them, and for reasons that still baffled him. You had to have faith. Even if Morarg didn't have much in the god, yet, he could still trust the one who had saved them from Barbarus.

He began to walk again, lifting one mud-clogged boot, then the other. It would take him a while to get where he needed to be, but that was fine by him. He had already experienced eternity, already gone to the universe's end and back, already died and lived and died again.

That tended to give you a sense of proportion. After all that, in the midst of all this, and into whatever pristine hell was due to be served up at you by the uncaring cosmos, you had to see the funny side.

Whenever you killed, he thought to himself sometimes, wondering if he was the very first to entertain the notion, it helped to laugh.

It was all so fascinating. A new world, opening up like a budding flower, and all within his grasp.

Zadal Crosius breathed it in, tasted it, felt it. His body responded, soaking up every new sensation, absorbing it all, feeling things that he had no words to describe. The sky was dark grey, hanging heavily with smog. The earth was black, choked with ash. Every surface, every brick and block, was coated with filth. And yet, if you knelt down, pushed your helm close enough, you could see the variation there – the tiny glints of crystalline carbon, the movements of insects across the dirt, still struggling on, despite the poisons everywhere. Crosius would reach out with a finger, toying with them for a moment, then crushing their glossy shells.

He had been an Apothecary, before. Back in the world that had been dull and dutiful, he had spent his time patching up lacerations and repairing bones. He had thought himself content with that, at the time. A Space Marine was an astonishing thing, capable of self-repair in all but the most catastrophic circumstances. The warriors of the XIV Legion were exceptional even by those high standards, having made a virtue of extreme physical endurance. The ones who had come from Barbarus had set the pace, having lived in a world of poisons for as long as anyone could remember, but the Terrans had caught up fast. The message had come right from the top, from the primarch, repeated over and over.

You are my unbroken blades. You are the Death Guard.

In hindsight, Crosius wondered how he had ever really taken pleasure in that old life. True, the position had been an honoured one – the Apothecaries of the XIV had been treated almost like the Techmarines of the X, charged with watching over the Legion's jealously guarded specialisms. But his subjects had been so dour, so relentless, so... uniform. They had never smiled at him, nor offered thanks when he had stitched them up and sent them back to the front. There had been a cloud over them all, a kind of heaviness, dull as stone, turgid as oil.

Now, though. Now.

He limped across the broken ground, his boots sinking deep into sucking clay. Pain flared with every movement, but it was interesting pain, something he could reflect on and marvel at. His body, once such a source of pride, was falling apart. His muscles were loose, his skin sallow. When he swivelled, his armour complained, already beginning to fail. Rust had crept across the face of his plate's metalwork, spidery and multi-hued, and he no longer scoured it off. Better just to let it all degrade, to slide down into a greasy mass. You could take real pleasure in that – the release! The freedom from all that endless, endless drudgery.

Now his mind worked differently. He regarded his fellow battle-brothers, and saw that they were changing, too. It was almost childlike, this emergence into a new world, each one of them treading carefully, discovering slowly what they had been turned into, and what they might yet become. So appropriate, that it was taking place here, on the very world where everything had started. The Legion had spread out across the galaxy, waging their dreary war over two hundred years, and were now back again, improved, released, on the cusp of marvels beyond imagination.

The term 'Apothecary' was no longer really suitable, he thought. Something better would have to be concocted, to reflect more closely the biological explorations that were now possible. For now, though, the old title would just have to do. There was, after all, a war on.

'Crosius!' came a shout from behind him.

He turned, watching as an armoured column trundled out of the mists, tracking alongside him. Infantry marched in ragged mobs, rags hanging from their exposed skin, their expressions vague and ill-focused. Full battle-brothers, the ones who still called themselves the Unbroken, marched alongside those wretches. They were bloated creatures now, swelling up at the armour-joints, their ceramite crusted and filmy. A column of Legion tanks rocked and swayed across the uneven terrain, chucking lines of thick smoke into an already hazy atmosphere. The growling formations of heavy vehicles stretched off down the road, finally disappearing into the curling mist. Crosius halted, waiting for the one who had hailed him to crunch down from his tank's top hatch and lumber up to him.

Gremus Kalgaro had always been a taciturn, closed kind of character. He'd served as the master of ordnance for the Legion fleet during the opening years of the Great Uprising, and the cold of void-war had suited him. Now, though, he'd loosened up. He'd taken his helm off, exposing a puffy riot of pink flesh that looked ripe to spill down his chest. One eye was closed, hidden by a cluster of tumours, ones that Crosius found himself itching to examine.

'Going my way?' Kalgaro asked, spittle hanging from a swollen lower lip.

'Depends,' said Crosius. 'Where are you going?'

'Over there,' said Kalgaro, gesturing ahead vaguely, into the boiling clouds of dust and steam. 'His new Manse.'

Crosius knew what he meant. The primarch's current resi-
dence, co-opted from his brother Perturabo, the staging point
for the final push. It had been a port, once. A space port. So
vast, they said, that it scraped the edge of the atmosphere. Cap-
turing that had allowed the Warmaster to bring Titans down
quickly, ready to deploy against the Palace walls. It remained
an important asset, a conduit for resupply, though the Lord
of Iron had clearly failed to see its continuing value, and so
now the place was theirs.

'I'll get there,' Crosius said. 'Though I prefer to walk.'

Kalgaro grinned. 'Good day for it.' He wiped the back of his
hand across his forehead, leaving a dark smear on the skin. A
wound across his right temple was stubbornly refusing to heal.
'Better there than Colossi, anyway. What a mess.'

'Ach, it would have fallen eventually. If we'd kept going.
Priorities change.'

'They do. Just wish they'd tell us why, eh?' Kalgaro laughed
harshly. Crosius had never, ever seen him laugh before.

'I was fighting with Caipha Morarg,' Crosius said thoughtfully. 'Out past Marmax, where they tried to flank us. We
were slaying anything that came up. They were cowering
behind the high walls, at the end, and we were just chewing
down the trench lines, taking our time about it. We could
have razed the whole place.'

'So there's something better being planned.'

'You'd think so.'

The tanks kept trundling by, one after the other. They were
obese things, for the most part – angular Spartans, low-slung
Sicarans, a few specialised transports and bombards. Every
surface of them was caked in muck, clogging the intakes and
staining the exhaust pipes. Their commanders slouched in
the open top turrets, their armour glistening with engine oil,
streaked with bloody patches. One unit clattered along with

its left-hand track flapping loose, the plates knocked out of true. It hadn't been fixed. Crosius guessed it would right itself, at some stage. That seemed to be the way things worked, now.

'I wanted so much to be the first, you know that?' Kalgaro said, scratching at his chin. 'First over the walls. I thought we'd earned it.'

'Doesn't seem to matter now, does it?'

'No. Strange. It doesn't.' He seemed briefly troubled. 'I don't even hate them much, to be honest. I just fight because it's… interesting.' Then he shot Crosius a guilty look. 'But ignore me. I didn't mean that.'

Crosius laughed, and slapped him on the shoulder guard. 'Relax. I'm not an informant. Anyway, I feel much the same.' Mucus pooled at the back of his throat. 'Hatred is for the past. This is just an obstacle, something stubborn and stupid to be cleared away. And then – then, my old friend – we can start to build again.'

'But I don't know what.'

'No, I don't see it yet either. Maybe only the primarch does. I trust him, though. He'll have it all worked out, just like before. We knock this place over, bury the tyrant under His own walls, and then it starts. We create it all again, but right. Explorers, truth-seekers, just like we were promised the first time around.'

Kalgaro laughed again, with genuine pleasure. 'I like that, Apothecary! I like the way you talk. We should do it again, when we're all up at the Manse.'

'Surely.'

The master of ordnance stomped off, still chuckling, to where his big Spartan waited for him. 'I'll hold you to it, and don't dawdle – he'll want you there in time.'

'For whatever he has in mind.'

The Spartan's engines spat oily smuts, and then the tracks churned, grinding back up on the dirt track. Kalgaro clambered up the handholds and took his place again at the top turret. Crosius watched him go. He watched the rest of the column go. It was a big formation and took a long time to pass by. When it had gone, it left furrows in the mud, glistening with scummy water.

Crosius started to walk again. His limp was more pronounced. A new pain was curdling in his stomach, as if something had started to ferment. His helm's tactical display started to malfunction, and everything up ahead became blocky and blurred.

As he limped, he started to hum. A little tune, something to repeat to himself, something cheerful.

Fascinating, it was. Everything up ahead, all within his grasp, just waiting for him to come along and discover it.

On some days, he believed he had become immune to doubt. On others, he felt as if there was no other state left.

To be a primarch – what was that? Was it physical strength? Yes, partly. There had always been so little that he was not an equal to in combat, and even less now. The power currently at his command was almost too much – overspilling, bursting at the seams of his stretched armour.

But it had been more than that, in conception. They had been made to be generals, not just warlords. Commanders. Governors. In some unrealised future, they would have been the satraps of an eternal realm, committed to the rediscovery of ancient truths as their civilisation went from strength to strength. At times, using the gifts he now possessed, he even thought he caught glimpses of that ruined future, like mockeries. Maybe his new patrons sent him those, as a kind of dark joke. Or maybe whatever was left of the soul his father had crafted for him was still active somewhere in his broken psyche, struggling to revive an alternative causality that became more distant with every passing day.

Now, though, he had made a bargain. He had traded away that future for another one, one that was more magnificent and expansive than any promised by this dying Imperium. Every time he breathed, every time he blinked, he saw more snatches of that possibility unfolding, one glorious aspect at a time. He remembered things that had taken place before he had been born. He perceived things that were yet to occur as if they were cemented into history.

Because he had made the choice. That was the important thing. For so long he had skirted at the edges of it, chafing at the impossible demands placed on him, gnawing at the injustices that had always been heaped his way. He could have stayed in a twilight state of indecision – fighting for the Warmaster without ever truly embracing the powers he had unleashed. He could have held back, indulging witchery only when it was needed, never committing, never submerging himself into its cold, dark waters.

What would that life have given him? He would have preserved more of his old self. He might have found a way to pick through the contradictions, maintaining something of his original form and temper while still breaking free from the strictures that had both suffocated him and kept him safe. Some of his brothers were still trying to tread that impossible line. Perturabo, he thought, would probably try it for longest. He would fail. Anyone who tried it would fail. Once you began to teeter, no matter how slightly, you were destined to fall.

Or rise. That might be a better way of putting it. Rise up, become an immortal, play a part in the highest level of drama. He was still a general. He was still a governor. He had no masters at all now, except in the sense that the god was a part of him, suffusing him, animating him, and he was a part of the god, albeit with a will of his own and a soul that remained discrete. These were the paradoxes. These were the gifts.

He could turn his agile mind to what came next. He could begin to think about a world without an Emperor in it, and what that would mean. Would Horus take the tyrant's place once all was done, becoming Emperor in turn and ruling from the ruins of the Throne he had destroyed? Or would everything dissolve again, when the common enemy was crushed, all of them going their own way, like ants without a queen?

If Horus had a vision for the future, he had never articulated it to him. He suspected, deep down, that the Warmaster was so consumed by the present, so gorged on the gods' vindictiveness, that he could see no further than his own horizon of vengeance. Let the galaxy burn, so long as the tyrant was overthrown. Everything else could be attended to once the Emperor's throat had been cut.

Whatever the truth of that, he himself could not be so cavalier. He had to think about the dawn of the new age. He had to shepherd his faithful children through it, ensure that no new Barbarus was erected over the smouldering wreckage of the old. He had to guarantee that the god was honoured, and that its realm was extended out from the immaterium and into the world of the senses. Fulgrim could fritter away his debauched life if he wished to, Angron could howl in lost rage all he wanted. He had to be different. He had to make the sacrifices worth something.

Now he looked out across the world he was helping to destroy. He stood alone in one of the space port's control chambers, a huge, high-vaulted space strewn with wreckage, half-lost in darkness as the sun set on another day of pain and struggle. Tall windows in the western wall burned red from its final rays, golden on the edges of the shattered panes. Everything in that place still stank of the IV Legion, a lingering stench of burning, of oils and grinding metal. The Iron Warriors had only vacated the operational levels a few hours

ago, following the petulant commands of their lord. Many of
them, he guessed, would choose to fight on somewhere else
on Terra, whatever Perturabo did. But not in this place. This
was *his* citadel now. This was the mountain he had conquered
at last, the highest peak, the one from where he would crush
the last flickers of resolve among the unbelievers.

As the sun slid wearily down into the burning west, he
watched the ongoing battles rage across the northern Katabatic
Plain. The flatlands were cloaked in dust and smoke, but his
eyes saw more clearly now than they had ever done before.
He perceived the results of Legio Mortis' brutal advance,
smashing its way across the wastes until their engines stood
in the shadow of the Mercury Wall itself. He saw the outlines
of the Titans, mere specks against such colossal emptiness.
Even *Dies Irae*, greatest of them all, was a minuscule dot, lost
in the vast arena of ongoing combat. Down there, though –
down at ground level, they would all be leviathans, splitting
the air apart with their war-horns, starting to drill and cut
and hack, undermining the last solid perimeter between
them and the enemy. Only moments remained, now. Just
slivers of time, counting down, almost gone. In the shadow of
the god-machines marched the uncounted hosts – the faithful
and the mercenary, the warriors of the Free Legions, the creatures of the New Mechanicum, all champing at the bit, all
yearning for the first break.

He had been at the front himself. He had fought up close,
bringing his scythe to bear on the necks of the faithless, settling
old debts and seeing to the demands of vengeance. Some
scores had been difficult – even painful – to settle, but the
ledgers had been scraped clean all the same. He could have
stayed out there, stood against those quaking wall-foundations,
ready to clamber up the slopes of rubble once they were
toppled. But no. His place was here. His duty was clear.

His gaze scanned upwards, westwards, away from the incipient breach and across the still-flickering corona of the Emperor's great ward-shield. He observed the high spires, crowded together under its faltering protection, climbing higher and higher until he caught sight of the pinnacles of his father's private domains, night-black against the bloody sunset – the Great Observatory, the Investiary, the Tower of Hegemon, the Bhab Bastion.

He extended his right claw, stretching the talons out as if he might pluck the summits from those fortresses and scoop up the cowering inhabitants inside. His tarnished gauntlet compassed the blunt parapets of the bastion, command centre of the most dull-witted, duty-obsessed lackey of them all.

'This is the gift I bring for you now, my brother,' he breathed, his metallic voice rattling against the strictures of his corroded rebreather. *'The gift that only I could bring, the reason the god set me here, in this place, at this time.'*

He closed his hooked fingers over the bastion, snuffing it out, masking it with his sealed fist.

'The last sensation you will ever have. The last emotion you will ever feel. And you will understand, in your soul, who gave it to you, and why you *remain powerless against it.'*

The sun slipped away, drenching the entire Palace in darkness. All that remained was the vice, the grip, the merciless application of pressure.

'Despair,' rasped Mortarion, ascended daemon-king of life and death, plague-maker, hope-ender. *'I send you despair.'*

THREE

Praetorians
Too soon
Day of wrath

And he felt it.

Rogal Dorn had been feeling it for days, weeks, building up, up, up, rising over him like a black fog, dragging at his limbs, clogging his mind, making him question every decision he made, every order he gave.

He hadn't had any respite at all, of any kind, for three months. Three months! His sharpness was going now, his reactions were slower. A billion functionaries depending on him for everything, reaching out to him, suffocating him with their endless demands, pleas for help, for guidance. A billion eyes, on him, all the time.

And he'd fought, too. He'd *fought*. He'd fought primarchs, brothers he'd once thought of as equals or betters. He'd seen the hatred in Perturabo's eyes, the mania in Fulgrim's, stabbing at him, poisoning him. Every duel, every brief foray into combat, had chipped a bit more off, had weakened the foundations a little further. Fulgrim had been the worst. His brother's old form, so pleasing to the eye, had gone, replaced by bodily corruption so deep he scarcely had the words for it. That degradation repulsed him almost more than anything else. It showed just how far you could fall, if you lost your footing in reality completely.

You couldn't show that repulsion. You couldn't betray the doubt, or give away the fatigue. You couldn't give away so much as a flicker of weakness, or the game was up, so Dorn's face remained just as it always had been – static, flinty, curt. He kept his shoulders back, spine straight. He hid the fevers that raged behind his eyes, the bone-deep weariness that throbbed through every muscle, all for show, all to give those who looked up to him something to cling on to, to believe in. The Emperor, his father, was gone, silent, locked in His own unimaginable agonies, and so everything else had crashed onto his shoulders. The weight of the entire species, all their frailties and imperfections, wrapped tight around his mouth and throat and nostrils, choking him, drowning him, making him want to cry out loud, to cower away from it, something he would never do, *could* never do, and so he remained where he was, caught between the infinite weight of Horus' malice and the infinite demands of the Emperor's will, and it would break him, he knew, break him open like the walls themselves, which were about to break now too, despite all he had done, but had it been enough, yes it had, no it could not have been, they would break, they *must not break*…

He clenched his fist, curling the fingers up tight. His mind was racing again. He was on the edge, slipping into a fugue state, the paralysis he dreaded. It came from within. It came from without. Something – *something* – was making the entire structure around him panic, weaken, fail in resolve. He was not immune. He was the pinnacle – when the base was corrupted, he, too, eventually, would shatter.

So he searched, as Rogal Dorn always did, for something to

do, some way to fight back. The klaxons were going off around him, wild and loud. Men and women were running, their discipline failing. They were trying to shut down the plasma reserves in the foundation interiors, drain them, prevent the penetration cascades that would critically weaken the Mercury Wall's substructure. Even as they ran, shouting, tripping over one another, the Titans were *there* – unwrapping their drills and energy-hammers, powering up forbidden drive-weapons augmented with daemon-essences, clawing, scraping down the outer skin like rats.

'My lord!'

And then, hearing that voice, he remembered. He had already acted. Typical Rogal Dorn, anticipating his own momentary weakness, he had already put the necessary move in place. He had summoned Sigismund here, to Shard Bastion, to speak to him in person, to give him the command, because he could never falter in front of his son, not *this* son.

He turned, just for a moment, away from the confusion of the command station, and faced him. Sigismund wore the black of the Templar Brethren. He had come up to the command level with others of his order, a dozen, and they all looked as grim as one another – fatalistic, hammered into a kind of permanent, shell-shocked fury.

Sigismund's own expression was wary. He had reason for that – Dorn had run him hard, borne down on him, bathed him in disapproval, ever since Isstvan. The reasons had been sound. Neither of them could have expected any less, given the codes of honour that made them who they were, and Sigismund had never complained.

But there had always been something else, under all that – not quite a test, but maybe a tempering, like that of the best blades. To see if the steel could withstand the fire, be more hard-wearing for it.

'This is the end,' Dorn told him flatly. 'All that could have been done, has been done. Every delay, every counter-strike, every anticipation. Now, they get in. Mercury will fail imminently, then Exultant, then the others.'

Sigismund's unwavering expression never flickered. He was a cold one. Almost too good an Imperial Fist. Almost a parody of their entire philosophy.

'Faster than we might have hoped,' Dorn said. 'Not as fast as we might have feared. Soon the shape of the battle will change – we will be like dogs in the rubble, scrapping over every habitation. The reserves are ready. You have their coordinates, they have their orders.'

Sigismund nodded.

'I will return to Bhab,' Dorn said. 'Communications are collapsing, and the Sanctum must remain operational. You, though.' He smiled coldly. 'I remember your ambition. To be here, whatever the cost.'

No reaction. Just that unbending devotion to duty. It could be almost scary, sometimes, to be in the presence of such a hyper-controlled psyche. Maybe other souls saw much the same monomania in him, too, but Sigismund was... well, Sigismund had always been something else.

'It has all come to pass, I suppose, just as the remembrancer girl told you it would. Coincidence? I have to believe it.'

Did he, though? Clinging too closely to the old rationalist cant felt pointless, now. Even Malcador was beginning to waver, marking the slide back into superstition.

'So many wars. So much blood spilt, all to reach the point that she foresaw from the start. I gave you hell for it then, but the new doctrines must give way to the old, it seems, and we can worry about what that means if any of us get out of this alive.'

Sigismund just stared back at him, the steel-trap gaze, the same mask he wore when he duelled.

'So the discipline is ended, the leash is off,' Dorn told him. 'March out. Take the wall defences, take the reserves and rally them. They will be blind and deaf out there soon, and so will need a leader.'

Sigismund nodded again. No other soul would have noticed it, but there was something other than the usual dutifulness in his eyes just then. Something like hunger. 'Any specific objectives, lord?' he asked.

At that, Dorn almost laughed. Not from humour, just from emptiness, the caustic recognition of what would come next.

He had given everything. He was already empty, drained to a husk, and the hardest test still lay ahead. The Lion had not come. Guilliman and Russ had not come. They were out of time, out of luck, and what remained now was only defiance – only bloody-minded, bloody-handed defiance.

'No, I set you free, my beloved, my best, son,' said Rogal Dorn, never taking his eyes off his First Captain. 'Do now what you were made to do.'

He smiled a second time, the expression as icy as the despair that gripped his hearts.

'*Hurt* them.'

Bran Koba sprinted, straining so hard that his lungs throbbed and his boots slipped. His squad came with him – thirty troopers, all in the carapace armour of the 13th Astranian Void-Jackals.

His heart was thumping wildly, both from the exertion and from a healthy slice of fear. General Nasuba's orders had filtered down the command chain too slowly, hampered by the faulty comms, by the general collapse in morale, by the rising tide of panic that seemed to be engulfing everything. Each of Mercury Wall's four great bastions was a gigantic citadel, stacked with level after level of internal complexity, and you just couldn't keep control of all that without the confidence people would actually answer their damned vox.

He could hear the thunder from outside now. His entire squad could too, swelling up against the exterior of walls so immense that by rights no noise at all should ever have been able to penetrate. But they were a long way down – close to the very base of it all, buried deep in a core foundation section. The ancient piles were sunk into the raw stuff of the terra-former's art here, and resonances travelled a long way, echoing in every chamber and knocking dust from the narrow-arched roofs.

The overhead suspensors blanked, then blacked out, just as something colossal struck the outer wall-skin again.

'Helms!' Koba yelled, switching on his forehead-mounted lumens.

After that they were haring through the darkness, relying on thirty-one bobbing pools of weak light, tripping and blundering like lost children.

The walls of the Inner Palace were not, as might appear from the outside, monolithic blocks of solid matter. They were honeycombed inside with all the machinery needed to keep the integral heavy gun platforms working – the energy conduits, the cooling vanes, the access galleries and service tunnels. They were like subterranean cities in their own right, manned by tens of thousands of technicians and wired-in servitors. If, in theory, an enemy were ever to come close to cracking the outer layers of defensive plating, then protocols existed to depower the entire spider's web of control chambers and flood them all with flame-retardant chems. In such an eventuality you would lose the wall guns – again, in theory – but negate the risk of catastrophic chain reactions in the – highly theoretical – case that something explosive managed to worm its way through hundreds of metres of solid adamantium.

All so much theory, Koba had always thought. A typical piece of over-engineering from the lord primarch, whom they all knew had built so much redundancy into every single bulwark and every single rampart that the chance of system failure across an entire wall section was as close to zero as made no difference.

But now he'd seen what the enemy looked like. He'd watched through his magnoculars, alongside thousands of gallery-mounted defenders, as the marching hell-machines had chewed their way across the open plains. It wasn't their size that had been so horrific – even though that had been bad enough – but their *speed*. The horizon had been filled from north to south with a tidal sweep of explosions, advancing faster than should have been possible – sheets of rippling fire through which those damned monsters had just kept on striding. A kill-zone that should have taken months to subdue had been compassed in days, an appalling spectacle, one that had blown all the defenders' careful fallback scheduling out of the water. Everything sent against those things had been crunched into fragments. Koba had imagined that an individual Titan was something close to being invulnerable, a weapon so outrageous in form and heft that its very presence should be enough to quell anything conceivable, but to see them destroyed, not in ones and twos, but in their *hundreds*… There were no words for that, no ways to articulate the things he'd seen.

They had been caught napping, a situation made worse by the degradation of every command conduit in every control tower. It wasn't just the augurs and the comms-tech that had failed them, but the defenders' *nerve*. Something had got inside the walls before the physical enemy had – a surging tide of hopelessness, a mounting pall of desperation that made men throw themselves from the high parapets and women slit their throats with their own bayonets. Until Dorn had deployed four hundred of his own Legion warriors to restore order it had looked likely the entire section might slump into complete anarchy, but even now things were balanced on a knife-edge. You couldn't rely on a voxed order being carried out, you couldn't rely on an augur reading being accurate or a section report being anything other than gibberish. You had to send armed teams to oversee everything, to make sure things were done, then come back in person to confirm it all, and somehow make sure your troops didn't go mad or kill themselves in the meantime.

That dragged them down. That gummed them up. And that was the weakness, the decisive flaw – the protocols were too slow, and the enemy was too fast, and suddenly it was all going to the hells. The generators had to be shut down, their power intakes killed, their reservoirs drained. And it had to happen *now*, before those hell-machines managed to force a breach and get their vile weaponry inside.

'Faster!' he shouted, making it to the end of the corridor, stumbling, catching himself, scrabbling around the corner, then running hard for the security hatch at the far end of the next one.

Now he could hear the plasma generators roaring, making the walls shake, filling the cycled atmosphere with the tang of chems. He could hear the shouts of anger and confusion from up ahead. He could sense the fear.

'Emperor guide me,' he muttered. He didn't know whether that would help. The Emperor was just a man, they had always said. But when Koba whispered it, for some reason, it gave him a little boost. It kept him going.

He reached the security door, punched the access code, then burst through.

The chamber on the far side was very big indeed – a

yawning chasm set inside the wall's core, soaring away both up and down for a hundred metres. Koba and his team emerged onto a platform perched on the inside edge. The platform's deck was already crowded with functionaries and guards, some wearing Mechanicus colours, others in the ochre yellow of the Palace technical cadres. Control machinery, most of it boxy and human-sized, took up the rest of the space. A man lay on the floor, bleeding. Another man, in the longer robes of a senior technician, had been pinned up against a sensor bank by three menials, his hair and clothes disarranged. Others were shouting, jabbing fingers at one another, faces flushed.

Beyond the safety railing, out in the gulf beyond, were the generators themselves – each the height of a multi-storey hab-unit, glowing internally with vicious levels of power, strung up in a web of cabling and support beams. Arcs of energy crackled and spat between the immense coils, making the entire space flash and jump with vivid light. It was noisy, echoing, and smelled of piped coolant.

'Shut it down!' Koba shouted, switching off his helm-lumens and levelling his lasgun at the member of the mob who looked the most senior.

'No, it's a mistake!' one of the operatives yelled back. Her face was wild, her eyes staring. 'The enemy *wants* them shut down! We need the guns operational!'

'Throne, just *listen* to him!' pleaded the senior technician, still pinned against the wall. For the first time, Koba saw the bruising on his face. 'They were *genuine orders.*'

Koba gestured for his troops to advance, guns trained. Time was of the essence. 'Shut them down,' he ordered the woman. 'I won't tell you again.'

'Never!' she retorted, reaching for her own weapon. 'You're just another–'

Koba shot her in the shoulder, hurling her back against the railings. His squad opened fire in support, aiming high, making the rest of the technicians scamper for cover. Then Koba was at the command terminals, trying to make sense of the controls. The generators thundered, less than fifty metres away from him, lacing everything with static, booming, making it hard to think.

The senior technician, freed from his captors, scrabbled across to him. 'That one!' he blurted urgently, gesturing to a glistening control column. 'Plunge it!'

Koba seized it two-handed and slid the column into its sleeve. Nothing much happened. An alarm briefly sounded, and a monitor bank blew out, but the generators kept on booming, the plasma silos kept on feeding out, the power lines remained fully activated.

'What in the–' he started, before seeing the woman again, on the deck now, just a few metres away, grinning at him.

She had a cluster of wires in her hand, yanked from an open access panel. Some of the conduits were still live, and tiny flickers of electricity squirmed to the deck, making her start and wince.

'You'll never do it, traitor!' she screamed triumphantly, wriggling away and pulling the gaggle of cabling with her. Blood ran from her mouth, bright red in the plasma-flare. 'You'll never do it! The guns must fire!'

He stared at her, horrified. For a terrible instant, he had no idea what to do. He wasn't a technician – he was a soldier, just sent to ensure orders were followed.

'Blow the main power intakes!' the senior technician shouted, yanking at Koba's arm to show him where he meant. 'That'll trigger a shutdown! Blow them out!'

Above them, maybe thirty metres up, six massive tubes jutted from the wall and ran horizontally out towards the generators. They were encased in polished metal jackets, well protected, but Koba guessed lasguns might puncture the outer skins.

'You heard him!' Koba yelled at his squad. 'Knock them out!'

But then the entire deck rocked, shivered to its foundations, and half his troops lost their footing. A web of fissures crackled outward across the wall section directly overhead, spreading with astonishing speed. Blown masonry chunks cascaded down, crashing off the deck and bouncing into the gulf below. Spears of fire shot out from the fissures, and the ear-splitting sound of military drills broke out, echoing eerily as the main wall structure was pummelled from the outside.

The enemy was almost through. The generators were still barrelling along at full tilt.

Koba gritted his teeth, aimed upward at the power lines, and fired. He hit with every shot he took. Others of his squad hit them too. Even as they emptied their power packs at the links, the walls above them bulged obscenely, cracks widening, the cacophony of the drills rapidly crescendoing until nothing else but the grind of adamantium through rockcrete could be heard.

He fired through it all, his finger clamped onto the trigger. He found himself willing a las-bolt – just one – to cut through. He found himself asking the Emperor to grant him that. That one small thing.

It was never going to be enough. He'd have needed much longer to cut through the power line casing with a handheld las-weapon. Maybe a bolter could have done it. Maybe the lord primarch should have sent one of his sons for this work. Then again, there were dozens of generators, and the Space Marines could not be everywhere.

A wall-plate above him blew out entirely, vomiting debris at the plasma chambers. The scraping whine of the drills screamed off the scale, followed by the howl of incoming air – superheated, acrid, blasted in from the raging battlefields outside. Shattered metal-faced ouslite blocks thunked and pinged from the generator's housing – huge pieces of the wall's external plating, sent spinning into its core like bullets. Then came the beams of energy weapons, blistering into the chamber and igniting on the already gas-infused air.

As the first of the mainline beams struck home, piercing the outer skin of the nearest plasma chamber, Koba knew that his time was over, and that he had failed. Still firing doggedly, he managed to mouth four final, horrified words.

'Throne preserve us all...'

And then everything turned into fire.

The Nails bit deep, goading him, driving him to a heightened pitch of frustration. He had to kill. He had to kill *now*, to bury his chainaxe into something living, or the Nails would just spike at him harder, punishing him, those glorious barbs against weakness, the things he both hated and needed.

For so long, there had been nothing to kill. Skarr-Hei had raced across the wreck-strewn plains in the wake of godmachines, first inside the stinking hull of a foetid old Land Raider, then on foot, desperate to fight. Hundreds of thousands had come with him – legionaries, mutants, cultists, all the varied servants of the gods, all slavering to get across the threshold. Some had the light of faith in their staring eyes, others were animated by a baser kind of bloodlust.

He barely felt anything now, save for the blinding waves of agony. His vision was cloudy, tinged with red, juddering whenever he moved his head. His hearts were already pumping, flooding his system with violence, and yet there was nothing to hurt, nothing to test him, nothing to go up against.

He wanted to scream. He wanted to roar. It would come,

soon. Surely. The primarch had promised them that much, showing them the way.

Skarr-Hei wondered, briefly, where the primarch was now. He wondered where the captain of the Eighth Assault Company was. Everything seemed to have dissolved so quickly, the battalions disintegrating and pursuing their own targets. His own squad were close by, somewhere, but he couldn't see any of them in the murk. Okasha had gone on a bit of a rampage, hacking his way through a detachment of beastmen, his frustration at having nothing better to kill getting the better of him. Ghazak and Nham had lumbered off in the shadow of a gang of Knights, perhaps sniffing something to hunt down. The rest should have stayed close, but he couldn't see them.

Smoke rolled up around him, smothering the landscape in clods of shifting blackness. Every so often those blooms would ignite, lit from within by some detonation, hearts of blood-red amid the deepening night. The Titans were still grappling out there, he knew – the last of the False Emperor's slave-machines, selling their unquestioning lives without honour or commitment. He didn't care about that kind of combat. He didn't care about ranged mega-bolters or lascannons. He wanted to get up close, the kind of fighting he'd been made for. You needed a Titan to open the first crack, but you needed flesh-and-blood warriors to actually make use of it, to take it and hold it, to push on and turn the ground red.

So he'd come alongside Mortis on their rampage, his Land Raider skidding and gunning around their mighty feet, coming so close to them that he might have been crushed more than once. When the transport had been hit sufficiently badly that its armour had peeled off and the tracks jammed, he'd leapt from it eagerly, knowing he was near enough now to make it on foot, to *be there*, to witness the moment when they would get their reward and start the proper slaughter.

Just then, even in the midst of the combat-madness, inside
his closed sphere of fury, he'd retained just enough awareness to be momentarily daunted. From ground level, up so
close, those walls were gigantic. Far bigger than anything he'd
gone up against before, difficult even to process. The vanguard of the Mortis Titans were up against the base of them,
void shields crackling with the debris that showered down.
The terrain was broken-up and sodden, cratered by the march
of the leviathans. Mortar shells fell incessantly, throwing up
sprays of boiling mud where they thunked to earth. Uncounted
thousands of helm-lenses pinpricked the gloom, blinking in
and out as the smoke rolled across them, marking the ragged
advance of the swarming infantry-tide.

They were caught in the open ground now. You couldn't go
back, or you'd end up mired in the ongoing Titan-brawls on
the plains. You couldn't advance, because those damned walls
were still intact. The parapet guns had mostly fallen silent, but
a thick storm of artillery still looped over the summit. The
longer this lasted, the more likely it was that they would all
die out here, in the slime, having achieved nothing.

Skarr-Hei lumbered up closer, breathing heavily, watching
warily as the curve of the high perimeter swept up into the star-
less night. He panted in the smoke, tasting the thick cocktail
of engine fumes and weapon discharges. He felt as if he would
burst apart, spill out of his armour's confines, become just
another swirling ball of flame to score the darkness. Gangs of
warriors milled around him in the shadows – Lorgar's fanatics,
Perturabo's now leaderless technicians, the Warmaster's own
sea-green killers. More troops were arriving all the time, spilling
from the guts of transports, forming up into straggling columns
and sent trudging up the slope towards the wall-shadow.

A singular colossus stood above and ahead of them all –
an Imperator-class Titan, surrounded by a phalanx of its

giant escorts, vast and fire-shrouded. Its hide was corrupted, blistered, weeping from metallic sores. Liquids poured from its vents and sluice-gates, foaming down its immense legs, mingling with the sludge-trail it had left on its advance. It smelled fouler than anything else on the entire befouled planet, corrupted to its core, leaking ruin like a living thing would leak sweat. Skarr-Hei didn't know its name. He barely knew his own, by that point.

Getting so close to it was dangerous. If that thing moved by just a fraction, a single tread could wipe out a whole infantry company. But Skarr-Hei didn't care. He pushed up, pushed on, his breath coming in animal growls now, sensing the static prickle of void shields far above. The Titan's bulk stretched away, looming over him, just like the other god-machines gathered there – fifty at least, more coming all the time. It felt like being lost in the shade of some metal forest, dwarfed by the boles of impossible, twisted trees. The engines' combined shield-aegis had mingled properly now, forming a giant film of interference-drummed protection in the sky overhead, one that burned and fizzed and flexed as projectiles crashed across it.

As Skarr-Hei crept along beneath their feet, the earth reeled. The night-gloom was ripped into slivers of dazzling light and smoke. Drills, propelled by mighty arms, gouged and tore into adamantium plate and piled rockcrete. Energy beams and melta-bursts pummelled and atomised, opening up caverns and cutting ravines. The scale of destruction was tremendous – a symphony of concentrated annihilation, focused and overlapped and poured onto the fracture points with remorseless single-mindedness.

On another night, Skarr-Hei might have admired the skill of it. But now, with the Nails biting deep, he was only conscious of his frustration. It might take days to blast through that barrier. Maybe weeks. Someone had miscalculated. He didn't care who, or why, but he was being denied his prey.

He almost turned back. He could hack his way out across the plains again, he thought – track down the rest of his god-cursed squad, make his way to some other battlefront in the ruins below the Anterior Wall, somewhere he could actually do some fighting.

But then the drills abruptly silenced. The beam-weapons went dark. The Titans' war-horns, deafening since he'd arrived at the front, echoed out.

Something had penetrated. Something had ignited. The entire battlefield, crammed with hundreds of thousands of armoured warriors, held a breath. Even the metronomic beat of the artillery seemed to falter, as if the world itself suddenly found itself on the edge of a cliff, horrified, poised to drop into an oblivion from which there would be no return.

Skarr-Hei peered into the murk. He could hear explosions, buried deep, muffled by layers upon layers of protection. He could feel the torture of the earth underfoot, more profound than the tremors provoked by the constant impact of munitions. He could see forks of lightning flickering, racing across the enormous black expanse, scampering like daemons across the face of an oily mirror.

The Titans started to withdraw, cumbersomely, awkwardly, causing havoc as they slowly turned. The war-horns started up again, as did the screams and shouts of stimm-crazed cultists. Skarr-Hei remained rooted to the spot, watching as the explosions fed off one another, building and building, still trapped under all that weight of wall. Shafts of light burst out from the fissures, blue-edged, angling into the gloom like floodlumens.

'It's… happening,' he slurred, feeling the tectonic instability begin to accelerate, to turn the soils into a drumming mass of dirt and ash. He smelled the telltale tang of a plasma breach reaching critical explosive mass. He heard the howl and bang of escaping gases, followed by a roar so massive that it nearly floored him. Blisters of flame burst out, shooting up the wall-surface and sucking at the parapets. Armour plates detached from the outer skin, disintegrating as they slid down, accelerating the collapse. The rumbles merged, swelled, became roars like starship engines kindling.

Then it blew, the long-awaited apocalypse, the almighty chain-linked explosion that blasted the outer plates clean away, sending thousands of tonnes of defensive architecture hurtling out into the night, backed up by a blast wave that radiated out from the epicentre and sent the structure around it crunching and slipping and tumbling over itself, spawning a debris cloud that reared higher than the parapets, surging into the heights, extending over even the pinnacles of the great spires, coating everything within kilometres in a layer of hot dust.

Skarr-Hei was laughing even as the storm swept across him, tearing at the tethered skulls on his armour. His axe was raised, streamers of fire flailing from its killing edge, whipped back as the hurricane screamed past.

There was no complete collapse, no total flattening of such an enormous structure, but a mighty landslide, a stately implosion of internal layers, a see-sawing of toppling observation towers and a subsidence of support piers. The dust cloud kept on rising, fuelled by its own mass now, lit up internally by secondary fulguration. A tidal wave of detritus spilled from the high breach, scraping down the slope in an avalanche that went on accelerating. The infantry vanguard fled from that, stumbling away from it, wiping their visors and trying not to lose their footing in the swirling miasma. Even the god-machines stumbled, rocked by the maelstrom they had unleashed.

Skarr-Hei remained defiant, arms outstretched, roaring back at the deluge. He swayed into the press of the wind, revelling in its intense pressure.

'For the Lord of Rage!' he cried, the Nails spurring him, now with the joy of what had to come next.

Even before the avalanche had stilled, he was running again, clambering, slipping and scrabbling up the piles of rubble. Alongside him, he could hear the massed roar of many thousands more, all rousing themselves from their stupor, stirring into action and calling on their gods and daemons to aid them.

The Titans couldn't follow – not yet. The incline was still massive, still steep. Even for Skarr-Hei, the ascent was testing, as the red-hot rubble slipped under his boots and clattered back down the slope. He was only dimly aware of those coming up with him – his crimson-tinged focus was firmly at the crest of the breach: a jagged heap of blown rockcrete, maybe three hundred metres wide, flanked at either end by the sawtooth edges of the intact parapets. Reaching it was like struggling to crest a mountain pass, beset all the while by the searing pressure of the superheated wind.

But then he did it. As the artillery fire started up again, as a stunned corps of defenders started to recover their wits and race to activate what defensive positions were still intact, Skarr-Hei of the World Eaters crested the final rise of twisted metalwork and smouldering masonry. For a moment, he stood on the cusp, staring out ahead.

Behind him lay the wastes, crawling with innumerable fighters. On either side of him were the walls, penetrated here but otherwise intact. Ahead of him, unravelling under a heavy shadow of dust and smog, was the object of all his tortured dreams, the promise of which had kept him going, year after year, even when existence itself had become so agonised that only death had felt like a possible release.

Spire up against spire, basilica up against basilica, a press of buildings so tight and so dense that it felt like you could shelter an entire world's population within its precincts. It was stuffed with life, now – fearful, timorous life. Skarr-Hei looked out at it, gazing across the vista of fear, taking in the intoxication of its abjectness, its ripeness.

It had begun here. Everything had begun here. But he didn't see any of that. He didn't see the place truly at all – the citizens huddled in the basements, the young and the old gaping with horror at the noise and the stench. He didn't even see Terra, just then. It could have been any citadel on any world, albeit a civilised one, one full of the rich and the weak and the cruel.

Now *he* was here, Skarr-Hei, Eater of Worlds. He had already killed many souls in this battle, but many more lay before him at that moment, in numbers undreamed of, herded together like cattle into the abattoir.

He gunned the teeth on his chain axe, and the familiar whirr made him want to roar with pleasure.

'Inside!' he slurred, his half-seeing eyes blearily fixed on the distant Sanctum Imperialis. 'God of all murder, we're *inside!*'

FOUR

Restorer
The Sage
Superiority

Inside, back within the walls, the sanctuary he'd worked so hard to reach, sheltered from the maelstrom for just a short time.

He didn't remember the journey from Marmax South very well. The entire front had been in disarray, collapsing around him, and he had flitted in and out of consciousness the whole time. A man had been there with him, one called Katsu-hiro. It was he who had managed to raise the alarm, get him dragged from the front line and sent back through the warren of trenches. That was the last he'd seen of him. He found himself wanting to go back, now – to seek him out again, give him thanks for it. But at the time he had just moved on, carrying the corpse of the other man he'd encountered, Cole, only for long enough to bury him. The child, the one Cole had been caring for in the wastes, he had left behind. How could he have done otherwise? There were no better sanctuaries now than those trenches, and no better carers for him than those people. He needed to return to the fight, to take his place beside his brothers once more.

Still, he thought of them often. Cole, and the child, and the man, Katsuhiro.

Shiban Khan stood up. He extended his right arm, then his left. He tested the reactions of his power armour, the interface with his muscles, paying particular attention to where those muscles were bundles of Martian metalwork rather than products of Terran genecraft. He walked, just a few paces across the stone floor, letting the weight of the battleplate test his still-raw wounds.

He was recovering quickly. Part of that was his Astartes physiology, part of it was the superior augmetics he'd been given on his return to Terra. He was hard to kill. He always had been. Not as great a warrior as Hasik or Jemulan, to be sure. Certainly not in the class of Qin Xa or Jubal. But they were gone, all of those names, swept away by this murderous war. Somehow, he was still intact, his wounds knitting up, his weapons reconditioned, ready to go again.

Withdraw, then return, he thought.

The chamber was a small one – windowless, buried deep in one of Colossi's many thick towers. Even so, he could feel the thrum of constant bombardment resonating up from the floor, making the slabbed stone walls shiver. The lumens blinked every so often when a big hit came in, and dust trickled from the whitewashed ceiling.

His knowledge of the wider battle was incomplete. The last he'd known, Colossi was where the Khagan had chosen to make his stand, and where much of the ordu's strength had been gathered. Clearly, for the time being, that defence had succeeded. Marmax, too, was in the defenders' hands, though the situation there had felt precarious in the extreme. Beyond that, he had little certainty. His long trudge through the outer wastelands, territory lost to the enemy, had shown him only what depravities waited for them all, should they fail here – it had been a desperate place, a fog-wreathed swamp where only the corrupted could linger.

The Eternity Wall space port was like that now, in all probability, for this enemy did not merely occupy territory – they changed it, twisted it, made it an incubator for their perversions. The bodies of those who had fallen at Eternity would be sunk deep into the warp-sick muck by now, denied an honourable burial or – for the White Scars among them – the rites of *kal damarg*.

He could so easily slip into hatred, for that. He had flirted with it, during the long years of the fighting to get back to Terra, his soul ravaged by the constant losses, but never quite given in. Nothing could ever be as carefree as it had been for them on the White World, back when the only enemy had been xenos, but if Yesugei had taught them anything at all, it was that the greatest failure was to lose yourself, the core of your being, the essence of the thing.

So he guarded it carefully now. Maintain the balance, remember that war is an art, treat it like the curve of a brush on paper. The Legion was not quite extinguished, and its numbers had been swelled by those hastily inducted into the ranks, neither Chogorian nor Terran, but gathered up and made use of from a dozen worlds before being thrown into the furnace here. They would need guidance, if they were not to fall into the trap that he himself had danced around. In the absence of the giants of the past, the ones who had forged the Legion in its infancy, they would still need schooling.

He didn't feel like an exemplar. Perhaps, just after Prospero, when many had been clamouring for him to assume greater influence, he might have seized the chance, but the injuries just then had been so great, so debilitating, and after that the poison of betrayal had soured everything for too long. It had always been the Khagan's choice to make, and Jubal had been the right one.

So what did it mean, then, to be the last one standing? Was there any particular honour in that, or were the flaws all still there, ready to be exposed in the final analysis?

It would have been good to speak to Ilya about it, though he doubted if it would be possible now. He didn't even know where she was – not here, at the front, surely. But just then the chamber door opened, as if prompted by the very thought of her.

It wasn't Ilya, of course – fate was never quite that neat. Stooping, as he always had to in these fortresses built for baseline humans, the Warhawk of Chogoris, Jaghatai Khan, his primarch, came inside.

Shiban bowed low. 'Khagan,' he said simply.

The Great Khan appraised him. 'You seem better, Tachseer. I'm glad of it. Welcome back.'

'Thank you.'

There had been a time when Shiban had been so eager to lay eyes on the Great Khan that he'd have fought his way across half a planet to be there. Jaghatai had been a force of the universe then, something to marvel at as much as to serve. In some ways, Shiban still felt the same way – the devotion was just as strong – but the endless conflict had ground away at all of them, and even Jaghatai had not been spared. He had always been lean; now he looked rangy. He had always spoken softly; now his voice was hoarse. Something had changed in him after Catullus – he was not diminished in raw power, as far as anyone could have gauged, but there was something colder in him now, something frozen. His ivory warplate was chipped, the gold lining had faded. His hair was loose and hung lank against his copper skin. The scar on his cheek seemed darker, more like a birthmark than something he'd cut himself.

The Khan looked around the sparse chamber – the narrow cot, the table, the chair, the comms-box and the sensor-jammer. 'I never truly thought you'd died,' he said.

Shiban raised an eyebrow. 'Then you had more faith than I did. Some of the time, at least.'

'I've begun to recognise the signs. The way I feel, before a soul of my people is lost.' He smiled thinly. 'So many gone now, I've had the practice.'

'But Colossi holds. I didn't know if you'd still be here.'

'We won't be. Not for long.' Then the Khan stirred himself, drew in a long breath, shook off his torpor. 'Tell me of the Eternity Wall port.'

Shiban recounted how it had been – the overwhelming assault, the gradual wearing down of the defences, the progress of the resistance, the price they had exacted from the enemy before the outer gates had finally fallen. He spoke quickly, precisely, giving only the information his master would wish to know. 'At the end, we were trying to use the port's tugs, to turn the drives into weapons. That was what kept me away from the final assault, as well as what launched me away from the fighting. The last thing I remember, after being hit, was striking the outer edge at speed. I woke up somewhere to the south of the curtain wall, I think. Then it was just a matter of finding a path back.'

The Khan nodded. 'Just a matter. My guess is there's a story in that, all of its own.' He had been staring down at his clasped hands, and now looked up. 'But I'm proud. Truly, I am. We needed a representative there, someone to remind my brother just what we contribute to his endeavours. I never believed in ceding the ports. I would have fought for longer at the Lion's Gate platforms, but at least we learned our lesson from that.'

'Maybe we should have done.'

'But we did.'

Shiban hesitated, unsure how to respond to that. The words

confused him. Could it be true? Had his master truly not known? In some ways, that made things easier. In others, far more difficult.

'Then, you...' he began. 'You believe we were meant to hold it?'

'Of course. You did what you could.'

'You and the Lord Dorn both?'

Jaghatai's dark eyes pinned him. 'What are you trying to say, Shiban?'

It would have been impossible to conceal anything from his gene-father, even if he'd been minded to try. Still, trying to find the words, to determine how to break this painful truth, that was tortuous.

'I may have been wrong,' he said weakly. 'That is always possible. But I spoke to Niborran, the commander. He made things as plain as they were ever likely to be.' He took a deep breath. 'Eternity Wall space port was allowed to fall. It could never have been held, not with what we were given.'

'No. If that had been true, you would have been evacuated.'

'We couldn't have been. The enemy had to believe we were fixed on keeping it. Eyes had to be focused on it, to prevent them from lighting somewhere else.'

Shiban remembered then how he had first felt, knowing that truth. It hadn't been so bad, back then – dying in battle, for whatever reason, was something that would come to all of them, sooner or later. Trying to reconstruct it all now, though, after all the deaths – that was miserable.

'I don't know what it was. Some other front, some other gambit. But, when I went up for the tugs, to buy us a little more time, I did so knowing that it wouldn't be anything other than a stalling of the inevitable. I never expected to come back. None of us did. That was what a few of us learned. We were sent there to die, my Khan. It was a ruse.'

For a moment, a single moment that felt everlasting, Jaghatai said nothing. His scarred face remained rigid, digesting that. His lips remained sealed. Shiban suddenly remembered how the primarch had been during the Legion trials, when he had wielded the blade against those of his own people who had been tempted by Horus, and had been more deeply wounded than any of those he had passed judgement on.

'The bastard,' the Khan breathed softly. His eyes darkened. The mournful look hardened quickly into anger. 'The lying, deceitful *bastard*.' He turned away, fists now clenched, looking suddenly, alarmingly, as if he might tear the entire chamber apart. 'He looked me in the *eye*. He stood right before me, closer than you are now, and lied. What did he think? That I'd blow his secret? That I'd prevent him? Damned right, I would have.'

Shiban almost had to suppress a smile then – not from amusement, but from a kind of relief. His primarch was still a force of the universe, after all – still as alive and passionate and fiercely protective as he had ever been.

'They should have been told. *You* should have been told.' The Khan shook his head in furious disbelief. 'A warrior may sell his life for a cause, but he must *know*. When we created the *sagyar mazan*, we never lied to them. That foul habit is what got us into this damned mess in the first place – thinking the truth was something to be kept under wraps, to be hidden from those who did the work.'

'If we had known,' Shiban offered carefully, 'the truth would have got out. The gambit would have failed.'

'You really think that? You trust those you fight alongside so little, even now?' Jaghatai's lip curled in disdain. 'Since this thing began, I've seen baseline detachments face up to horrors they had no business even being in the same galaxy with. I've seen them stand up, keep their weapons straight, stare down their own annihilation. Soul of the Altak, they have schooled us all. They should have *been told*.'

Slowly, the Khan brought himself under control, though anger still simmered under every gesture. He slumped back against the far wall, his long arms slack against the rockcrete. His chin sank against his chest.

Silence fell across the chamber again, and Shiban knew better than to break it.

The next thing he heard was unexpected – a low, sourly amused laugh.

'But then, what kind of example am I, really?' the Khan murmured. 'My brother does what he has to. He cannot break his nature, any more than I could. I understand some things better now.' His lips twitched into a wry smile. 'He was right, of course. Saturnine, I'm guessing. That does not make it any less contemptible, but I am sure he was right.' He pushed back from the wall, stood tall again. 'And I was always indulged beyond belief, you know that? Rogal spent his life denying himself everything, curbing every urge that might have actually given him some kind of joy, and all that while we were given our head, cut loose, treating an order from the Throne like it was some kind of insult.'

'We were true to our nature.'

'We were lucky. And we were selfish.' His expression became darker again. 'So this is where we make amends for that. The cost has been too high already, and there are more payments to come, but now I am angry, I am *furious*, for no one has been listening, even while the source of our sickness is as plain as the scar on your face. If we fail to act now, we will die behind these walls, another wasted defence, and that cannot be borne, for wherever and whenever I am destined to meet my end, it will not be behind a damned wall.'

It was good to hear such words. Even if the Khan's anger

was colder than it had been, less joyous and harder-edged, it was still magnificent to behold.

'Then you will call *kurultai*,' Shiban said. 'You will summon the khans.'

'The call has already gone out,' the Khan said. 'Not just to the Legion. To anyone, anything, that can help us.' He grinned then, the old expression of dangerous anticipation. 'Which makes me glad you are back in time to join us, Tachseer. The hunt has been called. It will need its masters.'

It was still a city. You had to remember that. Millions of people still lived here, crammed up against one another, terrified, doing their best to stay alive as the tides of unreality crashed against the faltering barricades. Many, perhaps even most, were no sort of warrior at all. They were the scribes, the administrators, the operatives and the civil servants who had come here first to govern an empire. Nestled up against those were the refugees from the Outer Palace and the sprawl beyond, who were far too diverse to classify, and had now merged into the already crowded tenements and spire trunks, starving, terrified.

Ilya Ravallion watched the immense, interlocked buildings pass by in the night. The sky above her was lurid, inked both by the orbital assault against the shields and the closer explosions of terrestrial artillery. The few remaining street-lumens strobed and guttered. It was all filthy, coated with ash, piled up with rubbish that could not be collected. They were hemmed in, a sealed system now, surrounded on all sides.

She leaned against the condensation-fogged window on her armoured transport, watching the narrow streets slide through the darkness. Crowds were everywhere. Troops ran and shouted. Administratum vehicles occasionally nudged their way through the clogged-up transitways, sirens wailing, some of them grav-plate skimmers, most old-model groundcars. If you looked carefully, you could catch snippets of more mundane forms of life in the gaps between the urgent war-business – queues for rations, huddles around burning promethium canisters, children in rags scuttling through the legs of the adults. You could see arguments, fist fights, couples holding on to one another desperately, glass-eyed loners stumbling amid the refuse. Despite the universe ending around them, they were still doing what they had to. They had to eat. They had to keep warm. They still squabbled over their place in the ration-lines, bickered about whether they should have taken that shuttle off-world four years ago when there had still been time, wondered if their overseer position at the tooling works would still be secure by this time next month.

This time *next month*. That made her smile.

It had taken humanity two centuries to spill out from Terra and smother the entire galaxy with its hubris. It had taken seven years for it to contract again, pulling all of that reckless energy back to a single city on a single world. Now, only days remained before it would all be over, one way or another. The few comms-bursts she managed to get from the Legion command indicated that the Mercury Wall had been breached, less than a hundred and sixty kilometres to the north-east. The war had been uncomfortably close to these citizens for weeks; soon it would be rammed down their throats, surging up every thoroughfare and through every hab-cluster.

But Ilya was not much different to all those scared souls, she knew. The long fight to bring the V Legion home had hollowed her out. She had been near the end of a distinguished career at the start of the war, and the privations of the extended void campaign had done the rest. She didn't have any of the advantages of the Space Marines she worked alongside. They still deferred to her, called her *szu*-Ilya – even more so than before, especially the newbloods – but it had almost become irritating now, because she was so obviously dying, just like this world, just like the Imperium, and there was no real point in any of it any more.

They wouldn't change, though. You had to love them for that. All the daemon-terrors of the species' nightmares could be pouring through the air vents and scrabbling at everyone's throats, and there would still be a White Scar on hand to ask if, szu, are you most well? Is there anything you are in need of? Can I be of any assistance?

'We are almost there, szu,' said her driver, right on cue. 'Commencing descent to yard two-forty-one.'

The speaker was one of the ordu, a warrior named Sojuk. Such experienced fighters were like gold dust at the front right now, but still the Khagan had insisted on her being accompanied on her mission by a full battle-brother. When she'd protested, insisting that a standard Imperial Army escort would be sufficient so far back from the main combat zones, he'd fixed her with that heavy, unarguable stare of his, and said, 'It'll all be engulfed soon. Just take him.'

So she had. Now she was glad of it. The Inner Palace felt more dangerous than she'd ever known it, suffused with an air of mania that got under the skin, and having Sojuk at her side was a comfort. It was hard to pinpoint exactly what was going wrong. Civilians in warzones often panicked, but this was different. It was almost as if they'd begun to give up entirely, their vital spirits drained out of them by some vile, unseen miasma.

'Very good,' she said, adjusting her uniform jacket, glancing in the rear-view mirror to check her appearance, tucking in a stray wisp of grey hair. She was very thin now. However old and useless she felt these days, though, you had to look the part – sharp, together. 'Bring us down.'

The transport swerved off the main transitway and trundled down a shallow rockcrete slope. A pair of heavy blast doors drew up, manned by sentries and gloomy under low lighting. Sojuk spoke briefly to the senior guard, and a moment later the doors were hoisted up, revealing a wide tunnel running further down below ground level.

Sojuk travelled another few hundred metres before the incline brought them out into a subterranean cavern, sunk deep into the solid bedrock of the city foundations. The air smelled strongly of exhaust fumes, and the space echoed with the ringing clang of power tools. He drew the transport up at a vacant berth, killed the engine, dismounted, and opened the door for Ilya. She stepped out, feeling her muscles ache, and looked around.

Yard 241 was huge, running back into shadowy depths that her eyesight couldn't penetrate. The cavern roof was about twenty metres up, rough-cut and hung with sodium tubes. Long chains of atmosphere processors snaked across it, sucking up the noisome air and blasting the worst of the toxins back up to ground level.

Across the rockcrete deck stood tanks. Hundreds of them, by the look of it. They were decked out in a range of colours and bore many different regimental badges. Most were standard Leman Russ battle tanks, arranged in rows, their panels open for servicing. Other variants clustered here and there – Medusa artillery pieces, Chimera armoured transports, even a few giants such as the mammoth Baneblades and Stormlords. Technical crews clustered around many of them, hammering at the engines, clamping fuel lines, welding fresh armour plating. Interspersed with the static units were the long lines of support vehicles: the tankers, the platoon groundcars, the maintenance and medical wagons. Gangs of Imperial Army personnel were everywhere, running to and fro, shouting at one another, or just lounging against the tracks of their vehicles looking exhausted. It was noisy, reverberating and stinking. After only a few seconds standing there, Ilya felt as if her skin had been freshly coated in grease.

Sojuk pulled up a functionary in a staff uniform and asked for the commanding officer. The two of them were led through the lines, past the long rows of tanks, some idling, some in decent condition, some barely working at all, until they encountered several dozen senior officers crowded around the blackened chassis of a Hellhammer super-heavy. The functionary scampered up to a woman in a khaki uniform, who looked up, recognised Ilya's rank, and strode over to meet her.

'Greetings, general,' she said, making the aquila and bowing. 'Colonel Jera Talmada. Can I be of any help?'

She was a stout, olive-skinned woman with a harassed air about her. Her uniform was grimy and fitted poorly – all of them had lost weight over the past few months – but her eyes were alert and she didn't have that awful defeated expression that you came across so often now.

Ilya glanced at the Hellhammer. Its panels were broken open, and lexmechanics were tugging at its innards. The side plates were heavily damaged, as were the nearside tracks. Bloodstains ran down from the top turret, long and black.

'What happened to it?' she asked.

'Stationed south of Aurum Gard, with the Hundred-Thirty-Fourth Kalans,' Talmada replied. 'Pulled back five days ago with the rest of the division – they took a beating. We've got six hours to turn them all around and get them back out.'

A Hellhammer was a formidable machine, valuable in the kind of close-range urban combat they were being forced into. Properly supported, it should have been tough to knock out – Ilya had always rated them, back when supplying the Army had been her main concern.

'Will you do it?'

The colonel laughed grimly. 'We'll send them what we can.' She leaned in closer, lowered her voice. 'They don't last long, out there. Not any more. You should hear the reports we get from the survivors. Half of those we can't even–'

'I'm aware of the general situation, colonel,' said Ilya, glancing back along the rows of damaged and rebuilt vehicles. 'You can't be thinking of deploying back to Aurum.'

'Last orders we got informed us all assets to be retained for Inner Palace, southern zone. We're still waiting for our detailed tasking.'

'The waiting's over. I come from the primarch of the Fifth. One-third of your main strength is to be deployed to Colossi. You have twelve hours to make preparations.'

Talmada blenched. 'One-third? General, there's no–'

'You can do what you want with the rest, but I need intact squadrons, capable vehicles, seasoned crews who know what they're doing. No mobile artillery, just the main battle tanks, all with loadouts optimised for confined spaces. I'd take this thing here, for a start. But they all must – and this is important – *all* must have full chem-rating. That's gas masks for the crews and working tox-filters on the hulls. No exceptions. Anything you give me without complete coverage, you might as well shoot the drivers now.'

'But, I've got my–'

'Colonel, the comms are down across half the city. No one knows where anything is, or where anything's going. Unless someone as reckless as me actually comes down here in a transport, even the Lord Dorn himself isn't going to know what you had here and where it ended up, and very soon no one's going to be out on the streets at all unless they're dead.' She slowed down. This wasn't Talmada's fault – there just wasn't enough to go around. 'So it won't come back to you, is what I'm saying. But you do have a chance to make a difference. There's a plan. It makes better use of what's sitting here than anything you'll get out of core command now, because it'll have a chance to *do* something, something that has a hope of hurting the enemy. Like I say, this comes direct from the Lord Jaghatai. You know that name, yes? Heard it before? Good. I have the holo-seals and everything.'

Sojuk took a step forward, held out his gauntlet palm up and the hololiths flickered into life. They were all above board, regulation, checked over by herself personally.

'I have the requisition details here,' Ilya went on, as Sojuk reached for a dataslug and handed it to Talmada's adjutant. 'What we need, how much of it, where and when. You were spoken of highly, colonel – I'm sure you'll step up to this now, given the urgency of the situation.'

Talmada, to her credit, started to recover her composure. 'This isn't the only depot you're visiting, is it?'

'You're fourth on the list. And I've got more to go.'

'That's a lot... hells, that's a *load* of tanks.'

'It is.'

'It'll leave holes.'

Ilya just maintained eye contact. 'If they weren't absolutely critical, I wouldn't be here.'

And then, somewhat unexpectedly, Talmada's demeanour shifted, just by a fraction. She looked suddenly enthused. 'Counter-offensive. That's right, isn't it? Throne, tell me that's it. Tell me someone's going out after those bastards now, because we've been falling back for so damned long now that it crushes you, after a while. You see that? Tell me you're launching–'

Ilya laid a hand on the woman's crossed forearm – gently, firmly. 'We just need them at Colossi, delivered in twelve hours.'

And, just like that, the enthusiasm was snuffed out, replaced by that old fug of worry and doubt. It was everywhere, all the time. 'But they've got total air superiority. Total. That's what's knocking them out – you push out of the Inner Palace rim, beyond the working wall guns, and they start throwing it all down. That's your problem, general. That's why we pulled them back.'

Ilya left her hand where it was. This was how it had been at the other depots, and how it would be at all the rest. It didn't matter much – the Khagan would get what he required – but better to do this the right way, through the right channels, as resolutely and quickly as possible.

'Just get me what I need on the ground,' she said. 'Air support is someone else's headache.'

Jangsai Khan took a Kyzagan speeder out from the Colossi bunkers, rumbling clear of the subterranean hold-pens and along the tunnels leading back towards the Ultimate Gate. Once free of the fortress' tangled foundation level, he boosted up onto the main supply route running back west. Most of this avenue was underground, heavily shielded from mortar and shell impact. He had to weave through the heavy traffic going both ways around him – wounded fighters and damaged vehicles limping back towards the support bases at the Lion's Gate nexus, patched-up fighters and reconditioned vehicles limping back to the front. The procession of supply ground-trucks was thinner than it had been at the start of the siege – everything, from basic rations to ammunition, was running low now. Over it all came the constant *crump* of gunfire, the earth-tremors of impacts, the steady thunder-rumble of the kilometres-long enemy advance.

He couldn't make out much of the wider tactical situation from so low down. Only as he neared the Lion's Gate itself – the penultimate bulwark before the Inner Palace – did the route briefly sweep up to ground level, giving him a few moments' glimpse of open terrain. The sky overhead was black, of course – it had been black for weeks – making the ruins of the great buildings look like bleached bones. Fires smouldered in the cleft shadows, most kindled by incendiaries, some from ruptured fuel bunkers or holed transports. The horizon to the west was vivid with angry plasma-flares over the orbital void shields, a flickering inferno that never went out. The pinnacles of the distant spires spiked up into that furnace, looking very fragile under its ceaseless ripple and bloom. To the north, past the ruined slag heap that had once been Corbenic Gard, there stretched a blasted realm of flaywire and trenches, most in the hands of the enemy now. He'd fought out there for a few weeks, part of a holding operation to prevent Colossi being entirely cut off from the Lion's Gate. That had been hard fighting – a nerve-wearing grind that had seen too many warriors crushed into the toxic mud and rubble. Still, it had worked. Supplies still got through… just.

For how much longer, though – that was the question. Every hour of defence they bought cost them in lives and materiel, whereas the enemy was free to resupply at will. Jangsai had seen landers coming down to the Lion's Gate space port, the towering structure that was just about visible from the defensive portal that shared its name. For as long as the besiegers held that place, the torrent could not even be slowed, let alone staunched. They all knew it. They all knew what they wanted to do about it.

The road ducked back underground, and he re-entered the shadowy realm of flashing lumen lines and clogged asphalt. The closer he got to the interior, the more frequent were the checkpoints, the more intrusive the questions and the more comprehensive the ident-checks. One of the big barrier-stations was comprehensively on fire when he got to it, with no sign of anti-flamm teams or reconstruction units. Saboteurs, they told him. Enemy agents, perhaps. Or maybe just a trooper going mad. There was a lot of that about. It took a special degree of madness to capitulate to this enemy, once you'd seen what they did, but the soul-sickness was everywhere, and it was getting worse.

Eventually he pushed through it all and emerged deep into the Inner Palace itself, that city-within-a-city, the last portion of the Palace proper to remain entirely in the defenders' hands. The great ward that kept the worst of the *yaksha* – the daemons – out was still intact here, as was the main orbital aegis overhead, but the physical damage from ground-level artillery was still heavy. Jangsai drove as fast as he could, weaving through the constant press of military traffic, swinging away west when the transitways allowed and heading towards the industrial zones on the inner sprawl of the Adamant and Europa wall-angle. Even without the crowds it would have taken him a long time – you forgot, sometimes, that the distances between salient points were so vast.

He caught sight of his destination when he was still some way off. It was hard to avoid it, hanging low in the fire-streaked atmosphere, less than six hundred metres above the tallest spire-tops, shrouded in the crackle and arc of grav-plate-induced lightning storms. The thing had been even larger in the past, before being part dismantled and refitted as part of Lord Dorn's orbital plate scuttling programme. Only this one station had been spared, he knew – less due to its formidable array of ship-killing cannons than for its innovative immersion drives, which had allowed it to be lowered steadily through the atmosphere until it hung just above the high limits of the cityscape, hard under the protection of the Palace's void shields, ready to angle its remaining cannons out at the armies on the plains.

The Skye plate, it was called, presumably in homage to that atmospheric capability. Despite its extensive reductions and modifications, it was still a truly gigantic slab of metal – more than eleven kilometres in diameter and over three hundred metres thick at the rim. It was blackened across its entire upper face, scorched to pitch by days of solid incoming fire, back from when it had been stationed at high altitude to take part in the early defence against the mass void-drops. Its guns had mostly fallen silent now, either blasted to scrap by enemy fusillades or starved of ammunition, and so it had ceased to be a major part of the Palace's defensive cordon, reduced to not much more than an array of airstrips for the defenders' ever-diminishing fleet of atmospheric flyers and a static backup for the main wall gunlines. It would still have dominated most other cities, hanging like some unfathomably large capstone over the buildings below, but here, at the very centre of humanity's realm, it was just another megastructure in a landscape already stuffed with excess, a throwback to a prouder age, forlorn and derelict.

But its engines, for all anyone knew, were still intact. Its power generators had never been knocked out, and it still harboured a skeleton crew of a couple of thousand. Skye brooded, immobile, over a landscape of munitions works, manufactoria and refineries, all very much in operation and working to feed the ever-thinning defensive lines. Burn-off towers and cooling vents jetted in the plate's shadow, turning the entire urban sector into a hell-hot vista of tumbling smut clouds and gusting spark plumes.

Jangsai made his way through those industrial clusters, boosting as fast as he could towards the epicentre of the hovering plate. The parapets of the Adamant Wall rose up some eighty kilometres away to the south-west, backlit from the constant barrage. They said now that Mercury had been breached – it wouldn't be long, surely, before the rest of the perimeter could no longer be relied on either.

Once at the agreed coordinates, he fed power to the Kyzagan's boosters, and rose up steadily above the rooflines. He transmitted and received the handshake comms-burst, then felt the shudder as his speeder's momentum was taken over by the plate's own grav-lift drives. He killed the engines and powered down, ascending now in an invisible column of energy. For a little while, suspended above the buildings around him, he had a panoramic view right across the south-western zones of the Inner Palace, and saw the swathe of fighting running in an arc from Western Hemispheric to the Saturnine Gate and beyond.

Then he was swallowed up by the plate's underside docking apertures, lifted gently into the receiving hangars and set down on an empty apron. Jangsai jumped down from his seat, feeling the emptiness in the space around him. You could have housed a thousand fighters in that hangar. Apart from his speeder, the only other occupants were a few lighters and a defunct Marauder bomber with its landing gear blasted clean off.

He was met by a few dozen crew, all in the pale grey tabards of the now obsolete Terran Orbital Command. They took him to a mag-train terminal, from where they were whisked down tunnels and out across high viaducts. It was all shabby, dust-blown, poorly maintained. Jangsai was no Techmarine, but even he could see the rapid degradation. A few well-placed shots, and the whole place looked liable to come apart.

Eventually they reached a command tower sited on the upper face of the disc, and took an elevator up to the topmost level. They emerged into what looked to be an observation chamber, with wall-high windows on all sides and flickering screens of augur equipment embedded in a wide central column.

Most of the escorts withdrew, leaving just two to guard the slide-doors they had come through. The chamber's only other occupant was a man, standing in front of the west-facing wall, staring out into the night. As Jangsai drew alongside him, he immediately recognised the telltale signs – the slightly too-tall body, made lissom by Ar Rija's low gravity; the faint hint of yellow on the exposed flesh of his face and neck.

'Greetings,' Jangsai said, looking out of the windows.

'Be welcome, honoured khan,' said Ayo Nuta, major general of the Terran Orbital Command, master of the Skye plate. 'We have not had any visits from core command for... well. More than two months, I think. Forgive the way the place looks.'

Jangsai looked out of the tower's windows. From that vantage you could see the flat disc of the orbital plate extending outwards in all directions, studded with sensor vanes and gun towers. It was like a landscape of its own, with its own topography, its own scars, all as empty and airless as a moon's.

'I read the reports of your action during the void-drops,' he said. 'You performed admirably.'

Nuta smiled sadly. 'We had dozens of these things, once. Dozens. They cut them all up, shipped the guns back to ground level. I mean, I understood the arguments. Lord Dorn does nothing without reason. But still, it broke my heart to see it. Even this one... it's just a shadow. A shadow of what it was.'

'You managed to maintain the main systems, though?'

'As ordered. And we can still launch six fighter wings from the wall-facing strips.' He shook his head wearily. 'Down from fifty-four.'

Would this man – a senior military officer – have talked in such a way, two months ago? Jangsai doubted it.

'But the immersion drives are still operational?'

'Just about. Three of the four reactors are powered, so we can hold this position for as long as ordered.'

'But if you had to shift position?'

'Shift position? To where, khan?' He finally turned away
from the window and looked at Jangsai. The flashes from the
battles outside lit up his tired face. 'We're static here because
there's nowhere else to put us. I haven't had a tasking for
weeks. We're almost out of supplies. I was wondering just
what to do when the power starts to fail. I thought I might
shift position then. Maybe straight into the Katabatic Plain.
Take a few with us, at least.'

'Look at this.'

Jangsai opened up a lithcaster, and a spectral map of the
eastern warzone spiralled into shaky life over his open palm.
It was marked with a trajectory vector. Nuta took it all in,
snorted, and shook his head.

'Impossible.'

'You didn't study it for long.'

'East of the Ultimate Gate? This thing doesn't have any teeth
left. What good would it do out there? They've got Titans
walking west of the space port now, they tell me, and, in case
you hadn't noticed, we're a hard target to miss.'

'Also hard to bring down.'

Nuta laughed humourlessly. 'To what end, though? Eh? To
what end?' He rubbed his temples, making his skin crease. He
looked exhausted. 'I was ordered here by the Lord Dorn. To
eke out the last of our useful existence while we could. Unless
I hear from him to the contrary, that's what I plan to do.'

'This comes from Lord Jaghatai, of the Fifth.'

'Last time I checked, Lord Dorn was in overall command.'

Jangsai felt irritation rise up, and quelled it. This man was
one of very few left – perhaps the *only* one, now – who understood fully how to operate an orbital plate. When Naranbaatar
had tasked him with this mission, he'd felt a similar irritation.
The fact that he hailed from the same world as this man should

have made no difference, not in the Imperium of Unity where the only mark of allegiance was membership of the species, and to have it suggested that, in this case, a pre-ascension heritage might carry any kind of importance was almost something he could have been offended by.

But this was, clearly, no longer the Imperium of Unity. The spiritual sickness was everywhere now, dragging everything down, making good men and women weak and querulous. In such times, given such stakes, a warrior made use of every weapon to hand.

'So what commune were you raised in?' Jangsai asked.

Nuta blinked, surprised. 'Which what, now?'

'Which commune? Uyani, I'd say, by the way you pronounce your Gothic.'

Nuta chuckled. 'Well, then. Either you're very well prepared, or you're a Rijan White Scar. I didn't think such things were possible.'

'Most things are possible, if you put your mind to them.' Jangsai was not wearing his helm, but most of the giveaway signs of his original heritage had been overlaid with the heavy musculature and gene-imprint of the V Legion, so Nuta could be forgiven his surprise. 'I was born on Gyuto, and I do not recall all the Dictates from your commune. Ours were derived from Praefectora Talyi, a heritage you would consider less than reliable, and anyway I was a child then. But I do know of one Dictate, one that stuck in my mind, and I am sure it was from the Uyani thought-strain. Tell me if I have it right – the traveller is the one who takes his truth with him into strange lands. The moment he forgets his truth, he ceases to be a traveller, and becomes the strange land.'

Nuta blinked again. This time, though, it was not from surprise, and his eyes glistened. 'Ah, Throne. I never thought I'd hear the Dictates again. Least of all here, on this terrible world.'

'What was your truth, commander?'

'That I had command of this thing. That I had worked for it, and that I deserved it. That I would use it to give honour to my commune, to my home world. To the Imperium.'

'You are not a part of this terrible world yet, commander. You can still do all of that.'

Nuta looked rueful. 'No guns left. No supplies left.'

'Did I ask you for any? I only asked that you move the plate.'

'And what good will that do?'

He was still resisting, but the tone had changed. He wanted to be told now, to be reminded of who he had once been, and where his old ambitions had once taken him, and how he could recover all of that. Not that Jangsai had ever thought it, but Naranbaatar was no one's fool.

'So listen now with your whole mind and soul,' said Jangsai, adopting the litany-rhythms of the praefectoras. 'This is what the Khagan wishes you to do.'

FIVE

The sword
The saint
The sinner

So he knew what he had to do.

Sigismund jogged down the corridor, his heavy armour clanking on the metal deck. Alarms were going off everywhere, resonating down the maze of interlocking passageways. The few active lumens were shaking on their chains now, rocked by the volume of ordnance slamming into the fringes of the Mercury urban zone. Fafnir Rann came with him, as did his brothers of the Templar order – not at full tilt yet, their gait heavy and purposeful. Their black-and-white plate was hard to pick out in the flickering light, like ghost-edged shadows, glinting from the chains that held their weapons.

Since leaving Shard Bastion, Sigismund had done a hundred things. He had given unit commanders their orders. He had despatched reserve companies to their stations. He had enacted destruction plans for key bridges leading into the city core. He had chosen battle-brothers of the Legion to lead counter-attacks, measuring each threat against the characters of the warriors in question. It was nothing he hadn't been doing since taking part in the defence of the Lion's Gate space port, except that now there was no deferral, not to Rann, not to his primarch. He had sole command.

And it was glorious. He couldn't lie to himself – this was the moment he had been yearning for. The words of his gene-father still echoed in his ears – *the leash is off*. For so long it had felt like he had been compromising, holding back, second-guessing every decision he made lest it somehow worsened the censure he'd been operating under. In the past, during the Crusade, there had been none of that, only certainty. That was what he had always thrived on, the surety of purpose, the absence of choices or hesitation. It was what had made him so deadly, and he had revelled in it, fully aware of what other warriors in other Legions had said of him. He had duelled them all, and beaten them all, and taken a pure martial pleasure in every moment of it – not in the disgrace of his opponents, mind, but rather in the edging closer to total mastery, to the knowledge that there was nothing more to learn or discover, and then he could simply exist in that truth, as an aspect of it, as a face of it.

He had always wanted the world to be just like that – no doubts, no lingering areas of hesitation or equivocation, just *action*, purity of will and deed, the knowledge that whatever he did could never be, and could never have been, otherwise. From the first day of this rebellion, everything had shaken that single-mindedness. The things he had relied on with total surety had proven to be illusory and weak, and things he had thought of as being fictive and simple-minded had proved to have unexpected power. He had been forced to recalibrate, to reorientate. As every sword-brother knew, the time of greatest weakness was during the correction of a defective technique. He had started to fight... and lose. He had faced Horus Aximand and had been made to withdraw. He had faced Khârn, whom he had not yet been able to bring himself to hate fully, and been beaten. He had even taken on a primarch. Had that been hubris? Or just frustration, a desperate bid to recover his now-so-elusive sense of superiority? If he had somehow done the impossible and bested Fulgrim, would that have finally banished the whispers of doubt?

Probably not. The fault had never been external, he knew now – it had always been within him, slowly metastasising, becoming impassable the longer he ignored it. He had needed to hear Dorn's words of release to understand it. They had, all of them, been fighting with one hand behind their backs, trying to hold on to a dream that had already died. The enemy was utterly changed now. They were physically stronger and morally intoxicated, eagerly drinking up gifts that should have been shunned as poison. And yet, those who remained loyal had tried to cling on to what they had been at the very start. They had still mouthed pieties about Unity and the Imperial Truth long after fealty to such virtues had become impossible. Once he grasped that, once he faced up to it, he had what he needed to remove the fetters in his mind.

I no longer fight for the Imperium that was, he told himself. *I fight for the Imperium as it will become.*

So now, as he neared the exit ramps, the portals that would take him out into the night of fire and blood, all he felt was eagerness. Everything that had held him back had been destroyed, burned away, immolated in the consuming fire of this certainty.

But at the inner barbican entrance, just before the last of the sealed gates, he saw troops waiting for him, lots of them. They were heavily decked out in arcane armour patterns he didn't recognise – dark green, smooth-faced, lined with gold. As Sigismund motioned for his escort to come to a halt, their leader made the aquila. The man flipped back his helm, which folded up and withdrew into the armour's collar-array in a sliding series of servo-motions. The face it revealed was slim, dark-skinned, dark-haired, with the Sigillite's mark prominent on one cheek.

'Battle calls, adept,' Rann growled, clearly unwilling to have the squad's momentum halted. 'Stand aside.'

The man bowed in apology, but addressed Sigismund directly. 'I have been seeking you for some time, First Captain. Khalid Hassan, Chosen of the Sigillite, operating on my master's behalf. This will take but a moment.'

He gestured, and one of his soldiers brought up a weapon. The trooper held it two-handed, cumbersomely, barely able to keep it aloft despite wearing what looked to be a kind of power armour. It was a sword, still in its scabbard, far too large for a baseline human ever to have wielded.

As soon as Sigismund laid eyes on it, a faint shiver passed through his body. He almost thought he heard something emanate from it – a faint murmuring, unquiet and veiled. The body language of the man who held it up gave away what he thought of it – he was desperate to be shot of it.

'What is that?' Sigismund asked, doubtfully.

'A gift,' Hassan replied. 'From my master's own repository. Forged a long time ago, when the world was a different place.'

Sigismund found it hard to take his eyes off the blade. He could sense immediately, even before it was drawn, that it was beautifully made. Everything about it – its size, its profile, the fine gold-and-black decoration that ran from tip to guard – screamed of excess, of extremity.

'I have a blade.'

'You have *a* blade. This is *the* blade.'

'Then give it to someone who wants it.'

'It is for you.'

'Who says it?'

'The Emperor.'

Sigismund found himself gazing at the black hilt. He had to make an effort not to reach out and seize it. The damned thing was seducing him. A mingled sense of revulsion and awe froze him in place. 'He speaks not.'

'You truly believe that? The sword is yours. It has always been yours.'

Rann laughed harshly. 'Witchery.'

'Nothing further from it,' said Hassan, never taking his eyes off Sigismund. 'The hour is come. Take it.'

As if in some kind of trance, almost without meaning to, Sigismund did so. As he grasped the hilt, a shiver ran up his arm. He took the rim of the scabbard, and drew the blade smoothly. The metal was as black as jet, hardly reflecting the lumens. He lifted it to his face, and saw nothing. The surface drank in light, giving nothing back. It was selfish, this thing.

'Why me?' he asked, almost for the sake of form. Now that he had it in his hands, he sensed the truth of it all.

'I have no idea,' said Hassan, smiling wryly. 'My orders were only to deliver it.'

Sigismund angled it, turned it, switched it to horizontal and looked down the blade's length.

Heavy. Far heavier than any sword he had borne before, but something told him it wouldn't slow him down. Its weight was just another aspect of its savage nature. The murmuring carried on, just beyond the edge of hearing, almost intelligible as he swiped it in practice arcs. It might have been his imagination. It wasn't his imagination.

'It has been here, all this time,' he murmured.

'Many ancient things are guarded in my master's chambers.'

'No, you do not understand me.' Sigismund finally looked up at Hassan again. 'When we went into the void, preaching the end of magic, this thing was already here. It had already been made. By Him. What does that tell you?'

Hassan shrugged. 'I'm not minded to speculate.'

Sigismund laughed. With a deft movement, he unchained his old blade and handed it over to Rann. Then he shackled the black sword's grip, and locked the scabbard at his belt. 'Well, you are fortunate that it pleases me. Give my thanks to your master, and tell him that it suits my new mood.'

'I will. And what mood would that be, captain?'

Sigismund moved past him. He could smell the promethium even before he crossed the threshold.

'Murderous,' he growled, and started to accelerate up the exit ramp.

Running, always running now, scampering into culverts and cubby holes, clamping her hands to her ears to muffle the stomach-churning bangs, wrapping rags around her mouth to stop her breathing in nothing but brick dust.

Euphrati Keeler fled from hideout to hideout, bedraggled as a half-drowned dog, barely able to pause for a moment to think properly about why she was there at all, back in the thick of things. It had been safer – sort of – in the Blackstone. At least in there she hadn't had to zigzag across mortar-blown streets as the undermined walls around her were blasted apart. Dealing with monsters like Fo had been intimidating in its own way, but at least she'd been fed and watered in there, given a data-slate to work with, something to fill the hours. And after the trauma of the escape itself there had been more trials, more horrors to witness. Some encounters – *one* in particular – she could hardly bear to recall.

What had she been thinking? Why had she let them persuade her that it was a good idea to leave? It had all gone predictably wrong so quickly – a confusion of guns and transports, shouting and screaming, the spark of pure terror. Then she'd just run, run hard, never working out what had come after her, never looking back to check. She'd outpaced those faceless hunters, but now whole armies of killers were everywhere, swarming through the city-palace like flies. She'd be lucky to last a day or two out here. She didn't even really understand why they'd ever tried to get her out.

Just don't preach, they'd said. *It's you that's important. So don't preach. Just… be there.*

At the time, it had been a way out, sent to her as if by providence, and she'd not argued, because you didn't argue with providence. You let the river take you where it would, turning and kicking in the gyres, but never resisting. You had to trust that the current was taking you in the direction it was meant to, otherwise what was the point?

She scuttled across the face of a wide impact crater, skipping through the debris of something huge and metallic, before skidding under the shadow of an intact hab-block. The eternal night sky above her was lurid with the splash-patterns of munitions hitting the defensive aegis, underscored by the ground-mounted guns that were now being deployed liberally within the suspended barrier. It was so *loud* now, all the time, a tidal-wall of noise that crashed and reverberated from every intact surface, making her arms vibrate, making her teeth throb.

She crouched down, arms around her knees, panting hard. She was wearing nothing more than the prison fatigues they'd given her in the Blackstone, but she was still hot. The volume of explosives going off had made the Himalazian air as humid as the tropics, and slicks of sweat stained her tunic-top.

She had to rest there, just for a moment, despite the obvious danger. She had no idea which zone of the city this was, but the enemy was advancing through it, or close to it, because crowds of people had already surged back the other way, panicked as rats from a fire. Like everywhere in the beleaguered Inner Palace, the press of high buildings was close. The unlit towers around her were all massive, but half of them were mere shells now, and the rest had all sustained fearful damage. There was nowhere for all that disintegrated rockcrete and steel to go, so the transitways choked up, and even the flimsiest remaining frontages were propped with piles of rubble. It seemed to her that all the enemy was doing was creating a denser, more tortuous landscape to eventually bludgeon their way through, though millions of souls were probably still hunkered down in the semi-demolished husks around her, hidden from view or buried deep, gnawing at their own terror in the munition-lit dark.

She wormed her way backwards, pushing between two heavy beams that had come down from some shot-to-pieces balcony, letting the metal cool her skin. She was hungry now, and very thirsty. She'd have to move off again soon, if only to find something to drink. She had no plan, no direction. It would only take one stray mortar or las-beam, and she'd be gone, snuffed out, with nothing achieved.

Well played, Euphrati, she thought to herself. *You've really excelled yourself this time.*

It felt strange, despite everything going on just then, to think that somewhere up above her, probably at high orbital anchor, was the *Vengeful Spirit.* It had been years now since she'd been on that ship, but the memories were still so vivid that it felt like moments ago. She knew enough of the enemy to doubt whether any of the dorms and mess halls and recreation stations were anything like they had used to be, but she could still vividly picture how they had once been, with the civilians and the regular ship crew jostling up alongside the transhuman giants and Army personnel – good-humoured, for the most part, full of optimism, free to jibe and dispute, yet part of something, an endeavour, all pulling in the same basic direction.

That little band of explorers was diminished now. They had all been so young. Like children, really, sent off to caper around the galaxy, wide-eyed and ignorant. Mersadie was gone, Ignace was gone. Kyril still pursued something like his old trade, though it was so compromised that it bore little relation to what he'd once been proud to do. Did he really think that Dorn wouldn't just yank the leash back, if he somehow prevailed in this desperate scrap for survival? The idea that they had been there to freely observe, record, report – that was dead now, and Sindermann surely knew it, deep down, in some part of his soul that he didn't look at very often. She wondered what, exactly, he thought he was up to.

She gazed upward, squinting against the neon-flare of the distant aegis. Yes, somewhere up there, hanging amid the other void-giants, was the old home from home, the old haunt.

And you are on it, still, she thought. *We all left, but you're still there. I can sense you, you devil. Maybe you can sense me too. I don't care. I never want to see you again. I have enough images, too many I wish I could erase. I never want to see just how bad you've become.*

Suddenly, she tensed. She felt something stir, up ahead, somewhere in the clouds of dust that drifted and swirled in the flickering half-light.

She squinted out at the streetscape. Nowhere to run to – not without giving herself away. She squirmed back up against the angle of the two beams, seeing if she could shove herself through the gap between them and find some way down into the building's foundations.

No good – she was stuck there, her spine hard up against the masonry, in the shadows but hardly protected from prying eyes. All she could do was make herself as small and still as possible, hardly daring to breathe.

Away ahead, some fifty metres off, the curtains of smoke

split open. Figures emerged out of the haze, marching steadily, not hurrying. They were all huge, and with the telltale hunch-shouldered profile of Space Marines. For a moment, Keeler dared to hope that they'd be from the loyal Legions, but it only took seconds to see that they weren't. Their battleplate was gunmetal-grey, blunt-edged and utilitarian. They clunked their way heavily through the rubble, hefting their huge guns two-handed, scanning carefully as they came. Eight of them were there, bearing the black-and-yellow chevrons of the Iron Warriors, helm-lenses glimmering in the shifting light.

Keeler felt her heart thudding. A line of sweat ran down her temple. She clutched her hands together, drawing her body in tight, as if she could squeeze it down so small that no one would ever see it.

The Iron Warriors marched down the transitway running alongside her position, clambering over the heaps of debris and kicking through the muck. Their armour was heavily marked with battle-damage, and two of the warriors were limping. Some of them had Space Marine helmets hanging from their belts – the crimson of the Blood Angels and the ivory of the White Scars.

They weren't looking in her direction. They seemed to be heading straight down what remained of the central avenue – perhaps a scout squad of some larger formation, or maybe just a gang of freelancers looking for loot and glory. At this rate, they'd pass less than a groundcar's length from her position.

Thirty metres. The crack and rumble of the artillery carried on the whole time, masking the faint noise of her breathing. She pressed herself harder under the crossed beams, hardly daring to look at the monsters as they neared. They were horrific things, fusions of genecraft and techno-weaponry from some industrial nightmare-factory. The play of light over their armour made them seem somehow less than fully real, like hololiths, but she saw the rubble-chunks burst into powder under their boots, and smelled the hot-metal stench of their armour's reactor cores.

Twenty metres. They would see her. They had to see her. It didn't matter that she was tiny, and crouched down, and lost in a fog of dust and darkness – they had sensors, ways of picking up heat and fractional movement. There was nowhere to go, no route of escape. They would see her.

Ten metres. She thought about bolting. That would surely be the end of her, but at least it would be clean. A single mass-reactive shell didn't so much as stop a human body as obliterate it. She wouldn't feel much.

Then one of the Iron Warriors held up a fist. The squad halted. The one with the clenched gauntlet moved its enormous, slant-faced helm, very slowly, in her direction. A pair of red lenses pierced the darkness, staring straight at her.

She couldn't breathe. She stared right back at it. She was frozen, her heart hammering, pinned like an insect to a card. All it had to do was lift the muzzle of its weapon. Or maybe just stride over and grab her by the neck. Or maybe, if it wanted to give her a heart attack, just carry on glaring at her like that for a little longer. Somewhere under all that ceramite and beaten iron, she knew, was a withered transhuman face, a withered transhuman soul, a corrupted being of boundless malice and infinite cruelty, the stuff of Old Night rendered back into reality. If she was lucky, very lucky, all it would do was kill her.

The red lenses. For an eternity, staring at her.

Then it lowered its fist. It turned away. It started to walk again. The others came with it, clanking along on their corroded servos. They trudged down the long, detritus-strewn avenue, overlooked by the ranks of eyeless hab-blocks. It took them a long time to pass out of earshot, and only a little longer for the stench to fade away.

Keeler stayed where she was, shivering, her body locked in place. Only once she was sure that they were well out of sight did she manage to unclench her stiff limbs and unfurl out of her hiding spot. Shakily, she edged out along the wall's length, clear of the shadow of the beams. The empty transitway stretched off in either direction, a battered wasteland of twisted rebar and pitted asphalt.

It had seen her. It *had* to have seen her. Even a pair of mortal eyes would have been able to pick her out at that distance. Why had it moved off? Those things didn't know pity. They no longer even comprehended it.

She was still shaking. Gingerly, she clambered back up the rubble-slope, until she was up at the level of the transitway. On the edge of what had once been its kerb, a single skull was perched on a tiny cairn of stones. There were skulls aplenty in the ruins, of course, but most of those were still flecked with flesh-patches and attached to spinal cords. This one was on its own, bare to the bone, glistening faintly as if someone had cleaned it. It had been facing away from her, angled back to where the Iron Warrior had been standing, interposed between them like a guardian totem.

She picked it up, turned it around and looked into its eyeless face. There was something oddly appropriate, even comforting, about its presence. A death's head in the city of death, the symbol of human mortality, the last and permanent remnant of an unremarked life.

They stared at one another for some time, flesh and bone. As they did so, Keeler felt her composure gradually return. Her hands stopped shaking.

Why had she ever doubted? She had already faced the worst the realm of the false gods could throw at her, and had never faltered. She had faced the wrath of primarchs and regents, and never backed away from it. Of *course* the Iron Warrior hadn't seen her. She had been *chosen* for this. She had a duty to perform, a mission to accomplish. Even now, amid all that was collapsing and falling apart, He was yet mindful of her, warding her, ensuring that she didn't stumble at the final hurdle.

She looked up again. Gauging distances, even gauging directions, was next to impossible. The firefights looked to be most severe towards the cluster of high towers she had been heading towards. She could hear the rattle of small-arms fire from up ahead, perhaps even the cries from human throats.

Some souls were still fighting, then, even here. Some who would need their faith bolstering, if they were not to be swept away.

Just… be there.

'Come on, then,' she said, wrapping the skull up in a rag-length and tucking it into her belt. 'You and me. Let's do this.'

Basilio Fo had no business being alive. He had no real business being on Terra, and certainly no business at all being free of captivity. Life was strange like that. Just when you thought it couldn't get any more implausible, something would show up and teach you a little humility.

Or, at least, it might have taught another man a little humility, but Fo had never been a humble soul. He was rational enough to see the twists of fate for what they were – dumb luck, for the most part – but it was still difficult not to feel a swell of pride every time he evaded his no-doubt-very-much-deserved comeuppance and trotted off towards his next opportunity for intellectual growth.

His fellow travellers were mostly gone – all the warlords and splicers and sociopaths, the ones he had either traded with or run away from as they eked out their hardscrabble life amid the ruins of Old Earth. Just him and the old man left, plus those few flunkeys and hangers-on of His that lingered within the Palace like leftover parts for a machine. Just the two of them now, an argumentative old couple, worn out, nagging at one another around the edges, their best years long gone.

He didn't mourn many of the others. Narthan Dume had actually been good company, in his early years at least, but the majority of them had been wearisome. Survival on Terra during the turmoil had been easier for the brutal ones, and brutes generally made poor acquaintances. Only a very few had made it through via cunning and subtlety, and he was by far the best of that breed.

Now the endgame. All the schemes and stratagems had come to nothing, bulldozed by that juggernaut on the Throne, the dullest and the maddest brute of them all. So much had been destroyed, so much irreplaceable and unreproducible had been rendered down to dust, it was enough to make a cultured man scream. What did it matter if this gigantic city was similarly pulverised? It was *ideas* that mattered, and they were already mostly wiped out, replaced by a sterile contest between two rival horror shows of almost equal slack-wittedness.

But it wasn't quite over yet. He had his freedom, he had just a little time, and he knew where he was going. The Inner Palace had been knocked about a bit, by the look of things, but he had a good memory and the street patterns were more or less as they had been when he'd last visited. It remained very dangerous, but he was used to danger. He liked it. You had to have a little danger in your life, when you were his age – something to keep the blood pumping.

By then he was dressed in a staff uniform of an Interior Departmento armaments inspector. Its original wearer had been unfortunate enough to run into him soon after his release from the Blackstone, and had died almost insultingly quickly. Fo had made a few adjustments, managed to access his victim's augmetic data-tables, even tweaked his own facial configuration a little, so that in a poor light, at a distance, even people who'd known the real owner wouldn't take a second look. Now he was hurrying through the corridors, adopting the preening strut of a self-important functionary. Millions of officials laboured in these labyrinthine structures, and the chance of actually being recognised as an imposter was minimal.

That would only get him so far, though. Where he was headed was secure. Very secure. There were ways inside, of course – he'd done it before – but it wouldn't be easy, and time was against him.

He went quickly, surely. He ignored the cohorts of minor scribes and officials racing from one station to another, their eyes staring from lack of sleep and fear. He ignored the sector-wide vox-casts, endlessly warning of incoming barrages or urban-zone evacuations. He didn't head straight for his objective, because the clearances and passes he'd inherited were nowhere close to being good enough to get him through all the interposed checkpoints and biofilters.

He'd need to get close to the centre. Not the *very* centre – that would have been impossible, even for him – but part of the secondary chain of laboratories, the same ones that poor old Amar Astarte had helped put together before she'd begun to lose her mind, and the ones that, with any luck, still had bits and pieces of serviceable material lying around that he could use. He'd need to scope out the habs east of the Sanctum Imperialis, where the Clanium Library dominated and where clusters of the old research and development cadres had once based themselves.

He could have raced over there right now, if he'd been too stupid and too eager. See, though, there was no chance at all that Amon, that blank-souled old golem, had lost his scent yet. The Custodian Guard might be many things, but they weren't dupes. It was entirely possible that Andromeda-17 had been working for them all along. Or even if she hadn't, Amon would have been on to her quickly. That was their job – to know, to predict, to triangulate. Yes, the likelihood was that Basilio Fo was being watched, right now, with a view to seeing where he'd end up, what he'd produce, who he'd talk to. It was a dangerous game, letting him loose, but things were so straitened now that only dangerous games were worth playing. Valdor's people had a real liking for this kind of thing. Let the subject get in close, let them test the defences, maybe even let them right into the heart of the place they wanted to get to. That way, you learned everything about your potential weaknesses, all the while keeping the whole shooting match under close observation.

Blood Games, they were called. It was a nice concept, but Fo was good at games too, and he liked blood very much. The problem with letting an enemy get close was that he might slip the tail just when you didn't want him to, and then you had a problem.

He'd need to be good. He'd need to be able to change his appearance, his mannerisms, make himself impossible to track. He'd need to stay on his toes. He'd need to draw on all his experience, and still take a few chances.

It all got very complicated. He headed away from the Clanium District, and traced a switchback route around the base of the Widdershins Tower. He dropped out of circulation entirely for a few hours, then popped up again in a groundcar, which he abandoned three zones away before picking up an identical model and heading back towards the interior. He killed four more times, twice in secret, twice ostentatiously, and changed his clothes and facial arrangement. He left an obvious trail on a cogitator terminal, and then a hard-to-find one, and then arranged for the entire network to blow once he was on the move again.

All that bluster bought him enough breathing space to home

in on his first true port of call – an Imperial Army medicae supply depot, buried deep within the makeshift garrison-hub under the Viridarum Nobiles. The place was crowded, stuffed with frightened troops making ready to push on out, but they paid him little heed as he shoved his way past them. Why would they have done? He was in the uniform of a full regimental colonel by then, and the only thing they might have expected, if they'd caught his eye, was a barrage of unwelcome orders.

He made his way several levels down, jogging confidently along metal stairways to where the lumens hung against bare rockcrete and the numbers of personnel finally thinned out. The medicae depot was placed right at the bottom of a deep shaft, kept cool by industrial refrigerators and barred by heavy plasteel doors. The two guards on duty made the aquila as he bustled past them.

Inside was a narrow chamber crammed between rows and rows of supply crates, poorly lit, claustrophobic and frigid. Behind a despatch desk were the big walk-in units. A lone attendant was on duty at the desk, surrounded by requisition slates. She looked young, harassed, frightened. Her job down here was probably mostly filled with officers shouting impossible things at her, since supplies of everything had been running critically low for a long time. It was terribly unfair, what this war had done to people. Still, her troubles would soon be over.

'In His service, soldier,' Fo said, shooting her his most sympathetic smile. 'I'll need access to your secure storage.'

She stared up at him nervously. 'Uh, do you have the clearances, sir? I can't give you the codes without them.'

He looked straight at her the whole time – not aggressively, with consideration, but firmly. 'Been on duty for a long time?'

She nodded. 'I don't know what happened to the next shift. I was supposed to be off-rotation seven hours ago.'

Fo tutted. 'I'll look into it. Are those your rotas?' He pushed his way around the edge of the desk, to where a clutch of faded papers had been pinned to a board.

'Sir, you really shouldn't–'

'My, you *have* been abandoned down here. I'll look into getting you some relief. Still, while I'm here, best I take a look at that storage. I'm after some of your surgical recon-structive tools, some derma-work philtres, pheromone masks, that kind of thing.'

She had the presence of mind to look surprised. 'There's not been much… call for that. I'm really not sure I can–'

He pressed up against her then, placed a single finger on her lips. He'd forgotten how much fun this kind of thing was. 'See, I'm on important business, and I'd really appreciate some help – time's already short.' He smiled at her again, his best benevolent-paternal look. 'And do stop worrying about procedure – we're at war. Help me with the codes, and we'll get this over quickly. Really, now, what's the worst that could happen to you?'

SIX

Destroyer
Aika 73
Sons of the Storm

That the primarch had changed – that would be the very worst thing, the one thing he couldn't live with. Morarg knew that his master had physically altered – by the god, they'd all *physically* altered – but you had to hope that his old essence was somehow intact. He'd seen him on the battlefield since the great transformation, and that had been impressive enough, but you never really knew how deep the alterations went. For him, for Caipha Morarg, it felt like every cell in his entire body had been flipped around, stretched and pummelled into something indescribable. But a primarch… well, who could ever be sure? They were exceptions to everything.

He was at the Lion's Gate space port now. The great ravaged edifice vanished into the darkness of the spoiled atmosphere, its terraces rearing away and upward, one on top of the other, on and on, far beyond the limits of even his vision. Every facing wall was darkened with filth. Much of that was from the munitions used by the Iron Warriors, but not all. Ever since the Death Guard had moved to occupy it, mats of mould and algae had spread across otherwise undamaged parapets and battlements, further blackening and corroding what remained. Landing platforms now hung with creepers and webs, clogged and sagging. Flies buzzed and clustered in the angles of the walls, breeding so fast they formed living carpets that slithered over the masonry like waterfalls. The entire structure, so vast that it was hard to even contemplate, let alone visualise, had begun to degrade, to fall in on itself, to dissolve slowly into the biological. Its innards glowed with a pale green light, points of vivid colour that punctured the darkness that hung across it. The more it changed, the longer they all occupied it, the closer it all got to... Barbarus.

Was that deliberate? Surely not. They had all hated that world – Mortarion more than any of them. Maybe they were doomed to bring it with them. Or maybe this was just a passing phase, something that they would eventually move beyond once the true nature of their strange gifts became apparent.

Still, it all conspired to make the fortress even more formidable. Its physical defences, many of which had been preserved during the conquest, rose up from the tangle of ruins around it, still solid, still immense. Some of the sky bridges had been demolished, but a number of raised viaducts still ran from the Anterior hinterland into the maw-like access tunnels. Ships still landed on the upper stages, though virtually all of them were XIV Legion landers now, since the other elements of the Warmaster's armada had opted to use the Eternity Wall and Damocles entry points instead.

Squeamish of them, thought Morarg, making his way steadily up through the lower galleries, wheezing in the turgid air. You got used to the stench, after a while. You started to gain an appreciation for the fecundity of it all, the splendid variety of phages curdling in the deep pits. If the Death Guard's allies failed to appreciate that, clinging to their less enlightened habits, that was their loss.

He climbed up very long flights of stairs, trudged his way around gigantic supporting piers, clambered deeper in and higher up. Every chamber within the space port's lower levels was filling up. Tank squadrons were digging in, thickening the airways with fume-palls. Infantry companies had filed into high-vaulted muster chambers, where they were being steadily resupplied. The bulk of these troops were the Unbroken – the Space Marines – since most of the baseline human crews had died in the warp. Their numbers had since been boosted with sundry mutants, beast-creatures and cultists, but the value of such soldiers was marginal, and so the core strength assembled within the cavernous interiors was now overwhelmingly power-armoured.

All, that was, apart from the daemons. Those spectral presences skittered and flickered in the dark galleries, dropping out of instantiation only to shudder back in again, wobbling and shaking like poor quality vid-films. Most of them were slack-bellied lurchers – parodies of obese or pox-infected mortals. They bellowed incoherently as they staggered around, or just slumped in the corners gnawing on bits of flesh. Morarg avoided them as much as he could. No doubt they were deadly, and no doubt the primarch had his uses for them, but he didn't like them. Maybe he'd change his mind once he saw them in action against the enemy, but for now they were just in the way, struggling to remain intact as the remnants of the telaethesic shield made things difficult for them.

As he climbed up towards the receiving chamber, they grew in number, chattering and whispering like frightened children. The air grew even more miasmic, and the flies clambered over everything in sight. The last traces of the IV Legion's occupancy had been thoroughly erased in those places – you couldn't even smell them any more, nor catch sight of any forlorn abandoned objects that might once have been theirs.

He drew up to a pair of high doors, closed and barred. Two of the Deathshroud guarded them, standing silently with their scythes crossed over the portal. Morarg didn't need to say anything to them – as soon as he reached the top of the stairs, the scythes were withdrawn and the doors slid open. An ankle-deep film of pale green condensation tumbled across the threshold, slinking over the granite, and it got noticeably colder.

He went inside. The chamber on the far side was huge. Maybe in the past it would have been some kind of major command-and-control centre, crewed by hundreds, but now it was virtually deserted, its floors strewn with smashed equipment and broken glass. Through large windows set into the western wall you could see many of the heavy landing stages as they fanned out across the space port's lower levels. Beyond those, flashes of massed battles flickered in the distance, a rippling constellation against the now permanent darkness.

Mortarion stood in the gloom, a hulking figure, cloaked in shadow. Semi-formed daemons wavered in and out of reality around him like a ghostly chorus. He was vast now, his gauzy wings splayed up to the vaults, his patina-crusted armour glinting in the gloom. Faint hisses came from his rebreather, frosting against the corroded bronze of the intakes.

Why did he need that, now? For that matter, why had he ever needed it? Morarg didn't know. He'd never asked, and he probably never would.

Aside from the two of them, the only other presence was semi-real – a hololith transmitted in from somewhere out on the front, swimming with interference, depicting a single individual. The outline of that individual was extremely familiar to Morarg, though, for as with Mortarion – as with all of them – it had been transformed by the harrowing in the warp.

The profile was larger now, crammed with gifts, extended and bulked out until the old armour cracked under the strain of it. Flies buzzed around the perimeter of the lithcast, spilling out of the battleplate's orifices, breaking up and scattering the poor transmission.

Typhus. The one who had done all this to them. Morarg had clearly arrived in the middle of a heated discussion. It seemed to be coming to its end, but he waited some distance off, his head bowed.

'They're ripe for it now,' Typhus rasped over the hololithic link. *'We have what we need.'*

'Not yet,' Mortarion replied, sounding weary of the conversation. *'There is little to be gained, and much to be lost. Have patience.'*

'Patience! Is that the only thing you ever–'

'Hold, now.' The primarch's voice suddenly dropped, becoming a warning growl that made the hairs on Morarg's scabrous flesh stand up. *'Watch your tongue, lest I see fit to tear it out. This is a delicate juncture, and you do not perceive the whole picture. Not as I do.'* The primarch drew in a long, painful-sounding breath. *'My father's beacon has been retaken, all due to this careless haste. It would be helpful to have the resistance there snuffed out. You might be interested in that, Calas – the ether tells me Corswain of the First commands the Mountain.'*

Typhus hesitated. *'Corswain?'*

'The same.'

The hololith briefly ruptured, then re-established. Morarg tried not to look too closely, but Typhus appeared to be mulling it over. *'If you will not authorise the offensive–'*

'I have given you my reasons.'

'–then it is something concrete, at least.'

Mortarion smiled. You could only tell that from the wrinkling of the grey flesh around his eyes, and it wasn't a pleasant thing to witness. *'It would be a simple thing for a commander of your talents, to take it back. By the time you return, I anticipate being ready for the main assault.'*

Typhus was no fool. He never had been. He pondered the offer before him, alive to the possibility of being despatched away from the main event like an unwanted irritant. Still, Morarg knew something of the history between him and the First Legion. It would be hard to turn down a chance to gain his revenge, and no one could claim that the Astronomican was a minor objective.

Eventually, the hololith crackled as Typhus bowed – a curt, dismissive movement. *'Very well,'* he said. *'But I will continue to monitor the front. If I discover–'*

'If the front moves, and you are required, I shall be the first to summon you,' said Mortarion patiently. *'How could it be otherwise? We will march across the threshold together, you and I. I promised the Warmaster that – the commitment has already been made.'*

Typhus hung on a little longer, looking like he might speak again. Then, abruptly, the link cut out, and the hololith scattered into a cloud of fading grey-green sparks.

Only then did Mortarion's gaze turn to Morarg, and only then did Morarg finally ascend the final set of steps up towards his master's position.

'Caipha,' said the primarch, as warmly as he ever said anything. *'Heard all that, did you?'*

Morarg bowed low. 'Not much of it, my lord.'

'Just the part about our deployment.'

'Just that part, yes.'

Mortarion adjusted position, and the various devices and philtres dangling around his archaic-looking armour clattered together. *'You probably agree with him.'*

Morarg decided to tread carefully. It didn't sound like his master was in a particularly good mood. 'I have no complaints.'

Mortarion snorted a harsh laugh, and flicked something coiled-up and glistening from his breastplate. *'Calas is a simple soul, really. He'd have been better placed in another Legion – a stupid one, where he could indulge his taste for needless drama.'* He placed his great hands together, scraping the patina from his gauntlets, staring moodily into his interlocked fingers. *'We are doing so much damage to them, and he barely even sees it. Every hour of every day, the god sends us his great gifts, all channelled through this place. I can virtually see the tip of the Sanctum Imperialis from here, and whenever my eyes alight on it, a little more of it crumbles away. Most of those inside will never know where the sickness comes from. They will have no name for it, aware only that such a weight of nothingness makes it hard to think, to sleep, even to lift a weapon. And for those who do understand? They have neither the strength nor the will to strike at me. The Red Angel is at their throats, their walls are breached, and their defences are falling into ruins around them.'* His rheumy eyes flickered back up to Morarg. *'We are killing them so very expertly, from a distance, and all Calas wishes to do is rush up to the walls. He is blind to the danger of it.'*

Morarg wasn't sure whether he was expected to say something then. He took a punt. 'Which is, my lord?'

'Our own side,' said Mortarion darkly. *'All know that this will be over soon. Maybe a week. Maybe less. And then what? Who has a vision for that? Who, in this rabble of monsters and madmen, truly gives a damn what must come afterwards?'* He shook his head dismissively, making the cables around his neck jangle. *'I did not bring us out of one living hell to plunge straight into another. Whatever happens, we will remain intact. When my father's throat is cut at last, we will carve our place*

in the new Imperium from a position of strength. Perturabo has quit the field, Fulgrim has given in to his whims. Angron's war-dogs are already tearing themselves apart, and Magnus' witches are too few to matter. When I choose to breach the walls, when all others are exhausted or scattered or ready to surrender, I will have you all with me. I will have my Legion at my side, unbroken and magnificent, united in the god's glory.'

'I understand,' said Morarg. In truth, save for the one great doubt, the one that had plagued him since the transformation, he'd never had much less than total faith in his master. Having things spelled out was, if anything, something of a luxury he didn't require.

Mortarion smiled again. *'But you still feel it a little, do you not? That faint tug? Shame. You wanted to be first, strike the initial blow.'*

Morarg thought on that. He'd spoken to Crosius about it, back when they'd been fighting at Marmax. It had felt, just after making planetfall, as if that was their destiny, given all they had suffered to be there. But now… No, he could no longer be so sure about it. His bloodlust seemed somehow dulled, replaced by a strange kind of numbness.

'I am not sure,' he said truthfully. 'And yet…' He looked up at his master, fearful of pressing too hard.

'Go on.'

Morarg swallowed. 'There are those… Some, in the Legion, I mean. There are those who say, well… that the Lord Typhus has set this… There are some who would be… *close* to him, if things became…'

He trailed off. Some things were too hard to find words for. To his relief, Mortarion didn't seem put out by what he'd said. If anything, he was amused.

'Let me help you out, Caipha,' Mortarion said. *'You have heard whispers that Typhus is the true master, here. You*

have heard that he was the one who forced the transition to our current form. That he tricked me, tricked all of us, pulled the veil over our eyes, and still runs things much as he likes. Is that right?'

This was so dangerous. 'More or less, lord. Only whispers, mind.'

'I see. And you do not know any names behind those whispers. That, also, is as it should be.' He drew in another of those long, rattling breaths, and the daemon chorus in his shadow chattered away, freshly agitated. *'I will not justify myself. That time on the ships was difficult. Painful. Hard to reconstruct.'* The primarch's eyes briefly showed that pain – a fractional flash of it, glimpsed over the lip of the rebreather. *'I will say only this. Nothing that happened on* the **Terminus Est** *was an accident. I loved you all too much. That is the only error I will admit. Calas was irrelevant – just an instrument, one the god was pleased to use. Does that reassure you?'*

Morarg didn't understand much of that. He wasn't sure if he had been meant to. Perhaps it was merely a challenge – a test of faith. Or maybe there was some truth there, an opaque one, that he was intended to grasp.

'I am content, lord,' he said weakly. 'I always have been.'

'And that is why you are here, and he is not. Loyalty matters to me. It matters to me a great deal. It is why you will learn the plans for the attack now, and he will only do so later.'

The primarch drew a little closer, his immense form shuffling forward, his wings trembling.

'Because this is where history turns in our favour,' he said. *'Stay true, Caipha, stay patient, and you will witness it all unfold, right from here, by my side.'*

The underground mag-train hissed in the enclosed siding, filling the high-arched space with steam and smoke. Its caged flanks were ten metres high, and the long run of uncovered wagons stretched back into the noisy, semi-lit confusion of the loading terminal. Officers bellowed orders, warning klaxons sounded, heavy transports drew up at the buffers and began to unclamp their loading doors. Everywhere you looked, people were running, gesticulating, banging fists into cupped palms, jabbing fingers at subordinates.

Tank commander Talvet Kaska watched it all unfold, taking a long drag on his nicotine-stick and feeling the cheap smoke clog up his lungs a little more. He was sitting on a pile of ammo boxes, feet crossed, a half-empty canteen at his side. His crew lounged around him. Vosch was asleep. He had no idea how she managed to catnap, given the clangs and bangs of the terminal, but somehow she always seemed able to grab a few minutes. Jandev was reading a slab-book, while Merck chewed on a protein-block. Dresi sat alone, her knees drawn up to her chest. Kaska didn't know much about her, yet. If he'd been more diligent, he might have asked, but he was dog-tired, irritable, and anyway there'd be plenty of time once they reached the forward muster yards.

'So there he is,' said Merck dryly, his big jaw working away slowly. 'Right on schedule.'

A tank was a strange thing. The crews always personalised them. In some battalions, they were female. In the Jadda 12th Armoured, most usually they were male. Sometimes they were given affectionate names, or joking epithets, but the Jadda squadrons were a serious-minded bunch, and stuck to the hull designators given to them on delivery. Kaska's tank was called *Aika 73*. It was a standard Ryza-pattern hull. Decent engine, decent cannons, no sponson gunners on this variant. Some commanders would have missed those – handy in a close fight, they said – but Kaska was glad not to have them. The innards of a Leman Russ were hot and cramped enough once the shells were loaded, before you tried to cram in two more sweaty bodies.

'Ugly old bastard,' murmured Kaska, with a mix of disdain and affection.

The hull was being hoisted by a loader-claw now, transferred from the flatbed transporter and swung over the transit wagon amid gouts of valve-steam. That operation in itself was something to witness – a Leman Russ main battle tank weighed almost sixty tonnes, unladen, and was eight metres in length, cannon included. Seeing whole squadrons of them plucked from the flatbeds and smartly dumped into position, one after the other, was impressive. The loader-claws were cumbersome things, each one manned by seven bolted-in servitors, the control units capable of being rolled up and down the siding-edge on sunken rails before their long cantilevered arms unfurled. The only thing that dwarfed them was the mag-train itself, which must have been eight hundred metres long.

Kaska watched it all. He paid attention to how *Aika 73* looked. He studied the repairs made at battalion command to the forward lascannon – you could still see the marks around the mantlet. The long scratches, dents and gouge marks were all present and correct, painted over quickly but impossible to remove now. He noticed they'd replaced all the tox-filters. *Aika 73* had been in some tough old fights. More than once, Kaska had made his peace with existence and prepared to face whatever state came next, but somehow the crew had always managed to claw their way back to safety. All save Jugo, of course. The poor wretch had shot himself only a week ago, leaving them without a driver.

Kaska glanced at Dresi again, who seemed to be staring blankly into nothing. He didn't even know which hull they'd plucked her from to replace him, nor why she had been free for redeployment. Everything was getting ragged and out of sorts. Still, he was lucky that they'd been able to find anyone at all. Some battalions were so short of units, fuel and crew now that they were effectively grounded, stuck in the depots and scrabbled over for parts. You wanted to be fighting, if you were still alive. Chances were they were all going to be dead soon anyway, so better to go out doing what you'd been trained for.

'Makes no sense,' grumbled Merck. 'We get pulled back, get our orders, they haul us over to Europa, and now this. They've lost their minds.'

Kaska took another drag. Merck could be a real pain. 'Orders change, trooper.'

'Yeah, but these make no sense. What's left beyond the Lion's Gate, eh? Rubble and ruins, that's what.'

'Counter-offensive,' said Jandev quietly, never looking up from his book. The front-gunner's pale face was impassive. 'It had to come.'

Merck snorted. 'Nah. Just another shore-up, somewhere. Not enough left to attack with.'

Trooper Merck, the loader, the most junior rank in the crew, didn't usually say much worth listening to, but on this occasion Kaska had to agree with him. They were strung out. The last time division command had ordered them to retake ground, they'd lost over a hundred units inside less than an hour. Air support was gone now, infantry support was patchy, and you stood a real chance of running into Traitor Space Marines if you travelled any distance. Those were properly scary things. Kaska had seen a squad of them rip their way into a Baneblade, gnaw right through it before emerging out of the other side crackling with disruptor energy and drenched in blood. And then there were the... other things. The things that nobody talked about but everyone had seen. The monsters, the creatures that shimmered out of the air itself, the beasts with nine eyes and blood-red spindle-legs and transparent skin.

Kaska remembered when he'd first reported a sighting, weeks back. Xenos, they'd told him. Just use the lascannon on them. But they weren't xenos. No xenos of any kind were stuck in the middle of this bloody, muddy shitshow. These were something else. Something that made everyone terrified, no matter how long you'd been fighting for.

'There's plenty to attack with,' said Kaska dryly, not wanting to think about that. 'Just look at the train.'

It was indeed filling up now, wagon after wagon, every tank chained down and ratcheted tight, the exhaust ports covered up and the gun barrels taped over. Scheduled departure was less than an hour away. They might even make that. Then the whole contraption would trundle down to the underground mag-lines, driving deep before clattering out south-east on the subterranean expressway. The crews would follow soon after, stuffed into personnel compartments on other mag-units, the kind of places you'd struggle to get any kind of rest at all. It'd be noisy, cramped and stinking. Then again, they were tankers. They were used to that.

'We'll last all of five minutes,' said Merck. 'Total waste of time.'

'Not the Lion's Gate,' said Jandev. 'No point stopping there. It'll be out east. Corbenic Gard, I reckon – the hole in the line.'

Vosch woke up. She stared around herself for a moment or two, then swallowed, coughed, and rubbed her eyes. 'When's our transport getting here?' she asked blurrily.

Kaska took another drag, and smiled. 'Nice to have you back, corporal,' he said. Vosch might have been a sleepy soul, but she was a good main gunner and one of the crew he actually liked. When she wasn't around, things got grumpier. 'We're heading out now. Just wanted to see him loaded up all safe.'

Aika 73's loader-claw had now finished with it, and was grinding jerkily down the tracks to the next transporter berth, where another Leman Russ waited for its attentions. Beyond that, everything was clouded with smoke, through which the dim outlines of loader-arms and flatbed cabs came and went.

Vosch yawned, then reached for a canteen. Her face bore the telltale 'gunner's spectacles' – the twin loops of redness around her eyes where the sights jammed in. 'Good. I was getting bored.'

Kaska looked over at Dresi again. The driver hadn't said a single thing. Just stared into space.

'So who's our force commander, then?' asked Merck. 'Anyone know that yet? Who the hell's pulled us out of Europa and sent us on this damned stupid rat-chase into the ruins?'

Kaska took a final drag of the nicotine-stick, savouring the acrid rolls of tobac, then flicked the stub onto the deck. He got up, stretched, and reached for his own canteen.

'No idea,' he said, now just waiting for the vox-alert that would see them all trudging over to the personnel mag-trains. He wasn't expecting to be told any time soon – even when the vox-channels were working, not much useful ever came down them. 'Stay cheerful, though – we all remain alive for a few more hours, we might just find out.'

Shiban had made his way up to the front at the first opportunity. Colossi was under constant fire, but its thick walls had yet to be cracked. The real fighting was to the north, under the shadow of Corbenic Gard, where the enemy was trying to force a passage behind Marmax and Gorgon Bar in order to open a direct assault on the Lion's Gate fortress. Detachments of the V and IX Legions had been despatched to staunch the flow for just a little longer, although they all knew that the territory would have to be given up soon.

In the face of that, the strategies of the two allied forces had started to diverge. The Blood Angels, under First Captain Raldoron's command, were retreating back across the battlefields towards the Ultimate Gate, from where they would be quickly re-stationed within the Inner Palace perimeter. Before long, all of them would end up there, joining with their primarch for the final defence of the core. The White Scars made the opposite journey – when their field positions were finally abandoned, they fought their way east, back to the Colossi staging grounds. Thus the V Legion command post was becoming ever more isolated, encircled by the lapping tides of the general advance. When the Ultimate Gate's tributary fortresses fell, that lone salient would be totally cut off, a single citadel amid an ocean of enemies. The long-standing Chogorian tactic of rapid encirclement was being applied to them in turn, and it was consciously being allowed to happen. Such were the ironies of war, Shiban thought.

He had taken a speeder out through the wreckage. In the past he might have waited until nightfall before risking leaving cover, but all hours of the day were dark now, drenched in permanent gloom under the ceaseless roil of the tox-clouds. Fires burned freely everywhere, igniting on hidden caches of promethium and flaring up into the murk. Sudden flashes illuminated a totally destroyed landscape – kilometre after kilometre of mountainous detritus heaps and tangled flaywire bundles, criss-crossed with trenches and groundworks, all life scrubbed from it, the few remaining wall-edges standing like sentinels amid the rubble dunes. These zones alone would once have housed hundreds of thousands, before all this started. Now they were just immense graveyards, brawled over by two sets of increasingly exhausted combatants.

The command post was not far – less than eighty kilometres west of Colossi's western barbican. As Shiban neared it, the locator-rune blipped on his helm display, guiding him in. He dropped down low between the empty corpses of two large storage silos, heading for a fortified gap at ground level. Ahead of him loomed the skeleton of what had once been a big manufactorum, its reinforced walls still intact in places, though its arched roof was gone and the glass in its hundreds of windows was all shot out. His tactical display picked up the presence of several dug-in mortar units and sniper details, hunkered down under cover for now, weapons silent.

He dropped through the gap and threaded his way underground, descending several levels to what had once been the undercroft of the manufactorum's assembly layer. As the rockcrete ceiling lowered, he brought his speeder to a halt, shut it down, and walked the rest of the way.

The forward base was spread across several subterranean chambers. Walls of sandbags were everywhere, as well as signs of hasty repairs to the place's cracked foundations. Tunnel entrances gaped at regular intervals, running off north and south to give rapid access to the zone's network of egress points. A few vehicles – Chimeras, mostly, plus fuel tankers, supply trucks and armoured groundcars – were parked up beside stacked crates of supplies and munitions. The whole place was crowded with Imperial Army troopers in dirty uniforms, some on guard duty, many more flat out in an exhausted sleep, lying head-to-toe in the crowded makeshift dorm-chambers.

Shiban headed straight for the command bunker, sited in a reinforced chamber further down in the manufactorum's echoing old undercroft. It was there that he saw the first warriors of the Legion proper. As he entered the bunker, they all bowed respectfully. Their armour had turned dark grey, covered in a thick film of dust, and all of it carried visible and heavy damage. These fighters were of the Brotherhood of the Storm, his own minghan, the one he had led since becoming khan. Those few he had taken with him to the Eternity Wall space port were all dead now, making this diminished concentration the very last of them. The brotherhood had once numbered nearly four hundred blades, but was now down to less than a third of that, and with a sizeable chunk of the remainder being recent newblood reinforcements

As a result, most of those in the room he barely recognised. In total there were ten scarred warriors of the ordu, plus a few dozen Legion menials operating the augur and comms equipment. The bulk of the brotherhood's troops were out fighting in the long tunnels, buying a little more time for the Army to withdraw from two positions further out west.

Their field commander, Yiman, was waiting for him at the heart of the low-roofed chamber, looking just as dishevelled as the rest of his retinue. All around him, baseline staff studied tactical hololiths or wrestled with faulty comms-boxes.

'Be welcome, my khan,' said Yiman, inclining his head. 'I trust you are recovered.'

Shiban flexed his augmetic hand, feeling the joints snag, the residual pain. 'Perfectly. How goes it?'

Yiman turned to a hololith column, bringing up the tunnel network in a spidery tangle. 'They have been advancing for two days now, without pause, here and here. We demolished these sections to slow them, but it only buys so much time – they have plenty of excavators. Increased numbers coming down over the past two weeks. Though, if I am honest, not as many as I feared.'

Shiban nodded, taking it all in. 'The Inner Palace walls are breached – they are swarming for the main prize.'

'We guessed as much. Then we will be asked to hold for longer?'

'No. The Khagan is accelerating the withdrawal. How long were you ordered to maintain position?'

'Another twenty-four hours.'

'Make it four. Anything you can't retrieve by then, leave it. All Legion assets to make for Colossi, all auxiliaries to head for the Ultimate Gate.'

Yiman hesitated. 'Four hours,' he said, in a low voice.

'It is all we will get.'

Another hesitation – clearly calculating what could be salvaged. 'Maybe that is for the best. The Army units… they struggle to operate in this.'

'You encounter yaksha down here?'

'More and more.' Yiman patted the tulwar at his belt. 'We ourselves are getting better at ending them. That satisfies me. But the auxilia cannot face them, and it is cruelty to ask.'

Shiban looked around the bunker's interior, studying the faces of those hard at work. The V Legion menial cadres had always been exceptionally tough and well trained, the equal of any non-Legion military unit in the Imperial Army. Now, though, their expressions betrayed the extent of their ordeal. None of them looked to have slept enough, if at all. Their skin was sallow, their movements sluggish. In another theatre, he might have reprimanded Yiman for allowing such an environment to fester, but this was different. He felt it himself – the constant pull of weariness, of mental strain, dragging at him, whispering of every failure he had ever made, all the time, on and on. Even when you knew it wasn't natural, and that its source was understood, it was still hard to counter, and that was with all the advantages he had been given. For the auxilia, who had been fighting a losing battle for months, it would soon become impossible to bear.

'I see it,' Shiban said. 'They should be given the chance to escape from this, even if only for a while.'

Yiman turned to his adjutant then and shot off a series of battle-sign commands. The warrior bowed, and hurried off to implement them. 'I am honoured that you delivered these orders in person, my khan,' he said, as the augur-units against the far wall lit up with renewed scans. 'But now, if four hours is all we have, I must depart for the tunnels – there will be hard fighting before we can extract our own.'

Shiban smiled, and unclamped the long *guan dao* power-glaive from his back. He brandished it deftly two-handed, enjoying the accustomed weight of the blade. It was the same weapon he'd carried since the campaign on Chondax seven years ago – just like him, tough to kill.

'I didn't come here just to pass on orders,' he said. 'This is still my brotherhood, Yiman – show me to the daemons.'

SEVEN

Gold under shadow
The Prince of Baal
Cthonia on Terra

But they came to him now, the Neverborn, needing no invitation to bring them into strike range. They wanted it. For some reason, they wanted to die on his blade, or at least to face him briefly, to laugh, or to feel some rush of fear, or maybe just to be there, at this time, in this place. It mattered to them. For once, they seemed to take it all seriously.

He still killed them, because that was his vocation: Constantin Valdor, captain-general, spear-bearer, threshold-keeper. He stalked through the narrow walkways of the Sanctum Imperialis, the deep vaults, the hidden places, waiting, watching. And then they came to him, sooner or later, rushing out of the dark to sink their fangs into his chest. His spear became bloody, its blade coated with the thick essence of creatures who had no true need for real blood. They died – or, at least, they were sent back to the place that spawned them – and then he would start again, going silently, hunting.

The fighting had been hard enough on the Outer Wall, where he had served alongside Raldoron of the IX and the

Great Khan of the V. Raldoron had impressed him – a fighter after his own manner, measured and artful. The Khan had been the Khan, peerless in some respects, frustrating in others. Now, though, the time for manning the far ramparts was over. The perimeter had shrunk steadily, pulling back towards the Inner Palace, and now within that too. It had never been a tidy process – large tracts of territory had been encircled and stubbornly held – but the shape of it was established.

So he could delay no longer. The order was given for all surviving Custodians to fall back to the Sanctum Imperialis. Valdor had informed Dorn, of course, who had barely acknowledged the courtesy. Perhaps he hadn't been aware that so many had been fighting for so long in exposed positions, so occupied was he with his many duties. Still, it was done. The Ten Thousand, who now numbered but a tithe of that nominal complement, had taken up arms within the very core of the Emperor's domain, ready for the assault on the last walls of all, both visible and invisible.

More than most, Valdor understood the true nature of that conflict. Any conscript in the trenches knew that the enemy was coming at them over ground, but would have been wholly unaware of the struggles going on the whole time under their feet. The battle for Terra had been going on a lot longer down there, and was a degree more vicious. For the most part, it was the Emperor who held the hordes back, and whose matchless power blocked the one stable passage up into the foundations of the Throneroom itself.

Every barrier was leaky, though, if placed under enough stress, and now the pores were opening. Much as it pained Valdor to admit it, his master's control was slipping. The great ward-shield erected over the Palace was failing. The counterpart barriers sunk into the earth were failing. The daemons could worm their way in now, darting out across the battlements, spinning down from the firelit air, thrusting up from the toxic soils. There was no single battlefront any more, no cleanly defined line behind which the defenders could shelter, but a heavily perforated sphere of imperfect control. With every hour, the chance of that residual protection disappearing entirely increased a little further.

He found himself almost wishing for the moment to come. He knew it had to arrive soon. Guilliman had not made it. Even if the Ultramarines somehow appeared, it would surely be too late to make a difference. Everything would come down to the Throneroom, the fulcrum of the entire grand drama, just as it had always been destined to. The Emperor was there. The Warmaster was closing in. The rest of the galaxy felt entirely irrelevant beside the chance to control that one minuscule speck of territory, that one tiny enclosed chamber, buried deep amid the fossils of earlier empires, the one location on Terra Valdor was sworn to defend at all costs.

And then he paused, suddenly alert.

The corridor ran away ahead, black as pitch. The walls here were bone-like, ridged and gnarled and thick with dust. He was a long way down, far below even the Dungeon's deepest levels. These places smelled of older, stranger civilisations, ones that had lived and died thousands of years before his own had fought its way to prominence. Not all traces of those forgotten cultures had been completely erased – the tunnels went down a long way.

He narrowed his eyes, remaining perfectly motionless. The tunnel was silent – down here, the perpetual thunder of the surface guns could no longer be made out. He could smell something, though, just barely, a faint whiff of… burning.

He crept forward, his auramite boots sinking softly into dust layers ten centimetres thick. The walls of the corridor, delved for mortal dimensions, pressed close. You could imagine being buried alive here, smothered by the millions of tonnes of rock above and around you. His shoulder guard snagged on an outgrowth, and he adjusted his position. It felt as if the route ahead was narrower than it had been. He looked up, searching for stress fractures on the rock-cut roof, and saw only the thick coating of ancient filth, black as oil.

A few more steps, cautious now, every sense alert. The smell grew more intense. He thought he heard a faint hiss from some way back, but paid it no mind. Something was in the tunnel with him now, a presence without a soul, coiled up in the darkness. It would try to trick him, if it could, distract his focus, send him down the wrong path.

He made it to the end of the tunnel. He saw a stone arch ahead of him, grainy in his helm's night-vision. The keystone was low – he'd have to stoop to enter. On the far side of the arch was a tiny chamber, mottled with mould spores, clammy and damp. An altar of some sort stood against the far wall, engraved with characters and images he didn't recognise. A single candle stood on the altar-top, burning with a blue-white flame that seemed to give out no illumination at all.

The place was cold. Very cold. Lines of frost rimed the rough-cut stones. Despite that, the smell of burning was overwhelming.

A presence was in there, hidden from view for now, but occupying it nonetheless.

He activated the disruptor field on his guardian spear, and the space flooded with vivid light. Shadows leapt away from him, all except for a ragged patch of darkness just in front of the altar, a clot of non-reflective blackness, low down.

'*Go away,*' a voice whispered, childlike, impish. '*I am praying.*'

Valdor did not move immediately. You could learn things from these creatures, if you were patient. 'There is nothing to pray to, down here.'

'*But plenty to pray* for.'

'If you say so.'

The nugget of darkness writhed, expanded, then started to twist around. A pale grey head emerged, as if from under a cowl. It was hairless, eyeless, noseless. A single mouth took up most of the space, and it was ringed with ranks of tiny teeth. When it spoke, flabby wide lips rippled obscenely.

'You could leave me be,' it said. *'I am quite harmless. And I have lived here for a very long time.'*

Valdor remained watchful. The candle flame had stopped moving, caught as if in a freeze-frame. 'Nothing lives down here.'

'You and me. We do.'

'Only one of us is alive.'

The mouth stretched into a wide grin. *'For now. You're not safe. Not even your master. We will feast on Him, when He is sent into our realm.'*

'I think not.'

'You think? For yourself? I see no evidence of that.' The vile mouth gaped wider. *'But let's see how quick you are!'*

It suddenly jerked upwards, outwards, the teeth-filled mouth gaping and dividing with horrifying speed. Valdor slashed straight into the tumbling wall of darkness, scything his spear diagonally and dragging its tip across the splayed maws. The expanding daemon's flesh split apart, scattering into new coal-black slivers that quickly pooled and reformed and wriggled back up into fresh bodies. For an instant, it looked as if the entire chamber would be suffocated by them, as they reared up and slobbered over the lone Custodian and drenched the entire space in void-like streamers of darkness.

But Valdor had only made the first cut to get closer to his real target. His second swipe, crossways, bisected the candle and snuffed out its frozen flame. The multiple daemon-forms immediately screamed in agony, then splattered into flying gobbets that coated the walls in black mucus. Valdor swept around towards the original glut of pseudo-flesh, still bearing the remnants of its uncanny mouth, jabbed down and pinned it to the chamber floor.

It writhed and spat. For a fraction of a second, Valdor felt its essence shudder up the shaft of his spear. He had a brief glimpse of another world, an infinite one, made of pain, made of malice, swirling, transmuting. He understood then that this presence was a petty one, a wayfinder, a prober of weak links, a slave to greater denizens of that pain-world and now destined to be consumed by them for its failure. He experienced a slice of its terror at that prospect – so much more acute than a mortal could ever have experienced.

He thumbed the disruptor trigger, and the last slug of its physical extrusion exploded in a crackle of gold.

'*That* quick,' he said grimly, and extinguished the flame.

Afterwards, he took a few moments to recover. Not from the physical exertion – that had been trivial – but from the exposure to such raw truth. Every time he did that, every time he opened himself up to those visions, it got a little harder to stomach. He could feel the foulness polluting him, introducing the ghosts of doubt where none should ever have been possible.

To kill with this blade, it took a toll. If he had been capable of doubting his master, he might have spent more time wondering why he had been given such a weapon. It seemed that the Emperor had forged a whole brace of such things, only to give them away to His servants, liberally, like the battle-trophies of some ancient warlord. They all had powers, some brazen, some subtle, some yet to be uncovered, none of them straightforward.

He looked down, where the last dregs of the daemonic essence pooled at his boots. Such creatures were the worst. The death of a mortal might expose a brief, uncomfortable truth – something to check you, make you reflect. The Neverborn, when they were sent screaming back to the other side of the curtain, gave you something much more disturbing – a snatched glimpse of something ineffable, vile, beyond reason. Perhaps, if he'd been gifted with a more vivid imagination, he might have found himself overwhelmed by such visions. Even so, you didn't forget them. They hung around afterwards, repeating through your mind, nagging reminders of what they all fought against, and what they had striven to build, and what they currently seemed destined to lose.

'*Captain-general,*' came a priority burst through his helm-mounted comm. It was Amon. Just to hear his voice – a steady, calm, *loyal* voice – came as a relief.

'Speak,' Valdor said, withdrawing from the chamber.

'*An update from the Blackstone. The woman Keeler is loose now, position unknown. Her supervised release was interrupted by the presence of an unexpected party. Identity unconfirmed. Judged to be of the Legiones Astartes.*'

'And this party is after her now?'

'*Assuredly. I enquire after authorisation to intervene.*'

'Negative. If she has any role to play now, it will be outside our control.' Valdor had never particularly seen the wisdom of this programme, but it had oversight at the highest level, so it was best that it ran its course.

'*Understood. Which brings me onto the other subject.*'

'The bio-criminal.'

'*I have him under surveillance still, but he is skilled. If things were not otherwise, I would place a Tier-three watch-guard on him, but the power to do so no longer exists.*'

That was almost certainly true. Soon they would no longer be able to exert any kind of control over the Palace beyond the Sanctum itself.

'Then your judgement?'

'*Given the circumstances, I cannot promise to keep him under observation for much longer. This may require a more… expert intervention.'*

Valdor thought on that. He had his duties here. Few could hunt down the daemonic with such precision, and the need for vigilance would only grow. If he left the narrow limits of the Sanctum now, it could only be for a short time. Despite all that he had seen in the Dungeon since the start of the siege, the criminal's presence still filled him with considerable and growing unease.

At the start, he hadn't even been convinced that Fo's boasts were anything more than bluster, a way to get out of his predicament. Now, though, he was no longer sure. The tantalising possibility existed, even in this galaxy of lies, that he had actually meant what he'd said, and could do what he claimed.

Generate threats, respond to them. Place our minds in the situation of those who wish to do Him harm. Let them in close, accepting the risk in return for the knowledge we gain.

That had always been the principle, ever since the affair with Astarte. The fact that they were still conducting such exercises even now, when the very gates of hell were opening in front of them, might have been considered either brave or foolish, depending on your particular appetite for risk.

'Maintain a lock on his position,' Valdor said, making his decision. 'I will come for him myself.'

He crashed down onto the eleventh high parapet of Aurum Bar's eastern face, slamming into the rockcrete walkway and scattering the armoured bodies clustered there. They were liveried in crimson, just as he was, their armour drenched in blood-red and gold and brass, superlative warriors from a tradition of splendour and devotion.

They had done well, to get this far. Six days of intense bombardment, followed by an armoured drive that had smashed through the fourth defensive circle, then the third, and now

Lorgar's zealous sons were into artillery range of the high walls of the Bar proper. Three such offensives over the past few months had been launched and had failed. Now, though, the resilience of the defenders was broken at last, and the mongrel horde of traitor legionaries, cult fanatics, Dark Mechanicum engines and their increasingly brazen daemon allies had reached the curtain barrier, dragging their siege machines into range and unleashing their devil-weapons at the structure. They had the numbers, and they had the supplies, and they sensed that this was the moment.

Perhaps it was, thought Sanguinius, as he grabbed a Word Bearer by his gorget and flung him out over the edge. Then he swept into a second, ramming his spear through the fighter's breastplate. The rest of them came at him, never hesitating, straining every genhanced sinew to land a blow on a primarch, heedless of the risk to themselves. Each one would have happily died, just knowing that he had done nothing more than that – scored a hit, extracted a little strength, contributed in just a fractional manner to the victory they had been promised and now expected.

Sanguinius might have admired such remorseless focus, had it been for some other cause. As it was, the zeal was empty, devoid of meaning other than resentment, slaved to a faith in gods that had no business being worshipped by any living thing. He despised them for that, perhaps more than any of the others he fought. You could readily see the weakness that had led to, say, Fulgrim's Legion's spiral into madness, and perhaps even understand it – they had been fools, trapped by their own desires. These, though – *these* – they had always known what they were doing. They had grasped the hidden theology of the universe, the dark foundations on which it rested, and had then freely given it their conscious allegiance.

'Traitors!' Sanguinius roared, crunching a third warrior into the battlement's merlon and breaking his neck. 'Oath-breakers!'

Even as he fought, carving his way across the overrun parapet, the sky above him was lit with down-lumens. Four Stormbirds came in low through the murk, turbines blasting the exposed wall section. Hatches slammed open, and legionaries spilled out – in crimson too, but the brighter hue of the sons of Baal, his own.

The Blood Angels assault squads smacked down around him, their flamers and energy-sheathed blades already snarling. Without a word, they fell into battle alongside their primarch, and together the IX Legion elite worked to clear the wall section. The pace and fury of it was relentless, a blistering surge across the five-metre-wide parapet, a whirl of blades that clanged and resounded from ceramite. The Word Bearers fought back hard, screaming denunciations of their own, the air around them charged with the shimmer of half-summoned daemons, their blades made deadlier with cantrips and ether-poisons. Those combinations made them lethal, and so the force of the charge was checked, with Blood Angels blasted apart or hacked to the ground or hurled from the wall's edge and into oblivion.

But the primarch was there with them, and under the shadow of those grime-streaked wings there could only be one outcome. The Word Bearers were gradually driven back, their rune-carved plate cracked open and their garbled spells silenced. The daemon-ghosts were scattered, sent howling out of the physical. The last of the fighters – a great champion clad in Tartarus armour surmounted with an iron crown – was cast down by Sanguinius himself, his axe-blade broken into pieces and his neck snapped. Sanguinius whirled his spear-tip around, angled it vertically over the stricken champion, and plunged it through his primary heart. The blade flared with energy, making its prey's limbs jerk and spasm, before the primarch yanked it free again and killed the power.

After that, the flamer teams went to work, methodically making their way across the enemy corpses, ensuring that

everything was rendered down to ash and no unnatural remnant remained to rear up suddenly and resume slaughter. The
bodies of the loyal fallen were taken up and carried towards
the hovering Stormbirds, which were already pivoting and
whining up for extraction. The raid had lasted just moments,
but they could not afford to linger – dozens of similar attacks
had been planned, each one aimed at snuffing out a critical
pressure point, blunting the exposed spearheads of the enemy
advance and eliminating their key command units.

Sanguinius himself walked up to the edge of the ramparts,
facing out over the Anterior wastes and the devastation that
had once led up to the old processional quarter. Already his
helm's comm-feed was filling up with pleas for intervention,
one after the other, a torrent that never let up. He, too, would
have to take wing again shortly, surging up into the poison
clouds alongside his Legion's few remaining attack gunships.
It was the best they could do now – no longer mount major
operations, but only run pinpoint strikes aimed at preventing the withdrawals becoming a massacre.

He studied the territory they were ceding. The approaches
to Aurum, heavily contested ever since the Lion's Gate space
port had fallen, were now overrun entirely. The outworks were
barely visible, mulched down to a sea of blackened mud and
trampled under millions of boots. The ground trembled, both
from the drum of enemy guns and the booby-trapped chambers
being detonated far below him. Columns of smoke twisted up
from a thousand points across the ravaged landscape, each one
marking the corpse of a big lander or a super-heavy vehicle, and
the wind was hot, tasting bitter even through his helm's filters.

They were no longer fighting to hold this line. The blood and
materiel expended on the long ring of outer fortresses had all
been to slow the enemy, to cause them pain, not to prevent them
ever breaking in. Now that the Inner Palace walls were ruptured

in more than one location, the defences east of the Ultimate Gate had become unviable. Massive evacuation columns were underway, streaming out from the bunkers and picking their way across the shell-blown terrain towards the dubious sanctuary of the innermost portals. The remaining combat was to protect those columns for as long as possible, to maintain a fragile defence-screen to ensure that most of them could get clear before the gates were kicked in and the monsters charged inside.

Sanguinius focused, looking further north, peering through the drifting smog banks to make some sense of the landscape. He could see the precipitous walls of Gorgon Bar, the place he had worked so hard to preserve, now ringed with stuttering firelines, its heart being gutted by the enemy troops rampaging within it. Beyond that, faint in the overcast haze, was Marmax. As far as he could tell at such range, it seemed to be holding – if they could keep it from collapsing entirely, even for another hour or two, that would be something.

That was the limit of his eyesight. He had not had one of his visions for some time – those disturbing glimpses straight into the minds of his brothers. Perhaps he had simply been too occupied with the fighting, or perhaps that unbidden and unwanted facility was fading of its own accord. Most likely it was just a temporary respite, a momentary stilling before the winds of the ether gathered power again. For the time being, he only had the vaguest of psychic sensations – impressions of souls, all caught up in the tempest of the eastern battle-front as it steadily imploded, some defiant, some terrified, most in a state of abject misery. That had been the key change, over the past month of unremitting fighting – the shift from fear to resignation. He could even feel it himself. It was different to how it had been before – the pain, the visions. This was a vaguer ailment, a kind of numbness, creeping up from his limbs and into his torso, making him want to hesitate, to doubt, to check himself. If he closed his eyes, he almost fancied he could see the sickness, creeping out of the heart of foetid darkness, crawling over the graveyards and the charnel fields and reaching out to throttle them all.

He couldn't indulge that. He had to keep moving, keep vital. And now, here, on the very edge of the shrinking arc of Imperial control, there was one thing he had to try again, before the growing distance made it impossible.

'Brother,' he voxed, using the most heavily encoded channel, the one that was kept clear even when the rest dissolved into shrieking static.

For a long moment, the space of three deep breaths, he got nothing back. And then, just as he was about to give up, a hiss and a crackle spat back at him.

'He's sent you to haul me back in, then?' came Jaghatai's voice, distorted and faint over the whirr of interference.

Sanguinius smiled. Ever suspicious, the Khan, verging on the paranoid – little changed. 'If he'd asked, do you think I'd have agreed?'

At the other end, a grunt of amused scorn. *'Maybe. You're a helpful soul.'*

'The Ultimate Gate is on the edge of being compassed. Your window for withdrawal shrinks.'

'Yes, I'd noticed.'

'And though you have a reputation for sneaking back at the last minute, I fear this may be slipping out of your grasp.'

'We're not coming back.'

'You are almost entirely surrounded.'

'Yes, we are.'

Sanguinius clenched a single fist, willing himself to remain calm. He admired Jaghatai, he had laboured long with him on the elements of the Librarius, he had fought alongside him more than once, but still the pig-headedness could irritate.

'Then you, too, have given up.'

'Far from it.' A long pause, as if he were searching for the right words. 'I know you respect dreams. The ones that speak truthfully, at least. They will win, I foresee, as long as he is active. The Warmaster cannot rely on much, for our estranged brothers are losing their minds. All save one.'

'But we are stronger together. At the core.'

'Under your strategy, maybe.' A faint, dry chuckle over the comm. 'Forgive me. This is not about character. It is about what we need to break the hold. The hold that crushes our spirit.' Even across the interference, Sanguinius could hear the urgency in his brother's voice. 'They do not plan, any more. They rush at the barriers set before them, barely knowing where they are, barely knowing their own names. But he is waiting, beyond our reach, as careful as he ever was. When all else is ashes, when we think that nothing worse remains, he will come. And that ends our last hope.'

Sanguinius weighed his own words carefully then. 'Mortarion has been… changed, brother. He is not what he was when you met on Prospero. Could you stand against him now? Could any of us?'

'I do not know. But then, if that is your counsel, when the moment comes, and you are called to face one of them, I shall expect you to stand down too. Hand over your spear, make your excuses. Fall back again.'

Sanguinius laughed. 'We are running short of places to retreat to.'

'We should never have let it be taken.'

'You still think that?'

'The guns are intact, and could be used. They're landing at will. And we will need a space port ourselves. When Guilliman comes. When we have victory in the cusp of our palms, he will need the swift route down.'

Victory. The Khan was still thinking of victory. How was

that possible? Had he, too, gone mad, just like the traitors who raved with joy as they dismantled the home of their own species? It was always possible. He had always flirted with it.

'In that,' Sanguinius said, 'you are at least consistent.'

'Not something I've been accused of often.'

Sanguinius looked up. To the north, fresh spikes of fire punched through the cloud cover. He would have to go now, to do what he had been doing since this thing had started – hold it together, keep the troops fighting for just another day, another hour, another moment.

'I did not make contact to summon you back,' he said. 'Much as it would gladden my heart to have you with us. Rogal always said you'd make your run, sooner or later, and he's usually right about the rest of us. That's why he's organising things.' He watched the burning lands, the spoil of a once proud galactic civilisation, brought low by its own vices. 'I made contact because, if you do this, it may be the last time we ever speak. And so I wanted to send you my blessing. I wanted to wish you luck. And I wanted to express the hope that you'll ram that damned scythe so far down his throat that he'll never find his stupid rebreather again.'

The Khan laughed hard at that. Even distorted by the poor link, Sanguinius heard that it was the right kind of laugh – not cynical, not knowing, just a brief break in the suffocating tension.

'We will meet again, my friend,' the Khan said. *'We will build all the things we ever dreamed of. Until then, do what you must. Keep them hoping. Hold the walls.'*

The link cut. Sanguinius stood for just a little while longer, alone on the parapet, watching his birthworld burn. He looked over his shoulder, to where the great massif of the Inner Palace rose up. In the darkness, against the gathering glow of the many fires, it looked more like an ossuary than a fortress.

'I plan to,' he said softly.

And then, with a leap, a clap of wings and a powerful thrust into the skies, he was gone again, spear held ready, streaking towards the next battle that needed him.

They were weak. They were compromised. Their will to fight was gone, their defences were falling open.

It had been so hard over the last seven years. Every gain had been contested, every triumph paid for in blood. Now, though, right at the end, resistance was falling away.

They had ceased to believe, that was the problem. For as long as they had been able to think that something was coming to rescue them, or that their enemies would somehow fall apart of their own accord, they had stood up and fired back. Now, though, they abandoned their posts, they ran down the long chasms between the smoke-filled spires, their nerves shot, their spirit broken.

Not his counterparts in the Legiones Astartes, of course. They still held their positions, still made hard work of it, but even they were missing something. It was as if they fought out of habit, almost – a kind of automatic response. They no longer believed they could alter the result. They were going through the motions. Seeing it out. He had killed so many of them – veterans, company captains, champions of renown. Even as they had diminished, he had grown, adding to a reputation that had been formidable during the years of the Crusade itself.

Indras Archeta, captain of the Third Company, Sons of Horus, reflected on that for a moment. In his left hand he grasped the neck of an Imperial Fists warrior. In his right hand, his beloved longblade, the one that rippled with beauty and whispered truths to him. The warrior's armour was decorated with veteran honours, telling of a long and storied career, but now he was almost dead. Blood ran from every seal

on his armour, trickling across plate that was more dirt than
ceramite, punched-through with bolt craters, its power gone.

The Space Marine was trying to say something. Archeta
lowered his head a little, prepared to indulge him, since he'd
fought well enough. 'What's that, eh?' he asked. 'Spit it out.'

'Emperor… damn… your… faithless…'

'Ah, nothing interesting,' said Archeta wearily. He let the warri-
or's head fall, and severed his neck before it hit the ground. Then
he watched the fighter die, slowly, life gushing from the deep
wound at his neck, seeping into the chem-saturated earth below.

He looked up. A long procession of armour and infantry
rumbled down the avenue ahead of him, flanked on either side
by the shattered walls of ruined hab-towers. The vehicles were
Legion Land Raiders and Sicarans, their hulls in the sea-green
livery of the Legion, in serviceable shape despite the punishing campaign to reach the main incursion points. Their tracks
churned up the remains of the choke-point barricades, even
as the last batch of krak grenades blew up the pill boxes
on the northern edge of the avenue. Tactical squads marched
through the debris, going watchfully but confidently. Behind
them clunked a big Contemptor, its heavy treads crushing the
remnants of yellow battleplate further into the mud.

He had not expected to reach this position for another six
hours. It was a confluence between two major thoroughfares,
the key to unlocking the next urban zone battlefront, the kind
of place a disciplined enemy would fight tooth and nail to
hold on to. If the pinnacles at the intersection had not been
blasted to pieces, you might almost have been able to clamber
up and make out the perimeter walls of the Field of Winged
Victory from them.

Maybe the defenders had run out of ammunition. Maybe
the main garrisons had already fallen back, exposing this
position. Maybe the fighters here had been sacrificed for a

front elsewhere. Even so, it shouldn't have been quite so easy. If he wasn't careful, the pace of the advance would run ahead of the supply lines and the tanks would grind to a halt for lack of fuel.

Archeta watched his troops file past, marching their way into the heart of the city-palace. From up ahead, all he could hear were screams and explosions. From behind, nothing – a total absence, as if they were erasing everything entirely, wiping the planet clean.

And then, from the north, where a second avenue met the first, more vehicles suddenly rumbled into view, all of them of the XVI Legion too. With a calm efficiency, the lead tanks swivelled on their axes and swung around to join Archeta's advancing squadrons. A few section commanders shouted out orders, but otherwise it was performed without fuss. A choreographer would have been proud of the way they all integrated, merging strength before ploughing on, driving further west, onward, into the heart of the conurbation.

A Damocles Rhino revved out of the shadows, heading straight for Archeta's location. At the last minute, the command transport shuddered to a halt, the hatch swung open, and a single warrior emerged. He crunched down to the rubble and strode over to Archeta, clenching his fist and extending it in the Legion salute.

'Captain!' he shouted. 'Here already, eh?'

Archeta watched him approach. The warrior was kitted out much as he was – fine artificer-crafted battleplate, long fur-lined cloak, the Eye of Horus on his breastplate. They were equals, the two of them, as far as rank went, but Azelas Baraxa was captain of the Second Company, just one step closer to the master of the Legion. In another time, given the prodigious tally of throats they had cut for the Warmaster, both of them might have expected to have played a part in the Mournival, but in the aftermath of the disaster at the Saturnine Gate there had been little enthusiasm to revive that old convention. What purpose would it have served, now? The Sons of Horus were the creatures of a living god, the warrior-slaves of an immortal deity. You did not advise a god, and you did not seek to give counsel to an immortal. They had all become just soldiers again, the tools required for the task at hand, with the last of their Crusade-era pretensions swept away.

'Aye, we're making good time,' Archeta said passionlessly.

He didn't like Baraxa. The Second Company captain was a visionless soul, wedded to how things had been before the great break with Terra. Like so many of the senior Sons of Horus, Baraxa looked on the gifts of the new dispensation with suspicion, clinging to the way things had been on Cthonia when they had all of them claimed not to believe in such things as gods. To maintain that view now was a failure of vision, a conservatism that did them no favours. When Torgaddon had been slain, the position should have gone to someone with similar gifts, a creature of the gods they now fought for, not another Ezekyle-clone, stubbornly refusing to acknowledge the inevitable.

Baraxa came to stand beside him. 'They're *broken*, brother,' he said. 'The Sanctum is just lying there. Ready to take. And I find I can hardly believe it.'

The captain's voice rang with enthusiasm. Despite his distaste for the man, Archeta knew what he meant. This was the heart of it, the soul of the old empire. Most of his troops had never set eyes on Terra before, let alone walked down the streets of its ancient capital. The galaxy was full of wonders, millions of them, but nothing truly compared to this place, even in its ruin. At times you would catch yourself, sometimes even in the midst of combat, and remember where you were. You would glance up at the vast buildings around you, the urban profile that was so familiar from a thousand propaganda vid-reels, the carved insignias of the Crusade-era triumphs, the mighty edifices raised to fuel the momentum of that incredible, unrepeatable feat, and wonder how things had ever come this far.

'It isn't over yet,' Archeta said, not willing to get swept up into euphoria. 'We're being drawn further in – they still have three primarchs in there, somewhere.'

Baraxa laughed. 'So cautious.' He pushed his cloak back, flexed the fingers of his sword-hand gauntlet, gazed down the long avenue towards the mountainous building-clusters ahead. 'Bastion Ledge has been breached – you knew that? Three fronts, all converging. They can't handle that.' He drew in a long breath, as if the air was something that might invigorate him rather than tear at his helm's overworked tox-filters. 'Thousands are coming through Mercury Breach alone, every hour now. It's a flood. The Red Angel is inside, doing what he does best. This is overwhelming. We just need to get there *first*, now – break the last gate before the World Eaters render it all down to blood-slurry.'

That was indeed the objective. The fragile unity between Legions and factions had already broken. What little cohesion remained was contingent on the target before them all – the hated Emperor, the Deceiver and the Cheater of Birthright. Once He was slaughtered, it would all dissolve again. The XVI Legion, greatest of Legions, the ones who had propelled and sustained this thing from the very start, would have to keep things from collapsing, and to do that they had to be in control of the centre, secure within the very same bunkers that they were now trying to prise apart.

'Then he'll need to be back,' Archeta said.

'He already is.'

That was a surprise. 'Abaddon? He's recovered?'

'He was fighting the Apothecaries, they told me, making their lives hell until they did enough to get him back to the front. He's landed at the Eternity Wall, heading for Mercury right now.' Baraxa clapped Archeta on the upper arm. 'It's all we need to finish this. Our leader.'

Archeta bristled. 'Our leader is on the *Vengeful Spirit*'

'Of course. Of course! But then, down here–'

'What does that matter? Ezekyle's just a mortal. Just like us. You should watch where your words take you, Azelas – the Warmaster sees all and hears all.'

Baraxa looked at him for a moment, taken aback. 'And is beloved by all,' he murmured.

'What?'

'Hells, brother, what's chewing at your guts? You should be pleased.'

Yes, what was ailing him? Why was he not exultant, relishing the last push into the heart of hypocrisy? He had never withheld his blade-hand before, never regretted a kill. The closer he got, though, the more ill-humoured he became.

Horus was not with them. Maybe that was it. Archeta had witnessed the primarch fight, once, a long time ago now, and it was hard to imagine anything alive being able to stand up to that. If Horus trod this ground, here, now, the whole thing would be over in hours. Oh, Archeta knew all the cant that the sorcerers spouted about the great ward-shield, how it kept out those with the greatest gifts, but that barrier was in tatters now. If Angron could somehow rampage his way inside it, then surely the Warmaster could.

As long as Horus remained absent, the fissures in his Legion would grow steadily wider. You would have power brokers like Baraxa whose heads had been turned by the dynamic First Captain. Sycar, the new Master of the Justaerin, was said to be Abaddon's creature too. Maybe Ikari, the much-disliked captain of the Fourth Company, was also. What would they all do, if Horus never emerged at all? Would they start, steadily, to think about where their loyalties truly lay?

Horus still commanded the allegiance of the Legion, that was true. Some had even begun to talk of him, as Archeta did, as a member of the true Pantheon, something elevated far beyond the merely human and worthy of a more strenuous kind of adulation. Beruddin, captain of the Fifth, was of a similar mind. Malabreux, the new leader of the Catulan Reavers, was fervent in the faith. But they were all so *new*, all so callow. The entire leadership layer of the Legion had been scraped away. The old great names – the Torgaddons, the Kibres, the Ekaddons, the Aximands – they were extinguished. Those that had replaced them, Archeta included, were poor copies, divided among themselves, beginning to doubt and bicker even as the greatest prize of all lay almost within their grasp.

All except Abaddon. He had come through it all, if not unscathed, then still himself, the last link with the heritage of the Luna Wolves. No surprise, then, that he was listened to more than ever, looked up to by both the newborn and the old hands.

Horus had to come soon. He had to snuff this nonsense out. He had to remind the faithful why they were spilling their blood for him. He had to be the Warmaster. He had, in due course, to be the Emperor.

'Just keen for this to be over,' Archeta told Baraxa, sheathing his whispering blade and making ready to march again. 'We've destroyed enough. Time to start building again.'

EIGHT

Old dreams
Betrayer
Kurultai

Impossible, though, to imagine anything being built again, not here, not like it had been. By the time Ilya made her way back to Colossi, the scale of the eastern warzone's disintegration was painfully apparent. The subterranean routes leading out from under the Ultimate Gate were still operational in sections, but there had been raids in many locations, puncturing the vital supply lines and diverting scarce defensive resources away from the surface. The big mag-train contingents she'd commissioned had got through, mostly, but they had been the last ones – any remaining reinforcements or supply-runs would have to be made overground, and that was now insanely dangerous.

She had seen that for herself. When the time had come to leave the Inner Palace and head back to the fringes, Sojuk had become increasingly concerned. Somehow he'd managed to cobble together an escort of three outrider speeders and a backup Chimera for the journey. He'd done it without consulting her, and when she remonstrated with him he could barely look her in the eye.

'My apologies, szu,' he'd said. 'Next time, I shall be sure to.'

She'd had to crack a smile at that. Sojuk was a sly old fox – there would be no *next time* for any of this.

It had been a hard stretch, once east of the big Imperial formations clustering together at the Ultimate Gate. The bombardment there had already started – you could feel the earth shudder even deep underground. The further you went, the worse it got. The little convoy had needed to break topside for a couple of hours about fifty kilometres north of the Lion's Gate, and that had been like emerging into a vision of hell. The portal itself was on fire, a huge raging glow that had made the southern horizon throb. Strange cries had echoed across the pummelled wasteland, making the pools of acrid water in the craters ripple.

'Yaksha,' Sojuk had spat, driving hard through the filth.

They had been lucky, though – they hadn't run into any of those horrors directly, or much else in the way of serious opposition. They had needed to skirt wide around a formation of VIII Legion infantry heading west through the ruins, but otherwise the worst they had encountered were bands of cultists and traitor auxiliaries, who could be hit hard and then outrun. As soon as he was able, Sojuk had got them back underground again, right down into the crumbling tunnels that threaded their way east to the tributary fortress-perimeter.

When they had finally reached the Colossi receiving ports, guarded in lamplit darkness by heavy lascannon towers and static V Legion tank lines, Ilya had breathed a long sigh of genuine relief. This place might have been isolated now, surrounded on almost all sides by a nigh-infinite expanse of enemies, but they were her people, an island of familiarity, a tiny echo of Chogoris.

She'd taken her leave of Sojuk after that, and had made her way up to the north command tower. Her reports had already been compiled and sent out through the comm-grid, but there was no guarantee they had got through – in these confused times, you had to actually speak to someone in person to have any confidence that you'd been heard. The bulk of the military staff left in the Colossi operations chambers were of the Legion, now – almost all the Imperial Army staff had been evacuated. Occasionally you ran into an officer in non-Legion colours, and always exchanged a brief smile or a nod with them – those were just like she was, the gone-natives, unwilling to leave the company of these strange off-worlders, prepared to die out here with them rather than back among those they had been raised with. That was how it was with Jaghatai's people – you could be infected, if you weren't careful.

Once in the main watch-chamber, which was full and bustling with a kind of febrile energy, she spoke to Qin Fai, noyan-khan and commander of the northern-zone defences. He listened to her despatches carefully, nodding here and there, occasionally pressing her on a detail, checking what she said against the ledgers his own officials brought him.

They've got better at this, she found herself thinking. *Then again, they've been forced to.*

At the end of her briefing, he bowed to her. 'Our sincere thanks, szu-Ilya. This could not have been done without you.'

That was probably true. The White Scars had never enjoyed the contacts she had – the routes into the Imperial command structure, such as that was now. Though it was good to feel useful again, the idea of it made her feel a little mournful, like an old tool that had steadily become worn out until it could only do one thing well. If this was the final task she ever did for them, it felt cheap – an errand of collection, a rounding up of damaged assets.

'It's the last we'll get,' she told him. 'The routes west are all closed now.'

'If that is what we have,' said Qin Fai, 'then it must be enough.'

And then she'd suddenly felt weak. Her stomach was empty, she was dehydrated. She'd been moving from place to place, often under fire, without pause, for days. It would have been nice to speak further with the noyan-khan, to gain a better understanding of how the plans were evolving, but she feared she might pass out if she did. She made an excuse, withdrew, and hurried down to her own reserved chambers, ones set deep inside the inner core of the fortress. Back inside them, she reached for a cup of water with trembling hands, unbuttoned her general's coat at the collar, sat down heavily in her chair, closed her eyes, and let her limbs go limp.

It was only after she'd been sitting in silence for a few moments that it slowly dawned on her that she was not alone. Something else was in there with her, something outsized and monstrously dangerous, something that scarcely belonged in the same sphere of existence as her, let alone the same room.

'You could have knocked,' she murmured, eyes still closed.

When the Khan replied, the out-of-character awkwardness of it made her chuckle.

'Forgive me. When you came in, you did not look well, so I… well, I did not know how to warn you.'

She opened her eyes, shuffled up in her chair. He was standing against the far wall, beyond the meagre light of her sole lumen, too big to fit onto any of her furniture pieces, looking as self-conscious as she'd ever seen anyone look.

'I'll be recovered in a moment,' she said. 'Come, speak to me.'

He started to make for the door. 'You look tired. I should not have waited for you here. I will return later.'

'No, really.' Ilya reached out for him, her fingers brushing against his gauntlet, tugging him back. 'You will not have the time later. We haven't spoken for weeks. Not properly. Please.'

He hesitated, looking down at her. They made a ragged pair – the battle-ravaged warlord, his exhausted emissary.

'How do you feel?' he asked.

'Old,' she said. 'I feel very old. How do you feel?'

The wisp of a smile flickered over his proud face. No one else would ever have dared ask him that question. None of the tens of thousands of warriors under his command, none of the hundreds of thousands of auxiliary troops who marched under his banner, would ever have presumed.

'I feel... settled,' he said thoughtfully. 'The pieces are arranged. The calculations have been made. Very soon we shall reach the point when nothing else can be done, save for the action itself.'

She found that she didn't really believe that. He had said similar things on the eve of other battles, and she had believed it then, but this was different. The stakes were higher, the likelihood of devastation overwhelming. This was not a voluntary decision in any meaningful sense. She had studied the same reports that he had, sat in the same council gatherings. This was desperation, a final spit in the eye of fate, and if any were to benefit from what they did, then it would not be them.

'But not quite, of course,' he added wryly. 'There is always doubt. Even more so, now. He clouds everything, and even when you know the origin of the sickness, it is hard to remind yourself that it is artificial, some of it, and can be fought, and must be fought.'

'It's worse in the Sanctum,' Ilya said.

'I can imagine.'

'But that's not all, is it?' She took a swig of water. 'I mean, it's not why you came here.'

The Khan moved away from her, headed to a shelf where she kept the few old things that had been preserved – the seals marking her entry into the Departmento Munitorum, the cheap plasteel memento of the Triumph she'd taken from Ullanor, a priceless dagger that Qin Xa had given her, never drawn from its sheath.

'Never do the easy thing,' he said, looking at the trinkets without really seeing them. 'We suffered, for that. And now, in a way, this is the easiest thing of all. To stop holding back, cut loose, just like we've been promising we'd do ever since Prospero.' He placed his hand gently on the shelf. 'Yesugei saw it. He dreamed of it, he told me. That I'd end my journey, fighting a creature of the dark, on a world of embers. And I tried to dismiss it, but it kept coming back to me. That's the problem with the dreams of Stormseers – you wonder if you work to make them true. So, despite everything that makes this seem inevitable, and right, it might just be me, deep down, tired of compromises, eager to get it settled. The easy thing.'

She watched him as he spoke. He stood erect, just as always. In his armour he was still imposing, but she had the sense that there was more hollowness under those plates than there had once been. The warriors of the Legions were all the same – they had been made to keep going, no matter how starved and damaged they became. A baseline human would give up on a task, after a while, but the Emperor's own would just keep fighting until the exceptional machinery of their bodies finally fell apart. Death meant nothing to them. Dishonour meant almost everything. And so it was possible that they could talk of an impossible trial, one which promised nothing but pain on the greatest conceivable scale, as the 'easy thing'.

'Why did he tell you of it?' she asked.

'I don't know. Because it troubled him, I think.'

'Or because he believed that he had to. To give you the means to make a choice.'

'Maybe.'

Ilya drank a little more. She was starting to feel more like herself. You could forget what a privilege this was, to be spoken to with such frankness. Over the years, the Khan had done so only occasionally. He sounded now much as he had sounded just before the Catullus Rift – musing on the past, fretful of the future – so to talk to him felt like a greater service than rounding up tanks.

'You know I never had a family of my own,' she told him. 'I never really knew if I wanted one or not. By the time I thought about it seriously, the opportunity had gone. I don't regret it. I did what I needed to do. And just when I thought I'd got to the end of all that, I came to Ullanor, and found myself tangled up with you. So I got that family in the end, and you made me furious and anxious and exhausted – all of the things I thought I might have missed.' She smiled sadly to herself. 'But the last lesson was the hardest one, because then you all began to die, and I learned how much that hurt. I was the weakest, but somehow I'm still here. Now I begin to wonder if I might still be here when you're all gone. I'd mourn you, if I lasted that long, like I mourn Targutai and Xa and Halji.' She looked up at him. 'But I'd be proud, too. Throne, I'd be proud. Not because you're the bravest or the best, but because you do this. You ask the question. I taught you how to keep your ammo dumps from running out, but I didn't teach you that. You always did it.' She edged upward in the chair, painfully, feeling her body betray her. 'And it is time now, my Khan. This is why we came back.'

He came over to her. In order to reach her level, he had to kneel. He extended his great hand, and she put hers out, and each one clasped the other.

'I will make you as safe as I can, here,' he said.

'If they come for the place while you're gone,' she said, 'I'll give them hell.'

'See that you do.' He looked at her with those deep-set eyes, the ones that could ignite with battle-fury in an instant, the ones that had witnessed both the realm of the gods and the charnel pits of mortals. 'Because I plan to come back.'

'Good.'

'There is much to do.'

'There always is.'

'So be here, then. Intact, and ready to serve again.'

'As you will it, my liege,' she said, gripping his gauntlet tightly, 'so it shall be done.'

Crosius pulled, and a long string of flesh and fat slipped out, glistening with a thin sleeve of blood. He held it up, turning in the light of the fires, marvelling at the transformations taking place within it. His eyesight had always been good, but now it seemed to be homing in on biological matter with an almost outrageous clarity. He would squint, and the cells themselves would pop into the edge of visibility, fizzing and dividing away in a promiscuous frenzy of mutation.

It was happening in real time – that was the exhilarating thing. He had prepared a philtre just an hour ago, applied it intravenously, and now the skin and muscle was shivering into new forms, some of them obviously useless, some of them possibly very handy indeed. He peered closer, using the cracked lens of his helm visor to zoom in tight. There were so many paradoxes, here. The sinews he studied were clearly atrophying fast, riddled with some kind of destructive pox, and yet their structure showed no signs of coming apart. If anything, the rapid disintegration was making it all stronger, more durable. That was impossible. He could not deny the evidence of his senses. It called for much more investigation.

Just then the man's eyes opened wide, staring in a feverish panic. You couldn't really blame him for that.

Crosius let the loop of entrails fall back into the incision he'd made in the man's stomach, then reached out and patted his sweaty brow.

'There, now,' he hissed. 'Quite remarkable. I don't even know why you're not dead. You should be, but you're not. Isn't it marvellous?'

The man tried to scream, to writhe away, but the gags and bonds Crosius had wrapped him in were quite secure. This could go on for a very long time, and every moment of it would unearth some new revelation. Even the pain would abate, eventually. The old Imperial uniform the man wore would rot away, his eyes would lose their pupils, his skin would turn grey-green, and then he'd be one of *them* – on the border of life and death, so hard to kill, so hard to revive, a kind of halfway house between the realms of experience.

Crosius reached for a rust-spotted scalpel, ready to make another cut, only for a noise outside the chamber to disturb him. He looked up, across the dingy old storage vault within the space port's basement that he'd turned into his little den for experimentation. Something was stirring around the heavy steel door, worming its way through the tiny gaps in the frame. Buzzing started up, a dull whine that seemed to be coming from everywhere at once.

'Ah,' he said to himself, understanding what this was, and put his instruments away. He thumbed a rune on his hand-held control-box, and the door's many bolts all slid open.

Typhus clambered through the gap, and his attendant cloak of flies spilled in with him. Those flies were all thick, black and furry, alighting everywhere and thudding in thick clods to the deck. Their master emerged through them as if slipping out of a thick mist, only ever part visible, the sharp edges of his outline now blurred and constantly moving.

'*Apothecary,*' he rasped.

Typhus had always been a caustic soul. His voice had been more of a croak, his humours sour. That, at least, had not changed.

'My lord Typhus,' Crosius said, bowing. 'This is unexpected.'

Typhus glanced at Crosius' experimental tables, all two hundred of them, every one occupied. Impossible to tell what he thought of it all, but nothing indicated that he found it very interesting.

'*I am leaving this place,*' he said curtly. '*This night. The primarch has ordered it.*'

'Now? Before the assault?'

Typhus snorted. '*You know the hour, then? I do not. He waits too long. He was always too cautious. That was why he needed me.*' Then he seemed to twitch, to jerk back into the present. '*But I won't be going far. I care nothing for the beacon. Why would I? I want you to stay in touch with me, to let me know when to return.*'

Crosius blinked. This was all very strange. He had no special knowledge of the primarch's intentions, nor of the Legion's disposition. He had never had close dealings with Typhus, either – as far as he knew, no one had. He considered himself somewhat removed from any politics the Death Guard may ever have had, and was uncomfortable about finding himself thrust into them now.

'I am not sure...' he began.

'*Calm yourself – I do not ask for anything untoward. Communications are unreliable. Messages are lost. I do not wish to find myself stranded when the moment comes.*'

That was true – their equipment was falling apart, their

cogitators no longer functioned, all of which accentuated what had already become a difficult arena for getting orders to where they needed to be. That was why the primarch had gathered so many of them here, in one place, so that the commands could be given in person.

'You understand,' he said carefully, 'that I am not a Tech-marine.'

'No, you are beginning to make use of better gifts. I judge you have the imagination for it.'

At that, Typhus retrieved two objects from the fly-swirled depths of his armour. Or maybe they retrieved themselves, for they were creatures of some kind, fat little things, pocked with sores and boils, with mouths that took up almost all their bulk. They were noisy when they moved. It sounded like they were giggling, or whispering to one another, or just spitting and slobbering. They wobbled up to Typhus' outstretched palms, one on each, and gurned at each other.

Crosius found himself instantly captivated. They smelled strongly, and were as hideously ugly as any dream-goblin of his imagination, but he had to fight not to take them both up into his arms, to pet them, to stroke their spiny backs and fondle their horned scalps.

'What are these?' he asked.

'Fragments of the god himself, it appears,' said Typhus, sounding uncharacteristically affectionate himself. *'The tiniest reflections, but they are appealing, no?'*

One of them was almost black, its skin shining dully. The other was almost white, as matt as chalk. They cooed and smirked beneath his gaze, rocking back and forth.

'Fascinating,' said Crosius. 'Utterly fascinating.'

'These are twins. Two sides of the same entity. They are extremely sympathetic to one another. Tell something to one of them, and the other knows it.'

Crosius understood immediately. 'Then may I take the dark one? I like the glint in its eye.'

Typhus grunted a coarse laugh. *'If you wish.'* He handed the little creature over, and it hopped from his hand, landing in the crook of Crosius' elbow with a wet splat. Once there, it snickered and wriggled, making itself comfortable against the rotting armour. Crosius couldn't resist a chuckle of delight, and cradled it avidly.

'I ask for nothing more than this,' Typhus went on. *'Look after it. Learn about it. Ensure it comes to no harm. And, when the moment comes, make use of it.'*

Crosius looked up again. 'And what moment will that be, my lord?'

'If you need to speak to me, you will know.'

Then Typhus made to leave. The clouds of flies gathered themselves up, circling him, buzzing furiously. He turned back to the open doorway, and the trains of whirring insects followed him out.

Crosius barely noticed him go. By then, he was rapt, tickling and cosseting the squatting creature on his arm. It blinked at him, welcoming the attention. He stared at it for some time, before the muffled groaning of the subject on the table snapped him out of the reverie.

'Come then, my little lord,' he cooed, reaching out for the scalpel again, taking care not to dislodge the creature from its perch. 'Stay here and watch. I am learning myself, more every day, and we have only just begun.'

By the time Jangsai made his way east again, the situation had become much worse. He skimmed through the panorama of burning buildings, staying as low as he dared, going as fast as the speeder's engines would take him, and saw fighting erupting in all directions. It looked formless now, spreading like wildfire on dry grass. In several urban zones the long-gestating sense of hopelessness had morphed into total panic, resulting in abandoned defence lines and huge civilian crowds streaming down the few unblocked thorough-fares. In more than one location he'd seen the guns of the city's defenders turned on those crowds, lest their sheer num-bers overwhelm positions further back. That just created more panic. The air rang with desperation, filled now with a kind of starved-animal frenzy that scoured away the last pretensions of civilised humanity.

From the inner Adamant angle he'd headed north-east, hug-ging what remained of the interior's secured sections, before boosting along what had once been the Gilded Path proces-sional avenue. The checkpoints he'd had to negotiate on the way in were now either empty or in disarray. At one of the last ones remaining intact he'd been frantically flagged down by the sentries, who were no doubt bewildered by the sight of a valuable Legion speeder heading straight into wholesale killing grounds without an escort or heavy support. He'd ignored them, boosting hard to veer away from their guns before shooting clear over the habs ahead. They'd even fired at him, perhaps thinking he was some kind of deserter.

From then on it got worse. Any Imperial formations east of that point were either destroyed or were being destroyed. Jangsai witnessed entire infantry divisions being steadily pum-melled amid the ruins, cut off from help, their only remaining service to make their demise as difficult as possible for a ram-pant enemy. He himself was soon tracked by traitor forces, and speeders belonging to both the XII and VIII Legions ended up on his tail. A few of them got close, nearly snagging him inside a nasty maze of collapsed viaducts, but there were few who could fly a speeder like a son of the ordu. He pushed the Kyzagan to its extremities, screaming at full tilt through the rapidly narrowing gaps until even the World Eaters gave up. It helped that he wasn't much of a target for them – they had far tastier objectives to the west, where the main concentrations of Imperial armour were still putting up something of a fight.

So he made it to Colossi in the end, his speeder's engines worn out and his own breath ragged and shallow. After stowing the vehicle in the hangars and handing over the confidential data-slates, there was no time to report to Ganzorig as intended, since everyone he met told him the same thing: kurultai is called.

He had to hurry, to wipe the worst of the caked slime from his helm and breastplate, clanking his way down the winding tunnels towards the council chamber. The entire fortress was in a stir, with menials and legionaries clearly gearing up for action. When he had left, the mood had been grim, infected with the same torpor that seemed to bleed into everything. Now, though, it had shifted. Not by much, and perhaps not for long, but still a palpable change.

By the time he reached his location, he could already hear voices from the far side of the chamber walls. He pushed his way through heavy doors and emerged into the main council room – a bare, circular space surrounded by concentric rings of banked stands. There were no windows, only suspensor lumens, and the surfaces were unpolished rockcrete and pla-steel. A faded banner of the Imperial Army's Colossi command hung forlornly overhead, but otherwise the sigils on display were those of the assembled brotherhoods – axes, bows, lightning strikes, hawks. Jangsai edged along the nearest curving row, taking position at the stand closest to him.

He glanced quickly about him to get his bearings. The speaker, on the far side of the circle, was Naranbaatar, chief of the zadyin arga. Next to him was Namahi, master of the keshig honour guard. Ganzorig and Qin Fai were present too, the two most senior noyans-khan. The rest of those assembled in the stands were khans of the various brotherhoods. Jangsai knew all their names. Many had distinguished themselves during the long period of void war, and had reputations that resonated across the Legion – Ainbataar, Khulan, Tsolmon. Terrans were there, as were Chogorians, even a few newbloods like himself.

None of them, though, had anything like the presence of Shiban Tachseer, who stood just a few places away from the primarch. He seemed to have picked up a few new scars on his exposed face since Jangsai had last seen him. No one could have called that visage beautiful – the old Chogorian compactness had been replaced with a patchwork of metal, raised tissue and tufts of a scratchy beard. If the ordu had needed a symbol of the many trials and transformations it had undergone during the war, Shiban would have served well enough. On Rija, they had told Jangsai that the khans of the V had once been famous for their joy in combat, their freedom and their flair. Now they looked much as grim and battered as any other warriors of the wounded Imperium, their exuberance beaten out of them, their joy blunted. Looking at Tachseer just then, it was hard to see how any of it could possibly come back.

The Khagan himself occupied the place of honour, standing just to the right of his chief Stormseer. Alongside him was the Sage, one of the few non-Space Marines trusted to attend. The primarch himself seemed pensive, staring at the floor, his hands clasped together loosely.

'We know where it comes from,' Naranbaatar was saying, just as calmly and evenly as ever. 'The primarch of the Fourteenth has ascended into a new form, one that expands and strengthens his power. He is new to this form, and so that power is the greatest now that it may ever be. As he gathers more of his kind around him, the strength only grows.

Even if he chose to never leave his new fortress, the despair he projects from it would be as potent a weapon as anything the enemy possesses.'

'But why remain hidden?' asked Tsolmon Khan. 'Why not use the power openly?'

'Because he is not a fool,' said the Khagan. 'He knows the carnage being unleashed within the Palace. He knows that destruction on such a scale unbalances all things, and that even the greatest may be undone there.' His mournful eyes flickered up to look at Tsolmon. 'He is doing what a good general does – drawing his full strength together, not wasting it, readying for the moment when both his allies and his enemies are exhausted.'

'Then he remains a coward,' said Tsolmon coldly.

'He remains what he has ever been,' the Khagan said. 'Careful. Patient.'

'Even so, he must launch his assault soon,' said Naranbaatar. 'The augurs tell us that. When the full force of that comes, it will hit the Palace just as the momentum of the Sixteenth and Twelfth Legions is at its greatest. Every simulation we have run, every possible future we have interrogated, indicates that this combined offensive must overwhelm whatever defences remain intact. Over and again, we dream the same words. *The Lord of Death must not cross the threshold.* If he does, then no hope remains.'

'Does the Lord Dorn not see it?' asked Khulan Khan.

'My brother sees it well enough,' said the Khagan. 'But what can he do? He has the Red Angel tearing down the Sanctum around him, and the greatest mass of Sons of Horus assembled since Ullanor right at his door. The Palace is already falling with every sword at his disposal deployed. But he knows we are here.'

'And the enemy does not,' said Naranbaatar. 'At least, they cannot be sure of our numbers, not until they assault this place directly again. For a single moment only, there is uncertainty. We have seeded every comm-channel we still use with movement reports indicating a full-scale withdrawal to the Ultimate Gate. Most of the auxilia we sent west had vehicles in Legion colours with them, both mock-ups and genuine. Some of our warriors were even allowed to be captured, all with the aim of spreading false accounts of our disposition.' The old Stormseer's composure faltered then, just for a moment. 'Their sacrifice was as great as any yet made in this cause. The names will be written in honour in Quan Zhou when victory is achieved.'

There it was again, Jangsai thought – that quiet, irritating certainty.

'The deception will not last,' said the Khagan. 'Even amid all the confusion of the main attack, we will be discovered soon. And so we must act. Every preparation we have made, every contingency, has been for this hour. The plans are laid, the objectives assigned, the vehicles are being made ready. We must strike hard, fast and true, with no other target in sight or mind. We fail here, and all fails. We succeed, and it will be for others to complete the main task.'

'We cannot rely on unaugmented troops,' said Namahi. 'We know the upper reaches of the space port were depressurised, and the lower ones will now be infested with both plague and yaksha. It is as challenging an environment as we have ever fought in. For that reason, our only support will be from the mobile armour assembled by szu-Ilya.'

The Sage, who alone in the chamber was seated, stirred herself. 'I got you as many hulls as I could,' she said. 'All tox-sealed, crewed and refitted for close actions. I pulled some strings where I had to.' She smiled wryly to herself. 'There are a hundred regiments in that gaggle of guns. We ended up reclassifying them all, amalgamating the command. You'll be going to war with the First Terran Armoured. First and last, maybe, but it still has a nice ring to it.'

'Tanks?' asked Tsolmon, respectfully but sceptically. 'In a space port?'

'You haven't seen it from the inside,' said Shiban. 'The place was built for void-ships – you could run Baneblades through it five abreast and never risk chipping the stonework.'

'Colossi is eighty kilometres from the port's edge,' said Namahi. 'A straight run across occupied territory, all transitways destroyed. Our only chance is speed. We get bogged down, and we will all die in the open. Break into it, though, and at least we'll have a roof over our heads. We retake the main orbital arrays, and we can start to make their landers fear planetfall again.'

Some of the khans, making the mental calculations, looked uneasy. 'There are enemy forces dug in all across that stretch,' said Ainbataar cautiously. 'They won't all be swept away.'

'No, it'll be fighting from the start,' said Shiban, his metal-edged voice sounding like he was looking forward to it. 'Our concentrations will be high, though, and we're not looking to hold ground, just break through it.'

'Even so,' said Khulan. 'We might be able to take on the ground forces, given surprise, but our air cover's gone.'

'Not entirely,' said the Khagan, looking up at Jangsai. 'At least, I hope not.'

'The objective was secured, Khagan,' Jangsai said, bowing. 'The plate will move, as ordered.'

'The Skye orbital fortress, last of those scuttled by my brother,' said the Khagan. 'It has been reduced, but has immersion drives, and can shadow the advance at low altitude. Together with what remains of our Legion atmospherics, we can mount at least some defence in the air. It won't be perfect, but it will be something.'

The chamber fell silent. Jangsai glanced at his fellow khans. Some were as new as him, commanding a hundred or so blades. Some were veterans of the Crusade, and led twice that number. Each one of them trusted their primarch more than they trusted the evidence of their own senses. They had followed him in every battle since the breaking of Unity, and that trust had been repaid with survival against the current of the darkest tide. They were as loyal as it was possible to be. They were united in purpose. They knew no fear.

And yet, when Khulan spoke, it was as if he merely vocalised the same thought that they all had running through their minds.

'My Khan,' he ventured, not from any lack of resolve, but because it needed to be asked now, needed to be settled, before pulling away became impossible. 'Can we do this?'

The Khagan nodded fractionally, acknowledging the question. He pressed his fingers harder together.

'Not if we delay,' he said quietly. 'Another day, maybe two, and the moment is gone. Once he has everything in place, we do not have the strength to break him. It must be while he is consumed with his own conquests. He has the numbers, he has the gifts, he has the power. All we have is what we have always relied on. To be faster.' He smiled darkly. 'See, what can we really do, for this Imperium? Can we sustain it now, bearing its weight on our shoulders? Not the way we were made. But we can kill for it. We can break, we can burn, we can unmake.' The smile disappeared. 'We have done everything they asked of us. We have held their battle line, scored it with our own blood, and it has not been enough. If we are to die here, on a world that has no soul and no open sky to rejoice in, then we will die doing what we were schooled to do.'

He looked out across the entire chamber, making each khan feel as if he were the only one there, the only one to enjoy this final confidence before the war-horns were sounded and the engines were gunned.

'But get me to my brother,' the Khan said, 'and as eternity is my judge, I shall scour his stench from the universe forever.'

PART TWO

NINE

No certainties
Catching up
The empty nest

It took a while for the smell to fade. Oll Persson had experienced many bad things during his unnaturally long life. Some of the worst of them had come recently, during all of that haphazard lurching through space and time. Those encounters blurred into one another, just a procession of ever more lurid scrapes and escapes, never quite anchored in any kind of secure history or steady sense of location, never made coherent or predictable or comprehensible.

That had always been the fate of the soldier – long periods of boredom, sudden flashes of terror. For Oll, though, his long periods of boredom had lasted centuries, making the recent flash-sequences of terror seem all the more vivid and unmanageable.

And yet, for all that, none of the things he'd ever lived through, in this war or any other, had been worse than Hatay-Antakya Hive.

He sat in the lighter's main hold, sweating, feeling feverish, unable to stop his hands from shaking. He knew what ailed him – delayed shock, the accumulation of adrenaline and cortisol, now flooding him with fight-or-flight. Or maybe just an ordinary sort of breakdown. He was overdue one. In the paradise-hive itself he'd been fighting so hard to stay alive, to stay clear of those sickly-sweet nightmare gardens, that collapsing hadn't been an option. Now the consequences were catching up with him, and collapsing felt like a very likely option indeed. He could still smell it, on his clothes, on his skin, his hair.

But he couldn't let it take him over. Not yet. In a few days, perhaps, he could give in, finally seek some kind of a way out. Now, though, he was closer than ever to being where he had to be. It was all coming together.

Just a little longer, Ollanius, he told himself. *You can fall apart when we get there, if you want. For now, you have strangers with you. Complete strangers. Don't make a scene, not in front of them.*

He tried not to. He kept his head up. He sweated, and swallowed hard, but he didn't pass out.

Zybes was in a bad way, too. He'd started to rock, very slowly, his hands clasped around his ankles, the back of his head bumping against the hold's inner wall. Katt was morose – suspicious, Oll guessed, of the new people they'd taken with them. Graft, of course, was oblivious to it all. Krank, though, looked semi-destroyed, with his external hard shell still, but the emptiness inside evident. He'd miss Rane. They all would.

And then there were the newcomers. Leetu, the prototype Space Marine John had taken up with. Oll had recognised Erda's old bodyguard the instant he'd laid eyes on him, despite the long passage of time since the two of them had properly spoken. Very strange, to be in such close proximity again. Leetu, for his part, took it all in his stride.

The final two were the strangest of all. The sorceress called Actae, who had appeared like some kind of summoned djinn just when it looked like they might never get out of Hatay-Antakya at all, and her companion, the one who called himself Alpharius. Unlike the rest of the group, those two seemed to know where they were going. They seemed like they had a plan.

Though maybe that was just bluster – Oll had learned the hard way that those who seemed most clearly in control of things were often the ones with the shakiest grip. Except for Him, of course. He'd always known exactly where He was going.

Oll coughed, clenched his fists hard, tried to clear his mind. Survival had been achieved. They had to work out what to do now.

So he just said that out loud. You had to start somewhere.

'What do we do now?' he said.

Krank didn't look up. Katt looked away, disgusted. Actae laughed, though not unkindly.

'Your friend's the one piloting this thing,' she said. 'Maybe ask him.'

'He's just getting us the hell away,' Oll said. 'When we next put down, he'll ask me the same question. I'm canvassing opinions.'

'We all know where we're going,' Katt said sullenly. 'Where we've been going since Calth. The Palace.'

Zybes nodded. 'The Palace,' he mumbled.

'Are we, though?' said Oll, worried about Zybes but having to ignore it for now. 'I mean, what are we planning? Just to show up? Say hello? See if they can squeeze in a few more combatants and find something useful for us all to do?'

'You only need to be there,' said Actae. 'At least, that's what I believe. The scattered fellowship, coming together just as the sun goes down on it all.'

Oll snorted. 'But I didn't want any part of it. John can be persuasive, when he has a mind to be, and even he's flying blind. Now we're running short of time.' He ruffled up his hair. It still stank of that awful perfume. 'So let's start with the basics – who are you, why are you here, and who is your travelling companion, and why is he?'

'I am Al–' the Space Marine started.

'Don't even *think* of saying that again, or so help me I'll open the bloody doors and kill us all,' snapped Oll.

'He's the last remnant of an old play,' said Actae calmly. She adjusted position against the metal of the bench she sat on, her bony body making her long dress pool. 'Sent to Terra to keep an eye on things for his master. Our paths crossed, and since then we've made common cause.'

'To push the old Cabal line again?' asked Oll sceptically.

'No, that thread was cut,' said Alpharius. 'Orders are always liable to change. My current duty is to take the lady to where she wishes to go.'

'The Palace,' said Katt again, just as irritably.

'Of course,' said Actae.

'But *why*?' asked Oll. 'And why make so sure to bring us with you?'

'Because I learned that there are no certainties in this drama, only probabilities,' said Actae. 'If I knew *what* I had to do, and *how*, then I'd be doing it. But here's the thing. There are archetypes here. Certain kinds of people. Some very powerful' – she looked at Katt – 'and some very basic' – she looked at Graft. 'We have, in this flyer, a snapshot. Something pulled together by fate, randomly, but still catching all the basic categories. We have women, men, states in between. We have a servitor, a farmer, a psyker, a soldier, a Perpetual, a Space Marine... you see what I'm getting at?'

'Not really.'

'That it's not an accident. That it's a summoning. A bringing-together.'

'By who?'

'I don't know.' She smiled, and rolled her unseeing eyes. 'Really, I don't. It doesn't help much, living and dying and living again, to make the best kind of sense of this. You just have to guess what's going on, most of the time.' Her expression became serious again. 'But some of you have been active, like John. Like me. Others have been unwilling, or caught up in the ride. I don't think that matters. What matters is that we're *here*, heading towards where we need to be. And we all do need to be there – not just you, not just Leetu, but all of us.'

'Because you're hedging your bets,' said Oll.

'Because she's making it up,' said Katt. She looked up, and shot the other woman a vicious stare. 'She doesn't know a damn thing. I can sense it.'

Krank stirred at that, glanced at Katt, then moved a hand gently towards his holster. If this got ugly, he'd be firing at Actae, never mind the fact they were all in a pressurised hold.

'Easy,' said Oll, beginning to get a pounding headache on top of everything else. God, he felt terrible. 'Even if that's true, she's no worse off than any of us.' He gave Katt a weak smile, intended to be supportive, because he sympathised. 'Look, we only followed our nose, didn't we? Hoping that John would have the answers. But guessing, I suppose, that he wouldn't.'

'I was just trying to get away,' Katt said.

'That's how it starts,' Actae said.

'Oh, shut *up*,' said Katt.

'Fine, enough!' said Oll. He needed to move. He needed to stretch out cramped legs and get some time to think. 'This has started well. But let's take the positives. We're alive. We don't – mostly – want to kill one another. We have some time. And we all want, one way or another, to get back to the Emperor.'

'No, no,' said Actae. 'That's what I've been trying to say – this isn't a simple action. There are many strands in the bind, as they used to say on Colchis.'

'What do you mean?' asked Oll, feeling he was going to regret asking.

'You can go after the Emperor if you need to,' said Actae. 'And I'll help you. I'll get you as close as I can. But that's not why I'm here.'

She gave him a strange look, then – part triumphant, part haunted.

'Because *I'm* coming for *him*,' she said. 'I'm coming for Lupercal.'

Some time later, Oll clambered up from the hold and made his way up the steps to the lighter's cockpit. He wormed through the tiny hatch and managed to twist awkwardly into the co-pilot's seat.

John was in the pilot's seat, staring ahead at a darkening sky. It was still daytime, but the northern horizon – the one they were heading towards – was rapidly sinking into a red-tinged shadow. His expression was fixed, his jawline tight. Maybe concentrating on keeping them all in the air was good for him. Maybe it stopped him thinking back to the place they'd escaped from.

'How are you doing?' Oll asked.

A long pause.

'It's not how I thought things would go,' he said eventually.

Oll nodded. 'No, me neither.'

They flew on for a while. Below them, a dry land of dirt dunes and cracked earth sped by, greying as the light failed. The engines whined, struggling as dust hit the intakes.

'So what did you find out?' John asked.

'I don't know what to believe,' Oll said. 'She claims to have been born on Colchis. Then died. Then reborn. Like you.'

'Not any more.'

'She said she's been conscious in the warp.' Oll shook his head. 'I don't know. What does that even mean? How could you check it?'

John shrugged. 'She knew where to find us. I'm guessing that wasn't random.'

Then silence again, save for the grind of the engines. It was difficult to talk. Finding words to use – commonplace words, small talk – after what had happened, felt almost improper. And yet Oll didn't know how to progress the other thing, either – the reason they were here, what they had to do next, how they were ever going to stay alive with the meagre resources at their disposal. He was so tired.

'Look, I'm sorry,' he said finally, weakly. 'That I wasn't there, where we agreed to be. And that you ended up in… that place.'

John just kept his eyes fixed ahead. 'Not your fault. And you came back.'

'Yeah, but it was–'

'Hell. Yes, it was. In every way. But you came back.' He turned to Oll, and gave him a forced smile. 'And now I know things I'd never have discovered before. Silver linings, eh, Mister Warmaster?'

Oll looked at him with concern. Just a sly dig, a way of coping? Or was he losing it now, too, driven over the edge by what he'd seen? 'Maybe I should have told you a long time ago.'

'Maybe.'

'I preferred being a farmer.'

'Yeah, well, we don't always get what we want, do we?'

'I guess not.'

More silent flying. The sky kept on getting darker. The wind got up, the outer skirts of a storm, blowing right at them, and dust-clumps hit the forward viewer harder.

'She says we were meant to come together,' said Oll, after a while. 'And that we're all archetypes, of one kind or another. A kind of representative sample.'

John snorted. 'To plead the case for humanity.'

'Something like that. But whatever she wants, it's not what we want. I don't know what she thinks she's doing, but it involves getting close to Horus.'

'To kill him?'

'Maybe. She's hard to pin down. For the time being, our paths run parallel, and that seems to be enough for her.'

'Well, it's not enough for me.' John's voice became harder. 'I've felt it, now. I never felt it before. I listened to the xenos, and I understood the arguments. The ones about Chaos. But now I've felt it. It's been at me. I'll kill Horus. I'll kill the Emperor. I'll kill all of them, anything, if it gets rid of it.' He glanced back at Oll, his face twisted with fury and grief. 'It's got to go.'

'I don't think it's that simple.'

'It is for me. And I can speak the lingo now, remember? I can do all sorts of things.'

Oll didn't like looking at John just then. A long time ago he'd had a nightmare, one involving angels and daemons over a burning world, and it had scared him, but just then John's expression scared him more.

'You need to rest,' was all he said. 'We've been flying for hours.'

'I'm fine.'

'Just another hour or so, and then we put down.'

'Time is short.'

Yes, and it had been for as long as he could remember. Oll suddenly recalled it then. They had been being hunted, by something, just on the edge of perception. Every jump they had made, every shift in space and time, it had felt as if that thing had almost caught up with them. Something very dangerous, all right up until the escape from the hive.

'I wonder where it's gone,' he said aloud.

'What?'

'The thing that...' He trailed off. 'Never mind.'

And after that, they didn't speak. Oll just watched the dust fly against the panes, the empty lands bled clear of life. It was a long way still. A long time, for something to come up, to make things clear, to give them a solid plan.

But all the time, while he was trying to work on that, he couldn't shake off the memory.

What was it? he thought. *And where has it gone?*

Once they had all left, the place felt too big again, too empty. An old curse for mothers. Not that she considered herself one any longer, but still. It brought back memories, and for a very short time her isolated hold-out had felt a little more connected to things again.

Now she watched her attendants. Some of them were dancing, ringing the fire, throwing long shadows across the sand. Above them all, the great circles of quartz glittered under the stars.

It was a rare break in the weather. For days, sandstorms had boomed in from the east, black-hearted and sour-smelling. She'd wrapped up during the onslaught, kept her head down, lashed the cloth coverings more tightly to their poles and made the best of it. The storms made her think of John, who had come there and stirred everything up again, making her relive things, remember things, and then had been off again, into the eye of the oncoming turmoil, taking Leetu with him, plus a great deal more besides.

She knew the break would not last. Given what was going on, it might be the final time she saw clear stars for a very long while, and so she sat on the bare rock and looked up at them. Their light was ancient. Anything reaching her now had set off on its journey long before she was born, before she'd done any of the things she'd done, and yet it was still out there – out *there* – that the intervention had been made to happen. The results of that scattering were all now back on Terra in order to raise their awful havoc, but still the clear light of those home systems burned up out of the past, as if nothing had ever taken place there or ever would do.

She had almost forgotten it all again, perhaps deliberately, until John had come back. And now she could think of nothing else. What she'd done. What she'd had to do.

After another hour or so, the fire burned down. The shadows merged into the dry, cool darkness of the night, and her people slipped off to their homes. She herself lingered longest, long legs pulled up in front of her, trying to set all the old memories into their correct order.

Eventually, as a bloody moon rose over the high dunes, she stirred herself, got up and padded back to her stone lodge. She ducked under the low lintel, poured water from a ewer into a bowl and splashed it over her face. She moved towards the innermost chamber and unwound her cowl, pushing her way through silk curtains. Only a single candle burned inside, the wax pooling and making the flame sway.

She sat on her low bed, resting her head against the cedar frame and feeling the wooden slats flex under her. The room was warm still, smelling of agarwood, cloaked in shadows that danced to the jerk of the single flame.

She reached out to snuff the wick, leaned back and closed her eyes, resting clasped hands lightly in her lap. As she drifted into sleep, all she could hear was the faint snap and flap of the cloth awnings outside, the rustle of the grass as the night wind moved through it, the sound of her own steady, deep breathing.

Until the words uncoiled out of the darkness, making her eyes snap open.

'Hello, grandmother,' said Erebus, standing at the foot of the bed. 'I think you and I need to talk.'

TEN

Deathboxes
Siegemaster
Riding out

He woke with a start. Kaska moved immediately, his head still foggy but with the old reactions just about intact, swinging down from the bunk and shouting out to the rest of the crew to get themselves together. The chimes were going off.

The chamber was large, cold, mostly unlit and smelling of hundreds of bodies stuffed up against one another. The floor was lost in a jumble of kitbags and crumpled uniforms. Triple bunk-units had been arranged in long rows. A dorm-chamber in a defence bastion looked much the same wherever it was, though this one was shabbier than most, with a long crack running up the western wall. Kaska guessed that they were a long way underground, though since arriving he'd not been able to confirm that. Underground, overground, it made little difference now that the sky was black and the earth was black and everything was coated in muck – you were fighting in darkness, wherever you ended up.

Still, at least he knew their location now – the Colossi Gate, out so far east that he'd assumed nothing remained there at all but bones and bloodstains. It turned out he was wrong about that. A Legion was there. A whole one, or at least what remained of a whole one after seven years of unbroken fighting. Once he'd found that out, he'd got briefly excited. Jandev had been right, it looked like – a counter-offensive, something to get the blood up again and stop feeling so damned mopey about everything. Perhaps that was why everything had been so stretched back beyond Saturnine – command had been planning for this, ready to take ground again, open a new flank for the enemy to deal with.

Since then, though, he'd had the briefings. A succession of V Legion warriors had come to speak to the assembled tank commanders, every time a different one. They'd all looked properly battered, with dented armour plates and bruised faces. They were polite, though, bowing to the assembled troops before getting down to business. It became apparent that this wasn't about pushing the enemy back at all, not across the main fronts anyway. It transpired that the manpower for that had gone long ago. This was about taking the Lion's Gate space port, driving out the occupiers and getting the orbital guns back in operation, and then holding the place for as long as they could. Even if they achieved the first of those things, they'd be surrounded, cut off from any possible resupply and forced to dig in against an enemy who seemed to command virtually infinite numbers. And that was the one thing that you didn't try to do, with tanks. They were thirsty, temperamental beasts. If you couldn't keep them fuelled, keep them supplied with shells, repair their damaged parts when they blew, then you were basically living inside a slow-moving coffin.

And of all the possible tanks to be stuck in, a Leman Russ was probably the worst. People spoke of it as the Pride of the Imperium, the greatest battle tank in human history, the main-stay of the Great Crusade.

Was it shit. A Leman Russ was a rolling deathtrap. Its tall profile was so notoriously awful that no commander ever wanted to be squadron leader – the only thing big enough to shield a Leman Russ during operations was another Leman Russ, so better to keep the command unit ahead of you for as long as you could. Its fragile tracks were exposed and its armour was a mess of easy-to-hit vertical planes. The standard pattern sponson-bulges just presented another flat edge to destroy, another reason to be glad not to have them. The interior was noisy and prone to bursting into flames whenever a loader coughed too loudly. And, if you were truly unlucky enough to have those sponsons, there was only one escape hatch, right at the top of the main turret, and so the chances of getting out alive in case of all-too-likely disaster were practically zero.

No, whoever had designed the Leman Russ – Kaska had always assumed it wasn't actually the primarch of the VI – was a moron. Or a sadist. Or both. The only things it had going for it were cheapness, mechanical reliability and a certain rugged survivability in numbers. The design was so brutally simple that the Imperium was able to churn them out by the million. It mattered less that each individual unit was a study in self-harm when you could overwhelm a battlefield with hundreds of them. And a front mounted lascannon at least could keep firing as long as its power packs held a charge, which made running out of shells somewhat less of a disaster.

Still, all in all, the crews had few illusions about the tanks they rode into war. Deathboxes, they were called, and home-wreckers, and other, earthier, names too. Infantry troopers would occasionally look askance at them, jealous of all that thick armour they had around them, but a Leman Russ tanker knew how fragile it all was really, and how going out to a las-blast was far preferable to being burned alive or buried under a wall of mud or suffocated by trapped engine smoke.

The chimes kept on sounding. Jandev was pulling on his jacket, Vosch trying to wake up, Merck downing a canister of last night's water. Dresi just got ready quietly, making no eye contact. Kaska had really meant to speak to her properly, try to get to know her, but it was too late now, for this was it, this was the push, the first engagement of the optimistically named First Terran Armoured.

'*Moving*, people,' he barked, reaching for his helmet and kitbag, blinking the last of the scant sleep from his eyes. 'You know the drill. Vosch, get that damned skinny arse in motion. Throne, where're my boots?'

The entire chamber was doing the same thing. Hundreds of crews, blearily getting their act together, heading for the elevators and the stairways, trying to remember where their unit was stowed, what their orders were, what their new squadron designation was and where they were meant to be going. All the while, the chimes kept blaring – *chang, chang, chang* – making it harder to think straight.

Kaska and the *Aika 73* crew jostled and bustled with the rest of them down to the holding levels. As they went, the walls trembled harder than ever, showering them with dust. For a moment, he thought that the fortress must be taking a real pounding – it had been under bombardment ever since they'd arrived – but then he realised what was going on. The remaining Colossi guns were going all out, chewing through the last of their ammunition, hurling everything they had left out at the wasteland beyond the walls. By the time they were done, there would be nothing left in the feeder-chambers. This was the last function they would ever perform, no longer used carefully to blunt incoming assaults, but instead employed to flatten as much as possible between the fortress and the target. The barrage must have been going on for hours already, while they had all been grabbing what rest they could. Kaska had a wary respect for artillery operators. It was a skilled profession, requiring mastery of both abstract geometry and the human-scale vagaries of the battlefield. It they did their job right, the advance would be possible. If they screwed up, the tanks would find themselves running into intact gunlines quickly, and that would get messy.

As everything shook and boomed around them, they jogged their way down to the holding chambers, the caverns at the very base of the Colossi outer wall sections, the ones requisitioned weeks ago and cleared out and fitted for their new purpose. They were stuffed with vehicles, hundreds and hundreds apiece, all ranked up and fuelled and serviced and ready for action. The air filters were already churning in expectation of thousands of dirty promethium engines coughing into life – waiting for the orders to be roared out, for the regimental pennants to be hoisted on the squadron lead units, for the tracks to grind into motion.

As Kaska ran out along the lines, counting down the hull numbers, he took a brief moment, just one, to guess how many units had been assembled in this one holding chamber. He didn't get very far. It was a lot. A *huge* amount. All the White Scars officers, with their quiet voices and careful tactical run-downs, had been so diffident in the briefings, but this was clearly a serious endeavour, something that serious people had been working on for a long time. He wondered how high up it went. He wondered if the Emperor Himself, beloved by all, could have had something to do with it. Maybe this was something, after all, to get excited about. Maybe this was something that might turn the tide.

Steady, now. Steady. It hadn't even started yet. Kaska had been part of enough catastrophes and balls-ups in his time not to get carried away. Once things were in motion, the mud thrown up and the smoke gusting into your sights, that's when it all started to go wrong. Stay calm, stay focused. Keep it together.

He reached the tank. Just as always, he smacked its flank before clambering up to the top turret.

'For the Emperor!' he shouted.

'For His people!' the crew echoed, getting ready to mount up. All around them, the rest of the crews were doing the same – their little pre-combat rituals, their final checks.

Jandev and Dresi got in first, clambering in through the side hatches and worming down into the innards – Dresi to the drive controls, Jandev to the lascannon station. Vosch and Merck were next, taking positions up in the turret at the main gun mechanism. Kaska was last, the only one to keep his head and shoulders above the line of the open hatch. He snapped his helmet on, taking care of the seals at his collar. They had been insistent about that, in all the briefings. *Full tox protocol, all times. All helmets on, all filters sealed, all hatches down.* He'd do that the instant they were out of the gates. For now, though, possibly for the last time in a while, he'd keep his head up, the hatch open. He wanted to see this kick off with his own eyes.

All around him, menials and servitors were doing what they had to do, finalising the squadrons for exit. Ahead of them, three hundred metres away, the mighty external doors were still down. The deck trembled as the guns far above kept on spewing out shells. One by one, the tank engines engaged, choking out plumes of black smoke. The chimes kept on yammering, the last of the crews raced to their units, the forward lumens flicked on.

'Status,' Kaska voxed to the crew, taking it all in.

'Lascannon powered,' Jandev replied coolly. 'Feed levels adequate.'

'All good from me,' Vosch replied, her face clamped in readiness over the main gun's sights.

'Drives engaged,' Dresi said. 'Spirit is compliant.'

Merck chuckled to himself. 'Five minutes,' he said to himself. 'We'll last five minutes.'

'Stow that,' snapped Kaska. 'This is His work. That goes for all of you. His work. Let's see it out.'

Then, with a chilling suddenness, the guns stopped firing. Only when they'd ceased did Kaska realise how loud they had been. The vast chamber became ominously quieter, the slamming thunder-beat replaced by the lower-pitched snarl of hundreds of engines.

Kaska felt his stomach twinge. His palms tingled, and he gripped the handholds tighter. For what seemed like an age, the entire space remained frozen – columns of tanks, all idling, all static, locked underground, as if shackled on leashes.

This had to start now. This had to get going. Everyone was keyed up for it, prepped and ready. If they waited, they'd die here, confined, caged like animals. And still the doors stayed down, sealing them in, burying them, holding them back.

Hold your nerve, he told himself. *Cold, calm, ready.*

When the door locks boomed open, it made him start. The echoes of the mighty bolt-shafts slamming back into their channels rang around the hall. Then the giant blast screens started to slide upwards, grinding in their grooves, accompanied by the clanking of enormous chain-runs. The chimes ceased, and the engine tones changed, revving up to drive. Gusts of hot wind flooded in through the widened gaps, making the smog plumes twist and writhe. Far ahead, Kaska caught his first view of the outside world for several days.

It was night. It was always night on Terra, now – a pitch-black veil lit only by flame and mortar-blast, a hellscape of tortured earth and fire.

The order came over the comm-box, crackling with interference already.

*Full advance. Full advance. The Khan and the Emperor guide
you.*

The cascade of acceleration started from the lead units,
rippling down the columns as the big Baneblades and Hellhammers rocked their way off the ramps and out into the
burning murk. It felt like it took forever to reach *Aika 73*,
part of 16th Squadron, Sixth Battalion, but then the moment
came, and they were trundling with the rest, picking up
speed, bouncing and swaying towards the strip of ink-black
sky ahead. Kaska stayed aloft even as the other commanders
slipped down inside their armour, slamming the hatches and
trusting to their periscopes and augur lenses.

So when they emerged into the open again, for just a few
moments, he saw it all with his own eyes, filtered only by the
freshly cleaned lenses on his helmet. He looked up over his
shoulder, and saw the towering walls of Colossi stretch up into
the night behind them, gouged and cracked but still standing.
He looked ahead and saw the expanse of ruins stretch away
into the distance, the empty skeletons of once mighty hive
spires and hab-clusters, some burning, most dead and cold.
He saw the contrails of the first Legion atmospherics taking off,
ready to launch the bombing raids that would mop up what
the big guns had missed. He saw the starbursts of explosions,
the rippling of firelines, the broken silhouette of the distant
Anterior Wall, the aurora of the orbital aegis reflected in the
acres of shattered glass and steel. Around him, the press of
tanks was so great that it looked as if the ground beneath them
had started to roll forwards, gathering itself up in a tidal carpet
of iron and promethium, one that would crash and smash its
way towards the ends of the earth itself.

But then, and most imposing of all, just on the edge of
sight, he saw the mountain-sweep of the Lion's Gate space
port, dark as the night around it, shrouded in giant boiling

clouds of dust and grime, its flanks lit with crackling threads of lightning, its innards glowing with a sickly light, its twisted spires dominating the north-eastern horizon and stretching high into the heavens above.

So far away. So immense. So... horrific.

Kaska dropped down, sliding into his harness and pulling the hatch after him. The circle of metal shut with a clang, and he swivelled to bring up the tactical lens and get the periscope sights close. The familiar sounds and smells of the tank's tiny world immediately enveloped him. He found himself breathing a little too quickly, his heart racing. It would have been better not to lay eyes on it, not until he absolutely had to.

'Here we go, then,' said Vosch. She shot him a tense smile. 'Emperor be with us.'

Kaska smiled back, just as tensely. 'No doubt about it, corporal,' he said. 'No doubt at all.'

Gremus Kalgaro made his way steadily up the winding stairs, his heavy boots sinking into the carpet of grime on the steps. He'd trudged kilometres already, working his way from one chamber to the other, tracing a meandering path through the labyrinthine innards of the space port. Its vastness was striking, even on a planet dominated by the absurdly outsized. The Legion was not close to filling it properly. Even in those spaces where they were gathered in numbers, the emptiness yawned away above and below, echoing dankly. Some of the dry-docks still had the carcasses of void-going craft in their maintenance cradles, half-finished and empty, ready to be propelled up by the elevator shunts to the take-off pads. It was a world within a world, a procession of gigantic assembly halls and service pits, all linked by immense shafts and transit-tubes. It would have been riotous, once – filled with the jarring crash and whine of machinery, the boom of engines kindling, the grind of lifters and servitor-rigs. Now it was quiet, almost dormant, inhabited by the slow shuffle of Legion warriors and their creatures, all grimly filing into their service areas for retooling and re-equipping. The edges had been softened by growths, by creeping moulds, by the loops of black-veined creepers, muffling it all, sinking it into a hot, perspiring somnolence.

Kalgaro wasn't the only one to notice how much the place now felt like Barbarus. The mists had started to slink up through the ventilation grilles, thick as milk. The tang of the air had become tarter, suffused with the poisons they had brought with them. At times, when at the base of one of the many multi-level shafts leading up into the heights, Kalgaro would look up and see how the toxins clustered in clouds, thickening steadily with altitude. And then he would remember how it was on the home world, and how they would all stare up at the peaks, both fearing and desiring them. Some vestige of those old emotions must have been imprinted on him, somewhere. He still liked to keep his feet on the ground whenever he could. He still breathed more carefully when a long way up, as if his lung muscles couldn't quite believe that it was possible.

He shook his head in irritation. Stupid, to keep those old twitches and reflexes. They needed to move on. Forget about the old nightmares. Still, they followed them around now, the ancestral bad dreams, like kicked curs coming back to the fireside.

Kalgaro reached his destination, the main observation tower on the western wall-edge. As he lumbered into the command chamber, four Unbroken saluted. A few dozen Legion menials worked away at their augur stations, their uniforms so filthy that they were barely indistinguishable from caked dirt on pale flesh. They were all very sick now, encrusted with sores and lesions, though it didn't seem to hamper them much.

'You asked for me?' Kalgaro said, addressing the sergeant in command.

'You should see this, Siegemaster,' said the sergeant, an old Barbaran called Gurgana Dhukh. He gestured at a large circular lens, clouded and greasy but still functional. Points of light were creeping across it, all streaming from positions concentrated to the south-west. Kalgaro screwed his eyes up, trying to make sense of the vague phosphor-blips.

'Another malfunction?' Kalgaro asked.

Dhukh shook his head. 'Checked several feeds. Those are movement indicators.'

Kalgaro clumped over to a larger-range cartographic unit, and activated the scanners. He looked at them for a while, then checked the geo-locators. 'They had fallen back,' he murmured.

'Yes, they had. It seemed.'

Kalgaro found himself smiling. The more he studied the signals, the more the picture was confirmed. The White Scars hadn't gone anywhere, and now they were out in the open again, streaming towards the space port, a coordinated spearhead that was already burning swiftly through the wastelands. 'A moment to be thankful,' he said. 'Our friends are still with us.'

He turned from the unit and began to give orders.

'Signal the primarch's equerry – ensure this reaches him. Order mobilisation of all defence forces and activation of reserves. Power up the wall guns and get me a readiness report on the flyers – if we have any useable yet they'll be needed immediately.'

Menials scurried to comply, using the comms-boxes. Two of the Unbroken headed off for the transit shafts to ensure that in-person orders were also delivered.

Dhukh, though, looked uncertain. 'There's no... plan,' he said. 'No defensive plan. We were due to move out again, the squads are still being refitted, they'll be–'

Kalgaro laughed, going back to a close-range lens and adjusting the gain-columns. 'This is better, sergeant,' he said good-naturedly. 'Much better. The squads won't need any encouragement – these are godless Chogorian bastards. We didn't finish them at Catullus, so we'll do it here.'

True, things had been bad at Catullus, and back then he'd been furious. Oaths had been sworn after that, ones that he'd fully intended to see through. And he would see them through still, with all his strength, it was just that now it would be something to relish, an act of sacred glorification.

Dhukh bowed. 'It will be done.'

'And signal the fleet,' Kalgaro ordered, starting on his calculations. 'We've nothing of any importance on that stretch. Request orbital battery, coordinates to follow. We'll blast them to scrap before they're halfway across.'

He couldn't stifle the grin. It kept on growing.

'After that, just watch,' he said, zooming the sensors in. 'I promise you, it'll be worth it.'

The Brotherhood of the Storm broke from cover as the blast doors lifted. All mounted on speeders – Kyzagans, Javelins, Shamshirs – the warriors streaked out from the hangars in tight arrow formation, staying low against the ground and pouring on the speed.

Ahead of them, the dust clouds of the tank columns blurred the dark line between earth and sky. The last of the artillery strikes slammed home, pulverising targets kilometres ahead. Shiban drove clean through the monolithic smoke plumes, leaving long trails of black behind him.

He had walked across this land, just days ago, though it might as well have been another lifetime. He remembered the last of the weak sunlight across those acrid pools, the ghosts of the wastes. He remembered the child. He wondered, once again, what had happened to him. And that made him think of Katsuhiro. Maybe they were both dead. Or maybe they had made it back inside the Inner Palace walls, where the last shreds of hope clustered.

He recognised nothing of the terrain now. It was a lost place, a haunt of daemons, its buildings merely grave markers over infinite killing fields. The only creatures abroad in those smoke-choked relics were the damned and the twisted, limping and shrieking under a moonless night.

'Targets sighted,' he voxed to his warriors, maintaining the punishing rate of speed. The blasted world raced by, blurred into stretched lines. 'Disperse for clearance.'

The speeder squadrons split up, angling and diving through the empty habs and spires. They flew past the vanguards of the armoured columns and shot clear of their rumbling stink and fume. Warning runes flashed across every helm, picking up threats in the debris. The pilots opened fire, spraying bolt-shells and las-bursts into the gloom, flushing out traitor infantry caught in the open and punching them apart.

'Ahead-right,' announced Chakaja, the Stormseer attached to Shiban's brotherhood, riding near the spearpoint alongside Yiman. 'Obstacle for the ground armour.'

Chakaja was not a great weather-worker, not like Naranbaatar or Yesugei, but his beyond-sight pierced a fraction ahead of time's veil, giving faint glimpses of possible futures. In these kind of actions, that contribution was priceless.

'Down low,' ordered Shiban, dropping hard. 'Shi'ir pattern – clear it out.'

His squadron skimmed down another metre, splitting up, still burning along. Every warrior pulled out two frag-charges. They sped down the long lane between two walls of empty rockcrete, skating over what had once been an asphalt transitway, ignoring the sporadic las-fire that spat and whistled past them.

'Here,' said Chakaja.

The warriors released the charges in a cascade pattern,

hurled from the barrelling speeders every few metres. As the charges struck the buried minefield below, the earth erupted into a bloom of liquid fire and earth-clots. Every sunken mine was caught, blown into plasma-bursts that threw soil and rockcrete high up against the glassless windows of the habs on either side.

'More signals ahead,' Yiman said calmly, driving his Shamshir through the whirls of flying gravel. *'Defence point.'*

'Take it out,' Shiban commanded, and the speeders instantly swerved into a wide formation, spread across the full width of the chasm. 'Jerun, Temuhan – this one is yours.'

Four missiles streaked out from two speeders, twisting away towards the distant target – an old defence bunker sat at the base of a derelict triumphal column. Each missile smacked home, shattering the rockcrete bulkheads and arrowing into the chambers beyond. The interior ballooned with smoke, and the surviving defenders spilled out, disorientated and firing blind. The speeders switched to assault cannons, crunching through both terrain and infantry in a splatter of hard rounds.

'Ahead now,' ordered Shiban, lifting the nose of his Shamshir and gunning to blaze clean over the destroyed bunker.

'Hold, my khan,' came Chakaja's voice over the comm. *'Something… dangerous.'*

'Belay – back out!' Shiban cried, hauling his jetbike sharply upward and round.

The rest of the squadron responded instantly, slamming on air brakes and jerking their mounts back into tight hairpins. The entire formation lifted, hovering on cushions of super-heated air and grav-buffers. More las-fire speckled in at them, the sources swiftly despatched by swivelling outriders.

'What did you–' Yiman started.

He never finished. From five hundred metres ahead, the very location they would have been travelling through had

they kept on speeding, the air itself trembled. The cloud banks
shuddered, the dust kicked up, and the atmosphere split apart.

A twenty-metre-wide column of pure destruction, rippling
and ablaze, crunched down from the heavens, drilling like a
thrown spear, shooting straight through the heart of a gutted
hive spire and delving deep into the foundations below. The
blinding impact wave shot outward, dashed with rubble and
tumbling hunks of plasteel, crashing through everything in
its path, demolishing hab walls and blowing through arches.

More las-columns slammed down beyond that one, pulverising and burning, turning the entire sector into a mess of
toppling balustrades and imploding wall sections.

'Away, away!' Shiban roared, hauling his jetbike away from
the rising dust cloud.

'Orbital strikes,' said Yiman grimly, following suit. 'Already?'

The squadrons scattered, running ahead of the overlapping
blast waves.

'So it seems,' Shiban replied. 'Signal command.'

'I think they're aware,' said Yiman, gesturing back the way
they had come.

All across the western horizon, the sky was on fire too –
not the fire of mortars or incendiaries or plasma shafts, but
a sky-born flame, thundering along in a horizontal line four
and a half kilometres up, as if the racing clouds had been
unzipped and torn apart by a lateral sword-thrust. Plumes
roiled and twisted around the rupture, spilling out in a steaming froth, splaying into fronds that flickered and danced with
friction lightning. Peals of artificial thunder cracked across
the vista, underpinned by a roar like the seas of all worlds
coming in at once. The cityscape beyond was obscured behind
that fiery shadow, blanked off by the kilometres-wide advance
that devoured all else, suspended on sun-red drives, hanging
impossibly low for its size and yet still moving, still grinding

towards them, wreathed in sparks and flares and gouts that stretched unbroken as far as the eye could see.

Ahead of the looming orbital plate came its support atmospherics, wheeling out of the inferno, their turbines whining at full tilt to stay clear of the lethal turbulence. And below them, the tanks still sped onwards, crashing along the attack-lanes cleared for them by the Legion outriders, supported by low-hovering gunships with heavy infantry squads poised to drop.

'So all is committed now,' Shiban murmured, allowing himself just a moment to appreciate what had been set into motion. 'Let us see how far it takes us.'

Then he pulled his jetbike around, powered up the drives again and made to plunge around the flaring mass of las-beams. Already more signals were clustering on the edge of his augur range, ones that would slow the ground advance if not eliminated quickly.

'Onward!' he roared, gunning back up to full speed. 'Keep it moving! Evade that las-fire, but keep it moving!'

ELEVEN

Hunted
The lesson
Contraction

No, no. Not that – that was the mistake. Find a hole, furnish it, hunker down. When you ran, that was when they got you, out in the open. He'd moved enough for the moment, leaving his false stink in every corner, letting them believe he was in a hundred different places within the Palace, and now he had this place, the one he'd been zeroing in on from the very start, the one where he'd stitch his potions together.

There were a thousand laboratoria in this city, and had been since the very start. Other cities had churches or war memorials, but the Emperor's home ground had temples to science, the great hope of the species. Fo had to hand it to the old man – that had been about as good a strategy as any other, given what He had had in mind. Only, you had to be sure that it was the right kind of science. The Emperor had always been obsessed with the stuff of biology, the helices and the cell cultures. Even before all that trouble with the abominable intelligences, the thing that had poisoned humanity against thinking silicon forever, it had been all about the petri dishes and the centrifuges with Him – the messy stuff, the liquids and the organs and the blood cultures.

Fo had occasionally wondered why. For sure, the old man had used His gene-meddling nous to conquer a galaxy. The programme had been impressive, in its own brutal sort of way. Maybe no one else could have done it. It certainly showed the power of what He'd been up to, closeted in those underground facilities for so many years with the ragtag gaggle of eccentrics He'd surrounded Himself with. It showed just what could be done with a few clever geneticists and some high-grade manu-facturing facilities, plus an infinite slice of self-belief.

But maybe it had been limited, all the same. Maybe some avenues had been closed down too early. A human could be made into a fearsome thing by that route, but unreliably, as had been amply demonstrated. Better, perhaps, if you were truly deter-mined to start over, to do away with the messy stuff altogether. The grey matter. The wobbly flesh and the faulty heart valves.

Fo suspected, though, that deep down the Emperor was something of a sentimentalist. There were some bridges He wouldn't cross, even if He could have done, because certain aspects of His programme were just the way they were. He had wanted His Imperium of Eternity to be inherited by beings that looked like He had done, once; that talked like He had done, that could share a joke or enjoy a glass of wine. Otherwise, what was the point? If you could build something indestruct-ible, something incorruptible, but no longer human, then why were you doing it? The whole point was survival of the kind, of the species, of *us*.

And even then, He'd gone too far. A Space Marine was an abomination of its own kind. A primarch a hundred times worse. Variety replaced with uniformity. Interesting weak-ness with glass-eyed strength. Possibility with uneventfulness. That was why He had to be stopped, somehow, before this entire gaudy shitshow developed so much momentum that no machinery ever conceived of could stop it. Perhaps that point had already been reached. Or perhaps this was when he, Basilio Fo, would have to step up and try to restore some colour to a rapidly greying universe.

And he could do it. It was possible. He looked down now at the long sterile bench in front of him, and saw the ingredients ready, all laid out.

The lab was some distance underground, like all the high security ones were. It had once housed thousands of workers. Those were gone now, fleeing in panic before the enemy advance – as if running a few kilometres further in would save them. The desks were overturned, the data-slates cracked and discarded. It hadn't been much trouble to gain entry, to work his way down, to locate the cold storage and the chem-vats and the splice-engines. None of that should have been left unguarded. At the very least it should have been destroyed, in case the enemy got its sweaty hands on it all, because it was all still good, useful stuff.

But everyone was terribly ground-down right now. Everyone was febrile, facing up to their own mortality, and that made their judgement poor. It had been the same with that girl in the medicae station. Even when he'd told her that she'd be helping out in a just cause, a noble cause, it hadn't stopped her crying about it. He'd been perfectly true to his word on that, despite her lamentable lack of vision – it wasn't his fault that the Imperium made so much use of retinal scanners and blood-cyclers on its door locks, and he could hardly go around leaving his own biomarkers out there.

Now, to business. He had to go fast. No room for mistakes now, not when the city was being demolished a little more with every passing second. If all his boasts to Amon were not to be for nothing, then this had to be done right.

He powered up the cyclers again, linking up the backup generators. He opened up the bioscopes and the mainline scanners, and got them to work. He emptied his bag of all the things he'd taken from the dozen places he'd needed to call at before this one, then rummaged around in the cold storage for more. He cranked up the lone cogitator with the power that he needed, and began to instruct its tetchy machine-spirit in new ways of crunching the runes.

Proof of concept, that was all. Something to take with him, to buy him safety. It wasn't easy. He found himself sweating. He could hear artillery the whole time, some way up but still resonating down the shafts and the tunnels. It reminded him of every time he'd ever been stuck in a city about to fall to barbarians – more times than he liked to admit – and it never got any better.

He shuffled over to the next close-viewer down, and turned on the zoom lens. He bent over the tube, and started to assess how his cultures were doing. Just as hoped for, he could see the cells dividing, bifurcating, splitting up into the spread-patterns he recognised from those first baby steps on much-lamented Velich Tarn.

It was working again. He was a genius.

But then he heard, from a long way off and some distance above, a crunch of ceramite on glass. He'd heard that noise too often as well. They were never particularly subtle, the Children of Astarte.

His heart skipped. Slowly, very slowly, he lifted his head from the viewer. He glanced sidelong, peering down the bench towards the lab's entrance, a hundred metres off in the gloom. Would it be a loyal one, or a traitor one? Which would be worse? The place was very dark, save for the pools of soft light at his workstation. It was almost deserted. If he stayed totally still, frozen in the lee of the main cogitator housing, it might just move on.

More heavy treads, coming down a debris-strewn stairwell. He caught sight of a red lumen-glow bleeding down the far wall, swinging with the movement of a body in motion. A vial shattered, crushed under a thick sole, and it made him start.

But it was only when he glimpsed what had come down the stairwell that his blood went truly cold. The monster emerged steadily, striding out into the open, one of the VIII, replete with flickers of witch-light over its nightshade armour, its helm stretched into contorted spines, its lenses burning dull red. Those eyes would detect absolutely everything in the murk, even more than its loyalist kin would have done. It would not be hunting for tactical advantage here, nor be amenable to bargaining. Fo knew just what it was here for, and also what it was capable of.

He grabbed his results, scrabbling for the vials with shaking hands, and ran as fast as his limbs would take him.

'They're going to break,' said Fafnir Rann.

The loyalist position was strung across a wide chasm between stripped-out power plants, barring one of the main intact routes further in. The bulk of its defenders were base-line humans, arrayed in a motley collection of regimental uniforms. They were bolstered by two dozen Leman Russ tanks and a single Malcador, Annihilator pattern, all set hull-down behind thick rockcrete barriers and rubble heaps. Forty fixed heavy gun platforms had been positioned on either flank, some behind the blackened walls of the twin complexes, others sunk deep into the debris and surrounded with barricades. Five hundred infantry were dug into foxholes and trenches all across the gap, armed with flamers, hellguns, lasguns, a few bolters. Additional squads had been positioned higher up and under cover, huddling in the wreckage of the power plant interiors, armed with the longer-range sniper guns, augurs and the best working comms units. Air support was long gone, but that mattered less in such claustrophobic confines – the sheer walls of the buildings clustered high and close on all sides, topped with the flickering interference of the aegis, made ground level feel almost subterranean.

By the time Sigismund and his assault group had reached the location – eighty kilometres north-east of the Palatine, out in the contested urban zones well inside the Mercury perimeter – the defence seemed ripe to fold. The armour and gun-points were low on shells, and resupply to the sector had been made perilous by deep traitor incursions to the north and south. The position commander, a woman called Misa Haak from the Gattlen 43rd who seemed to be running a high fever, had been struggling for days with waves of refugees flooding west, all of whom could have been harbouring renegades or worse and so had to be screened. Food was gone, comms were out, the air itself screamed in hard-to-pick voices and the stars were hidden by a wall of shimmering fire. By the time the true enemy had begun to filter into place at the far end of the long chasm between the heavily shelled power plants, her nerves were almost shot.

'Fan out,' Sigismund ordered, clanking his way towards the command bunker buried in the centre of the defence lines. 'Keep them in place until we see what's coming.'

He'd come with thirty of the Templar Brethren, Rann included. These warriors were all in black now, the last traces of gold erased from their armour by the smog, that thick rain of filth and dust that carpeted everything in all directions. Only their helm-lenses and their weapon-fields still glared into the seamy night, snarling like angry stars. Dozens of other Templar squads had been sent hunting through the hollow city-sector, each acting autonomously now and trying to shore up the faltering defensive marks, but this was the furthest east any of them had come, right up against the main thrust of the XVI Legion vanguard.

All but four of Sigismund's fighters took up positions along the line. Auxilia defenders looked up at them nervously as they lumbered past, wondering if they would halt at *their* squad, and if that was a good or a bad thing. None of them moved an inch, though. Not now. Not with those brutal, near-silent presences among them.

'You will *hold* this place!' Rann roared out, marching along the trenches. 'This is the Emperor's domain, and you are His people! You will *not doubt!* You will *not fear!* You will *fight*, and you will *kill*, for those who come here offer nothing but *oblivion!* You will *hold* this place! This is the Emperor's domain, and you...'

Sigismund remained silent. He moved up to the forward edge of the line, clambering up a steep slope of rubble and resting his chin on the lip. He let his helm-lenses zoom out into the murk, to the distant shadows of enemy infantry shuffling their way forward. Still a kilometre distant. They hugged the shadows of the buildings, creeping through their empty innards watchfully. Beyond the infantry he could detect the low rumble of approaching armour, smashing its way through rebar-clogged accessways further back. He estimated numbers. He gauged the speed of the advance. He tried to assess the quality of troops.

Then he glanced back at the defenders cowering in their foxholes. Then he looked up the sheer walls around them all. Then he looked back down at the crater-pocked ground level.

Rann took a break from his oration and moved up to join him. 'What do you think?' he asked.

'This could hold a while, if they had the will for it,' Sigismund said. Further back along the line of the chasm, directly east, outlines of power-armoured infantry could be made out now even without zooming in. The enemy were projecting confidence, coming on openly. 'They need to be shown the leaders can be beaten.'

'If the leaders are among them.'

'They're Cthonians. The gangmasters never hung back.' Sigismund shuffled back down the slope and went to find Haak. 'Maintain fire down the centre, when they come,' he told her. 'Force them wide.'

Haak nodded, numbly, cheeks flushed red under her helm. 'Aye, lord.'

'As soon as you see us again, cease firing. You understand?'

'Aye, lord.'

'You will see us again. Then cease firing. Just watch.'

Rann was looking out from one flank to the other as Sigismund rejoined him – the two soaring, bomb-marred walls of burned rockcrete, each enclosing the shattered remnants of their massive internal workings.

'Which side, then?'

Sigismund drew his blade, then gazed deep into its black surface. You could almost think that it was liquid – that if you placed your finger against its matt plane the tip would sink under the surface. It still fascinated him.

'South,' he murmured eventually. 'They'll come that way.'

The Templars moved out after that. Ten stayed at the barricades to keep the nerves of the auxilia steady. Sigismund, Rann and the remainder clambered up the scree incline along the chasm's southern edge and broke into the echoing chambers beyond the walls. The internal spaces had been abandoned for some time, the floors sodden, roofs holed, windows empty. All the inner corridors were jet-black and cluttered with refuse, making the going slow. Corpses of the old work-crews slumped amid the shell wreckage, mouldering in the humid dust-drifts. Other bodies littered the chambers and walkways further in – Imperial troops, most of them, but civilians also, as well as some scabrous forms that looked less than human. Startled, immobile faces were briefly illuminated as the Imperial Fists swept past them, a brief flash of red-tinged light, before sinking back into the gloom.

'Closing, fifty metres,' Rann reported, jogging heavily beside Sigismund.

'Total dark,' Sigismund ordered, and every one of the Templars killed the final light sources on their armour – the weapon disruptors, the glimmer from their lenses. They ran faster through the broken ways like ghost-images, black ripples across a world of shadow.

The Sons of Horus came on with less caution, crashing their way up through the open doorways. From outside, the sounds of Haak's steady barrage could now be heard. She was doing what she'd been asked to – making the full-frontal assault inconvenient, pushing the oncoming infantry into the cover of the old buildings. The invaders' attention would still be partially on where they wanted to get to, judging where they would break out again and start slaying properly. Not much of a distraction, but something to latch on to – the kind of fractional gain Dorn had always made his sons seek out.

Rann was first into contact, bursting out of the gloom with his twin axe-blades and crashing into the lead XVI Legion warrior. That instantly broke the near silence – energy fields flashed into life, helm-lenses blazed, ceramite clanged against steel in showers of sparks as the rest of the Templars engaged. The Sons of Horus squad was smaller – twelve fighters in Reaver configuration, with chainaxes and bolt pistols – but they'd be summoning more soon, so speed was of the essence.

Sigismund hung back for just a second, long enough to pick out the warband leader amid the lumen-streaked dark. He was in a veteran's Mark II plate, heavily scored and overlaid with battle-trophies. Chains swirled around him as he moved, each one capped with a bleached skull, and he carried a heavy chainsword fashioned into a serpent's-head design. Like all his squad, he still had that old ganger edge to him, the rough cut of the armour-trim and the crude blood-daubs over the exposed panels. The savagery was more pronounced than Sigismund could remember, though – they were degrading, reverting to an older type, their fighting style wilder, just as dangerous, but looser at the edges now.

He plunged straight at him, shouldering his way through the challenge of another warrior to get to the real prize, all the while calculating the distances, the angles he'd need. His whole body responded now, taut as a drum, every movement efficient, taking in the tactical data around him, processing it unconsciously, using it, turning it to his advantage.

He slammed hard into contact, his black sword screaming up against the teeth of the enemy's blade. One, two, three swipes, hard and fast, hammering the Reaver backwards and making him stumble on the loose stone. Sigismund's severe face twitched into a smile under his helm – a flicker of real enjoyment. He *hated* this enemy. This enemy was an unbeliever, fallen from the light of hard truth, a thing to be exterminated with joy. That was what had changed. It wasn't about skill. It wasn't about the abstract goal of conquest. It was about righteousness. It was about certainty.

He crunched and blasted the apostate further back, severing the chains and sending the skulls bouncing. His Templars came with him, using their greater numbers to drive the Sons of Horus back out towards the chamber's outer wall. They bludgeoned and shot and punched through the last remnants of the old perimeter, pushing the fight out of cover and into the old transitway between the power plants.

Haak immediately ceased firing, just as commanded, and

the chasm shuddered into dust-choked silence. The Imperial Fists and Sons of Horus fought their way right into the exposed centre, neither side giving any quarter, the exchanges vicious and heavy.

It didn't take long to end it. The Reaver commander was a decent warrior, experienced and canny. On another battlefield, he might have reaped a fresh tally of skulls. He was brave, as they all were – a kind of desperate bravery born in the lightless streets of his cursed old world, fuelled by the desire not to be shown as weak.

That wasn't enough. Sigismund forced him up a long heap of wreckage, driving him out of the dust-roil where the fight could be clearly seen. His sword-swipes were even sharper now, even quicker, all aimed with razor-edged precision. He smacked the chainsword completely away, checking the parry and sending it sailing end over end into the dark. Then the switch, the change of direction, so fast it felt like it must have been preordained, ramming up through the Reaver's breastplate in an explosion of disruptor charge. The stricken body left the ground entirely, propelled off its feet by the force of the thrust, and for an instance it hung like a marionette amid the snarls of angry lightning-forks.

'Faithless!' Sigismund snarled, the only word he had uttered since the fight began. He cast the corpse to the earth, letting it slam into the dust like a rotten side of meat.

It wasn't a kill. It was a demonstration. The defenders at Haak's barricades had been watching the whole time, seeing an enemy they were terrified of being casually, systematically dismantled.

There would still be fighting ahead. Enraged Sons of Horus were already advancing in numbers, and would be in range within moments. Survival at this position would still be tight, as all confrontations had to be now.

But that wasn't the point. Sigismund turned to the Imperial defenders, his bloodstained sword hot in his hands.

'Witness this!' he shouted, his hearts thudding with the glorious rhythm of exertion. 'They can be hurt. They can be killed.'

Haak was listening. Her troops were listening. They no longer looked terrified.

'So stand up,' he growled. 'And *do your duty.*'

The air inside Bhab had changed. It had been foul for some time, due to the general collapse of the atmosphere across the entire Palace, but now the stink had an element of more human weakness.

Fear had a smell. Illness had a smell. So did hopelessness. The men and women working for long shifts at the command stations had been unable to attend to basic hygiene for a long time. Their uniforms were filthy, their hair lank. Most of them were so sleep deprived that they barely knew how long they'd been there. And yet, through all that, through the mind-fog and the reek of it, they kept working, their hands numbly switching levers and turning dials. What else was there to do? Dimly, somewhere deep in their animal-stem brains, they remembered what it was they were fighting, and so they kept going, because the alternative was too horrifying for words.

And that was ironic, Dorn thought, taking a rare moment to look up from his own station to gaze across the signals pits. If the enemy had not been so consumed with its essential sadism, its extravagant orgies of cruelty, then perhaps these people would have thrown in the towel by now. As it was, though, fear remained just a little stronger than the despair. Every vid-feed they saw from the contracting war-front, every capture of what the World Eaters did, what the Night Lords did, that stiffened resolve just enough.

For all that, the painful truth couldn't be hidden. Every soul in the bastion saw how things were going. Even Archamus, solid Archamus, who had stepped up without hesitation when the first of that name was killed, was fraying now. Dorn didn't ask him when he had last taken a rest-period. It would have been hypocrisy to order him to stand down, since he himself had long burned past the point of normal endurance, and so he let it slide, just like he did with so much else.

In the past, he would have detected the Sigillite's advance before the man had even entered the chamber. Now, though, his weariness was so great that the cloaked figure had limped halfway up the steps towards the primarch's crow's nest station before he registered it.

'Rogal,' said Malcador.

Dorn nodded. It was still easy, even after all the long years he'd known the First Lord of the Imperium, to find the crabbed, wizened face disconcerting. Those eyes had seen plenty in their time. They had peered across a world that had existed before the Imperium, and had then peered across one shaped by its Crusade. Now they seemed destined to peer into its destruction, the final unravelling of plans that he had partly devised himself.

Dorn had always been a soldier, following orders as much as giving them. In the final analysis, his task was to preserve the work of others. Malcador, though, had built this place. The Imperium had been his creation, and this was therefore his defeat. What did he think of all that? Did it crush him? Or was he above such things, having scorched them out of his system over the thousands of years he'd been alive?

As ever, impossible to know. All you got was the exterior – the glittering eyes under the cowl, the long staff gripped by a bony hand, the low voice as dry as a lizard's.

'Lord Regent,' Dorn replied. 'Any change?'

It was almost an unconscious habit now, to ask. The answer was always the same, of course.

'He remains silent,' said Malcador. 'If it changes, I shall let you know. How stands the defence?'

Dorn smiled grimly. Having to outline it all explicitly felt like a punishment all of its own. And yet, where else could Malcador go for the information, now? With the final failure of all communications, only Dorn had any kind of grip on the wider tactical situation. Only he remembered everything that had been planned, where every last unit had been deployed, where they were likely to be now, given the rate of attrition. The sole measure of pride he allowed himself was in how accurate his projections had been.

If Guilliman had only made it…

'Falling back on all fronts,' Dorn said curtly. 'That good enough for you?' He took a moment, rubbed hard at his forehead. 'Three main enemy advances inside the Ultimate Wall, all moving fast. Sixteenth Legion spearheads are within three – maybe four – days' march of Palatine. Eighth Legion berserker units are not far behind them. Four zone commands are cut off entirely, their defenders now out of supply range. We have effective control over the Sanctum, Palatine, some of the Adamant and Europa sectors. The rest – gone.'

Malcador took it all in. 'Then the general order for withdrawal to the Sanctum–'

'Not yet. Not yet.' Dorn felt another wave of pressure on him, another voice of doubt to add to the hundreds that already whispered in his mind. 'We still command the key arterials. We can bring them back. But right now, we have to hurt them, while we can. Once we're penned in here…'

And that was the final trap. No escape. The shape of the siege, for all the surface complexity of its hundreds of interlocking walls and war-fronts, had always been simple in outline. Concentric rings: the Outer Palace and the space ports, then the Inner Palace, then the Palatine core, and then, last of all, the Sanctum Imperialis, the final bastion, guarded by the Eternity Gate itself. Once the Palatine strongholds were surrendered, the final ghost of hope would be gone – there would be no more room to manoeuvre, no room to breathe, no room to do anything but die, crushed up against one another as the walls were slowly driven in.

'I understand the strain you're under, Rogal,' Malcador said carefully. 'No one doubts your commitment. But do we really have–'

'No, we don't have anything like what we need for it,' Dorn snapped. 'Jaghatai's made his move now, you know that? A third of our Legion strength, gambled away on a damned port. We've had our armour reserves plundered to make it all viable, and what does it get us? Not enough. He could have been here, with us.' Just rehearsing it all made him angrier. 'It knocks out the Fourteenth, that's true. Having more Death Guard inside the walls wouldn't make me any happier. But now I'm searching for reasons not to think it's rank insanity.' Again, though, control, control. 'Sanguinius is with us still. Vulkan is with us. Throne, I'm thankful for that.'

'And Sigismund fights on.'

Dorn's gaze, which had been wavering, flickered up. 'On my command.'

'Rumours of it have reached the Dungeon. The Black Sword. They say he's making ground.'

'He's not there to make ground. He's there to give them something to fear.'

'Because the line troops are failing.'

Reluctantly, Dorn nodded. 'I can't even bring myself to blame them. Maybe you don't feel it. The... weight.'

'Oh, I feel it.'

'The Lord of Death, they tell me. Safe in his own fortress, making the world sicken.'

'And so maybe Jaghatai has a point.'

'Only if you think it's possible.' Dorn felt his lids growing heavy again. He felt the dead pull of all his fine armour, not put to serious use since encountering Fulgrim on the parapets. And there was so much to do here, so much to put right, just to squeeze out another week of resistance, another day, another hour, preventing him from arming up and charging out into the dark, doing what he burned to do, because someone had to keep a grip, to care about duty.

'But it is set, now,' said Malcador. 'Nothing can prevent it.'

'Just as you say,' muttered Dorn wearily. 'And so the world ends thus, not in defiance, but in madness.'

TWELVE

Atmospheric friction
Weak suit
Percentages

Yes, madness, thought Ayo Nuta. The only word for it. It had never been done, and there were good reasons for that. The Skye orbital plate's very presence in the lower atmosphere had already been something skirting the absurd, but *moving* it – dragging it hundreds of kilometres across an active warzone – was beyond anything he'd been asked to contemplate before.

Nuta had struggled to get some of the crew to follow orders, once they'd realised what he was asking them to do. He might have reprimanded them for that, but in truth he understood how they felt. They were run-down. They were scared. They knew that their chances of making it out of this alive, always small, had just vanished, and now came the insanity of making a powered run through the full atmosphere, something that had only really been theorised about in the constructor's tomes held securely in Luna's shipyard archives.

But then the immersion drives had always invited the

possibility. If you could lower a plate into the true atmosphere, keeping it intact and self-powered and able to function, why couldn't you push things a little further, and use it as a proper mobile platform? You'd wreak havoc on everything within a kilometre or so, churning up Throne-knows-what and making the weather run amok, but in the current circumstances that no longer seemed like something worth worrying much about. The entire planet had been stirred up into a permanent electric storm by the volume of ship-mounted las-fire loosed on the surface, and whatever physics had once applied to the atmosphere had been wholly superseded.

The ride was a horror show, all the same. Colossal resistance smeared across the forward plates, ratcheting up quickly into a full firestorm that tested the limits of the re-entry armour. The plate's structure, vaster and more cumbersome than the mightiest void-going battleship, shook and screamed and pinged rivets across its full expanse. The noise was incredible, a constant boom and a thunder that reverberated up from the drive-rooms and made thinking impossible. Every lens in the main control dome flashed crimson, telling the crew nothing much they couldn't already feel – that this was mad, mad, mad.

And for all that, Nuta couldn't help but enjoy it – the daring of it, the colossal, shameless audacity of the thing. They were *doing* it. They were making their mark on the battle just when they had looked destined to serve out time as a redundant atmospheric hangar. Who knew what was passing through the minds of the enemy now, having burned their way right up to the Ultimate Wall, only to see a fire-wreathed hunk of orbital salvage roar straight back at them, slicing the atmosphere in two and sending friction lightning raking for kilometres in all directions.

'Maintain course and speed!' he shouted, his voice already

hoarse. 'Clamp down on that power-drain – the upper voids are on the edge!'

He could see nothing on the realviewers, all of which were now portals onto walls of fire. Many of the ranged augurs were scrambled, but a few of them still gave him a shaky picture of the outside world.

They had ground their way across their mooring station in the southern Palace, across the Europa and Sanctus sectors, finally cresting the Ultimate Gate and veering due east. He'd witnessed snatches of the gradually deteriorating battlefields during that time, from the intense combat still going on inside the Ultimate Wall to the emptiness of the sectors outside the old Anterior barbicans. He wondered if the orbital plate's progress had disturbed any of those conflicts – if enemy battalions had been momentarily shaken by the sight of the heavens erupting above them and flooding their augurs with static. He hoped so. Every morsel counted, every slight twist of fortune.

Only once they had cleared the Ultimate Gate fortress, its heights still burning wildly, did the orders start to come in from Colossi. Nuta slowed the advance a fraction, aiming for perfect coordination with the planned land advance. That had been a complicated business – the Skye plate had truly colossal inertia, driven by its immense mass and limited-power manoeuvring drives, and so velocity had to be calculated with a high degree of precision. Around ninety per cent of its entire power output was devoted to the monumental repulsor-coils that kept it from crashing to earth, leaving comparatively little for anything else.

In the end, the timings had been as close as could have been hoped for. The plate crashed on eastwards, driving an incandescent path over the summits of the Colossi comms-vanes, just as the land assault snarled up to full speed and began its long race to the space port. The remaining squadrons of

V Legion fighters screamed out around them, shadowing them all the way out. The plate itself had minimal armaments of its own – it had been a platform for nova cannons once, all of which had been stripped out and used on the Palace walls – but its remaining atmospheric escorts flooded from the hangars too, and its residual heavy bolter arrays swivelled into action.

Then the void-to-surface las-fire started. Nuta had been braced for it. It was why they were there – to shield the otherwise exposed armour. The orbital plates had always been designed to withstand battleship-grade weaponry, and Skye's void shields were fully powered and operational.

Even so, the first impacts were shattering. Lance after lance shot down from the heavens, thrusting out of the racing storm fronts and jagging straight into the plate's upper disc-face. The void shields shrieked, flexing concave under the impacts and scattering into interference patterns hundreds of metres in diameter. There was no prospect of firing back, nothing to do but weather it, keep moving, keep the power feeds from shuttering the generators and exposing the physical hull.

'More spikes detected!' cried the master of signals, a Terran named Uwe Eisen. 'Impacts incoming across zones nine and ten!'

Nuta tensed, his fingers drumming on the arms of his command throne. Aside from rotating the harmonics of the void units, there wasn't much he could do. 'All hands, brace,' he ordered. 'Keep all forward sensors open and scanning.'

The lances struck again, smacking in sequence across the upper decks and sending impact waves rippling across the shields. Alert klaxons went off, just as always, swiftly clamped down on by the crisis teams who had heard enough of them. The lumens flashed out, plunging them all into total darkness, before flickering back on again. The deck shuddered, and the sound of something exploding echoed up from the repulsor chambers far below.

Those enormous las-beams had been launched towards ground-level coordinates, intended to wreak havoc amid the close-packed tank columns. With a wry grin, Nuta found himself wondering if the targeters on the void-ships even knew yet what their energy beams were running into.

'How much more of this can we handle?' he asked Io Sleva, his master of operations.

Sleva's slender head popped up from behind her bank of controls. 'Hits like that? We're getting knocked hard. A few more hours, if it doesn't let up.'

'It won't let up. Do what you can.'

A few more hours would be about right. The tanks were moving fast, shadowed by even swifter V Legion speeders. They were making good use of their improvised overhead cover, limiting casualties from long-range fire. Nuta started to think that maybe the whole scheme wasn't so mad after all. Maybe it even had a chance of working.

'Incoming comms from Legion command!' Eisen shouted.

Nuta patched it through.

'*Enemy atmospherics launched,*' came Jangsai Khan's static-drenched voice over the link from the airborne squadrons. '*Squadrons moving to intercept, but you will wish to make arrangements.*'

'Acknowledged, my lord khan,' Nuta responded, before turning towards Eisen's station again. 'Get me whatever you can from those forward viewers.'

A bank of lenses positioned around his throne blurted with white noise, hissing like a nest of snakes before some of them cleared to expose jumpy, grainy feeds from the prow-mounted augurs. The images were very bad, a mix of interference and poor processing from the night-vision compensators, and

for a moment or two it wasn't clear that anything much had
been picked up. Nuta had vague impressions of the looming
space port on the far horizon, barely perceptible amid the
slew and the dark.

Then he saw them – blurred points of light racing out,
whole clouds of them, soon surrounded by the spark-flicker
of massed las-fire. The numbers were immediately intimidating, the reckless flight-aggression even more so.

He took a deep breath, and patched a link to his commander of ordnance.

'Jafda, alert the air-to-air bolter crews, all sectors. Free-fire
on my mark.'

He kept his eyes fixed on the scopes, even as another
hammer blow landed from orbit, nearly throwing him from
his throne. The lenses went white, the lumens blanked out
again, something else exploded.

'Should have known better,' he murmured, shuffling back
into position and calling up fresh damage readings. 'Still
damned insanity.'

Morarg watched the flyers streak out of the hangars – Fire
Raptors, Storm Eagles, a few Stormbirds and Thunderhawks.
Some of them went erratically, as if their pilots were struggling
with the controls. Or maybe they had just changed too much
for comfort, their engorged limbs no longer squeezing into
the cramped cockpits. In any case, the XIV Legion had never
specialised in flyers. They maintained atmospheric capability, just as any full-spectrum army did, but they never loved
them, and those who crewed the machines were not held in
especial honour.

So he had little confidence in them. They would do some
damage, to be sure, but the V Legion were masters of this
warfare, and that ludicrous hunk of hovering adamantium

they'd somehow conjured up would take some beating before it finally broke up. The best they could hope for was to strafe the slower-moving ground forces, take out as much of those as they could and block the routes east, but even then he doubted the White Scars would give them an easy time of it.

For a moment longer he stared at the western skies, still unsure whether to believe the evidence of his senses. The orbital plate was not so much moving through the atmosphere as ripping it apart, bringing with it a low-frequency rumble that made the earth itself vibrate. Watching an eleven-kilometre-diameter void-platform thunder its way closer and closer, all the while taking sustained hits from the fleet and a constant rattle of fire from the ground below, was one of the more arresting sights his long service had given him. Sensors indicated that the plate was tracking the speed of the armour underneath fairly well, but from that distance it looked almost immobile, a violation of both physics and common sense, an affront to what warfare ought to be.

After a moment longer, he shook his head wearily, and went to find Kalgaro. It took him a while, for the ways of the space port were still unfamiliar, and everything seemed to be in a state of total disarray. When he finally located him, partly thanks to the prompting of a helpful daemon hanging like a clutch of rotten fruit from the roof-arches, he was pleased to see that the Siegemaster, at least, seemed to be taking things seriously.

'What word of the primarch?' Kalgaro asked, never breaking stride as Morarg joined up with him. Together, they trudged their way down towards the lower levels.

'He was intrigued, when I told him,' Morarg said.

'That's it? Nothing more?'

'Something to do with his new perspective, maybe.'

Morarg remembered just how Mortarion had been, once

the news had been broken. A sad smile, as if it was something that was somehow entirely expected, and could not be avoided now, but was to be regretted all the same. And then an injunction to make all ready, and refocus the Legion, do what needed to be done.

'And it is a drain on his soul. The art.'

Kalgaro grunted. There were some in the Legion who still had mixed feelings about 'the art'. 'I'm glad you're in charge, up there, Caipha,' he said. 'I can't even understand some of the others now. The ones that changed the most.'

The two of them lumbered heavily down a twisting stairwell, with the pale green witch-light flickering around them.

'I have serious concerns,' Morarg said, trying to remain calm about it. 'Nothing is in place. Half our units are stripped down for refitting. The Lord Typhus took a substantial force with him east, and we have too many detachments placed on the main battlefront, out of reach. Getting things moving is... difficult. We are not as strong here as we should be.'

Kalgaro chuckled. 'You worry too much.'

'Do I? That iron bastard did so much damage coming in there's no longer a hard perimeter left to secure. The outer walls are in ruins, the old void generators are blown to pieces. It's not what it was, brother, we never intended it to be, and now we've been caught napping.'

Kalgaro stopped walking, turned to face him. 'So they'll get in,' he said. 'Let them. Bring them. Have you seen what's happened to the interior? Down in the dark? This place is becoming a hell-world again, and if it's hell for us, it'll be worse for them.'

'They'll be expecting it. We've fought one another too often to be surprised now.'

'That's right, we have – we're like old sparring partners, heading to the pits just one more time.' He snorted a harsh laugh. 'I was worried we might miss it. I was worried the pri-march would take so long to give the order that there'd be none of them left to kill. So this is good, for me. They ran from us at Catullus. Now they're coming back for more, and I can't be sorry.'

Morarg almost pressed him on that. They had been on the front foot in the void, with the numbers, with the momentum. They had planned it, with all the care that they always planned offensives. That was where they excelled – the slow vice of control, meticulously conceived, everything accounted for. Now the situations were reversed, calling for swift response, for a rapid change of course, for improvisation. Even with all their advantages, after everything they had already achieved, those had never been their strong suits.

'At least release the armour we've got standing ready,' he said in the end. 'Something to slow them down while we rearm the rest. If they are to get in, I want them damaged while doing so.'

'Already done,' said Kalgaro, starting to walk again. 'They'll bleed for the passage here, and they'll bleed for the wall-crossings too.' Once again, that hard-edge chuckle. 'And then, once they're through all that, we'll truly go to work. Trust me, Caipha – we'll be knee-deep in Chogorian blood before their madness ends.'

Aika 73 blasted through a loose ramp of rubble, rocked a little, then boosted onward. Ernama, the commander of the squadron's lead tank, was setting a hard pace, barely pausing to take loc-readings, and the rest of the six-strong unit had to work to keep up.

'Steady,' Kaska told Dresi, still unsure exactly how to handle her. The driver was concentrating furiously – almost too furiously – and they were skirting at the edge of wearing out the main engine.

She didn't respond, just leaned forward in her seat and maintained the rate of speed.

Kaska turned back to the scopes. His narrow station right at the top of the turret was lined with them – a slew of greasy lenses with spider's webs of tactical data churning down them. Aside from the night-vision scanners, he had augur readings for the rest of the squadron and a battery of tactical data on the terrain and environment. A narrow armoured slit just ahead of him gave him his only realviewer on the action ahead, though he had the use of an extendable periscope when that failed.

For all that, he could barely see a thing. The atmosphere outside was a spewed mess of blown dust and smoke. The interior of the Leman Russ was its usual roar of engine noise, reverberating throughout the claustrophobic crew stations, and the whole thing rattling around like a kicked ration-can. He was under strict orders not to open the hatch, even before the enemy had been sighted, and so everything had to be done through the scopes and auspex, all of which flickered and jerked and kept disappearing into static-fields just when you needed them. It all felt so artificial, so dislocated. He could almost imagine they were in a training simulator again, a box wired up to faulty cogitators and motion-engines.

They were going too fast. He'd already voxed Ernama to tell her so, but she hadn't replied. His loc-readings were unreliable now, and he could barely keep tabs on the other tanks in the convoy. Messages from Legion command had filtered in a while back, telling them all that the air cover was in place, but aside from the fact that the few snatches of open sky he could see were darker and redder than usual he couldn't really tell what that meant – it wasn't as if he could stop, get out, and take a proper look.

'*Enemy sighted, dead ahead,*' came a comms-burst from Ernama over his headset. '*All units, move to engage.*'

Engage what? Damn Ernama. He caught glimpses of old walls and structural interiors, stripped to bare rockcrete amid a man-made sea of dust and masonry-chunks. The remains of the once huge buildings rose up on either side, enclosing a channel less than a hundred metres across. The squadron was uncomfortably concentrated, squeezed together by the urban cliffs on either side – it would have been better to fan out, free up room to use the guns without hitting a friendly. In this murk, under these conditions, Kaska could all too readily imagine a shell smashing through his tank's weaker rear armour, sent flying blind by an enthusiastic gunner with a nervous trigger finger.

'Vosch, make ready,' he ordered his own main gunner, who crouched beside him on the far side of the cannon's solid breech chamber. 'Targets ahead. Jandev – keep them peeled.'

A Leman Russ' armaments were crude but effective. The forward lascannon had a decent rate of fire and could pepper a target with high-power beams as long as the powercells remained active. The main gun had a much slower rate, but it packed a mighty punch when it scored a hit. Vosch knew what to do with it, too – Kaska had never served with anyone more adept at making sense of the incoming screeds of sighting data that her scopes fed her, expertly pulling the pistons and cranks to get the optimal angle out of the long barrel.

Kaska adjusted the auspex gains, and the main lens zoomed forward through a soup of black-grey muck. He was sweating now, both from the punishing warmth of the engine grilles below him and the close tension of the upcoming firefights.

'Keep us hard right,' he warned Dresi, who was working very hard to remain in formation at such high speed. 'We get in front of Frahlo's guns, he won't hold back.'

Then he saw it, eight hundred metres ahead, smashing its way straight through the remains of an old iron balustrade and dropping down onto the dirt with a crash. A XIV Legion Sicaran, followed swiftly by another, both of them armed with turret autocannons and sponson-mounted lascannons. Behind them came other indistinct outlines – heavy infantry, power-armoured, far taller and broader than any standard human troops.

Ernama, closest of the Leman Russ tanks, fired instantly. The shell from her main cannon flew long, exploding against the upper walls of the buildings beyond. Her lascannon's beams flashed out a second later, joined by those of the following two tanks in the squadron, streaking out in blinding lines and igniting the rooflines with stark white flashes.

'Hard right!' ordered Kaska again, quickly gauging the terrain through his auspex. If they maintained this position they'd neither get a clear shot nor guarantee getting out of the path of shells from the rear. 'Vosch – get your fix on the second one.'

The air around them exploded into a criss-cross inferno of interlocking fire-beams. The Sicarans were highly manoeuvrable and crewed by pilots with superior reactions and perception – they seemed to slip across the ruins like eels, despite their bulk. They were slippery in other ways, too – their shallow-sloped armour made scoring a decisive hit harder, not like the brick-square hulks of the Imperial tanks. Sicaran autocannons were ferocious things, twin barrels spitting out shells far faster than the manual gunners could respond in kind, backed up by the silent flares of lascannons.

The effects of all that were ruinous. A Leman Russ on the left – Alchak's, Kaska thought – was hit hard under the turret mechanism, the impact blowing it up and sending armour plates clattering away to the ground. Ernama got another shot away before her hull was slammed by heavy volumes of shell-fire, smacking into the engine intakes and immobilising her. The only remaining squadron vehicle ahead of *Aika 73* slammed straight into an autocannon storm that rocked it almost completely over. Having found its range, the second Sicaran swivelled to finish the Leman Russ off.

'Full stop!' Kaska yelled. 'Lock down that target!'

Grinding to a stop in a firefight was dangerous. Some commanders never did it unless they had to, but Kaska had learned the hard way that the targeting cogitators on a Leman Russ came up with the numbers faster when things were less complicated.

Dresi slammed on the brakes. Jandev calmly lined up the lascannon, and Vosch expertly ratcheted down the main gun.

'Fire!'

Aika 73 shuddered as the battle cannon blew. Kaska jerked away out of instinct as the breech shot back in its sleeve, filling the turret with clots of smoke. Merck got to work instantly, wrenching open the hatch and reloading. Jandev fired steadily in concentrated bursts, piling las-beams onto the target Sicaran. The enemy disappeared behind a wall of black smog, its outline totally obscured.

'Again,' ordered Kaska, peering into the scope and risking another shot while static.

Vosch responded, her second volley adjusted a fraction to bring it in hard against the bolter-mount on the Sicaran's front armour-slope.

It was a good shot, hitting the weak point full-on and driving the armour inward. Jandev followed suit, sending las-fire spitting into the wound even as Dresi got the Leman Russ moving again. By then, the other two active units of the squadron had also found their range, opening up at the beleaguered Sicaran and blasting at its compromised hull. Something in that barrage must have drilled straight through the enemy's armour plates, getting into the engine compartment and rupturing the fuel tanks. The entire heavy tank lifted from the earth for a moment with the force of the detonations, before collapsing back again, smoking and disabled.

That still left the first one. The Sicaran finished off Erna-ma's lead tank with a slamming rain of autocannon shells, stripping its victim's tracks into ribbons and punching holes along its hull length. It then closed on the third wounded Imperial vehicle, swinging its turret round to spray more armour-piercing rounds. Even as it fired again, however, the remaining mobile Leman Russ units trundled into position, each long barrel swinging round hard. The trio fired at once, sending three corkscrewing shells whistling into contact, followed by a flurry of las-bolts that zeroed in on any rupture.

The Sicaran disappeared behind another billowing cloud of black smoke, followed immediately by a muffled crash. Inky plumes gushed out from every orifice, every open barrel, and more bloody flashes went off as further systems ignited under the steady rain of las-bolts.

Both enemy tanks were down, but the danger wasn't over. The supporting infantry, recklessly outpaced by the lead armour, were now lumbering into range, more than a dozen of them, their stolid treads kicking up the dust. Kaska only had fleeting glimpses of the troops themselves as his sights juddered and skipped, but he saw enough to realise that something was very wrong with all of them – they dragged themselves along almost like invalids, limping and staggering, their armour stretched and twisted and glistening. A pale light glimmered around them – their eyes, their blades, their armour-joints – and that alone was enough to send his heart hammering, to make him want to pull back, to order full-reverse and somehow accelerate his way out of the path of those impossible, horrendous things.

Massed infantry had always been the danger. The schedule of the cross-terrain charge had been so tight that the usual mixed-armed support structures weren't ever in place. The instructions from the V Legion had been to send priority comms-bursts whenever enemy squads were encountered, but there wasn't time now, because those monsters were dragging themselves closer, and everyone knew what a Legion warrior would do once it closed in on a wounded tank.

'Forward!' Kaska cried, pushing his terror down, somehow. If he could ram into a couple of them, drag them under the tracks, that might give them a chance to break through.

He never got a chance. Shrieking like loosed falcons, blurred into pale streaks by their extreme speed, three V Legion jetbikes suddenly shot down the channel and wheeled around amid sprays of dirt. The residual smoke clouds were ripped apart by fresh bolter-trails, ploughing up the dust into furrows and cracking down hard into the oncoming legionaries. The Death Guard reeled under the lightning assault, stumbling, dropping back, blown from their feet or cut open. More speeders veered in, opening fire on the attack run before dropping infantry to the ground. The White Scars hit the dirt sprinting, energy weapons igniting while still in the air.

Ernama must have put the call in early. Throne, that had saved the rest of them.

Aika 73 ground its way onwards, Dresi following Kaska's direction, shadowed by the other two active tanks. The first two hulls in the squadron, Ernama's included, had been totally destroyed. A third was immobilised, which amounted to much the same thing. Now the traitors were being engaged by the White Scars all around them, and Kaska caught fractured, up-close glimpses of absurdly brutal combat, a wild mix of totally unrestrained hatreds. He saw a V Legion swordsman hacked virtually in half with a heavy-swiped chainblade, just as one of the twisted horrors was driven to its knees by two glaive-whirling fighters. You couldn't look at that for long, not without wincing, not without instinctively recoiling from the pitch of concentrated violence.

Jandev voxed up from his position. 'Support fire?' he asked, swivelling the barrel of the lascannon round as hard as he could.

Would that do any good? Would he stand a chance of hitting anything in that sprawling, messy, faster-than-thought brawl?

Before Kaska could reply, though, a Legion override came up on the comm, beamed from one of the speeders.

'Squadron to advance. All vehicles keep moving. Squadron to advance.'

That was just what they'd said, back in the briefings. Never stop. Never get bogged down. Keep going. We'll handle the anti-tank squads – just keep the engines hot, get to the portals.

Kaska took a deep breath, his sweaty hands slipping on the control levers. Ernama was gone. Nikkala, her deputy, was in the immobilised unit. That put him in command of what remained of the squadron. A couple of hours in, and they were already down fifty per cent.

'Negative – full forward,' he snapped down the squadron-wide vox-net. 'All gunners, reload and stand by. Drivers, move out, move out.'

They did as they were ordered, pushing around the hand-to-hand fighting and forging onward, revving and gunning through the broken terrain. As Kaska guided them out, trying to ignore the mix of wild battle cries and bestial war-growls that crackled up out of the augur-grilles, he picked up dozens of active signals on the auspex – more squadrons, just like his, surging onward, bulldozing through defensive lines, gradually converging on the objective ahead, all in motion, whatever the toll in lost and smouldering hulls.

Never stop. Never get bogged down. Ernama, Throne ward her, had been entirely right to push it.

'Full speed!' he ordered, astonished, on reflection, to find himself still alive, and determined now to keep it that way – any sense of artificiality had been wrenched away for good. 'Damn it all, keep us going! This is real! This is the real thing!'

THIRTEEN

Imagist
Within sight
Lady of Chaos

Nothing was real now, though, or anything close to it. The entire place had become a dream, Garviel Loken thought. Like a faded image of something physical, an after-echo of something solid. For as long as the Ultimate Wall had held, you could visualise the rough structure of the battle – the hordes at the gates, the defenders inside. Now that great barrier was no longer effective, and the flood had gushed in across the breaks, swamping the city within. Precincts were now wastelands. Some pockets fought on. Others had been forgotten entirely, left isolated as the hab-towers burned elsewhere. You could move from one place – lit up with combat, a roar of noise and movement – and within a heartbeat find yourself in a parallel world of eerie quiet, the dead lying in ranks, the dry wind moaning over open eyes.

He didn't know how much shape the fighting still had, if any. Comms were worse than useless, augurs were no longer reliable. It was down to eyesight and instinct, fogged by the endless surges of battle-hot dust that flowed down the narrow rifts between building-masses. He knew he shouldn't have gone out alone, of course, out of contact with core command. The Sigillite would be angry, if he had any spare capacity. Dorn too, maybe. Another blade would have been welcome at the centre, the environs of the Sanctum and its Palatine hinterland, in that narrow circuit of solid ground that had been shrinking even when he'd left it.

But he had needed to leave. As soon as he had discovered that they were planning to use her, he had needed to go. And he had almost caught up with her, too – almost managed to snatch her back at the last moment, stop it all happening. He'd killed plenty – both those who had thought of themselves as her protectors, as well as those who had clearly wished her harm. All that butchery had taken time, though, and so she had got away from him in the end, running off into the devastation of a city on the edge of annihilation.

Now he hunted through the shadow-realm, alone, exacting a price from those who had come to despoil it. There had been no real choice in the matter, only the promptings of what another age might have called conscience. He had to find her – it was that simple. Some kind of madness had seen fit to let her loose, as if she were a plaything for intellectuals to study. For him, though, she could never be that. She was one of the last threads that still bound him to a past he had never wanted to lose. She would die quickly, if discovered, and that could not be countenanced.

He had killed again, preferring Rubio's old force-blade for the most part, but switching to Aximand's longer sword when it felt right. Both borrowed weapons, with little flickers of their old masters welded to the steel, now his for however long he was granted use of them. He wore his Luna Wolves plate, possibly the only warrior on any battlefield who still did so. On one occasion he caught sight of himself in a smeary pane of broken glass, and was struck by how he looked in the reflection. The ever-present film of black dust hadn't quite erased the bone-pale glimmer underneath, making him seem like more of a phantasm than any of the horrors he slew – out of place, out of time, something to be forgotten and shuddered at.

Now he was heading north, following the half-scent of a semi-hunch. She had gone to ground quickly, disappearing like a wisp of smoke. Those damned fools had released her too close to the front. Or maybe they hadn't expected Mercury Wall to fall so quickly. Either way, it had been reckless.

You could still find information in these places, if you were patient. Some of the enemy would talk, before you killed them. Some of the defenders, where they still lingered, had seen things. Bit by bit, he constructed a picture of something strange happening. Civilians, who by rights should all have been dead, were still clustering together, huddling in flooded basements, clinging on.

Stories had begun to circulate. He encountered two of them over and again. The first told of a sword, a black sword, blessed with the divine will of the Emperor, seeking out the masters of the enemy armies and slaying them, one by one. Vengeance, they whispered, His vengeance, let loose against the unbelievers. If they could have found that sword for themselves, they said, they would surely have joined up with it and become part of the army of the faithful.

And then there was the other story – the lady of bones, the gatherer of the slain. She was immortal, they told him, had transcended death. The enemy could not touch her, and against her words of authority the fallen had no power. The tellers gathered up skulls – not hard to find, those – and cleaned them carefully, placing them in alcoves and on the top of wall sections. Some even escaped their hiding places to follow her into the dark. Others, left behind, remembered how she had spoken to them, and reverently tended her fanes with their flickering candles and empty eye sockets.

He went after rumours of her. He headed in a zigzag route north-east, picking his way through that dreamlike realm of stale destruction. Everything roared in those places, the dull sound of gutted buildings collapsing, of huge vehicles grinding slowly through the remains. Whenever he glimpsed the sky in narrow strips far above, he saw the failing aura of the aegis, and knew that it could not remain intact for long now. He avoided the major concentrations of the enemy, but slew any of them who had allowed themselves to rove freely, the most unwary of them no doubt believing that the war was all but won.

Eventually, he found himself inside the scraped-out residue of an old residential quarter, one that must have been bombed flat a long time ago because the rockcrete was no longer hot. Not much more than the foundations were left, plus an irregular maze of first-stage walls standing erect amid smooth sweeps of masonry dust. Billows of inky fumes swept across the labyrinth, the product of promethium fires still raging. It smelled strongly of death, with bodies piled almost as high as the remaining walls – men, women, children, servitors, all tangled together in an improvised architecture of stiffened flesh.

Loken went watchfully through it, force-blade drawn ready. The further in he went, the further down he was pulled, sinking through sliver-topped ravines and along narrow, twisting paths. The faint light of the underlit clouds faded away, replaced by near-total blackness. He began to sense something, stubbornly persistent under the stink of the dead. A presence, maybe, some kind of ambient soul-heat.

He reached a door – an old metal hatchway, buried at the foot of a solid internal wall, barely visible even to his eyes, rusted and riveted. He paused, listened for a moment, then ran a scan. Nothing. He sliced through the lock with his blade, snagging the edge of it on the corroded metal. Then he was through, climbing into a sour interior, perfectly dark.

His helm's night vision exposed a chamber beyond, one that seemed to stretch off underground for a very long way. Its support columns were square-cut and functional, its floor lost under an ankle-deep layer of black dust. The space must have once been a service area for the levels above, perhaps only ever inhabited by servitors. Now, though, its recesses bore signs of recent habitation – empty ration packs, ammo cases, piled-up bedding rolls. His armour-senses picked up no movement, his scanners no heat signatures.

He pressed on. The route took him down, always down. Before long, he was pacing along the centre of a narrower shaft, one cut between solid rock walls on either side. At the end of the long shaft was a pedestal covered in the detritus of a rockfall.

Only, as he got closer, he saw that the debris was not detritus of any kind – it was a heaped pile of skulls, all of them cleaned and polished, stacked up one on top of the other, all facing outwards. In the pedestal's facing panel was another single skull, set within a semicircular alcove. Below the alcove, words had been carved – crudely, as if by a combat knife: *Imperator Protegit*. And below those words was an image, scratched out in ink, showing a benevolent-looking man on a golden throne.

She had never been much of a painter, but she had always had a knack for the striking sketch, the effective composition, and he instantly recognised the style. That was what she did, one way or another – create images, icons, things that lingered in the mind.

Loken picked up the skull. It felt light in his hand, a hollow sliver of dry bone.

'Oh, Euphrati,' he breathed to himself. 'You would have laughed so hard, if I'd told you, back on the *Spirit*. You'd have told me I was making it up.'

He looked around him. Someone had tried to make the place look the part. Aside from the skulls, there were carvings, streaks of old candle flames against the stone. This was a piece of theatre, a sham play of seriousness, the kind of gothic fancy only a fanatic or a simpleton could have been awed by.

And yet. He looked back the way he'd come, and saw how many more skulls had been gathered on the shaft's walls, all glaring back at him with their sombre eyes. This had been the labour of many hands, over many hours, just when the world was falling to pieces around them. The owners of those hands had been convinced by her, evidently. Many more might be, too, if they continued to be scared enough.

'So why did I come down here, again?' he asked himself, turning back the way he had come. 'To save you from them?' He began to climb again, to clamber up out of the unmoving air and the grim rows of bone faces. He felt a new urgency now, one that was a fraction sharper than the drive that had brought him. 'Or to save them – and us – from you?'

Erebus hadn't really known how he'd feel when he laid eyes on her. Awe, maybe? Intimidation, perhaps – to the extent he was still capable of that? In the end, it was neither – more a sort of intellectual curiosity, as if he'd discovered a brand new breed of scorpion.

'Who are you?' she asked, her surprise giving way to indignation.

A name. Such a simple thing, but then he had taken so many across the years. Most recently, on the comet, he had been the Apostle of the Unspeaking. He still wore the same chain-draped black-and-red armour, still carried the sceptre of iron, though he had removed the eyeless bronze helm and had dispensed with the services of a voice-slave. That had all been subterfuge to keep Magnus' witches from divining his identity, no longer required now.

'I am the Hand of Destiny,' he said, without the faintest blush of shame. He knew that people laughed at the title he'd given himself, but he didn't care. No one else – *no one* – had done as much as he had to set all these things in motion, so he deserved it. He had destroyed the greatest empire the galaxy had ever known. Just him, working away for years, like a voracious insect gnawing at the foundations of a rotten building. He'd suffered for it. He'd been made to suffer. Even the armies he'd helped raise up no longer wanted anything to do with him.

But that was fine. A prophet in his own land, and all that. Redemption would come soon enough, once the truths he'd exposed were revealed to even the stubbornest souls, and so it was only proper that he was around to guide things at the very end, just as he had done at the start.

'The Hand of Destiny,' the woman replied, unamused. 'Well, then.'

She shuffled up in bed, gesturing briefly to her candle, which lit again. Outside, the wind had got up, and the awnings were flapping against their restraints.

'And what do you call yourself, my lady?' he asked.

'You don't know? You broke in here, all that trouble, and you don't know?'

'I couldn't ever divine a name. Not clearly. In any case, I suspect you have more than one. How do you wish to be known?'

'I wish you to leave. You were not invited.'

Erebus smiled ruefully. 'No one invites me anywhere any more. But there are laws of hospitality here, are there not?'

'Laws apply to those who respect them.'

Erebus glanced around the chamber. It was a strange

place – a modest setting, but filled with nice things. Some of the trinkets had the warp-stench of extreme age about them, their crude outlines twisting with the imprints of many souls.

There was power, here. Deep, time-worn power, hidden away carefully but still detectable to one with a good eye. It hadn't been easy to break in, even after months of preparation.

'I meant what I said,' he told her. 'I wish to talk.'

'They leave me alone for so long,' the woman muttered. 'And now the rush.' She shot him a weary look. 'I have nothing left to say to any of you. I played my part in this sorry game a long time ago, and now wish to retire from it altogether.'

'Yes,' he said, turning back to face her, gripping the foot of her bed with his gauntlets. 'That is what I discovered, and so I worked hard to find you, before it's all destroyed. I had to pay my respects, at least – you understand that?'

She looked properly bewildered then. 'Your… respects.'

'Nothing would have been possible. Everything we've done, all we've worked for, it all started with you. The choirs of the Pantheon still sing of it. You are *revered*, my lady, by those who know the truth. I had to make the time to be here, even though the trail was a long one, and I had to follow a gang of blind wretches through some tricky patches, in case I got lost forever in the mazes. But they're off on their own now, and now I've ended up where I wanted to be all along – with the architect. The mother of it all.'

'Listen, I do not know what portents you've been studying, but something has gone badly wrong with them.'

'No, I am never wrong. You are the architect. The scatterer. The instrument of the gods themselves.'

At that, she finally began to lose her composure. 'Gods! This again. What could you possibly know of gods? Look at you! You dress like some mind-touched devil-boy kicked out of the village for poisoning the well. Something has misled

you, and I do not care what that is. I only care that you leave
now, before I become truly angry.'

Erebus found himself enjoying this. She was as impressive as
he'd hoped she'd be. She worked hard to hide it, sure, but now
he could feel her power bubbling up from under the surface.
It was like nothing he'd encountered before – not an overt,
flashy power, but a subtle one, like an aroma.

'Maybe you don't even know it yourself,' he pressed on. 'Maybe
you believed that you acted alone, for reasons that seemed pure
to you. They relish it, when that happens. But it was them, all
the same. You crippled the enemy before He'd even properly
got started. Ha! When the Warmaster kills Him in turn, it will
be your name on the lips of the faithful.'

She got up. She gestured again, and the room lit fully. She
was tall – almost as tall as he was – and moved like a dancer,
imperiously.

'You have some cheap art about you, devil-boy,' she said,
her voice low and dangerous. 'You might scare a child, on a
good day, but you neither scare nor impress me. Leave now,
and never return.'

He held his ground. 'You were there at the start. You have
the power to throw primarchs across both time and space.
Wittingly, or otherwise, it doesn't much matter. Did you really
think that could just be ignored, now, only days away from
the birth of our new order? I needed to find out what you
meant by it. What you hoped to achieve.'

He spoke fast, aware of the danger. She'd stopped advancing towards him, perhaps intrigued, or maybe just appalled,
and he made use of that.

'Loose ends,' he went on. 'I seek them out, interrogate them.
Do you stand by your actions? Do you intend to follow them
through? That could open new doors. It could make you a
power we might do business with.'

Now there was no mistaking it – she was horrified – but this was the moment.

'Because I created Horus, see, raised him up, made him Lord of Chaos,' he said, delivering the offer, just as he had done on Davin. 'Think on it. I could do the same for you.'

Archeta broke from the cover of the crater's edge, just for a second, and unleashed his bolter. At the precise same moment, twenty-nine of his warriors did the same, all emerging from their various shelters and opening up.

Two hundred metres ahead, the remains of the wall sheltering the Blood Angels' defensive position blew up from the mass-reactive assault, pulverising into whirling shards of brick and rockcrete. A brace of grenades sailed through the night to complete the job, exploding on impact and blasting apart what remained. A scatter of fire shot back, sporadic now, but the old hab-block the Blood Angels were sheltering in had been rendered completely unstable. Archeta gave the command, and more of his troops filtered up through the ruins on either side, dragging heavier weapons with them. As the beleaguered Blood Angels fell back, those guns were brought to bear, levelling deep troughs between the few standing sections and sending debris-chunks splattering through the empty window frames.

This was how it had been for hours, now. The enemy was still withdrawing steadily, still overwhelmed by the sheer numbers coming at them, but the terrain slowed everything down for everybody. It was all devastated, all tumbling and crashing inward and sending up thick clouds of toxic ash and dust. The transit arteries were blocked. After every artillery strike it took time to plough through the smouldering remains. At every turn, in that jungle of dilapidation, you were liable to face an ambush, counter-push or suicide strike. Both the Imperial Fists and the Blood Angels were lethally good at that kind of fighting, and they knew every inch of the territory they were ceding. They knew where to leave the fragmentation charges, the anti-personnel mines, the booby-trapped hatches that would send an advancing squad plummeting down into the waterlogged vaults below.

Still, it was a game that the Sons of Horus could play, too. Archeta had fought his way through a thousand cityscapes across both the Crusade and the Rebellion, and success always followed the same pattern: keep pressing, keep pushing, keep the infantry and armour together, watch your flanks and don't get careless. Fast-moving warfare was exhilarating in its own way, but this heavy attrition, this slow grind of strangulation, it had its own attractions.

He dropped back into cover as returning bolt-shells whined overhead. Twenty metres off, his second and third squads were reloading and preparing to advance. His flickering tactical display told him the fourth, sixth and seventh were making good progress through the tangle of scrap to the north, and his lieutenant's supporting squadrons of Spartans would imminently crunch their way into range to the south, restoring the punch they needed to finish this block off.

'*Captain*,' came a priority signal across his helm's secure feed.

It was Beruddin, captain of the Fifth Company. Archeta signalled for his own squad to keep moving, then slid further down into the lee of the muddy crater-lip.

'Captain,' he replied. 'How goes it?'

'*Slow. Bloody. Satisfying.*'

Archeta smiled. Beruddin was a warrior after his own heart. 'You'll be with us, then?'

Their two companies were due to rendezvous thirty kilometres further in, just in sight of the already shelled Field of Winged Victory, the muster-point for the combined push into the Palatine.

'*Negative. Not unless you pull back now.*'

He didn't like the sound of that. 'My orders are—'

'*Sigismund, brother. Sigismund. He's been sighted, Mercury section. They lost a whole battalion with Reaver support down there, and it's got Legion command spitting bile. There's some life in this band of wastrels yet.*'

Sigismund. One of the mere handful of names that could be spoken of with unfeigned respect across any Legion, in any faction. It had been rumoured by some that his powers were waning, that he'd lost his nerve under the suffocating control of his primarch. No one wanted that to be true. You wanted to kill a beast at the apex of its power, just to show yourself what you could do. Such things mattered. They were the things that enabled a commander to rise through the ranks, to control the loyalty of the line troops, to alter the balance of power within a Legion.

'I'm within sight of the muster,' Archeta said, though without conviction. His mind was already racing. Baraxa, who had pushed ahead hard, might reach Palatine ahead of him. 'I still need to get to—'

'*Listen. Ezekyle is already inside the Ultimate Wall. They say he's clawing his way across territory faster than anything that's ever lived. He wants the kill. He can get it. But we're closer, my brother. We're much closer, and we deserve it more, don't you think?*'

Why wasn't this coming from the primarch? Hells, where *was* he? Why were they squabbling over prizes like gangers, when they should have been marching united in the shadow of his fur-lined cloak?

Still, Beruddin made a point. They were closer. And they had been bleeding for this battle, all while the First Captain had still been licking his wounds from the Saturnine debacle.

'*It's important. That he doesn't do it. You see that? They're already calling him Legion Master. Some openly – the blasphemy of it. So it can't be him – someone has to stand up.*'

That was all true. And it was a better reason to change course now. Archeta made some calculations, barely even hearing the crashes of gunfire around him. As he did so, his gaze alighted on the scabbard of his beloved blade, the one that whispered to him in the quiet moments. It had been a while since he'd unsheathed it. He'd been waiting for an occasion worthy of it, almost despairing of one coming.

'You have a loc-reading?' he asked.

Laughter at the end of the feed. *'Don't need one! He's the only resistance between here and the Palatine. Everyone's after him – to join him, or to take him down. Come, brother. We need to be there.'*

Archeta looked up. His tac-reading showed that his Spartans were almost in position. The Blood Angels were in full retreat now, leaving the bodies of their slain behind them. Even so, this front would take hours, maybe days, to reduce. It would be hard, thankless work, all of it in the shadow of the Great Potential Kill.

And when you put it like that, there was really no choice to be made at all.

'My sincere thanks, brother,' he said, stowing his bolter and readying to give the command. 'I'll give the order as soon as we're done here. We'll hunt him together.'

'For the honour of the Warmaster!'

Archeta smiled. 'Aye, that's right,' he said dryly. 'For the honour of Horus.'

FOURTEEN

Fragile
Not just yet
Remembrance

'For his honour!' cried Jangsai fervently. 'For the honour of the Khagan!'

The Xiphon was a beautiful, beautiful thing – a machine so perfectly crafted in the image of the V Legion's mode of warfare that it might have been born in the vaults of Quan Zhou itself. It was slippery in the air, jumpy as a colt, always liable to flip over or slide into trouble, but that was the very appeal of it. You had to learn how to handle that, to master its lightness and its fragility, and only then did it become truly deadly, a stiletto in a world of broadswords.

So many Legions had abandoned them entirely during the Crusade, preferring the more brutal charms of heavier atmospheric fighters, but even after the Mechanicum had ceased sponsoring new production, the White Scars had hung on to as many as they could. The great mass of those remaining in service had been destroyed in the first few weeks of the war, despite reaping a toll far in excess of their numbers. All those

remaining had been held back for this single exercise, and at
that moment Jangsai could only be thankful that they had.

His every nerve tingled, his every sense was alive. His
squadron screamed along, ten strong, in tight formation,
cutting bright white contrails through the filth of the atmosphere. When at the controls of this brilliant, temperamental
machine, there was no room left for anything but pure concentration. Let your mind drift for just a second, and you would
find yourself flying wildly out of control and smashing into
the onrushing horizon.

'Targets marked,' he announced, thumbing attack runes to
his pilots. 'Kill with joy, my brothers.'

They hurtled down between two horizons. The lower one
was natural, black as coal and scarred by months of combat.
The upper one was the enormous orbital disc, blotting out
what remained of the natural sunlight, a false terrain of
streaming fire that churned and rumbled, stretching as far
as could be seen in all directions. Being so close to it had
an exhilaration all of its own, racing between such vast solid
masses, making the narrow airspace between them into a fren-
zied killing zone.

Everything swung and swerved around him, tilting wildly as
the axes were hurled across one another. Enormous lances of
orbital las-batteries speared and flashed, some punching clean
through the Skye plate's outer armour and fizzing down, their
killing potential drained, to the terrain below. Debris splattered and pinged about them, crashing into unwary tanks,
fighters and gunships, igniting spontaneously before exploding
into perilous bursts of chaff.

The four and a half thousand vertical kilometres of airspace
were terrifying and marvellous, a bracketed, congested zone of
high-velocity combat. The orbital plate still absorbed the vast
majority of the void-launched las-fire, so the enemy had to

bring its gunships close to ground level to have a crack at the armour columns. That was already difficult, due to the turbulence the Skye plate brought with it, but not impossible, and so every remaining V Legion airborne asset had been loosed too, poised tight under the platform's fire-shadow and ready to take on the oncoming shoals of Death Guard flyers.

As a rule, the enemy preferred the larger, more cumbersome units – most of them gunships – perfectly adapted to unload air-to-ground fire. That made them dangerous for the tank crews, but vulnerable to the faster-moving true fighter squadrons. The bulk of the White Scars gunships had been pressed into service ferrying rapid-response infantry to keep the attack runs cleared, and so the task of securing the airspace had fallen to the Xiphon formations, who were thinly spread, but able to sweep across the battlezone at blistering pace.

Jangsai locked on to a formation of seven Death Guard Storm Eagles, skidding along at low altitude and gearing up to strafe a unit of Imperial Hellhammers. The gunships were almost in position to fire, but went unwarily – the colossal interference from the Skye's progress made augurs virtually useless, and you could use the firestorm above you just as you used the glare of the sun, staying high against it until the very last moment before spinning into kill range.

The ten Xiphons suddenly dropped, plummeting nose first and racing hard into contact. Missiles streaked out from the first four launchers, spinning away before smacking into the gunships and blasting two of them clean out of the air. Before the rest could react, the lascannons spat a furious volume of bolts in sharp lines, searing off like tracer shells and cracking across the gunships' upper armour. Three more gunships were knocked out before the Xiphons had to pull up again. By then, the rest of the enemy aircraft were scattering, all thoughts of ground assault replaced by a frantic run for cover.

'*Hai Chogoris!*' Jangsai whooped, doling out marker runes for the survivors over the squadron comm-net before swinging tightly round to finish them off.

The Xiphons split into hunting pairs. Jangsai dropped in behind a jinking Storm Eagle, its turbines kicking out huge clouds of smoke from an earlier hit, and locked on with all four of his inline las-cannons.

'For Catullus,' he breathed as he depressed the fire-runes, watching with savage satisfaction as the las bolts drilled home again and again. The Storm Eagle blew apart, its airframe cracking into pieces that tumbled over and over before splaying down to earth.

All ten fighters made it out of the engagement, all seven targets were neutralised. From far below, the lead Hellhammer let off a flare, which Jangsai interpreted as a gesture of gratitude.

'Ha!' he laughed out loud, genuinely pleased. 'Now for the next one.'

After that, it got harder. The flurry of initial fighter-strikes took the Death Guard by surprise, but despite their preference for ground combat they were no fools. The heavier gunships maintained ground attack runs while the more manoeuvrable units pulled up higher, ready to engage their attackers.

More dogfights followed in quick succession, the interceptors streaking in hard, aiming to knock out the target quickly and at range before heavier armaments could be brought to bear. A Storm Eagle could take a bucketload of punishment before breaking up, whereas a Xiphon might be crippled by a single clean shot. Thus Jangsai's squadron began to winnow down – Kojar's flyer blasted into shrapnel by the heavy bolters on a Thunderhawk, Xoi-Men's taking hits from a Stormbird that threw it up into the orbital plate's firezone, Hiban's struck by a machine-spirit-guided missile that ripped the right-hand wing right off, sending him corkscrewing out of control before smashing apart against the derelict flank of an empty hab-block.

But the exuberance was never dented. The fighters blasted more tonnage out of the air, one stolid hunk at a time, clearing the skies above the always-moving armour below them. Their momentum was unstoppable, the pace unflagging. Jangsai streaked in to rake a slow-moving Thunderhawk, smashing every system along its flank before his brothers sent las-bolts pounding into its cockpit. He outpaced a rare Corsair bomber, tormenting it with a missile strike before sweeping under it and spearing las-lines through its bomb-chamber and setting them all off.

Bit by bit, moment by moment, the tanks drew ever closer to their objective. The towers of the Lion's Gate space port grew nearer, swelling up to blot out the last few scraps of open sky ahead. Green lightning-shards scampered across the blackened earth, snagging against the inferno's edge kindled by the Skye plate, all of it polluted by the smoke-trails pumped out by the fortress' corrupted heart. The artificial night became darker and thicker, with every scope silting up and every turbine choking on ash. The Xiphons activated their powerful lumens, giving up secrecy for a sliver of extra visual clarity.

Somehow, in all that flying muck, Jangsai's wingman, Selik, spied an incoming formation of Stormbirds – three of them, burning fast through a churning bank of smog, seeking out targets on the ground. Those craft were big enough to be carrying infantry squads, and so were prime targets for neutralisation.

'Down at them!' Jangsai ordered immediately, yanking the control columns and banking steeply.

The seven remaining Xiphons swept earthwards, powerful thrusters booming as their wing tips tilted in parallel. They dropped like falcons, almost vertical for the dive, before the

lascannons erupted into their four-pronged assault. The
Stormbirds instantly broke formation, swinging away from the
incoming barrage with their own bolters cracking out return fire.

Jangsai pounced after the lead aircraft, driving hard to get
a missile lock. His reticules jumped and slewed, struggling to
clamp on to the wheeling target. A warning bleep sounded
in the cockpit, but he ignored it, knowing he was only micro-
seconds away.

But then bolt-shells crunched through his tail fin, knocking
the structure from its mount and blowing the Xiphon's balance
out of kilter. The world spun crazily, over and over, as Jangsai
fought to regain control. He hadn't even seen where the projectiles had come from – one of the other Stormbirds, maybe, or
even launched from the ground. It didn't much matter, though,
as the single strike had made his fighter unflyable.

He had a sickening view of the terrain rushing up to meet
him, the G-forces nearly blinding him entirely, before he managed to somehow swing the interceptor down into a forward
skim, only metres from the ground. The whole thing shuddered now, as unstable as a thrown discus. Jangsai saw the
space port towering over him directly ahead, its outworks
rising in messy terraces, all crowned with the flicker of gunfire and the spider's webs of ordnance striking. He gauged
whether he might be able to make it all the way – ram the
interceptor into one of the parapets and take out a defence
battery or two – when another hammer blow of bolter fire
blasted him lower, punching through his starboard wing and
ripping its meagre armour free. The Xiphon plunged earthwards, still rocketing along but now entirely uncontrollable.

Jangsai hit the eject controls, and the cockpit cover blew free.
He was kicked out next, thrown up into a vortex of streaming
fire-flecks. The pilot-seat's thrusters jerked into life, boosting him
clear of the impact site, where his Xiphon smashed to earth in a

furrow of ploughed-up dirt and rubble. More bolt-shells whistled past, maybe aimed at him, maybe just flying thickly from the dogfight, but then the ejector-unit sent him plummeting. Jang-sai pushed himself free before the chair itself smacked to the ground, landing in a heavy crouch with his blade already drawn.

The tormented sky roared overhead, furnace-bright and racing with interlocking contrails. Ahead of him were the outworks, ink-black, a rising terrain of scaffolds and bulwarks. The ground beneath his feet shook incessantly, rocked by the massed tracks scoring it for kilometres around. Already the gloom beyond the first line of ruins was pierced with pairs of pale green lenses, lumbering up out of the drifting murk with their corrupted blades glimmering.

Jangsai activated the disruptor on Ajak's blade, and the flaring energy field was like a pure white star against the smoke-screens of churning darkness.

'Come, then, you turgid filth,' he snarled, grinning under his helm and preparing to burst into motion. 'Let us see how you keep up with *this*.'

The full muster alert had annoyed him. Crosius had hoped for hours more exploration down in the basements – he'd just had another delivery of twenty more conscious subjects – but you couldn't ignore a priority-one summons. He'd looked at the tiny creature perched on the shelf above him, who was gnawing on a tufty bit of scalp-skin and dribbling adorably, and sighed.

'Come with me, then,' he said, and the creature hopped down to perch on his shoulder guard. It nuzzled into the cleft between pauldron-rim and breastplate, a gap that had widened as Crosius' body had swollen. 'Duty calls.'

He limped back through the doors, picking up his old chainblade as he went. Its adamantium rim was rust-addled and rotting, but something interesting was oozing from the outtakes now – he guessed it would be poisonous. Alarms were going off everywhere within the creaking space port, some of them part of the old Imperial network, some of them blaring out of newer Legion warning stations. The racket was irritating, and it didn't seem to make anyone hurry – legionaries clumped and clanged their way towards their positions as if half-asleep, barely speaking to one another.

The daemons were a different matter. Those flickering, realm-phasing monsters were rollicking along with real excitement, slobbering and snickering, occasionally losing their grip on the physical environment and slipping through the floor entirely. They looked almost drunk, or drugged, as if just being there – in such proximity to the Anathema and His continued wards against them – turned them into imbeciles. By way of compensation for that, the slow transformation of the space port's innards had ramped up greatly, with the old plain metal walls buckling into new and organic forms, leaking chems and spilling out with dark-edged creepers. The air around them all felt as thick as vomit, and visibility was down to a few dozen metres in the deeper pits.

He chuckled with enjoyment, and found himself cultivating the hope that, when the fighting was done, the Legion would never leave this place. Let Horus have the Palace he so craved to destroy – this intriguing tower of decay would be enough for them. They could turn it into an incubator, the greatest there had ever been, so ripe with power and virulence that the galaxy itself would be irredeemably infected.

First, though, they had to defend it. He wheezed through his rebreather as he climbed up the long stairs, gripping the rails to haul himself along. He emerged into a long hall, one that ran for hundreds of metres up towards the great gates at the western end of the ground-level galleries. A vast mass

of bodies was in motion, all of them stamping and lurching their way towards the ramparts – Unbroken marching in
squads, ragged bands of cultists dragged from the wastelands,
the candle-flicker daemons shuddering in and out of vision.
The floor shook under all that, its foundations booming as the
wall guns opened fire. The mobilisation might have been pre-
mature, done without sufficient preparation or foresight, but
at least it was underway, ratcheting up through the rusty gears
towards battle strength.

Eventually he emerged onto the south-western-facing parapets, three hundred metres up from the level of the outworks
and surrounded by heavy gun emplacements and defence
towers. More than half of those emplacements were out of
action, shattered by Perturabo on the way in. A few had been
reconditioned, and other cannons had been airlifted in from
the Legion's own supplies, but the impression was still one
of decrepitude.

Crosius adjusted the snarled-up controls on his helm visor,
and felt the mechanism clunk. For a moment, all he could see
was a fog of interference, before the sluggish machine-spirit
finally remembered its business and targeting lines swept over
a sharpening tactical vista.

Due west, the sky was on fire, and the source of it was
getting closer all the time, surrounded by the flash and dart
of duelling atmospheric squadrons. Below that oncoming
thunderhead, as wide as the horizon itself, the conquered
territories leading down to Colossi were now obscured by
a rolling carpet of dust – not the lazy drifts dissipating out
from sites of previous destruction, but the churned-up trails
of vehicles moving, propelled at reckless speed, swarming
through the remains of the old cityscape like a pack of rats.

Crosius was no master stratego, but the numbers looked…
troubling. The enemy had not launched a counter-attack of

such size for months, certainly not since their blood-soaked setbacks across the Anterior war-front. This, though, was concentrated. It looked determined, and it was moving fast.

He remembered Typhus' words to him, then. *You will know.*

So maybe he should summon him back. Maybe this was the eventuality he'd been concerned about. Crosius picked up the fat daemon, stroked one of its chins to make it giggle, and pondered. The tiny monster didn't seem concerned. It pointed at the advancing armour, then twisted around and farted at them.

Crosius laughed, and patted its spines. 'Commendable,' he murmured. 'And no more than they deserve.'

That reassured him. He put the creature back into the crook in his armour, and fumbled for the control switch on his weapon. Far below, the clouds of dust billowed closer.

'Race up as flashily as you like,' he said, clambering up the steps towards the rampart's edge. All around him, Legion warriors were cranking the gun barrels lower, hauling up gurneys of ammunition, powering the heavy engines that would swing the turntables around. The air crackled with daemon-outlines, the rockcrete flags trembled from the massed march of cloven boots.

'We will make you suffer for it.'

Naranbaatar leapt from the open hatch of the Thunderhawk. For a second, he was plummeting, surrounded by nothing but flame and air, before he smashed to the dirt and got to work.

To his right was the carcass of a downed troop-lander, an enormous tube of darkened metal more than a hundred metres high and long. To his left was a choked-up quagmire of twisted rebar and masonry sections, a piled-up nightmare of long-collapsed structures, all but impassable even for infantry. The avenue ahead, cleared just hours ago by V Legion

engineering units, was the only route in this attack-sector, and
already the assault was slowing down.

All the routes had been carefully planned. Weeks of research,
backed up by perilous scout missions, had given them a network of paths to the enemy. Three battlefronts had been
delineated – Gold, Ebony and Amber. The first was commanded
by Ganzorig, and had been tasked with driving an arrowhead
across the northern sections of the space port approaches.
Qin Fai led Ebony, hacking its way along the southern flank.
The Khagan himself led Amber, taking the most direct vector,
straight at the enemy's gunlines.

Within those various battlefronts were the hundreds of
cleared attack-runs, stripped of mines and flaywire and
trenches so that the tanks could rumble down them unim-
peded. For the offensive to hit its mark, to strike the walls
with necessary power and numbers to drive wounds into the
interior, more than eighty per cent of those runs had to be
completed on time. That target was punishingly hard, made
all the more so by the degradation of every piece of equipment the Legion still possessed. To be halted in the open was
death, and so the tanks had to be kept moving at all costs.

Naranbaatar swung his staff around him, gathering up the
kinetic force of the storm. The skull tip blazed with a pure
silver light, flooding out across the wind-blasted terrain.

'Ta makaj!' he cried, and thrust both arms ahead of him.

Twin arcs of raw fulguration streaked out, igniting the charged
air around them. His target, an enemy Spartan war machine
barrelling down the narrow channel, was hurled from its axis
and sent tumbling back into the path of a Rhino transport
behind. That snarled up the advance from the Death Guard
column beyond – ten tracked units, flanked by infantry –
allowing the Imperial forces at Naranbaatar's back – twelve
main battle tanks, plus three jetbikes strafing down the side

channels – to power onwards. Naranbaatar kept up the barrage, twisting on his heel to hurl more weather-magic into the
enemy, shattering gun barrels and blowing apart tracks. Once
the Terran Armoured's guns came into range, true carnage was
unleashed, with both traitor armour and foot-soldiers pulverised by a slamming cascade of well-aimed ordnance.

But then the air shuddered, popping like a bubble-skin, and
the earth erupted. A mud-streaked dome exploded out from
ground level, thrust apart by the emerging outline of something
monstrous. It was huge, taller and broader than the burning
skeleton of the Spartan. Its flabby, translucent body slopped
out of its birth-crater, steaming and weeping, before long, bony
fingers uncoiled from a dozen arms, and a white-eyed face
reared up from what passed as a hollow-chested torso, all of
it surrounded in bursts and smears of sulphurous gas.

'Withdraw!' Naranbaatar commanded the lead Leman Russ,
which was now gunning hard at the creature and engaging
with its lascannon.

It was too late. With a startling lurch of speed, the daemon-
form surged straight at the tank, latching on with its many
glimmering arms. It swung the hull around, lifting it up and
slamming it hard into the hull of the stricken lander. The
unit exploded as it impacted, showering the monster with
burning metal that ignited into green-tinged flames wherever
the gas-clots gusted.

The other Imperial units had ground to a halt or were revers-
ing. If they had been unaccompanied they would have been
frantically targeting the thing with their main cannons, but
Naranbaatar himself was by then sprinting hard into contact
and the engagement protocols were strict – they would not
risk hitting him. White Scars jetbikes streaked ahead to tie up
the surviving enemy ground troops, giving the Stormseer free
rein to take on the true threat.

The yaksha lashed out at him, surrounding them both with noxious plumes, grappling to drag him into its emaciated embrace. Naranbaatar used his staff as a spear now, wreathing it in crackling lances of storm-power. He thrust down, once, twice, severing unnatural sinews and cracking unreal bone. The creature tried to smother him, to wrap its watery limbs across him and squeeze his armour into cracking, but its movements were stilted, unaccustomed yet to the world of the senses and still part immersed in the dream beyond. It managed to extend an obscenely long tongue around Naranbaatar's neck, whipping it tight and tensing to haul him in, but the move had already been foreseen – the Stormseer slashed his staff sharply, severing the muscle completely, before spinning briskly to gain momentum for the killing blow. The snarling shaft plunged deep into the creature's throat, buried deep into the heaving sacs of glassy flesh, before Naranbaatar released its full power.

The daemon blanched, bulged, then exploded, shredded into gobbets of flying fat and gristle that slapped messily across every exposed surface for thirty metres. Naranbaatar himself remained braced at the very centre, head down and shoulders set, the remnants of the kill cooking into black slurry on his crackling stave.

Only once the last slops had landed, and the last echoes of its eldritch screams had died away, did he extinguish the flames, drop to one knee, draw in a deep breath and attempt to recover his equilibrium.

It had not been the strongest of its kind, not by a long way, but every step the army took, every kilometre of ground they covered, the creatures grew more numerous and more potent. Once they were at the gates themselves, down into the lightless shafts and the mouldering undercrofts, the daemons would be formidable indeed.

The Imperial tanks started moving again, their secondary

armaments ratcheting up to support the Legion jetbikes. Naran-baatar needed to call up the air support and take flight towards the next potential choke point. Every surviving zadyin arga in the Legion was doing the same, being hoisted from crisis to crisis, gouging and smiting and carving up the warp-gorged creatures that seemed to creep out of every shadow and crater's edge. It would all begin to tell, soon. Their limbs would become heavier, their mastery of the art less sure. Every exercise of power exacted a price, and this one could only rise.

As he got back to his feet, Naranbaatar found himself thinking of Yesugei again. None of the V had ever been as powerful as he; few psykers of any Legion had. If he had been with them still, if *he* had been commanding the conclaves of the gifted, would that have made the difference? Would they already be within the walls by now, following his bright star down into the depths with confidence?

It was still hard to believe that he was gone. His had always been the great guiding presence, the voice of calm and surety that had spoken to them from the start. Those who remained did not approach the same degree of patient command, and Naranbaatar, for all the long decades of service and deep combat experience, would never have disputed it.

We would have followed you cheerfully, my elder brother, he mused to himself. *You would have made the night a little less dark for us.*

But then he was stirred by the whine of a jetbike approaching. The machine juddered to a halt and the rider dismounted – a sergeant in dirt-and-blood-covered armour, all sigils of his brotherhood totally obscured, but with the height and gait of a newblood rather than a Chogorian.

'Do you require assistance, zadyin arga?' he asked, bowing low. 'Is there anything I can do for you?'

In the background, the noises of combat were still ongoing.

Troops were still fighting, the tanks were rolling again, and amid all of that, with the danger very much live, this sergeant had thought it important to ensure that his Stormseer was attended to.

They look to me as I once looked to him, Naranbaatar thought. *And they can have no memory of the time before, when all these things were begun, when we were children too.*

'You fight superbly, *darga,*' he said, returning the bow. 'Please continue it – I shall be fine.'

Naranbaatar moved off then, letting the sergeant remount and get back to the task at hand. Intermittent signals were blinking on his helm display – the Thunderhawk was coming around sharply, angling under fire, and would soon be making its descent. The next battle would then follow, and then the next, and then the next.

'Because we cannot match those who came before us,' he said out loud, clambering up to the landing site, repeating the mantra he had spoken ever since Catullus in the hope that he would one day truly believe it. 'Only go as far as memory and vengeance permit.'

FIFTEEN

The game
The cards
The Nails

He should never have got so far.

Valdor began to think ahead to a difficult possibility – a future in which, for the first time ever, he did not capture his quarry. If Fo somehow got away amid all the confusion, then the consequences did not bear thinking about. If he were taken alive by the enemy, then that was even worse. So he had to be found.

And yet the city was on the edge of capture. The enemy advance was now visible in all directions, a ring of fire that was steadily contracting, gnawing away at the softening defences and pushing ever closer to the core. Those battlefronts were already contested by armies of millions. As the hard hours passed, those millions would become tens of millions, further unbalancing an already one-sided slaughter. Time was running out.

Valdor crouched down for a moment, his long cloak draping over his knee. He let the killing edge of his spear dip a little, angling down into the darkness, glistering with a faint gold-silver light. Blood seemed to burn away from it, once the killing was done, leaving it just as pristine as ever. Amid all the squalor of the defeat, that one weapon remained pure, as hateful and stark as it had ever been.

He stared at the ground ahead of him. A thousand bootfalls had stirred the dust, blotting one another out and making the tracks unreadable. But then he wasn't there to read trails in the ash. He was there, at an intersection of possible futures, to take a moment, to place himself in the place of the hunted, to imagine the path he must have taken.

Valdor closed his eyes, and rehearsed what he knew. He had penetrated the deceptions of the murders, the false leads running off into already conquered urban zones, the dismal procession of broken equipment and misleading ciphers. The man he hunted was good at this, maybe as good as any he had ever gone after, but the pool of locations was shrinking fast now and no living soul knew the ways of the Palace better than he did. This was his territory, the one he had scouted out and marked over decades, all the while preparing for just such an eventuality. In the brief stillness, he gauged probabilities, considered what the man required for his work, where he could get it, what path he must have taken towards it to keep himself hidden and alive.

The spear trembled a little in his grip. He opened his eyes, now certain of the route ahead. He moved out, breaking from the shadow, out along the high-strung viaducts over the chasms of roiling fire. He ran swiftly, his heavy tread making little impression on the wind-blown filth around him. His armour was silent, a masterpiece of technomancy even by the standards of his order – save for the glittering spear, he was almost invisible in the murk, all that finery concealed by the palls of ash and grime smeared over every surface.

These were perilous places now, some abandoned ahead of the enemy onslaught, some already infiltrated by forward units. Dislocated body parts – fingers, arms, legs – were heaped up and protruding from the sea of rubbish, pale grey and black, the dead skin as hard as rockcrete and becoming brittle in the scouring winds. The currents shrieked and moaned around every corner, just on the edge of howling intelligible words, but prevented, just, by the frail wards still rattling in place.

Valdor ghosted across the high places, his cloak rippling in the acrid smoke, before dropping down steeply through the empty carcass of a storage silo, plummeting down shafts that had once carried industrial elevators and were now pits into pure blackness. He broke out near ground level, tearing along a parapet filled with silenced artillery pieces, their crews scattered face up, sightless eyes open to the heavens, outstretched hands locked in a rictus of supplication. He slipped through a long gallery of burned-out armour, all twisted barrels and broken tracks, overhung with a static fog of promethium vapour. Mist banks rose up on all sides around him, thick and curdling, smelling of chems, munitions and the dead.

He soon laid eyes on the enemy again – warriors of Lorgar's Legion, advancing through the unnatural dusk with raw confidence, surrounded by the spectral flicker of half-instantiated daemonkind. Their armour was carved with words of power, decorated with the bones and the flesh of those they had slain, their helms deformed into outstretched maws, or serpent's mouths, or the leer of some Neverborn warp prince. Their cantrips stank and pulsed around them, making the natural air recoil and mist shred itself into appalled ribbons.

They were engorged with their veil-drawn power, sick on it, their blades running with new-cut fat and their belts hung with severed scalps. For all that, they were still warriors, and they detected Valdor's presence soon enough. Nine curved blades flickered into guard, nine genhanced bodies made ready to take him down.

He raced straight into the heart of them, lashing out with his spear, slicing clean through corrupted ceramite. The combined

blades danced, snickering in and out of one another's path as
if in some rehearsed ritual of dance-murder, all with the dull
gold of the lone Custodian at its centre. A poisoned gladius
nearly caught his neck. A fanged axe-edge nearly plunged
into his chest. Long talons nearly pulled him down, ripe to
be trodden into the mire under the choreographed stamp of
bronze-chased boots.

But not quite. They were always just a semi-second too
slow, a fraction too predictable. The gap between the fighters
was small, but it remained unbridgeable. His spear slammed
and cut, parried and blocked, an eye-blink ahead of the lesser
blades, a sliver firmer and more lethal in its trajectory, until
black blood was thrown up around it in thick flurries and
the lens-fire in the Word Bearers' helms died out, one by one.

Afterwards, Valdor withdrew, breathing heavily, taking a
moment to absorb the visions he had been gifted with each kill.
Lorgar's scions were little different to the true daemons in what
they gave him – brief visions of eternal torment, wrapped up in
archaic religious ciphers and a kind of perpetually forced ecstasy.
They were steeped in some of the purest, deepest strands of
Chaos, wilfully dredging up the essence of its mutating, despoil-
ing genius and turning it, through elaborate tortures, into a way
of war. To fight them was to be reminded, more acutely than
with most others, of the consequences of defeat.

But he could not linger. He pushed on again, clearing his mind.
He ran harder into the maw of the advancing enemy forces,
fighting his way through the scattered warbands. None caught
him. Some of them barely knew he was there before he slew
them. That couldn't last – when the main formations of Traitor
Legions reached these regions then even he would have to withdraw – but for now the ragged interlopers scarcely slowed him.

He plunged below ground level, following his memory of
all the installations east of the Clanium District. He slipped

through narrow gaps blocked up by fallen arches. He slipped down deeper wells, on rickety steel clamber-frames, on spiral stairs, until it felt like he was almost back into the Dungeon stratum again, suffocated deep under the layers and layers of old construction and forgetfulness.

He finally entered the target laboratorium and witnessed for himself the destruction. The walls were cracked, the floors strewn with rubbish, the long tables covered in broken instruments. He walked through it all, and saw that some stations had been used very recently – the machine-spirits on the auspex devices were still functioning.

He paused at a station, brought the tip of his spear up, holding it laterally over the worktop. He closed his eyes, and listened to the resonances in the airspace.

Fo had been here. But he had not been alone. Valdor concentrated harder, letting his armour systems process every morsel of pheromone left in the stuffy atmosphere, letting his mind settle on the environment and its unfolding story.

His eyes snapped open. He moved further back, along the workbenches and into the deeper darkness. He saw blood on the far wall, and a broken door, and some fragments of an Imperial officer's uniform hanging below long gouge marks on the bare walls. Those marks were familiar, both in scale and style – a gauntlet-mounted claw, slashed wildly at a fast-moving target.

Night Lords.

He started to run.

They had to put down eventually. As much as John wanted to keep going, there was a hard limit on their progress. No one else – as far as any of them had admitted, anyway – could fly the lighter. He had been exhausted before they had taken off. It had to stop.

Keeping going, though, had felt like the easier option for most of the journey. It had meant that the memories could be pushed out, deferred in favour of keeping their little craft in the air. As soon as he set it back to earth, on top of a flat mesa of blasted scrub and blown weeds, he knew it would all come back.

The turbines wound down. The hold locks snapped open, the environment controls turned off. John deactivated the main power lines with a soft click, and then they were done, back out into the fresh air, their scant protection taken away again for the time being.

It was a hot night. Or a hot day – no way of telling now. The passengers made their way down the access ramp, going awkwardly with stiff limbs and aching muscles. They soon fell into their little groups – Actae and her bodyguard, Oll and his travelling companions. All of them took the opportunity to break open ration boxes stowed in the lighter's hold, and slumped wearily onto the baked earth with them.

Leetu brought some for John. 'You should eat,' the Space Marine said.

Yes, he should. There were lots of things he should do.

John looked up at the archaic warrior, that strange mix of the familiar and the unknown. He'd been scared of him in the beginning, knowing well enough what such creatures could do. He wasn't now. Now, he knew the right words. The words that could turn armour inside out, send his bolt pistol flying from his grasp, render his muscles to water.

'Thanks,' he said, and sat down.

The two of them ate in silence. To the north-east, the sky was alight – a wavering, flickering blush that never went out. You could smell the mix of chems and cooked flesh from here.

'I suppose I don't know why she kept you on,' John said eventually. 'I mean, if she hated all of this so much. Aren't you just… the worst kind of reminder?'

Leetu chewed steadily. 'Maybe,' he said. 'Maybe that was

a problem for her.' He never really smiled. His bull-necked, slab-muscled head was always held perfectly poised, almost expressionlessly. 'Or maybe she liked to remember a beginning. From when things were more optimistic.'

John raised an eyebrow. 'But, if you believe her, she was the one behind it all. No Erda, no traitors. Everyone raised properly in father's secure Palace, given the guidance they always needed.'

'What makes you think that would have gone better?'

'*Is* there a worse outcome than this one?'

'I would say so. There usually is.'

John chuckled, and shook his head. 'I envy your cast of mind. And now I wonder who you were, before they changed you.'

'It doesn't matter.'

'I think it probably does. I think that's what we're learning, here. You can give someone all the genework you like, but add a shitty upbringing and it all comes crashing down about your ears. Or a good one, we have to hope, and they can prosper through it all.'

'I really don't remember.'

'I guess you probably don't. I hope she kept some records.'

Something enormous flashed in the far distance then, followed a few moments later by a soft rumble. The scrub-bushes swayed around them, then got back to their shivering in the warm air. Above them, the faint stars burned, although most of the lights weren't really stars.

'I think I liked to draw,' said Leetu after a while, out of the blue. 'I mean, I still do. But I don't think the process taught me that. I think it's something I kept on. From before.'

Almost sheepishly, he drew out some small rectangles of material from a pouch at his belt. They were plascard, roughly cut. He handed them to John, who turned them to face the light of the aircraft's lumens.

Each one had a picture on them. The images were stylised,

bordering on crude, but in an intentional sense. There were ten of them. The likenesses were striking. Under each representation was a caption in an old form of vernacular Gothic.

The Magician. The Empress. The Hermit. The Fool.

'Very good,' John said, grudgingly impressed. 'I recognise all of us. When did you have a chance to do these?'

Leetu shrugged. 'They do not take long. I have more.'

'Hobby of yours, is it?'

'More than that.' He blinked impassively. 'Something to... keep on at.'

John looked up at Leetu's face. It was an Astartes face, the kind of face that wouldn't blanche at wiping out a village, or a fortress, or a world. And yet, once, it would have been a human face, softer, thinner, capable of going in a different direction if the genecraft hadn't meddled.

'Actae thinks we've been assembled,' John said. 'A spread of human types, off to the Palace to remind someone, maybe everyone, what's at stake here. You should do a card for yourself.'

'I would not know what to call it.'

John shrugged. 'Temperance?'

'The Devil, maybe.'

John chuckled. 'Hah.' He reached for another ration-stick, and started to gnaw at it. He needed to sleep, though that brought the risk of dreaming.

Some things, amid all the nonsense, had really flipped about. In the beginning, it had been John begging Oll to get involved again. Now the old soldier had taken charge, whipping them all into some kind of military shape for whatever came next. John had drifted to the edge of events, he felt, unsure what he was doing now, knowing that the next death would be the end of the line. And yet, for all the horror, Hatay-Antakya had given him the knowledge. His resolve had never been lower, his powers had never been higher.

What a bloody farce.

He got up, slowly and awkwardly. Leetu remained rooted to the spot.

'We'll need a plan,' John said. 'For when we get closer. It won't be an easy run.'

'I shall speak to my counterpart. The new Space Marine.'

'I think Ollanius will be the one calling the shots. Are you fine with that?'

'Of course.'

'My guess is we'll be improvising, even if a solid plan comes up between here and the Palace. You might think that went beyond the call of duty. If you wanted to bail, get back to Erda, I wouldn't blame you.'

For the first time, Leetu turned to look directly at him. 'I am with you now, John. Do not insult me again.'

John held his hands up. 'Just making sure.' He forced out a smile. 'I mean, I'm glad. I've seen what you can do with that pistol – better on our side, eh?'

But that was weak, and Leetu looked away again. When he next spoke, though, his voice was the same as it always was – unoffended, inoffensive.

'Reflect on what you can achieve now, logokine. I will be at your side throughout, just as I told her I would be, but your role is the important one.' He smiled, in an artificial kind of way. 'In any case, I wish to be there for myself, because I have not finished the set. How could I have done? No one, to my knowledge, has ever drawn the Emperor from life.'

Skarr-Hei was losing his grip. Skarr-Hei was becoming just a part of the whole, a fleck of fire on the orb of sun-fire. Skarr-Hei had to keep killing to keep the pain at bay, though you never really lost the pain, it only changed character – sometimes a goad, sometimes a reminder, sometimes like an old friend that you felt you needed even though nothing good ever came of knowing him.

The enemy weren't worth noticing. They were buckling, and had been running ever since the breakthrough at Mercury. Skarr-Hei had heard that Titans were coming through the gap now, a monumental effort given the huge amount of earth and stone that needed clearing. That wouldn't affect things for a while, though – a Titan would struggle in the cramped and ruined Palace interior, whereas infantry went fast, went hard, swarming across any barrier raised up against them, getting to the blood-spill.

Skarr-Hei had hoped for better fighting, though. He had hoped to find an enemy that would test him, one that would stand up and hammer back at the whirl of chainaxes. Instead, they had died weakly – in clumps, in squads, in droves. The World Eaters' advance was remorseless. They had no heavy armour to back them up this far in, no particular strategies or tactics, just a howling onslaught that burned its way in closer, closer, closer. They killed without compunction, without thought, out of reflex. Their old formations were nothing to them any more, they barely knew one old warrior from the other. Their armour was black-red, plastered with gore and dirt, all of it looking much the same, of a piece with the trenches of loosed flame that licked and rippled across the spoiled earth.

Skarr-Hei ran down a long viaduct with his many battle-brothers, the ash-wind tearing at them all. Below was murk and rubbish. Around him were the great towers, rising up through the reeking smog. Ahead was the rising massif of the Sanctum itself, still distant but visible now, ringed with fire and smelling of terror. Even as the embers of his rational mind sank into perpetual red-tinged fury, he still understood that this place was the target, the epicentre of the true pain. It had to be destroyed.

And yet, when they reached the end of the viaduct, at an

intersection tower where the ways ahead branched out in all sorts of directions, one of his own Legion was waiting for them, uncharacteristically still. His great chainaxe ran with streamers of gore. His bronze helm was splattered with it, his breastplate was covered in it, making the dust coagulate and clump across the ceramite.

Skarr-Hei knew this one. They all knew this one, and by the looks of things he'd been busy.

'My lord Khârn,' Skarr-Hei said, the words slurring through his clogged vox-grille. He came to a halt, as did those around him.

Khârn barely seemed to notice them. He barely seemed aware of any presence, even his own. He was facing north, away from the Sanctum's edge, off into the great cluster of tall spires that broke off from the Palatine urban zone and merged with regions already conquered. His stance was erect, febrile, as if suffused with some kind of electric current.

'I...' he grunted. 'He's... out... there.'

Skarr-Hei listened, but it wasn't easy. He had to keep moving, keep killing. The process had been set in motion now, and what little remained of his rational mind told him that it would never stop, whatever happened here – kill, and kill again, or be lost in futile excruciation.

'What are you saying?' Skarr-Hei tried. 'The primarch? You've... seen him?'

They all knew Angron was somewhere ahead. Skarr-Hei had heard the bellows from a distance, seen the carnage, but the Legion Master was off on his own, raging in his own private world of slaughter, neither commanding nor commanded, smashing through the unseen barriers against the netherworld. The best you could hope for was to witness it.

At the mention of the name, though, Khârn stirred. His bloody mask turned to gaze on Skarr-Hei. 'Something... worth our time.' His voice was breathy, thick with mucus. 'Something... got up.'

And then Skarr-Hei knew what had distracted him. Some staged fight, some encounter, not allowed to run its natural course, nagging away somewhere in that addled mind. An adversary who had been allowed to escape alive, now out there too, part of the slaughter.

'Who?' he asked.

Khârn struggled to vocalise it. 'The... Black Sword,' he blurted at last.

Skarr-Hei didn't know what that meant. There were a million swords out there, a great number of which were probably black. It wasn't much of a name, and he doubted Khârn would be able to tell him more than that any time soon.

But they had to move. Had to keep going. His own blades were cooling, the blood on them was drying out, the Nails were already spiking.

'We can find him, my lord,' Skarr-Hei said. 'There's no hiding, not now. We can find him.'

And slowly, dimly, Khârn seemed to understand. He nodded. 'You come,' he ordered. He looked at the rest of them. 'You all come.'

Then they were running again, not towards the centre but careering away like a pack of wild dogs, howling, growling, panting with machine-fervour. The movement would stave off the worst of the pain, but they all knew they needed to fight properly soon, to bury their blades into living flesh again, to kill, to maim, to burn.

Khârn led them now, driving them onwards, thick-painted gore flying free of his churning limbs.

'Find... you,' Skarr-Hei heard him mutter, over and over, obsessed now, consumed with it. 'And *finish*... it.'

SIXTEEN

Taking the chance
Learning to doubt
Wallbreak

Finished indeed. It had been fun while it lasted, Ayo Nuta thought, but this was the end now.

The gunners in orbit had adjusted their tactics, moving from strikes aimed at maximum-spread ground destruction to pinpoint lances designed to smash the inconvenient obstacle that stood between them and their prey. The orbital plate had begun to lose altitude badly, hammered lower by the series of incoming precision hits. Its void shields had been perforated in a dozen sectors, exposing the solid armour plates of the upper hull. Enemy atmospherics had launched missile after missile at their thruster arrays. Some of those attacks had been intercepted by V Legion fighters, but plenty had got through.

The damage all added up. The vastness of the orbital plate had been its main defence all the way along – it took time to batter through all that adamantium and ironwork, even once the voids were stripped away and the wounded thrusters were pumping gas-flares into the air.

The command bridge still operated, more or less. Large

chunks of the machinery were destroyed or non-functional, but the surviving crew were able – just – to maintain a grip on the motive controls, which was all they were really required to do now.

Nuta had given the order for course change two hours ago. That had been an exercise in prediction, really – it took Skye so long to shift trajectory that you had to make such calls far in advance. Only now, as the occupied space port itself filled every forward viewer with its malign outline, did the energy-feeds to the immersion drives take tangible effect. Slowly, painfully slowly, the entire suspended station began to swing south, away from the Lion's Gate fortress and out over the wastelands beyond.

Nuta stood watching the shift. He had been standing for hours, ever since his command throne had picked up some defect and started bursting with static electricity. He didn't mind it. It felt appropriate, somehow, to be on his feet.

Just then, another las-strike hammered in from orbit. It smashed clean through a damaged void shield section before carving up the ninth hull-sector and driving its way into the chambers below. The plate's chassis shuddered once again and dropped a hundred metres or so – a familiar pattern, by then.

Nuta smiled. They must have been spitting with frustration, up in those enemy void-ships. Skye had absorbed everything they had thrown at it, and for just long enough. The core structure was finally breaking apart, but its job was done. A few of the forward ground-armour squadrons had already raced ahead of the plate's protective shadow, confident now of getting into cannon range safely. Even those fanatics on the fleet wouldn't open up with las-fire so close to the one place they were trying to protect.

The deck reeled, and yet another power coupling blew. Nuta had once prided himself that he could determine every aspect of his little kingdom's health from the audible hum of its thousand systems, but these sounds were all new now, and all he could really ascertain was that it couldn't last much longer.

He tried to open a comms-link to Jangsai Khan, the one who had given him this chance to shine. Predictably enough, with all that was going on, the link failed. He hoped dearly that the warrior was still alive.

'If you can hear this, my khan,' he voxed anyway, 'be assured that I took my truth into a strange land. My thanks to you. You give honour to both your commune and your Legion.'

So that was that. The forward viewers were beginning to crack under the ever-increasing friction. Everything was shaking – the walls, the decks, the roof-arches. Another las-barrage swept down, possibly triangulated and launched before the plate had even changed course, but still hitting them on the extreme northern rim and blasting three perimeter sectors into puffs of splintered metal.

Nuta staggered across the pitching deck to reach the internal comms-station. He pushed aside the prone body of its operator and scrambled to bring up the distribution diagrams. Setting the spread to *whole ship*, he grabbed the mouthpiece.

'Crew of the Skye orbital platform!' he shouted. He had very little idea how much those still in the lower reaches would be able to hear, but at least those still living around him – Eisen and Sleva included – were able to look up and listen. 'You can see and feel the evidence for yourself, so you do not need me to tell you that we are at the end now.'

Out of the corner of his eye, in the realviewers, he could see the ground coming up to meet them. The onrush all looked so slow, so sluggish, and yet he knew that outside, in the real world, it would be accompanied by a hurricane of lightning-raked fury the likes of which even this world of superlatives could scarce have witnessed before.

'Protocol demands that I give you leave to head for the saviour pods now,' Nuta went on, 'but, in this case, I would not recommend it. The territory below is held by the enemy, and we know what they do to their captives. Our imminent demise will, I trust, take a few more of the bastards out, which is something to take satisfaction from.'

The shaking got worse. The outside view became entirely obscured by solid walls of flame. The roar that had been with them since the start became a scream of tortured metal.

'So we go down with our ship, like the seafarers of old. Your names may not be remembered, but *our* name, the name of the fortress you served on, can never be erased now. Be proud! Stand tall, as the end comes, and be as damned proud as any warrior of the Emperor!'

Another las-blast hit them hard, sending an enormous crack running across the width of the western section. The metal-scream grew worse, and Nuta even fancied he could hear the atmosphere howling in, racing up through the lower decks as the outer hull finally blew itself into tumbling slivers.

'All we ever demanded, in truth, was a proper chance to serve,' he said.

The flames cleared across the realviewers, and he got one final, snatched glimpse of the Lion's Gate space port, wheeling away to the north, its skirts glowing red with the fire of the White Scars' assault, the one they had helped deliver.

'We were given a chance,' he said, smiling in satisfaction. 'We took it.'

At last, the artillery was firing. The heavy breeches crashed back into their sleeves as the enormous machines erupted, whistling along the tracks and making the buffers clang. The trickle had become a steady barrage now, hurling shells hard and low into the encroaching pillars of rising dust. None of the gunners could see their targets clearly, but that hardly mattered – there were only so many avenues the enemy could charge up, given the chewed-up terrain, so you could discharge blind and be unlucky not to hit something.

Morarg was pleased to see it. He was also pleased to see the last squadrons of Legion ground vehicles leave the depots and roll out to engage beyond the walls. All of those tanks would be destroyed, he knew, but slowing things down was the objective now. Many things had changed for the Death Guard, but that core doctrine was still central to their philosophy of war. They were so good at it, turning every encounter into a swamp of endurance, ramping the levels of suffering so high that only a pure-bred contempt for life could see you out the other side. Slow it all down, grind it into stasis, sink everything into the swamp.

Attention now turned to the fixed defences. That damned orbital plate was falling fast, its work done, and the remnants of the atmospheric combat would be over very soon. The contest would come down to the ground forces after that, and whether they could establish bridgeheads in sufficient numbers.

Morarg had gone to Mortarion as soon as he'd finalised the defensive arrangements with Kalgaro. He'd half-expected to find the primarch arming up, ready to head for the front and take command in person, but nothing much seemed to have changed since his last visit. Mortarion sat on the obsidian throne still, his great gauntlets clutching at the hewn stone, staring intently at the red-tinged skies ahead.

'I believe they will reach the perimeter soon, my lord,' Morarg had told him. 'We will make them pay for the crossings, but they will get in.'

Mortarion had nodded. *'Then they wish to destroy themselves,'* he had said, his dry voice soft and sallow. *'We have*

*harried them for so long that they have given in to madness. I
had dreamed of slaying him within my father's house, to bring
our long feud to an end in the place where it all began, but
now it must happen here.'*

'He has not been sighted yet,' Morarg had said. 'Every unit
has orders to locate him, and bring him down before he can
breach the walls.'

Mortarion had chuckled. *'Ambitious. If you succeed in that, I
will be impressed, but also disappointed – his throat is marked
for my scythe, after all.'*

The primarch had seemed distracted, only partly paying
attention. The entire fortress was mobilised now, gathering
itself to repel the invaders, and yet he was still here, surrounded
only by shadows and the chattering glimmer of the daemonic.
Morarg had told himself that this impression of inactivity was
an illusion, and that the Lord of Death was engaged in combat
across planes of existence that he himself would never be able
to understand. The Emperor's own halls reeled with hopelessness, all due to the great vortices of power being channelled
here, in this very chamber, by his master.

But it would have been good to see him arm up, all the
same. To have his eyes light up with fury, as they had on Barbarus, when the scythe had swung to the rhythm of a million
soldiers marching. That would be have been good to see again.

'Then,' Morarg had said, unsure what was required of him
now, 'I should join the defence myself.'

'Yes. I suppose you should.'

And that had been it. Morarg had walked away feeling as
despondent as he could ever remember. This was a crisis, a
moment of acute danger, and those about him seemed either
to treat it as a kind of vicious game, like Kalgaro, or remain
blind to the peril altogether.

Had the void done this to them? Had the hidden bargain

made during the Sickness actually diminished their capabil-
ities, rather than making them stronger? It was hard even to
unpick how to examine that. Their bodies were becoming
this strange mix of disease and impenetrability, making them
so incredibly hard to kill even as their wits slowed and their
minds started to decay. Once the war was won here, it was
hard to guess whether that process would continue. Might they
eventually slide into the other realm entirely, becoming no different to the daemons that belched and capered around them?
And if that was their fate, what kind of victory would it be?

As he travelled down the arming chambers, such thoughts
plagued him, taking his attention away from where it needed
to be. So it was that he caught sight of the lurking daemon
very late, and that was dangerous, because they were not creatures to get close to without good reason.

Morarg froze instantly, staring at it, his hand hovering over
his combat knife. It looked up at him. He looked down at it.
For a long time, neither of them moved. And then it unfurled a
little, slinking wetly out of the gloom, and gave him a sly smile.

'*Disappointed?*' it asked. '*Are you?*'

'Who are you?'

'*You'll have to tell me, if you wish to learn more. Are you
disappointed?*'

The creature was extraordinary. Most of the Neverborn
infesting the space port were of a broadly similar type – obese,
covered in boils and scabs, slobbering and limping, clad only
in mouldering rags that hung from their slack frames like a
shedding epidermis. This one was nothing like that. It was
thin. Very thin. So thin, that if it turned away from you, you
could imagine it would disappear entirely, folding up into
the darkness and slithering away. Its limbs were long and
misshapen, its face was a landslip of sagging grey flesh. Like
many of its breed, it was phasing in and out rapidly, its outer

shell turning glassy, its skeleton exposed, before it turned solid again. It squatted in a pool of brackish water, its bony knees up around its shoulders, its knuckles cracking and its big, mournful eyes glowing like plates of corposant.

'Learn more about what?' Morarg asked, irritated. He was in no mood for this.

'Your master.' The daemon leered suggestively. *'The one you are losing faith in, this very moment.'*

Morarg drew his knife – a whip-fast movement. He could still do it, when angry enough.

The daemon stared at the blade, and blinked. *'I think you might actually try to use that. And it might even hurt.'*

'It would, trust me. What are you?'

The daemon shrugged. Every gesture it made, every half-snatched movement, emphasised its extreme skinniness. It looked like a famished corpse, a starved body, a dried-up rind.

'I am the Remnant,' it said. *'I am the last scrap, when all else has been consumed. I am the little slip of gristle that lingers, when you have chewed the steak. I am the memory. I am what came before.'*

Morarg started to walk again. 'I have no time for riddles,' he grunted.

'But we adore him!' the creature blurted, halting him. *'We adore him. Does that make a difference? You have to fight for him now, and you are wavering in your belief. But you should not. He is loved, in the empyrean, like few others.'*

This was disturbing language. The Neverborn were not well known to the XIV Legion yet. They were still unsettling phenomena, as much to be feared and distrusted as to be used as allies. Morarg did not know how to read them, but was astute enough to realise that they lied, and tricked, and made up for their ephemeral natures by playing on the doubts and hesitations of solid-fleshed mortals.

But he waited, all the same. 'You seem to know a lot about me,' he said warily.

'Because you are the most loyal of a loyal Legion,' the daemon said. *'You have endured the most, the pain, the Change, the descent into a world no one prepared you for. And yet you still serve, trusting that the cause must be just, because he has ordered it so. It would be a shame, if you doubted now, and had your head turned by lesser souls, ones who have taken credit for things they never fully understood.'*

Morarg kept the knife raised. 'You will need to speak plainly, creature, or I shall cut the truth out of you.'

The daemon smirked. *'You could try it. I am harder to finish off than most things, for I am what remains when the cutting is done.'* Its uncanny face, mournful and disordered, twitched. *'But here, as plain as I can make it. You believe your lord was deceived, that he was led by another, one who should have been called to heel long before any of it could happen. You suspect that he is a victim, and now makes the best of things, just as you all do, and thus you try not to despise him. But still you fear that he is weak, the worst of all the Barbaran sins, and has been a pawn in the hands of others.'*

'I have killed souls for saying less,' Morarg growled.

'Then it is good that I do not have one.' The daemon grimaced, getting to its feet, and the shadows jerked and snagged around it. Its round eyes were reflective like a felid's, but without any pupils. *'Take some comfort now, for the truth is more complex. That is what I came to tell you, for it matters that some stories are known. This is Mortarion's Legion, and always shall be. He is the master, and he is the maker. You should fight for him, Caipha Morarg, and do so without hesitation.'*

'How could you know all this?'

'Because you could not,' said the daemon. *'Even though you*

were there, on the ship, along with all the rest, but you would not have seen it, because you were looking elsewhere.'

It shuffled closer, and Morarg smelled its corpse-stink, rank in his nostrils.

'Just wait, for a moment, here, and listen,' it said eagerly. *'For only I will tell you what really happened on the* Terminus Est.'

Amber was the spearpoint, the moment of greatest risk, the first thrust into the heart of darkness.

Shiban gave the order for the charge, and three hundred jetbikes leapt forward, accelerating up to full velocity in a split moment, their drives shaking with white-blue flame. They streaked through the ash and the smoke, wheeling like thrown daggers, outpacing the lumbering heavy armour and racing straight for the ramparts ahead.

Already shells were firing, hurled high right up at the artillery positions. Missiles from the gunship wings streaked off into the dark. The unnatural night was torn open, shredded by light and noise, and half-dead things in the craters looked up, blinded, before the jetbikes blasted over their heads and coated them in waves of thruster-chucked smog.

'For the Khagan!' Shiban roared, whirling his glaive wildly.

'For the Khan!' came the thunderous cry from all those around him.

He whooped aloud, long and carefree. This was *exceptional*. This was the moment when all was unlocked, when the patient planning was put to the test.

Everything remained in the balance. Ganzorig, he knew, was struggling to make headway against the network of trenches and gun towers across the fortress' northern outworks. Qin Fai had had more fortune, but his task had been to launch feints towards the big artillery positions, to make the enemy think the main strike must be there and divert greater resources towards it.

Amber was the spearpoint, held back and held back and held back right until the Skye plate began its ruinous descent. As that immense sky-city of iron and plasteel had finally succumbed to gravity and damage, the jetbike battalions sprang out of the ruins in a single crashing wave, eating up the ground in a blur of red and white. Shiban's battalion was set at the very edge, driving harder than all the others, their pennants snapping wildly against their spear-shafts, their sword-edges glinting with the gold of a distant Chogorian dawn.

The enemy reacted, cranking the guns towards their position. Shiban grinned.

Too slow.

Even as the first shells loosed, the formations split open, filtering through the ruined outworks. The riders drove their steeds to the very limit – tilting over ninety degrees and hanging on one-handed, sliding and thrusting, their bolters already crackling.

'Hai!' cried Shiban, his voice cracking with the intensity of emotion. They had not ridden at the enemy in this way, with all thrown in and nothing held in reserve, since Kalium. This was all, or it was nothing. He pulled the nose of his jetbike up higher, letting fly with a riot of bolt-shells. His forward passage was bracketed with the sparkling dance of their detonations, an honour guard of destruction. His brothers streaked along with him, magnifying every hit with their own, blasting and gouging a path to the destination.

And it worked. The lead Imperial armour columns had made their forward positions, and were now pummelling the ramparts themselves. The many gateways into the lower fortress reaches, already damaged, were smashed apart. The nimbler tanks pushed on, slinging more ordnance into the inferno. Ahead of that barrage, out on the flanks where the firestorm did not risk hitting them, the Kyzagans and the

Scimitars and the Shamshirs and the Hornets and the Taigas surged straight up into the green-edged coronas, kicking their straining repulsors to boost above the burning earthworks.

Shiban locked on to the first target – the bastion tower over the main causeway leading inward. Beyond that were the ship-elevators and the hauler-shafts, the maintenance halls and the conveyer galleries, but this was the hard edge, the point the enemy needed to hold to stop them getting in. He could already see power-armoured infantry on the ramparts, and fixed guns swivelling towards him, and strange shimmers across it all, like electrified gauze.

Flares shot above the scene, sent up by the tank crews, flooding everything below blood-red. Explosions bloomed from the parapet beyond, the result of looped mortars and gunship missiles. The barrage was percussive and comprehensive, blowing up rockcrete and splintering across masonry, breaking chasms through which a speeder could thread.

'Follow my lead!' Shiban shouted, gunning harder.

The jetbikes screamed up the broken slope of scree and rubble, jinking and ducking under the blistering counter-barrage of projectile fire. Some were picked off, tumbling over and over before crashing into the racing ground, but others repaid the debt, laying down punitive bolt-streams that picked off gun-points and hull-down armour.

They seared their way towards the bastion tower, a squat low mass of interlocking walls, semi-ruined and barely patched up. A great rent in the outer fabric gaped directly ahead, glowing from within with that eerie green aura and silhouetted with night-black scaffolding struts.

Shiban blasted his way straight for it, shooting defenders clean from their positions before driving up through the rebar tangle and emerging at the parapet level.

He swerved round, clearing the flat top with a flurry of bolter

fire, just as his brothers shot up from the breach to join him.
Now they were constrained, hemmed in by rising curtain walls
on three sides. Shiban dismounted, leaping from the saddle
as the enemy began to advance at him out of their bunkers,
their own bolters bucking in their grips. His brothers did the
same, then charged into contact, whirling and spinning and
lashing out with their fire-edged blades.

Then it was the eternal shape of combat between Space
Marines – up close, bloody, fast, a sensory overload of sword-
work and gunplay, a swarm of power armour across every
exposed surface. The slaying was without art or grace, but
an animal frenzy of mutual hatreds, a raw desire to hurt, to
maim, to rip out a throat or puncture a lung or shatter a skull.

The White Scars were the storm unleashed, vital and desperate, flinging the long-ingrained muck from their armour
as their limbs pumped and thrust. The Death Guard were
as unyielding and lethal as they had ever been, only now
bolstered with their strange new resilience and the uncanny
cloaks of the daemonic. Each lone warrior of Mortarion's
Legion took two of the White Scars to bring down, and even
then they would stagger back up if not completely annihi-
lated. The assault ran up against solid walls, held back by the
dogged resistance of an enemy who had had time to prepare
and loathed their opposite numbers just as much as they
were loathed in turn.

More White Scars streaked up to the ramparts, running the
gauntlet of the wall guns to reach the breaches in the defences.
They poured out from their discarded mounts and into battle,
their ivory battleplate stark against the seamy shadows of
the foetid fortress-mountain. They were met by ever-growing
numbers of bottle-green leviathans, wading as if through oil
slicks to reach combat. Tulwars slashed against chainswords,
dao blades clanged against rust-streaked cleavers, and blood

spattered across stone flags already stained black from clashes between Dorn's paladins and Perturabo's engineers of murder.

Shiban despatched a lurching creature before him – a swollen mockery of a Space Marine with luminous tentacles hanging from its vox-grille like a ragged beard – before kicking it down the steps towards the rampart's edge. Then he was sprinting onwards, racing up a curving stair, Yiman and the rest of his brotherhood at his shoulder.

When he emerged up onto the next level, he was confronted by a sterner test. Traitor Marines, in ranks three deep, were trundling towards them across a shell-blown mess of upended rockcrete plates. They were so riddled with mutation now that the term 'Plague Marines' had started to become commonplace among those who fought them – a wry jest that had long since lost its humour. Yaksha came with them, taller and fatter, glittering and jerking as they phased in and out. An ancient Leviathan Siege Dreadnought, both its power fists leaking tox-clouds from between metal fingers, crunched its way through the mass, and behind it more troops were clunking down wide stairways to seal the breach.

Shiban tensed to charge, knowing that all this had to be cleared swiftly, but already doubtful of the numbers, when the sky overhead turned to pure crimson. A colossal boom followed, and then a ravening blast of forge-hot winds. A vast orange mushroom cloud rose up in the east, towering as imperiously as any spire of the Imperial Sanctum itself, before the rain of ash and dirt-clods started to thump down around them.

The Skye plate had crashed at last, driving a kilometres-wide gouge through what had once been the Imperial Fleet College and turning an entire urban zone into a molten pyre. And even as the ash rain swirled and the bow wave of its apocalyptic demise slammed across the entire space port, ten Sokar-pattern

Stormbirds thundered overhead, angling and tilting through the tempest in order to reach the drop-points.

'The keshig!' Yiman shouted. 'The Khagan! The Khagan is with us!'

Each mighty gunship swung in low, enduring steady torrents of incoming fire, their loader-doors already open. Giants of blade-art hurled themselves down, smashing up the ground as their heavy Terminator plate impacted. Namahi was at the forefront, wearing the golden helm that marked him as the greatest swordmaster of the Legion after Qin Xa. He crunched into immediate and savage combat with a whole squad of Plague Marines. Stormseers landed next, sending arcs of immolation lashing against the wailing daemons.

But it was the Khan himself who shone the brightest – clad in ivory and gold, his dragon-helm glinting with golden fire, his cloak whipping about him as he shot to earth. The famed *White Tiger* dao blade flashed out from its sheath, licked with lightning-forks and refracting the bloody nimbus of Skye's death throes. The storm winds kindled around him, lashing into a splintered vortex that shrieked with its own deadly chorus. Taller than the greatest of the enemy, faster than the swiftest of his own people, he crashed directly into the heart of the Plague Marines. Four were cut into smouldering, silver-edged pieces before they had even lifted their weapons.

Then he took on the Leviathan, slashing through its joints, severing the cables under its neck as it lurched for him, punching through the heavy protective faceplate, lifting it up one-handed, whirling on his heel and hurling it high over the entire battle-scene – thirty tonnes of solid ceramite tossed into the turbulent skies as if it were a mere child's toy.

For a heartbeat, every soul assembled there just watched it go. Even the keshig honour guard, inured by long experience to what their master could do when the killing mood was on him, gazed at it sailing overhead.

The crippled war machine smacked into the earthworks far below and blew apart as its reactor ruptured. As if a signal had been given, the keshig's standard bearer unfurled the giant banner of the V Legion, and planted it firmly on the ramparts. The sacred symbols streamed out, high and proud – the red lightning-strike of Chogoris, the eternal vengeance of heaven sent to bring judgement on the unworthy.

Simultaneously, every White Scar lifted his blade, and their massed roar outmatched the ongoing thunder of the armour barrage.

Khagan! Ordu gamana Jaghatai!

He had cried those same words on a hundred worlds, and across a hundred battlefields, but just then Shiban Khan poured his very heart and soul into them. The walls around them shook from the vox-enhanced battle cry, and the Death Guard themselves seemed stunned, falling back before the imperious savagery, the utter commitment, the soul-deep release of it.

And then Shiban was running, sprinting into battle alongside his primarch, with the pride of the Legion surging alongside him, and he was laughing again, he was laughing hard, just as he had done when the skies were clear and the sun shone bright and all there was in the world was joy and strength and the promise of glory to come.

For the Khan, he breathed as he swung his glaive into contact. *For the chosen people of Jaghatai.*

PART THREE

SEVENTEEN

Theology
Keep moving
Numbers

And she was laughing, too. It wasn't a laugh of pleasure, but of scorn and disbelief.

Erebus endured it. He was used to being scorned and disbelieved.

'So what do you say?' he offered.

'What do I say?' She shook her head. 'What could I possibly say? You have ambition, I will give you that, but little else.'

She walked over to a cabinet, one of the many stacked with idols and figurines taken from humanity's long past. She looked at them for a moment, as if consulting with them, before reaching for a bowl of dates and taking one. She chewed it slowly.

'I had my disagreements with Him,' she said at last. 'Somehow you discovered those, but they were hardly kept secret. We differed, and we still do.' She looked up at Erebus. 'But I always knew that He worked for the good of the species. He might have been wrong, perhaps, and arrogant, and

infuriating, but the threat was real. We had all lived through
it. Your masters, however – or, what you *take* to be your
masters – they are the end. They are the closure of the story.
I marvel that you could believe I would ever be tempted to
serve them.'

'Because you already have.'

'I acted to prevent an escalation – something terribly wrong,
a twisting of what our ascension was supposed to be. I never
acted to aid your cause.'

'What you *meant* matters little.' Erebus watched her carefully
as he spoke. 'It is deeds that resonate. You paved the way for
everything that followed.'

'No.' She turned back towards him. 'No, all choices were
still to be made. He could have abandoned the project – that
is what I thought He would do, but I underestimated His
pig-headedness. Or He could have killed His creations, once
I had shown Him how dangerous they were, but something
in Him must still have had affection for them, even then. And
your primarchs, all of them, they were still free to choose.
If they had not been dragged back into this awful Crusade,
pressed into action on His behalf like sullen children, what
choices might they have made for themselves?'

'They would have encountered my masters, sooner or later.'

Erda laughed again, just as scornfully. 'You *have* no masters,
you simpleton! There are no gods, not that deserve the name,
just distorted reflections of our own dreams. You prostrate
yourself before annihilation. You literally serve nothing.'

'And those sound like the sermons of Unity again, the ones
we found wanting so long ago.' Erebus sighed. 'If the gods are
not real, then how can their gifts be so potent? How can their
heralds give us so much power?'

'Because all you are doing is consuming your own,' Erda
said, disgusted. 'A daemon is nothing but a human thought,

a moment of human weakness, a piece of human pride. You can dignify them with names and titles if you wish, but all they are is the corpse-gas of our own kind.'

Erebus snorted, struck by the image. 'Ah, how wrong you are.' He reached for his sceptre. 'I told you nothing but the truth – you are spoken of with reverence in the empyrean. If you truly never wished for that, I could yet educate you on its ways, show you the scale of the power you are denying, and all the Anathema's folly would be undone. A new dawn of enlightenment is still possible, one in which we both might rise to heights undreamed of.'

Erda smiled sadly. 'This again,' she murmured. 'Always the quest for power, for knowledge, like some mania that should have been quenched after puberty.' She looked down at his sceptre, unimpressed. Then she picked up one of the figurines, a pot-bellied deity of some kind sitting cross-legged. 'I knew the sculptor of this one. She was a modest woman, barely knowing what art she possessed. She made it for pleasure, never thinking it would outlast her as it has done. Her life was hemmed in by close horizons, untroubled by envy or zeal. She died at peace, having given the empyrean nothing much to feed off. All she left behind was this, the mark of two patient, quiet hands. If I had to worship something from humanity, I might worship those hands. But she would never have understood it, and would have been mortally embarrassed if I'd tried. Those who demand veneration are never really worth it, in my experience.' She looked at it a moment longer, then put it back. 'Enlightenment was coming. That is the tragedy. It was always within us, working its way to the surface. Between Him, who wanted to rush it out, and you, who wouldn't understand it even if it was put right before your eyes, it has all been squandered now.'

She turned to face him, her arms by her sides. She was a

large woman, built solidly, and her gaze never wavered. Set against her, Erebus, with his spiked and gruesome armour, looked like a vaudeville reject.

'I apologise for nothing,' Erda said. 'I reject Him, and I reject you. You fuel one another, you need one another, and now you are locked so tight in your lovers' embrace that I can barely even tell you apart.'

Erebus drew in a long, sour breath. 'I had genuinely hoped for more,' he said darkly, activating his sceptre's harmonics. 'I had hoped for some awareness of the stakes, at least. Some indication that you realised what you had done.'

Erda looked witheringly at the weapon. 'I acted as my conscience dictated.'

'Then you were a fool, for conscience is no guide to anything.'

'You cannot have thought, for a moment, that I would ever ally myself with such as you.'

'Why not? You have already given us so much.' His grip on the hilt tightened. 'But if you persist in ignorance, then I shall have to remove you from the game. There can be no second scattering, no further intervention into schemes that are now divinely ordained. As things stand, my lady, you are a throwback, a relic, but if you will not reform your outlook then you are too dangerous to be allowed to endure.'

Erda smiled mirthlessly. 'So like all your kind – desires frustrated, and then quickly to the threats.' She placed her hands together, raising them up as if in prayer. The golden glow within the room intensified, and a strange harmonic began to thrum across the earth floor. 'But you should not have come here alone, monster.'

But even as Erebus' sceptre began to spark, the air around him crackled and shifted. Four great shapes began to curl into being around him, diffuse like water but thickening fast, with spines and fangs and the genesis of glowing, bestial eyes.

'I didn't,' he said, completing the summoning. 'And I think you owe my friends an apology.'

So some were still willing to stand up, to push back. Archeta was almost glad of it, though it slowed everything up, just when they needed to gain the last thrust of momentum.

Beruddin had been right – a kernel of resistance had been uncovered, an ingot of iron amid a world of pliant flesh. The XVI Legion forward units rushed towards it, diverting squads from a dozen objectives. Whole battalions from other Legions shifted course too, weary of merely killing, looking for a proper fight.

The effect worked the other way, too. Archeta had already marvelled at how easily some of the enemy formations had crumbled under assault. Many of those must simply have been weak and demoralised, but more than one of them, it now seemed, had picked up the same tidings he had – a leader is among us, someone is fighting back – and had abandoned their positions in order to join the resurgence.

And so, for all the Legion discipline, for all the great strategic visions of their commanders, a significant chunk of troops on both sides of the struggle had proved willing to make their way towards where the action was at its greatest, to where glory could be won. They were soldiers on the outside, but warriors at heart.

How far have we really travelled? Archeta thought to himself as he ran. *How different is this to what we did in the old slum-hives back home?*

Not very, was the answer. As ammunition ran out and tanks struggled to punch their way to the inner core, the fighting devolved into hand-to-hand struggles. It was vile stuff, really – no finesse to it, only an all-consuming desire to snuff out the life in front of you, to gouge out its eyes or pluck its windpipe free, then move on to the next one, just so you could keep moving.

So why do it? Why care so deeply about this war, when in essence it was just like all the others?

Archeta smiled to himself. Because names would be made, here. After the guns had fallen silent at last, you had better be able to say that you had done something good, something worth boasting about when the primarch finally stirred himself to making enquiries. There would be more fights to come, this time within the Legion, establishing who was up and who was down, so best to build a reputation while you had the chance.

He dropped down to his knees for a moment, breathing hard. He was deep within the honeycomb debris-piles of a demolished causeway. Its supporting pillars were still partially intact, rising a hundred metres above him like exposed ribs. Cliff-face buildings reared away on either side, all smouldering. A pair of downed Stormbirds framed his view ahead, their carcasses forming a triangular opening through which his brothers had been ordered to push on.

The rattle and crack of bolter fire was everywhere still, though at a lower pitch of intensity than it had been as the magazines emptied. Five hundred energy weapons glimmered in the murk instead, their illumination guttering as their power units felt the strain of days-long usage.

Archeta's own blade needed no such sustenance. It was hissing at him now, a low-frequency thirst for slaughter that he liked to hear. His senses were operating at their fullest pitch, his mind attuned to the targeting data streaming down his helm display. His brothers were filtering across the chasm floor carved by the causeway's collapse, wary of potential sniper fire and ambush.

Just getting here had been an achievement. They had cut their way through a full battalion of Blood Angels, supported by an Imperial Fists siege squad and the remains of an Imperial Army mobile infantry regiment. Those warriors must have been part of the Black Sword's offensive – they had fought with a kind of grim purpose he hadn't encountered until then. They weren't fighting for victory any longer, seeking to take and hold ground, but merely to deliver pain. They were bitter, nihilistic, spiteful and underhanded. And that was pretty admirable, all things considered. At least they weren't running away.

All of that told Archeta that he was getting close. The cityscape was almost impossible to navigate now, a maze of roads sunk into drifting cloud banks of filmy soot, its outline features scoured away, so you had to trust your instincts. Those instincts told him the command group was up ahead. He had already despatched flanking units out wide, moving into their familiar pincer formation, keeping in close comm-contact as they jogged warily through the ruins.

He started to move again. The risk was that his subordinates might flush the target out too well. He didn't even want them to wound him – it had to be a clean fight, one witnessed by his own kind so that the story of his victory would stick. So he ran as fast as the terrain would allow, his squad-brothers working hard to keep up. Hundreds of Sons of Horus fighters slipped like wraiths across the trash-clogged floor, hugging every scrap of cover, scanning furiously for movement-signals or heat-traces, even though they knew that in such conditions, with the air itself virtually on fire, they would be lucky to get anything.

Once they cleared the oddly sculptural arrangement of burned-out Stormbirds, the ground level ascended steeply, running up a wreckage pile that zigzagged towards the causeway's old terminus. The slope was overlooked on both sides, with high bridges criss-crossing overhead a hundred metres up.

As they advanced for the terminus, bolter fire immediately sprang out from hidden vantage points along the northern edge of the exposed run, striking a brace of Archeta's troops and forcing the rest to drop down.

Archeta signalled a halt, falling to the dirt, then ran an augur sweep. It didn't give him much, but he knew the place would be riddled with defenders, maybe in the hundreds too. They would be buried in the dust, crouched under collapsed beams, clinging on to the floorless levels above, just waiting for something to try the gap. Forcing a push towards the terminus that way would be bloody and difficult, as would ordering squads to fight their way into the interior of the buildings on either side.

Archeta signalled to his heavy support. 'Clear this out.'

Missile launchers set further back immediately whooshed out, followed by a percussive drumbeat of heavy bolter shells, obliterating the masonry wall the shooters hid behind. That familiar cushion of blown dust mushroomed across the expanse, filling the chasm from wall-edge to wall-edge. The barrage intensified, chewing through valuable ammunition but pulverising the vista heads and forcing the collapse of a long rockcrete support-pier.

'Now take them.'

As the thick dust still swelled up, Sons of Horus forward units burst out of cover and charged up the slope, using frag grenades to clear the route ahead before moving to secure ground. They went in low and fast, bodies tight to the ground as they ran before unleashing concentrated bolter fire at any sighted target. Archeta came with them, right in the vanguard, sprinting as fast as he could to make the next vantage, his bolt pistol kicking in his grip.

The effect on the defenders was overwhelming, the kind of shock-attack tactics the Legion had used throughout the

Crusade – hard to fight back when your surroundings had been blasted into powder around you.

Except that they did fight back. Somehow, they emerged out of the flying debris already firing. They were black-armoured, all of them, multiple squads wading through the shrapnel and picking their targets. The air filled with the whistle and whine of a thousand mass-reactive shells, followed by the clang and echoing crack of their detonations.

Archeta swore, even as he leapt up from his cover and sliced through one of them with his sword. The edge kindled on the armour, flashing with a red-tinged flame before it cut deep. He punched the dying warrior away and pressed on, driving hard. They might be prepared to fight here, but they had neither the numbers nor the support to hold on for long.

'Drive them back!' he cried, determined not to drop away into yet another holding pattern. He lashed out furiously, breaking the blade of another black-armoured fighter and sending him tumbling, where a volley of shells finished him off.

The Sons of Horus spear-tip advanced swiftly, cutting and blasting its way up towards the summit of the rise. For all its ferocity, the defenders were too thin-spread now, unable to sustain this pitch of combat for long enough, out-gunned and out-equipped. Archeta and his honour guard fought their way up to the terminus approaches, the secondary squads not far behind. His static-fuzzed tactical display showed hundreds more of his troops racing into position, filtering up through the buildings around, flushing out the last resistance as they came.

He reached the foot of metal stairs leading up to what had been the terminus command tower, flanked on either side by heavy rockcrete piers. The terrain around him was cluttered with machine parts – axles, wheels, tank tracks – all piled up like some conqueror's heap of skulls. Infernal winds raced overhead, blowing the dust into ever taller pillars, the howl of it masking the ongoing clamour of combat.

But then, just before it happened, he realised what he had done. He got the warning tingle, like an electric field across his back – the old ganger instincts that had been with him long before his ascension. Before he could call out a warning, the heaps of machine parts were thrust aside and sent sailing down the slope, bounding and thudding. Dozens of loyalists erupted from underneath them. Some were Blood Angels by their pauldron marks, some were Imperial Fists, but the grime had made them all as black as soot, set into stark relief by the flares of their disruptors.

Then the fighting really started. Archeta needed to give no orders – his vanguard hurled themselves at the enemy, pivoting instantly to take them on. Those coming on behind redoubled their efforts to reach the terminus, knowing that this was now in the balance.

He despatched the first enemy to reach him, slashing wildly with his hissing blade. Only as he moved to meet the next one did he see how far he'd come.

The fighter before him was an Imperial Fist, but arrayed in the coal-black armour of their Templar Brethren order. Something about his presence gave his identity away even before he'd laid eyes on the sword itself. Something about the way he carried himself, his stature, his movements – every figure around him unconsciously reacted to him, so that when he moved, they all moved too, like planets around a sun. His recklessly open stance might have been arrogant in any other fighter, but with him it merely fitted the aura he projected, one of complete and total focus, of immersion into the art of the blade to such an extent that no other way of being made any kind of sense at all. He strode across the wreckage in perfect silence, moving through it like a predator, his longsword eating up the meagre light and dragging it down into nothingness.

Archeta felt a spike of joy.

'The Black Sword,' he murmured, dropping into an attack stance even as his own blade screamed with hatred. 'I did not expect to come across you so–'

He never saw the blow coming. It smacked in transverse, so strong, so fast, smashing through his guard and knocking his whole body out of line. And then the follow-up, liquid like oil, punching up, cutting in, unbelievably powerful. The hilt cracked against his helm, stunning him, then a point-first ram of the blade, two-handed, a wrench, and blood was everywhere. The last thing he saw was a pair of red lenses swinging round at him, the ebon blade whistling for his neck, his parry nowhere near being close enough to–

Sigismund gave the decapitated body a brief glance as it crashed to the earth. Before he could press on, Rann, having despatched his own opponent, looked down at it too.

'A captain,' he noted, impressed. 'Who, though?'

By then, Sigismund was marching down the slope to take on the rest.

'No idea,' he said. 'Keep moving.'

It all came down to numbers, Keeler discovered. Nothing fancy, just some simple arithmetic. Two platoons of well-equipped Imperial Army troops, plus some heavy fire support – that stood a chance, in favourable conditions, of knocking out a single Traitor Marine. If you sent in the irregulars, the ones who were armed with power tools and had no proper armour, you were looking at over two hundred of them. In those circumstances, the kills were a matter of smothering, sending bodies en masse against a single target. All it took was one pair of turbo-pliers, right up under the helm-seal, to finish the job – all the rest were there to soak up the creature's rage, to weigh its limbs down, to bury it under a tide of the dead.

All of them, all her faithful, they went into battle with a skull clutched tight. Some had them hanging around their necks, others carried them on poles; some used them like morning stars, swinging iron-studded bone at the end of long chains. They had no other insignia, now. The aquila was never seen among them. This was the icon of the creed, the symbol they marched under. It didn't matter whether you had been a major in the Imperial Army, once, or just a worker in a munitions unit. Everyone under this new banner had been ripped from their old structures, made homeless by the war, ready to be reforged under new auspices.

She never preached directly – despite the temptation, she held true to her promise. Somehow, for all that, they found their way to her. They limped up out of the buried foundations of empty hab-towers, or the old sewer-tunnels, or the mud-filled shadows of sunken mortar-impacts. Any ration packs were distributed. Any wounds were treated. Guns were shared out, armour-pieces given to those best able to use them.

They were led into battle by men and women, old and young – those that had the fire within them, the willingness to bawl out orders. All led from the front. She'd insisted on that.

'Teach by word, teach by deed,' she'd said. 'They see you stand up, they'll do the same.'

Ranks started to emerge. She never had very good names for them. None of it was planned. Most of them were called 'preachers', because that's what they did. They had all read the books, the pamphlets and the missives, some of them circulated long before the great rebellion had even kicked off. The result was a mess of conflicting theories and beliefs, with the constant risk of arguments flaring up into conflict. The only thing that prevented it was the constant pressure, the ever-present risk of destruction. They lost every battle they fought, were forced back every time, but that wasn't a problem, because they extracted a little something each time. To lose was glorious, if it meant just one more enemy of the Emperor was taken out.

And the supply of recruits never dried up. There were hundreds of thousands of refugees everywhere, shuffling down the remains of the old processionals, desperate for somewhere to linger for just a moment. They weren't fools. They knew that the Sanctum couldn't hold them all. The only thing left was to find a decent path into the next life, one better than dying alone and in misery.

So they would listen to the sermons, then find a skull from the plentiful supplies on the open battlefields, clean it, polish it, take it up. And then its empty eyes would be trained on the oncoming enemy, a mass of hollow sockets, in their tens of thousands, silent witnesses to the apocalypse.

'This is the strength of us,' Keeler said. 'Our numbers. Willing to endure any suffering, asking no questions, resting on only one truth – that He protects. Nothing else matters. We must suppress anything contrary to it, root out any deviance from it. Individually, we are weak. In numbers like these, we are invincible.'

Her deputies nodded. Perevanna, the old Army apothecary-general, had long been pushing for a harder line against creatives inside the fellowship. Eild, an old manufactorum overseer, was less effusive, but held his tongue. Wereft, who had lived a life in the enforcers of the Provost-Marshal's office and believed in discipline, was as supportive as ever. The conclave had only been together for a matter of days, drawing together by happenstance and coincidence, but already the bonds were pulling tight.

'We're running short of serviceable guns,' Wereft said, his old face creased in the light of the fire. They were deep underground, in a corroded old chamber that had once been part of a water-treatment complex. It stank, it was unsanitary, but, for the moment, it was safe.

'Promethium is everywhere,' Keeler said, her voice softer and deeper than it had once been. 'Spills, old caches. We can make flamers, adapt the guns we have. Chechek, the lexmechanic – he's already on it.'

'The range of those things–'

'Is good for the soul. They will see the eyes of those they kill. Purify themselves as well as the enemy.'

She'd never have spoken like that, in the time before. She'd been wedded to a different concept of truthfulness, once – the veracity of the image, millions of them, all different, all pointing to incomplete fragments of reality. That had been her life, her training. Now all those things were gone, replaced by the purity of a single goal – survival, not of any one of them, but of the creed itself.

'But we'll have to fall back, even so,' said Perevanna, always thinking of the tactical situation. 'We lost most of Geron's congregation last night.'

'For the ending of a Son of Horus,' Keeler said, with feeling. They were the worst, the ones she would risk almost anything to see killed. 'A righteous bargain.'

Keeler saw the look Eild exchanged with Wereft at that. It didn't trouble her – they were entitled to doubt. All these things were new, forming out of the ashes of an empire that had done everything possible, in its infancy at least, to suppress the possibility of faith. Like water, though, devotion had found a way, seeping through the cracks, made stronger by persecution, until it was ripe to rise up and wash everything clean again.

'We hear stories,' Perevanna tried again. 'A commander, holding up the enemy, slowing them down. They say he's killing their leaders, one by one.'

Keeler nodded. 'The Black Sword. I hear the same things.'

'Then we should seek him out. If he has been chosen, then–'

'Chosen? How do you know he has been chosen?'

A pause. They were all learning to watch what they said around her.

'It's the name they're giving him,' said Eild. 'The Emperor's own champion, sent out to deliver His vengeance at the last hour.'

'We are His vengeance. We will outlast any hero.'

Another uncomfortable pause. They hadn't truly understood this, yet. They were thinking, out of instinct, about more than survival. They wanted to hit back, and thought that this Black Sword would give them that.

That wasn't how it would work. She knew that, with as much certainty as she knew anything at all. The important matter was one of belief, of adherence to a positive doctrine. The mistake, in the past, had been to preach a negative – there are no gods, there are no daemons. Humanity needed concrete things to cling on to. There is one god worthy of worship. Fear the alien, the mutant, the heretic. The Emperor protects. Once all that was established, set down in catechisms and enforced with the twin weapons of fear and fire, then the species had a chance. It was all about the numbers.

Two platoons could take out a Traitor Marine. An Imperium of billions, all under the sightless eyes of the skull, could wipe them from the galaxy forever.

Keeler sighed, and ran a weary hand through her hair. They would see the truth, in time. In the interim, compromises still needed to be made. This Black Sword might prove useful.

'Very well,' she said. 'If he's so important to you. Send

messages through the congregations, start the search. There cannot be many still fighting outside the Palatine, so it shouldn't take them long.'

They looked satisfied. It would keep everyone busy, which was also good.

'If we can find this Emperor's champion,' she said, 'if he lives still, we'll be there.'

EIGHTEEN

An excess of emotion
Distributed
Definitely not xenos

'You were not there,' Morarg said. 'You were not on the *Terminus Est*.'

'*Of course I was,*' the Remnant said.

'It was us, alone. The Legion.'

'*And a thousand other entities, all there to feed, or to revel, or just to watch, because it was a great day, a day of turning, and we dared not speculate which way it would go, right up until the moment of crisis.*'

'It was fated. It was destined.'

'*Just so. It had to happen, and it also might not have done. It could never have been otherwise, but it was also a choice. That is the nature of such moments. Oh, the beauty of them!*'

From above, from below, from all around them, the echoes of combat were growing in volume. Morarg had to leave, to take his place with the defenders. Every second counted.

'You speak as if I wasn't a part of it,' he said. 'As if what I saw was all a mistake.'

'*What did you see, Caipha?*'

And, instantly, as if a switch had been flicked, he was there again, in the heart of the deep dark, on the ship as it came apart around him. There was no time even to scream, to protest, because the pain came back, just as before, the all-consuming, all-enveloping agony that made it seem as if he had no limbs, no eyes or ears, only a raw lattice of nerves, all firing, all burning.

The howls rang down the corridors, the sound of Space Marines weeping and roaring, trying to vomit more blood up from empty guts, blinded and rendered lame, mutilating themselves in the madness of their agony. And it had gone on for days, months, years, forever, so that time itself had become just one more aspect of the pain, just another dimension of that unbearable suffering. It was beyond anything, not just damage, but erasure, annihilation, all of it fully conscious and never-ending and impossible to counter.

And then, just as suddenly, it was gone, and the two of them, Morarg and the Remnant, were on another world. Morarg fell to his knees, his mind reeling, his skin sheened in sweat. It took a moment to calm himself, for the howls to shudder out of his hearing, so that he didn't even notice at first how unbloated he had become again, and how pristine his armour now seemed.

'This is… before,' he murmured.

The two of them were high up on the edge of a huge amphitheatre. A vast conclave of bodies filled it – Imperial officials, legionaries, priests of the Mechanicum, even primarchs. One of them was speaking now, railing from a lectern. It was Mortarion, just as he was years ago, his body not yet transformed, the livery of his loyal Legion hanging proudly from the banners around the theatre's rim.

'Nikaea,' Morarg breathed.

'Where it all started. Or, at least, where this particular thread

started. See how fervent he is, your primarch! No voice was raised more strongly against the witch. He believed it, too. You can see that, even from here. Ah, how he hated the very thought of it.'

And then the impressions shifted once more, racing wildly through time and across space, until they were on Molech, that great clash of arms masterminded by the Warmaster himself. Mortarion was there too, but changed again, on the first stages of his long transformation. The sky rippled with sorcery, the earth split open with visceral exuberance. At the forefront of the fighting was Grulgor, that distended old monster, brought back to life in order to kill in quantities even the Death Guard had never dealt with before. He raged and raged, lost in his own world of daemonic excess and fury.

Then that, too, was gone, all the visions quickly swallowed up in darkness. Morarg took a breath, looked around himself. It was pitch-black, and the air smelled rank, a mixture of body odour and rust. He could see nothing, only hear a strangled sound, echoing strangely as if buried deep in a ship's hold.

'How did such a thing happen?' the Remnant asked, whispering softly in the enclosed space. *'How did this preacher against witchery succumb so completely to its spell?'*

'Because he learned its power,' Morarg said. 'It was necessary.'

'Was it?' The Remnant smiled. *'Or did he like it? Maybe there were days when he revelled in it, and others when he could barely look at himself in the mirror. Maybe that was the torment.'*

Morarg couldn't take his mind off the strange sound. It was as if an animal were trapped in there with them, but he couldn't see it yet. 'You have no idea what he suffered for us. He guided us out of hell, marching with us at every step. If he did something, anything, it was to keep us alive, so we would never have to go back.'

The Remnant nodded. *'Ah, now that is true,'* it said. *'Who, in this universe of suffering, has suffered more? Look at him. He is here, with us now.'*

Morarg still saw nothing. 'When is… now?'

'After the deed was done. After seven of his sons were slaughtered, all to create the monster you saw on Molech. This is the aftermath.'

The Remnant shuffled a little, and a pale grey light crept across the chamber. Morarg caught sight of Mortarion again, alone, crouched over the body of a slain Deathshroud warrior and racked with horrified sobs. Morarg got just a glimpse of the primarch's face, torn apart in a mask of anguish and loathing, before the vision switched out again.

Now they were on another war-torn world, with the Death Guard marching en masse towards another doomed Imperial fortress. All sorcery had been put aside – they were doing what they had always done, constricting, controlling, wearing down. The artillery boomed, the bolters laid down withering fire-lanes. Mortarion marched at their head, marshalling them all, issuing his commands in that habitual cold-as-death manner. His scythe swung about him, dazzling in its disruptor-wreathed power.

'He has put it aside again,' said the Remnant, gazing in appreciation at the scenes of slaughter. *'Just for a moment, he has convinced himself that he can live without it, and that Molech was a mistake he will someday be able to forget.'*

'The weapons were always chosen for the war,' Morarg insisted. 'When we required sorcery, it was used – when we didn't, it wasn't.'

'Or was it this – that he tried to push it away, but failed? That, like an addict who loathes his poison, he kept putting it behind him, and then coming back to the well? Did you never even question it? How, one moment he would be spitting with

fervour in his denunciations, only to slay his most precious sons just for the chance to outdo his brother on the battlefield? Did you never wonder at that? Did no one say a word?'

Morarg looked across the scenes of fighting. Even here, while abominations like Grulgor were banished, there was something different in the aromas. A sickening, a sense of decay. Their armour was so degraded, so filthy. And yet, they were winning.

'He did what he had to,' said Morarg, sticking doggedly to his mantra. 'We had to survive.'

'Yes, he did what he had to.' The Remnant blinked again, and the visions rippled away. Then it was just the two of them again, surrounded by complete darkness, complete silence, as if taken out of time and space entirely and marooned at the end of the universe. *'So imagine if you had learned these two truths, each of them necessary. Imagine if you learned that the only way to guarantee your Legion's survival was to immerse it in the most profound sorcery of all, thereby giving it gifts so potent that no force in the galaxy would ever be able to dominate it again. But then imagine that all your old fears were still true, that you had been in the right of it at Nikaea, so that any involvement with it would damn you all to suffering beyond mortal conception. Imagine knowing both those things. How could you live with it? What would you do?'*

'What was right.'

'But they were both right, and they were both wrong. Resist the empyrean, and you will never become as powerful as you were always destined to be. But embrace it, and the agony will be eternal. You can be pure but weak, or corrupt but strong. What a conundrum! What a perversion for a Barbaran to contemplate! And so there is the mystery of why your master swung from one pole to the other, never able to plot his course with surety. It was as simple as mortal indecision. He didn't know.

Every course ended in disaster. And he couldn't even pretend that he didn't care, because he did. God of Decay, no father ever cared more.'

At that, Morarg suddenly remembered what Mortarion had told him. *I loved you all too much. That is the only error I will admit.*

'But the decision was made,' Morarg said, though no longer with much certainty. 'He solved the riddle and brought us to Terra.'

'That he did, but not in the way you think,' said the Remnant. *'Which brings us to the final element.'* His grey face flickered into a warped smile. *'So let me talk now of Typhus.'*

The rumble of gunfire never stopped, even after the army itself was long gone. Deep down in the caverns under Colossi, Ilya Ravallion tried to put it out of her mind, to forget how vulnerable they were there, and concentrate on her work.

It was true that their precise location would be hard to find, hidden behind thick rock walls designed to look like tunnel collapses from the outside. Few souls would even be searching for them – the bulk of the main enemy attack was over a hundred and sixty kilometres westward, and the Death Guard themselves were fully occupied at the space port. But still, only the bare minimum of guards and weaponry had been left behind, just enough to keep a tiny portion of the old fortress in working order. If anything did sniff its way down here, the battle would be brief and brutal.

She leaned forward at her station, her head pounding. She needed something to drink, but suspected the reservoirs were virtually gone now. Best to leave it for the soldiers, in case they were called on to fight again.

She looked away from her terminal lens, unable to bear the glare from the glass, and let her eyes run across the cramped interior. A few dozen Imperial officers, maybe three times that many V Legion menials, all working away at the comms arrays and augur intakes. Ilya wondered if any of them were doing better than she was – the quality of the signals was atrocious, and getting worse all the time. Still, at least they were able to forward some scraps to the field commanders, to give them some idea of the tactical situation.

She heard the low hum of power armour behind her, and turned to see Sojuk. The warrior bowed.

'You have been working long beyond your allotted stretch, szu,' he said. 'I must request that you take a rest period.'

'Who organised the work-schedules, Sojuk?' she asked.

'You did.'

'Then I think I'm entitled to ignore them, aren't I?'

'Permit me to insist. If you require physical assistance to take you to your quarters, I am able to render it.'

Ilya laughed, and sat back in her chair. He was right, of course. She could barely see straight, let alone process the low-quality scanner signals. 'I don't need help,' she said. 'Come with me anyway, though.'

She pushed herself back up to her feet, feeling every muscle ache. Just walking unaided was an achievement. She should have used a stick, ideally, but didn't want to make the visible concession. Limping, she made her way past the ranks of huddled operatives, all of whom were too busy to notice her leaving. Sojuk clunked along at her side, knowing better than to offer her a hand.

'They're inside the space port now,' she told him, just in case he didn't know.

'So I understand.'

'We'll be lucky to maintain contact with them for long.'

'That is understood. Though we may indeed be fortunate – such things have happened before.'

They passed through the blast doors and into the narrow underground corridor. It was horribly hot and humid.

'I'm sorry you're not with them,' she said. 'I know you must long to be there.'

Sojuk smiled warmly. 'The honour is to be here. If one of my brothers had tried to take it from me, I would have killed him.'

Ilya laughed. 'Nice of you to say. Though I doubt your master would be pleased.'

'He would understand, I think.'

They reached the door to her dorm-unit, shared normally with two others, although empty for the time being. The remnants were all crammed together in this little hideaway, hunkered down and invisible as the earth burned above them.

She needed to sleep now. Even though the cot was hard, the bolster lumpy and filthy, she knew she would pass out as soon as her head hit the plasfibre.

'So do you believe it, then, Sojuk?' she said then, almost without meaning to. The thought ran through her head all the time, as if stuck on repeat, tormenting her. 'Do you believe he can do it?'

'Of course.'

'But I was there. On Prospero. They were matched, the two of them, and now the enemy has grown, and we have been worn down so much...' She leaned against the door frame. 'Sorry. I shouldn't say it.'

Sojuk didn't smile again. For all his equanimity, the worry must have occurred to him, too. 'He would not attempt it, if it were not possible.'

'But if he were... If he *died*? What then?'

'Another Great Khan would be chosen.'

That startled her. 'No. Not possible.'

'We would grieve, szu. We would be angry, like no force of the heavens has ever been angry, but then we would fight again. The hunt would continue. An outsider might never even know the truth, even for centuries after – there is always a Great Khan.'

'But I cannot… I mean, the way you say it…'

'Only the way he has always been with us,' Sojuk said, calmly but firmly. 'Some primarchs are bound up with themselves, wrapped in their own power. Jaghatai, though, always made us all stronger. He is of the Legion. We are the people of the Khan.' He looked straight at her throughout, as if warning her of how to be, should the moment come. 'The gift was never hoarded. It was shared freely.'

She didn't even want to think about it. She didn't know why she'd brought it up. Overtired, maybe, in need of a break. Or sick of it all.

'Oh, hells,' she said. 'This… waste. When I joined up, at least we were doing something constructive. Or it felt like that, anyway. But this… Even if we survive it, what will be left?'

Sojuk reached into the dorm-unit and activated the sodium-strip lumen.

'Rest, please,' he said, more firmly now. Then he seemed to relent. 'The Qo taught us that the universe is a cycle. One day, we construct, another day, we knock down. There is no end, no day when we can say it has all been achieved, only another day of struggle. But it is better to be there, to be part of it, all the same. And I very much wish for you to be there, with us, when we cease destroying and begin to build again. So I say for the third time, my lady, take rest.'

Ilya smiled, and placed a time-worn hand on Sojuk's enormous breastplate. 'Very well. You have been patient with an old woman. Wake me in four hours.'

Then she left him, wrapped a blanket around herself, and collapsed onto the narrow cot. Even before the lumen died she could feel herself slipping away.

'For all that, it cannot happen,' she murmured, tossing uneasily. 'Not him, too. I will not let it.'

'Fire at will! Fire at will!' Kaska shouted, trying hard not to lose it completely.

Aika 73 bucked and rolled over the smashed decking, its engine hammering as the tracks slipped before finding a grip. The terrain was nightmarish – a slick mat of faintly glowing vegetation, rapidly ground up into a black slurry as the tanks skidded and revved across it.

The crew were all sweating now, breathing heavily, working the air filters hard. Merck reached for another shell with shaking hands, fumbling the catch before shoving it into the breech. Dresi was as silent as ever, though the constant jarring motion of the hull must have been making things hard for her. Jandev had been firing constantly ever since they had driven up from the wastelands and broken inside the enormous port complex.

Kaska didn't like to remember the passage inside. He'd only had glimpses of the action anyway, locked down as they were inside their humid, overheated, already malfunctioning box of death.

The super-heavies had done most of the core lifting. Once the skies had cleared of the overhead firestorm, those had been the ones to smash a path through the ranks of enemy armour, using their numerical superiority to bludgeon the slower-moving traitor units. They had suffered for it, though, and Kaska had lost count of the number of burning wrecks he had had to skirt around. The impacts had been tremendous on both sides, with heavy-calibre ammunition ripping clean into thick armour and punching through crew-stations and fuel tanks. Some of the traitor units had kept on coming through firestorms that should have blasted them clean from their tracks, taking several direct impacts to finally bring them to a halt. Once the lead super-heavies had pulverised each other into straggling heaps of scattered machine parts, the main battle tanks had had to negotiate veritable hull graveyards, trying not to crash straight through the raging promethium slicks and ignite their own fuel tanks.

Las fire had been useful in that confused scrum – Jandev could fire faster than Vosch while the tank was on the move, as well as swivel his barrel more easily than a full turret-swing. *Aika 73* had scored two more hull-kills before the threshold had finally beckoned. Kaska, trying to keep his eyes clamped tight to the periscope sights as his tank rocked and jerked, had caught sight of the gaping maw of the objective from a long way out. That gate had once welcomed heavy ground-conveyers for void-ship components, and soared away sixty metres up. By then, its gun-points had been obliterated, its guard towers ruined and hollowed out, but it was still a daunting place to run at. If it hadn't been for the heavy White Scars presence, already up into the high battlements and tearing across them like wildfire, it might have been impassable.

Aika 73 was not the first across the gate's edge, though – it had broken through the barrier alongside the two units remaining in the squadron, in the lee of a trio of huge Storm-blades, all of which had taken heavy damage on the way in. More Leman Russ units had followed them, some partly on fire or with damaged turrets, but soon the numbers started to add up. You could begin to believe, Kaska had dared to think, adding up all the locator runes on the close-range augurs, that they might even pull this off.

Until, that was, they had got inside.

It had already been claustrophobic, stuck in that shaking, rattling casket for hours on end. Once under the shelter of the space port's colossal innards, it felt like being buried alive.

The air tasted foul through the filters of the tox-guards. The narrow viewer-slits silted up instantly. Black mould started to spread across the interior panels, almost in real time. The ground, which should have been solid rockcrete, degenerated into sloughs and mires. Visibility dropped to a few dozen metres, blocked by a miasma of dark green that barely shifted even as you fired through it.

The noise was the worst of it – a constant resounding thunder of confined engines and gunfire, one that never let up and soon had everyone wanting to scream. Enemy tanks had been stationed just inside the interior walls, hunkered down low behind thick razor wire barricades, and the slaughter taking those defence-lines was prodigious. After that the infantry had come, those massive power-armoured monsters that seemed able to shrug off hit after hit before coming into range. Kaska's second tank had been destroyed by just one of those creatures – it had got close enough to tear its way into the interior, using some kind of huge cleaver to hack through the armour plate and then carve up the soft bodies frantically trying to reach the escape hatch. Kaska had opened fire on the tank himself with the main gun, just to end the screams of terror from within. Vosch's shot had ignited the ammunition store, blowing up the whole hull, but *still* Kaska had needed to wait in position, ready to fire again, just to make sure the damn creature didn't limp out of the flames.

They were horrific. They were everywhere. You had to hit them at long range, laying down as much destruction as you possibly could, because if they got in close, nothing much was going to stop them. Kaska remembered his briefings back at Colossi, when he'd thought that sending hundreds of tanks into a single fortress, however big, might be overkill. He didn't think that now. The environment was such that exposed line troopers would have lasted only moments. The enemy was such that only devastating levels of firepower had any effect. It was almost comically miserable – a valiant charge into the jaws of an earthbound hell, opening up with physical weapons on something created by a malign force beyond all comprehension. All you could do was keep moving through it, keep firing, hope against hope that you'd finally smash your way through to some improbable sanctuary in order to take stock, to rest up, to catch your breath and rearm for the next melee.

The units ahead of him finally broke into an echoing gallery, and Kaska followed them in. Enormous chain-lengths hung down through the fog, dripping with condensation. The burned-out skeleton of a fleet tender hung in rusting loops within a lifter cage, itself more than five hundred metres long. Cutters, welders and industrial drills were suspended from blown-out crane rigs, all of them draped in that infernal rotting carpet of organic filth. The tanks ahead of him were already hard at work, pummelling a line of defence some three hundred metres off. The gallery heights flashed and echoed with the sharper sounds of Legion gunfire, causing the miasma to be joined by even thicker blooms of smoke that cascaded down to ground level and made it even harder to see anything clearly.

'Push right, driver,' Kaska ordered, concerned about a formation of Imperial tanks making faster progress along the left. As ever, you had to be as worried about friendly fire as that coming from the enemy. *Aika 73* struggled to make headway, trailed by its sole squadron survivor. 'And drop your speed – I can't see a damn thing in here.'

But he saw clearly enough what came out of the murk next, and it chilled him to the bone. It was one of *those* things – the things they had been told were xenos, but which definitely, definitely weren't. It was lit up, so he saw it lurch along amid a cloud of flies, semi-transparent and flickering as if unreal, but clearly able to affect the environment around it. Its face was almost human, though distended and warped like no human face had ever been in life. Its belly was ripped open, its grey-green skin glistening with a fever-sweat, and it lurched along on flabby legs as if drunk.

'Fire, fire, fire!' he shouted, feeling himself slip into panic.

Vosch got a shell away, blasting it in close and sending a huge geyser of superheated earth up out of the impact crater. Jandev, getting his range from the explosion, followed up with a sprayed line of las-fire.

The creature staggered through it all, taking hits but somehow able to survive them. Kaska caught its lone yellow eye through the periscope and almost vomited. Merck was already doing just that, even though the gunner couldn't see a thing – the deathly smell of the apparition seemed to get inside, despite all the other rival stinks it had to cut through.

'Fire again!' Kaska shrieked, powerless to do anything else. It would be on them in moments, and that would be it.

But then something intervened – a blur of ivory, with a blade that flashed in the darkness. Kaska could hardly make out the detail through all the white noise, but clearly something had interposed itself.

'Cease firing!' he shouted.

He adjusted the focus on the periscope viewfinder with shaking, clammy hands, trying to get a better view. He saw the creature bellowing, lowing suddenly like injured cattle, with an armoured warrior right up at its throat. A sword flashed out, back and forth, marshalled with incredible power and heft. A cry of wild aggression in a language he didn't understand rang out, and then the monster was gone, ripped from view as soon as it had arrived, leaving only fresh slicks of translucent slime across the scorched terrain.

'Keep those guns locked down,' Kaska repeated, swivelling the viewscreen and trying clumsily to improve the image.

His visual field jumped across a landscape of firing hulls, of advancing Traitor Marines, of more of the bowel-emptying nightmares spinning into existence. Just gazing on those things made him want to get out of there, to hare off as fast as he could before his heart burst from fear. The paths ahead and behind were all clogged up, though, blocked with the grind and thunder of mobile armour, or dazzling vehicle lumens in the dark, or the unearthly glimmer of spectral forces.

But then his close lens was filled with the grainy, shaking image of the Legion warrior – a white helm banded with blood red, already plastered with grime from the kill, still on his feet.

'Well fought, commander,' came the warrior's voice over the comm, as strangely accented as they all were. 'Jangsai Khan, Brotherhood of the Iron Axe. You are now with me.'

Kaska swallowed, trying to master himself. Was this better? Was this worse? Would this fighter keep them alive a little longer, or lead them quickly into something even more terrible?

Not that there was a question about it, of course. It was an order, and having one of them on the outside was surely better than going further alone.

'Aye, lord!' he shouted back across the comm, before switching back to Dresi. 'You heard him, trooper,' he ordered. 'Follow that one.'

The engines growled up a gear, and Merck reloaded, wiping his chin with his uniform sleeve. Everything rattled, everything complained, the engines coughed and spluttered, but *Aika 73* did as he was asked, allowing Kaska to take another look through the scope.

'A Space Marine,' he murmured, sweating profusely and still trembling from what he'd seen. 'We are fortunate indeed.'

NINETEEN

Lord of the Night
Sweet spot
Broken Angel

'A Space Marine,' Fo muttered to himself, his mouth full of blood. 'Of all the damn luck.'

His attempt to escape it had been farcical. He'd managed to get to the end of a long corridor, almost to a sealed door, before it had shot him.

It had missed, but not by accident – a Traitor Marine didn't miss at that range. It had missed because a mass-reactive shell striking him in his body would have killed him outright, and the creature didn't want him dead yet. The shot exploded at his feet, enough to break both his ankles and bring him crashing down to the deck.

Then it had scooped him up, using its long claws like a cargo-lifter, and loped through the doorway with him tucked under its arm.

He didn't remember much of what happened next clearly. He was in a lot of pain, and the stink of the armour around him made him want to pass out. He felt something wet and leathery flap against his face, and realised only slowly it was the vein-latticed surface of some fresh-flensed human skin.

His captor went rapidly, negotiating the shadow-realm of the Palace warzone more surely than Fo would have thought possible. It said nothing to him the whole time, just ran through the dark, ignoring the combat erupting in all directions around it. Fo jangled painfully in its one-armed grip, feeling like his ribs were being broken with every footfall – though at least that took his mind off the white-hot agony in his legs. He clenched his jaw tighter, he forced himself to keep his eyes open. If he lost consciousness, that might make things feel a little easier once they stopped, but it would end any possible chance he still had to get out alive.

After a while, he realised that he was being taken upwards, climbing high out of the dust and the smoke. He blinked hard, his vision still cloudy, and gained a glimpse of the internal metalwork structure of an old hive, stripped of its outer surfaces and its solid floors, the skeleton of iron stretching away from him both up and down. It all smelled of burning. The Traitor Marine scaled the struts and beams effortlessly, leaping when it had to, which made Fo's body scream with pain.

Soon they were at, or near, the summit. Fo only knew that because his captor threw him down onto his back and he saw nothing but ember-glow storm clouds streaming along above him. He tried to speak, but the traitor extended a single finger of its claw and impaled him to the steel below, pinning him just under his right shoulder blade.

Fo yowled, thrashing against the pain, before the shock passed and he realised that any kind of movement just made things worse. Panting, he forced himself to keep control, to face his tormentor, to clear his mind. Even as his heart raced and his stress hormones shot off into overload, he knew he had to keep thinking. There was always a way out. Always.

But then he looked into the skull-face of the creature's helm, saw the dull ache of its lenses, and the scraps of still-warm flesh hanging from its armour like ribbons. It reeked of agony – the agony of its prey, not just killed, but made to suffer first.

'You are the tyrant of Velich Tarn,' it said.

The voice was as horrific as everything else. It sounded as if the lips and tongue under all that armour plate had atrophied, seizing up in some kind of immune response to their owner's debauchery.

Fo swallowed a bloody mouthful. Lying, at this stage, seemed a weak strategy. 'I was. How on earth could you know that?'

The monster did not need to answer. Something in the far distance blew up just then, flooding them both briefly with a stark orange glow, and Fo saw esoteric runes carved across the traitor's armour. He saw the marks of what the old man had once called 'Ruinous Powers', the very powers He had taken it upon Himself to go after. This monster, if it was foolish enough to tap those, probably had access to all kinds of secrets.

'You exist in several futures,' the traitor told him, in a voice that was neither angry nor sinister, but just empty, as if its soul had been harrowed to the bone by the things it had done. 'And you do not exist in many more. By rights you should have been killed already, and yet here you are. A stubborn fly to swat.'

Fo smiled grimly. The hot wind tore at his uniform, making the pain worse. 'But you got me in the end, eh? Well done. Now what? You want the secret? That's it? My weapon?'

The traitor stared at him with soulless, pitiless eyes. Its armour, right up close, was a thing of awful fascination – the machinery never stopped making sounds, emitting heat, like a chained animal all of its own, only loosely held in check by the withered thing inhabiting it.

'I do not know what does the most harm,' the traitor said musingly. 'Letting you live, or killing you now.'

Fo laughed, then regretted it. '*I'm* not important. I can hardly lift a lasgun. But I can tell you what I know. I can build something for you.'

The Night Lord spat out a steel-hard laugh. 'You are deluding yourself with that. This is about *you*. What you might become.'

With a sudden clarity, Fo realised that the monster was genuinely undecided. The indecision was all that was holding it back – just a twist of its long claws would be enough to finish him off, but it still hadn't moved.

Then, with a terrible wrench, it pulled its talon free of his flesh, dragging long trails of blood with it.

'Enough. You must die. That is safer.'

The monster tensed to plunge its claw down, and Fo screwed his eyes shut, managing to curl up into a ball, as if that would do anything to shield him from the strike.

He felt a rush of air, heard a thud like a vehicle striking a bulkhead, and then… nothing.

He opened his eyes, just in time to see the creature fighting, lashing out with those claws in a frenzy of startled movement. It was locked in close combat with something much worse, much more powerful, and the contest was painfully one-sided. A spear flashed out, crackling with silver-gold energy, and the Night Lord was hurled, cartwheeling almost comically, out over the spire-top's edge. It called out, just once – a thin, strangled cry, fading away rapidly. The storm roared overhead. Far below, the city burned. The drop must have been nearly a kilometre. Even a Space Marine wouldn't get up from that.

That just left the matter of the other one.

'My lord Custodian,' Fo croaked, feeling the cumulative effects of his wounds. 'Back to Blackstone, then.'

Valdor gazed down at him. The oil-dark blood on his great spear was still wet. 'No,' he said.

'Then you're here to kill me,' Fo said resignedly.

'No,' he said.

Fo didn't know what to say next. He was still close to passing out from the pain. His nerves were fried. The after-effects of his time with that creature were rapidly catching up with him. After sufficient amounts of terror had been doled out, though, all that really remained was irritation – the desire to get things over with, to find out what fate had in store for him now.

'So you want to destroy the weapon,' Fo said, unnerved by his captor's eerie, implacable silence. 'Amon told you what it could do. Is that it? Just tell me!'

'You are coming with me,' Valdor told him. 'Into my care, not the Blackstone's.'

The captain-general picked him up, just as easily as the Traitor Marine had, and only slightly more gently. Then they were moving again, leaping down from the spire summit, a dizzying drop into the girders and struts.

Fo tried not to throw up, or to scream out loud, or to otherwise embarrass himself. His head shook, lolling painfully against his chest. He clenched his jaw, pressed his fingernails into his palms to keep himself conscious. A man could get irritated by all this… disrespect.

They reached ground level, where the air was almost unbreathable and the heat unbearable. Valdor hesitated for just a moment, gaining his bearings. That gave Fo his opportunity – perhaps the last he would get before the run back to the core.

'So what difference does that make to me, eh?' he demanded, struggling somewhat performatively against his captor's grip. 'A prison's a prison, isn't it?'

Valdor's golden mask gazed down at him, those jewelled eyes impossible to read. It wouldn't have made much difference if his real eyes had been there instead – the captain-general was a closed book, even to those of his own kind.

'Not quite,' he said, his voice as deep and rich as it was preternaturally calm. 'The Tower is mine to command directly. As are you now, criminal.'

The polished lenses never so much as flickered.

'I went to some trouble to find you,' said Valdor. 'So your vaunted weapon had better be worth it.'

The lighter was not a well-armed craft. It had a single las-cannon, low-powered, projecting out from under its angular nose-section, and some flimsy armour plates running down its flanks. The engines were reasonably powerful, and it was manoeuvrable enough for its size, but that was about it.

Oll reflected on that as the kilometres passed by. He spent most of his time up in the cockpit with John, watching the burned lands skate underneath them. Everywhere you looked, the destruction was complete. Cities, some of them so vast they would have been capitals on any other world, were little more than slowly cooling fire pits. The short-lived lakes and reservoirs reintroduced as part of the great programme to restore Terra's ecosystem were slowly boiling away again. Great tracts of agricultural land were on fire, their terraces smouldering with chem-encouraged flames.

Those places had once been prosperous, productive and heavily populated. Now they were all empty. Where had the people gone? Maybe they were still all down there somewhere, buried under the top crust of ruins, hiding away and waiting for deliverance. Or maybe they had left months ago, trekking off for places such as the paradise hive where they imagined they might be safe.

There was no question of setting the lighter down anywhere near the few remains of civilisation – whenever they had to drop to earth, they did so a long way from signs of habitation. The fuel tanks had needed refilling twice. Both times, they had siphoned what they needed from the larger wrecks of other craft. The two Space Marines had stood watchfully as the process was completed, bolters drawn, seemingly as suspicious of each other as anything that might emerge out of the shadows.

The hours of airborne monotony passed, and the sky grew darker and redder. The once pristine Himalazian plateau was now a twilight realm of smog and flame, its earth scorched and its low skies permanently overcast. With every kilometre they travelled, the blood-glow of orbital munitions increased steadily, until the nimbus flared across the entire horizon, casting long shadows across a terrain of blasted emptiness. Forks of amber lightning skipped under the palls, briefly illuminating the first jagged pinnacles of blackened spires.

'So there it is,' John remarked simply, as the towers of the Outer Palace slipped onto the magnified viewers.

Oll watched them come closer. 'Is it already over?' he asked, wondering if they'd come too late – the area looked devastated.

'Maybe,' said John. 'The place is hundreds of kilometres across, though – if they're fighting still, it'll be at the centre.'

Enormous walls of smoke hung in the air above the jagged silhouettes, kilometres high, drifting steadily higher up into the atmosphere from where they would be pulled across the entire globe. Oll was no terraformer, but it seemed impossible that a planet could ever recover from pollution on such a scale. Win or lose, he guessed, Terra would never enjoy clear skies again.

'How long before we hit the perimeter?' he asked.

John glanced at the scanners. 'A few hours yet.'

'Fine. I'll get the others ready.'

He clambered back down into the crew hold. Zybes and Katt were asleep, their heads lolling as the lighter fought its way through increasing turbulence. Actae seemed absorbed in some kind of meditative trance. Leetu was methodically preparing his weapon, which lay in pieces on his lap.

There wasn't much for Oll to do. He checked his own laspistol. He thought back over all the journeys he'd taken, just to be here, and how unprepared he still felt. The first task of a soldier was to understand the objective. Be clear about it. Know what you're trying to do. Here, though, it was all about the journey. Just get there in one piece, and things would become clear.

He shook his head, smiling grimly, perfectly aware of the absurdity of it all. As he did so, his eyes met those of the Alpha Legionnaire, the one who called himself by the name of his primarch.

'This all comes down to you, I guess,' Oll said.

Alpharius shrugged – just a tiny movement of those massive shoulder guards.

'You know a way in, Actae tells me,' said Oll. 'And so we're trusting that, without any proof, just because there's nothing better on the table.'

Actae looked up at the mention of her name. 'He isn't alone here,' she said. 'Dozens of his brothers were placed on Terra, down in the catacombs, ready to be activated.'

'For what end?' Oll asked.

'Numerous ends,' said Alpharius. 'As of now, their only purpose will be to aid us.'

Oll looked at him sceptically. 'So you can get us back?' he said. 'To where they are?'

Alpharius nodded. 'The pilot has the coordinates. If he is able to get us close enough, I can take you the rest of the way.'

Oll laughed dryly. 'And then we'll just walk on in.'

Actae didn't smile. 'It's all about timing,' she said coolly. 'If we'd arrived earlier, when the defences were still intact – impossible. Later, and it'll all be over. This is the sweet spot.'

'Nice choice of words,' said Oll, checking the power pack on his weapon. 'You should know that if I had any better options at all, I wouldn't even be contemplating this.'

Actae smiled. 'I do know that.'

Katt woke up. A little later, so did Zybes. That completed the set, the entire gang, ready for action. Oll never needed to give them orders – they got themselves ready, did what they had to. One way or another, this zigzag quest was coming to an end, just as the galaxy fell apart all around them.

'You all right?' he asked Katt. The psyker had been feeling worse and worse the closer they got.

She nodded, not meeting his gaze, and started to prepare. Zybes followed suit. Leetu completed his work, reassembling the archaic bolter expertly. Nobody spoke. The only sound was the rumble of the lighter's engines.

Oll snapped his own helmet on, strapped his flak armour into place. After that he spent a long time with his back against the shuddering hold-wall, trying to keep himself relaxed, and failing. He was tensed up, wound tight. If he closed his eyes he saw nightmares; if he kept them open, he imagined more of them. When the first hit came in, it was almost a relief.

A warning lumen blinked on overhead. The deck rocked, and then bucked harder as something else struck them. Oll heard the engines whine up, and the lighter tilted hard to the right as John began to make evasive manoeuvres.

'Take your stations, people,' he warned them all. 'We're going in.'

To kill, to kill, to kill.

There might once have been other things, other considerations. Hard to recall.

He remembered his name – Khârn. He remembered where he had been born – here, on Terra. So he was home, back on the soil that had first raised him up, though the place looked a bit different now – like every world he ever conquered, a desolation, fit only for bone fragments and whining ghosts. He would blink, and see the place then as it would become very soon – the great brass thrones in place of cities, the mountains of skulls, the skies of liquid fire. The barrier was so thin, now. Just a few more kills, just a little extra push on the tally of slaughter, and it would break entirely.

So where was Angron, just as the victory hove into view? Where was the gene-father he had coaxed and placated and tried to reason with for so long? Why were the primarchs, those squabbling brothers who had driven so much of this long, long war, suddenly careering out of view, as if embarrassed by their respective excesses?

Lost in madness, they said of Angron. Swallowed up by the permanent rage that had always been his destiny. There would be no more words spoken with him, not any more. He had risen to inconceivable heights, becoming a force of destruction the likes of which the galaxy had never witnessed before. His anger was almost a ritual now, outside time, something that would cycle for eternity. He was capable of anything and everything… except reason. The very thing that separated the humans from the beasts, and he had lost it.

To kill, to kill.

Did he regret the change? Did Khârn, the most faithful of all Angron's sons, wish for things to be different? Maybe. Except that he had never known his master undamaged. He had never seen him in his youth, before the Nails had been inserted, and so his loyalty had always been given to a broken angel. And after that, once he'd been given the same bad medicine as his master, it had been easier just to wash any doubt away with fresh blood. When you killed a man, a woman, a child – when you ended a fragile flame of life, when you took away the chance of any further development, of happiness, of sadness, or selfishness or vice or sainthood or intellect – when you did that, in that one moment, the torment ceased. Just a fragment, an atom of peace amid an eternity of rage. But at the same time, in that fleeting glimpse of sanity, you could recall everything you once were. You could remember discourse, and laughter, even pity. And so you had to start again, to move to the next victim, the next challenge, because that knowledge was the worst goad of all.

To kill.

This hunting ground had been the richest he'd ever encountered. His chainaxe had gorged on the blood of the mortal and the ascended. Some had run from him, some had stood firm. Some had screamed at him in hatred, some had wept from fear. It didn't matter how they died, only that they did. The kill-counter kept on turning, the only certain gauge of his achievement.

He was aware of bodies in motion around him. He judged they were of his own Legion, from the copper stench that came with them. Their old pale armour was now as black as every other surface in this despoiled world, blushed only with the mortal stain of those they had ended. He didn't remember their names, either. He might have even killed some of their battle-brothers, during the worst spells of orgiastic slaughter, but if he had done then no one seemed to hold it against him.

Together, they charged out across the old ruined viaduct, the one that speared right into the heart of the tiny Imperium of Mankind. A realm that had once spanned the stars, reduced to a few square kilometres of crumbling estate, soon to be demolished and refashioned into something more suitable for the Great God's triumph.

But, just then, he didn't care about any of that. He looked out, ahead, through the murk and the mire, his helm display overlaying the night with its redundant skein of runes and markers.

He saw a warrior standing tall among other warriors, right up at the terminus of the viaduct's span, his armour as black as his own, withdrawing his blade from the torso of a slain opponent. There was no flourish, no cry of triumph – it was a functional display, just something that needed to be done, but still artful in its spare economy.

The Black Sword had many fighters about him, a whole army, just as Khârn had his warriors by his side. None of those mattered – they were just there to prevent anything getting in the way.

For a second, Khârn paused in his headlong run, watching. He saw the Black Sword wave his fighters on, rousing them to more defiance. They were under heavy fire, but still they advanced through it all, dogged and unyielding. He sensed an old memory stir then, a distant recollection of a kind of fellowship under arms. He remembered a pit, and opponents, and fraternal laughter echoing into the high vaults above.

The memory didn't last. He singled out the Black Sword, the one he had come to kill.

'Mine,' he slurred, gesturing with his blood-soaked axe.

The others didn't protest. There was plenty for them, and they still knew just enough to defer to rank. He was Khârn the Loyal, Khârn the Faithful, the one soul capable of holding them all together for just a little longer while their gene-father ran amok. They were running again, the hounds of war, down the slope towards the enemy, no tactics in mind, no objective in sight, save the one goal, the one target that kept them a step away from total dissolution.

To kill, to kill, to kill.

TWENTY

Close enough
Ulysses contract
The mire

To remain restrained, to remember law, to limit immersion in the path.

Yesugei had always preached that, even in the midst of the worst and bloodiest combat. To lose yourself – that was the danger. Any village-witch could drive themselves mad by supping too deeply from the wells of power. Such practices might yield a moment's glory, but the price would always have to be paid further down the line.

The evidence of that debauchery was all around Naranbaatar just then. He strode through the knee-deep liquid mud, crackling with a nimbus of white gold, his staff spitting with storm-flare. On either flank, the keshig fought their way deeper into the enemy lines. The Khagan was at the forefront, as ever, and very little lasted long against his peerless sword-mastery. The rumbling squadrons of armour struggled to keep up with them, though their powerful guns were welcome.

The galleries and chambers they fought through became

truly colossal – assembly halls, dry-docks and lifter-shafts, all of them so vast as to have an almost ceremonial grandeur to them. Now tens of thousands of fighters swarmed across their swamped floors, making the internal spaces ring with the cacophony of massed combat. Hundreds of tanks rumbled into range to fire, the cannon reports deafening and their incessant engine growl making the decks shake.

Every inch of the path ahead was packed with hosts of the corrupted. The Traitor Marines were the most numerous, advancing in close-set ranks that glimmered with dancing slivers of corposant, but alongside them came far greater horrors – mighty Dreadnoughts, transformed into bizarre fusions of the organic and the mechanical, as well as the yaksha themselves, greater and more malign than any encountered yet. They leapt and shambled out of the black-green darkness, boiling up from every lingering shadow, slobbering and capering in some monstrous parody of mortal joviality.

Those creatures came straight at him, attracted like moths to a flame, just as they did with all the zadyin arga, knowing their peril but also drawn by the promise of a juicier soul to feast on. Their surface grins and capers were all a distortion – the leering mouths were filled with wicked teeth, and those swollen bellies were brimful with poisons. Every Traitor Marine they faced now was riddled with the warp's corruption, turning them steadily into shambolic echoes of the steadfast warriors they had once been.

Surely they must have been horrified. Surely some part of them must have been screaming in horror at what they had become. It made them powerful, to be sure. It made them resilient beyond belief – Naranbaatar had been forced to intervene in countless engagements where numerically superior White Scars units just couldn't break the enemy formations. So perhaps that power was enough for them. The advances

had certainly slowed across the entire battlefield. Ganzorig
was now inside the perimeter, the signals told him, but only
after paying a ruinous price to reduce the outer defences. Qin
Fai was struggling, trying to maintain momentum against the
defensive concentrations strung across the southern ramparts.
The intended link-up of forces had yet to happen, fracturing
the assault and leaving vulnerable points all along the line.

They had always known that breaking the hard external
shell of the space port would be the easiest part of the exercise – the ordu's expertise lay in such shock-attack moves,
and Perturabo had done a typically thorough job of smashing
up the fixed defensive architecture. Now they were into the
defence in depth, the endless series of energy-soaking firefights
to clear out chamber after chamber. Even the Amber spearpoint, blessed with some of the greatest warriors of the ordu,
found the going tough. The Death Guard could soak up tremendous punishment before turning around and doling it
right back. Their reactions may have been slowed, their souls
withered, but they were still fearsomely intelligent, staggeringly
committed, wading through volumes of incoming fire that
should have blasted them into flying clouds of ceramite flecks.

A formation of Terran Armoured Malcadors roared past
him then, throwing up waves of sludge as they rushed the
lines. Their battle cannons boomed in sequence, obliterating a high screen of ironwork behind which a battalion of
Death Guard was dug in hard. Enemy armour responded,
hurling back chem-shells and phosphex mortars. When those
exploded, the already seamy atmosphere became choking and
translucent, a swimming soup of poisons that gnawed at every
armour-seal and tox-filter.

White Scars infantry charged up in the wake of the tanks,
firing bolt pistols one-handed, staying close to prevent the
Traitor Marines from closing on the vehicles. Lascannon fire

lashed out from high up in the galleries, drilling into the corpulent flanks of plague-ridden enemy tank hulls. A squadron of jetbikes screamed along after the volleys, their underslung bolters spitting.

It was still too slow. The far end of the chamber was eight hundred metres off, lost in tox-clouds, with stubborn defensive redoubts all the way along it. At this rate, it might take days of slaughter just to reach the far end.

Naranbaatar rose from the deck, his armour surrounded in a corpus of spinning witch-light. He swept higher, feeling the whistle and whine of projectiles around him. His visual field was the usual mix of tactical overlays and ghostly foresight, a melange of projections and predictions that swam in and out of one another. In the middle distance, still shielded by heavy detachments of traitors in Terminator plate, he saw an astonishing construction grinding its way to the front. It appeared to be some kind of quadrupedal walker, a giant war engine built from the usual bulbous plates of adamantium and ceramite, only bulked out with pale grey flesh and surrounded in loops of translucent tubing. The unmistakeable aura of the daemonic pulsed and throbbed across its calloused surface. It carried massive fist-mounted cannons, and its ridged back was studded with gaping rocket launchers. It bellowed as it came, a roar of pain and fury. Whatever intelligence still remained at the heart of the thing was in misery and confusion, goaded into combat by those around it. It also carried massive fuel sacs under its fleshy belly, feeding what looked to be some daemon-fused reactor core. If it got into close range, it would raise havoc.

He whirled around, building momentum and extending his staff out horizontally. The storm wind quickened, catching on the calligraphic screeds lashed to his armour. His golden eyes went white, his hearts thudded into overdrive, his palms became hot.

'Shala'ak!' he cried.

The force left his body, bursting free of the skull tip of his staff. For a moment he felt as if he would be ripped along with it, sent sailing alongside its kinetic energy, but he battled to hold position, suspended high above the battlefield.

The warp-bolt he'd summoned, a writhing sphere of pure annihilation, leapt straight over the heads of the multitudes, striking the war engine in its fleshy underside. The daemon engine reared up instantly, howling blindly, before the burrowing immolation reached its swaying fuel tanks.

The explosion rocked the entire chamber, obliterating the daemon engine and blowing its hundreds of support troops from their feet. Artillery pieces tilted over, tanks were driven skidding into one another. A ravening impact wave streaked out, yanking chemical spillage along with it, clearing a huge undulating crater out from the epicentre. Everything struck by those flying chem-spatters roared into unnatural flame, and soon Traitor Marines were blundering into one another, blinded and burning, a lumbering rampage that threw their tightly disciplined advance into confusion. A cheer went up from the Legion forces closest to him, and the White Scars worked to press the advantage. The Terran Armoured units were not far behind, and every available gun targeted the newly opened breach with storms of cannon fire.

Naranbaatar withdrew swiftly before he was targeted by return fire, sinking to the ground again, light-headed and breathing hard. The summonings were getting more difficult the deeper they went. He did not witness how well the Legion was able to capitalise. He dropped to his knees, trying not to pass out, knowing that he was already dangerously overloaded. Foul vapours rose up over him, their fingers snagging at his limbs. He gripped his staff two-handed – he required time, just a little, and then he would be needed again. The daemons would already be limping in closer, alerted to his power. He sensed the rapid movement around him – Legion warriors racing to make the most of the respite, their boots splashing through the filth.

A gauntlet reached out then, and pulled him up. Naranbaatar clambered awkwardly to his feet again, looked up into the helm of his helper, and saw his primarch standing by his side.

'Khagan,' he breathed, bowing clumsily.

The Khan reached out a steadying hand. 'You honour your calling,' he said. 'That was powerfully done.'

Naranbaatar tried to clear his head. His body was already recovering – his mind would have to follow swiftly. He couldn't see any sign of Namahi and the keshig – had they gone on ahead?

'How may I serve?' he asked.

The Khan looked out at the battle. His dao blade ran with thick gobbets of slime, his armour was caked in gore. Ahead of them, around them, his Legion threw itself at the enemy, whooping ancient war cries as their blades whirled. They were dying for every metre of ground they took. For all that, they still hurled themselves onward, never hesitating, never doubting.

'I have already asked so much,' the Khan said softly.

'My lord?' asked Naranbaatar, unsure if he was hearing it right.

The Khan turned back to him. 'Are we close enough?' he asked. 'Can you sense him yet?'

Naranbaatar drew in a long breath. His senses were fogged with every kind of warp apparition, clamouring at him, yelling out their presence with every foul word they spat.

He concentrated. The space port's structure swelled up into his mind's eye, a colossal pinnacle of corrupted stone and steel.

From the inside, it was hard to focus on – the distilled horror of it made his retinas spike with pain. Webs of warp energy throbbed and flickered within its dark profile like disease in a body, a mass of green-tinged cells and tumours. For a moment, the fecundity of it was dizzying – he could scarcely tell which auguries were coming from which location. He forced himself to work harder, to filter out the extraneous echoes.

And then it fell into focus. There could be no mistake. The source of it all – the genesis of the despair, the lens through which the greater corruption was filtered. It did not hide itself. Maybe it couldn't – maybe power of this magnitude was akin to the Emperor's, overflowing, superabundant, impossible to conceal. Even to witness it from afar was daunting. It was a repudiation of all they had ever told themselves about the Path of Heaven. It was indulgence beyond reason, a wilful drowning in power, the surrender of all human control.

He snapped away from the visions. Around him, the auditory thunder of battle rushed back in to take their place. He stared up at the fixed point of the dragon-helm, as if that might prevent him from cutting loose entirely.

'I can,' he said.

The Khan nodded. 'Then he wants this as much as I do.'

'But Ganzorig is still too far off. We cannot yet give you–'

'Time runs out. Are you strong enough?'

And that was the question. The strain of it might kill him before completion. Of more importance, it might kill his lord. But time was already racing away from them while warriors died in the plague-sunk halls of the Lion's Gate. In that place, at that time, there was only one answer to be made.

'Give me the order, Khagan,' Naranbaatar said, steeling himself for what had to come next. 'I shall be as strong as the task demands.'

* * *

'Where are we now?' asked Morarg.

'*In a myth of this world,*' said the Remnant. '*One forgotten by most of the souls of the age. Soon it will be remembered by none at all.*'

The sun was bright. A sapphire sea stretched away in all directions, calm and placid. A single boat rocked on the swell – an ancient vessel, with a sail and oars. Under the beating sun, the crew were tying a man to its mast. He didn't appear to be struggling.

'*This ship will set sail for an island,*' the Remnant said. '*That island is inhabited by beings of such allure that no mortal man can resist their call. Any sailor straying too close is destined to dash his ship against the rocks. The man you see wishes to witness them for himself. What can he do? As of this moment, he is in command of himself. He knows, though, that once he reaches his destination, he will not be.*'

Morarg watched the crew stop up their ears with wax plugs, and pull the last knots tight. 'But he has surrendered command,' he said.

'*No, he is still giving the orders. The men obey him. He has made a contract while he still has the power to do so, one that will give him what he desires while preserving both himself and the ship. He knows his strength, he knows his weakness. That is an attractive quality in a commander, I would say.*'

The vision rippled away, just as the others had done. With dizzying speed, the scene rushed to the next one – the deep void, on board the *Terminus Est* itself. Its captain, still calling himself Calas Typhon, was on the bridge. The deck rocked as heavy broadsides fired. Every member of the crew was furiously busy. On the scopes, the markers of enemy battleships swarmed towards them. Each bore the sigil of the First Legion.

'This is Zaramund,' said Morarg.

'*But you were not there.*'

'No.'

The Remnant shook its flabby head in amazement. *'You never questioned it, did you? Your Legion's second-in-command, off on his own. Given his head to mingle with the sons of the Lion, even though he was such a strange one, an uncanny one. He never seemed to get properly injured, did he?'*

'It was not my place to judge the First Captain.'

'No, it wasn't. It was your master's. Only, he didn't seem to judge him much either, did he?'

Inside the vision, the void-war broke out in earnest, with Typhon overseeing it all dispassionately. The First Captain stood confidently, knowing just what he was doing.

'He's here for his own reasons,' the Remnant whispered, creeping up around the command throne, unseen by the other figures present. *'You see that now, don't you? There's no Legion objective here, only his own. He's already committed to his path. Why, in all the planes of suffering, was he allowed to do that?'*

Morarg permitted himself a flash of irritation. 'You ask a lot of questions, daemon.'

The Remnant laughed, then gazed up at the First Captain's daunting profile. Typhon's raw charisma was already obvious, even before the grosser changes that were still to come. *'Only because it fascinates me. You people never once raised so much as a query.'*

'Just the way they made us,' said Morarg.

'On Barbarus? Or afterwards?'

Before Morarg could answer, the rush of displacement came on again, a jarring swirl through space and time, a surge of cold dislocation, until they were back at a place Morarg recognised all too well.

'This is Ynyx,' he said.

'After Ynyx,' the Remnant corrected. *'The reunion of father and son.'*

Ahead of them, Mortarion now stood on the black sands of a world's ending. Before him was Typhon, looking little different to how he had been at Zaramund, except maybe even more self-possessed, even more cocksure.

Typhon bowed, prompting a scornful wince from his master.

'Do not bow and scrape,' Mortarion told him. 'I seek truth, not obeisance.'

'Truth,' echoed the Remnant. *'You heard that? He doesn't even ask where he's been! This is all very odd.'*

'I broke away,' said Typhon, 'because I needed the distance to see clearly.'

'Oh, the insolence,*'* breathed the Remnant, clearly admiring it. *'And yet it passes without censure. He is welcomed back to the Legion with nary a word of reproach. That is either very generous indeed, or your master knew more than he was letting on.'*

Morarg peered a little harder at Typhon's outline. There was something strange about it, a fluttering, just beyond the edge of true vision, like thousands of tiny wings disturbing the air.

The Remnant slunk up close. *'Oh, you can see it now, can you? I imagine your father saw it the first time. Remember, he had spoken to one of our number already. He had some art of his own, even if he hesitated to use it.'*

'But if... he *knew*–' Morarg began.

'Why did he *let it go on? Indeed. Something of a puzzle.'*

The next instant, they were back on the *Terminus Est* again, right in the heart of the Destroyer Hive attack. The thick screams filled the corridors again, the foul stench of rotting flesh, the bloody excrement sloshing across the decks. Just going back, even within the confines of a vision, was almost more than Morarg could bear. It had been timeless, that pain, cut adrift in an eternity of agony without end. But worst of all, far worse than the physical sensations, was the knowledge, in the present, that they had failed to endure it. It had been too much for them. They had capitulated.

He turned on the Remnant. 'Take me away from this place.'

For once, the daemon had no mocking response to offer. *'It had to happen,'* it breathed, as if awestruck by it. *'This was the great ritual. The thing that would change you. Once over, you could never be dominated again, not by anything and not by anyone, but he could never have taken the decision to inflict it on you. Remember what you saw of him on Molech. Never again! Never would it be* his *scythe at his own sons' necks.'*

Morarg looked up, only to see Typhus stagger down the screaming corridors, surrounded now by wholly visible flies, swollen with power and disease until it was spilling out of every orifice. This was the source of it, the incubator for the Destroyer, roaring with a mix of joy and horror, his battle-plate splitting open and dissolving into clots of pure spinning blackness.

'He did it,' Morarg said, unable to prevent a little hatred from colouring the words.

'Yes, he did,' said the Remnant. *'But who let him in?'*

The vision shifted, sliding up through deck after deck, showing freeze-frames of serried horrors – guts sliced open and forever spilling, eyes plucked out only to regrow and fester again, battle-hardened muscle sloughing from the bone and slapping wetly on the plasteel. Eventually they reached the highest pinnacle, the cathedral of misery, open to the void. The rest of the fleet hung amid the multi-hued abyss of the warp itself, flung across dimensions and becalmed in the neon embrace of living hell. The screams were audible out there, multiplying and folding over one another until you could hear them for what they really were: a hymn of unending praise.

And there was Mortarion himself, out in the void, standing

atop the spine of the *Terminus Est*. His arms were raised up, his head thrown back. The agony on his features was just as it had been on Molech – no triumph, only awareness, terrible awareness.

'My blood and my bone!' he was crying, beseeching the shifting curtains of the empyrean. 'The force of my will and the power of my spirit! These are yours to command, if you only grant my people deliverance!'

And in the deep vaults of the warp, in the darkest pits of the realm of dreams, something vast and ancient stirred, rising up through the tiers of experience to take the place it had been destined to take since the first decay of the first living cell, but, according to the paradoxical laws of that nowhere-place, only once a mortal decision had been taken.

'Enough,' said Morarg, unwilling to witness what was coming next.

'*I agree,*' said the Remnant. '*Quite enough.*'

After that, they were back in darkness. The screams were gone, the tortures were over. Morarg breathed heavily. The plagues were fizzing in his bloodstream, in his suppurating flesh, in his rheumy eyes. There was no going back – this was what he was, now.

The Remnant waited patiently, looking morose. In that darkness, its famishment made it virtually invisible again.

'Everything happened as we were told,' Morarg said.

'*It did.*'

'Typhus brought the Destroyer.'

'*He did.*'

'Mortarion brought us deliverance.'

'*He did.*'

Morarg looked up at the daemon. 'But there was no deception.'

'*How could you ever have thought it? Your father is a son of the Anathema. The warp gives no honour to dupes.*'

'But why?'

'*He tied himself to the mast while he still could. He could never have given you the agony, only the cure. There was a decision, but it was not when you think it was. The moment of crisis was on Ynyx, when he could have had Typhus slain, but only said* I seek the truth. *That was the crux. The powers were listening, and all then unfolded as it had to.*'

'But I was with him. The whole time. I saw his doubts – he didn't know what was happening. None of us did.'

'*You are right. He didn't. He never knew how, or at what time, or in what way. He only required one revelation – that Typhus was the vector. Let him in, then do whatever you wish, in whatever way seems apt to you – the god will take care of the rest.*'

Morarg turned away from the creature. He could sense the lie in the words. But, then again, it was a creation of lies – perhaps what he had been shown was real enough. What was worse to contemplate, that Mortarion had been a victim, or that he had been the perpetrator? The end was the same, but the means by which they all arrived there… it felt as if all had been upended.

'Why tell me these things?' he murmured.

'*Because you were already beginning to doubt,*' said the Remnant. '*You were already believing that your master was a blind fool. He was not. Whether he cursed you or redeemed you, it was his hand that steered the ship.*'

The daemon limped up closer, its wide eyes glistening in the dark.

'*So you must fight for him with utter commitment,*' it told him, '*or fight against him with all your heart. You cannot ignore* him, *you cannot pity* him *– he is your primarch, and your fate* *was shaped by his will.'* The creature's gaze was intent. *'So what will you do, Caipha? Knowing this, what will you do now?'*

Morarg looked back at him. Emotions warred within him, as turbulently as anything that had assailed him on the ship.

He wanted to reply, to settle it there, go back to the war and play his part. But he couldn't. Not yet. Because he didn't know.

The objective was out of reach. For a tantalising period of rapid advance, it had felt as if they might even take it on schedule, but then the resistance had thickened, like blood coagulating over a wound, and now the way ahead promised nothing but pain.

Shiban Khan had killed as prodigiously as ever. He had led his combined brotherhoods in from the walls, slaying enemy champions and foot-soldiers alike with his whirling, crackling guan dao. The White Scars had fought their way up from the bridgeheads and into the dark heart of the Lion's Gate space port. What they had seen there didn't surprise any of them – they knew enough of the Death Guard already to foresee the depths to which they would sink, and so the horror had been anticipated, just as the deadliness of Mortarion's terror-troops had been.

Shiban had forced a ferocious pace, using his assigned armour squadrons to blast open shortcuts to the big orbital arrays. Every khan knew the layout of the interior in exhaustive detail – they had studied cartoliths for weeks beforehand, memorising every elevator shaft and assembly hall. It was likely they knew even more than the place's defenders, who had only ever occupied it as a staging point. Shiban had ordered pinpoint strikes on isolated structural elements, risking section-collapse for the chance to burn swiftly inward. Several vehicle elevators had been taken, allowing transport of even the super-heavies up the levels. The brotherhoods had gone surely through the degenerating maze of chambers, cutting their way into the stinking and foetid caverns, keeping close together, guarding the precious tanks from counter-strikes and using the hulls' formidable gunnery to blast clear paths onward.

At every step, though, he remained conscious of the eyes on him – not the enemy, who knew or cared little for who he was, but those he led. The veteran Chogorians fought as hard to earn his esteem as they did to reach the target. The Terrans and the newbloods did the same, particularly those who knew little of the details of the sundered home world, and who worked all the harder to prove themselves worthy of the honour of belonging to the Legion. In every gesture they made, in every lowered gaze and respectful vox-response, he heard the same thing: *You are Tachseer. You are the Restorer.*

Torghun would have laughed at that. Shiban's old rival, his old enemy, the one who had eventually redeemed his errors through sacrifice, the one who Shiban still yearned to speak to one last time, to make amends for all that misplaced pride, all that resentment, Torghun would have laughed to see how things had gone: Shiban Khan, the wide-eyed and eager commander on the white battlefields of Chondax, risking everything for a mere glimpse of the primarch in action, now venerated by the next generation of stripling warriors as some kind of totem of the Legion's soul.

He couldn't protect them all. However hard he fought at their head, however much he tried to shield them from this enemy, his warriors died. The newbloods would throw themselves at the Plague Marines, their bladework immaculate and their fervour exemplary, but they would still come up short. You could punch their hides with bolt-shells, you could sever their sinews with tulwar-strikes, you could pepper them with frag-charges and mortar-blasts, and still they would come back at you, again, again, their impassive green lenses glowing in the deathly gloom, never complaining, never shouting battle cries or denunciation, just *existing*, as impossible to eradicate as despair itself.

The best weapon was speed, and now that momentum was falling away, leaving them open to the grind of attrition. Fury could only achieve so much against an enemy like this. They were never roused to anger, never provoked into rashness. Feints never drew them on, diversions never deceived them. The only tactic left seemed to be an equal and opposite willingness to suffer, to take them on on their own terms, to stare into those seamy, rheum-addled eyes and hold your ground right until the pale lights had been extinguished and the next one beckoned.

Shiban's spearhead had been charged with taking Orbital Battery Seven, one of over forty major surface-to-void artillery installations. It was the first of those within range of the Amber incursion point, one the Khagan had desired taken quickly. Control the guns, he had argued, and you could make the Warmaster's fleet start to fear again. Shiban had asked for the honour of taking it, knowing how fiercely the silos would be defended.

Now he could see the guns themselves. At the very end of a typically vast gallery, enclosed by a roof so high it was entirely lost in accumulated smoke-palls, he could see with his own eyes the first of the giant cannons, each one nearly half a kilometre tall, their immense barrels surrounded by a mini-city of shock absorbers and coolant circuits and ammunition loaders and guidance pistons. They were arranged in long rows, their snouts protruding somewhere high up, piercing layer upon layer of shielding. You felt as if you could almost reach out, now – stretch a hand towards the activation panels and begin to hurl vengeance into the heavens again.

In between him and them, though, was the hateful enemy –
advancing through the unnatural mists in numbers, their ranks
thick and their support dug in. They did not rush to the charge,
but instead soaked up attack after attack. The terrain around
them was now their ally – the port's internal atmosphere was
dripping with poisons, its walkways were rotting and treacherous, the walls themselves mumbled with the witch-words
of semi-formed yaksha.

The only option left was to press the attack, right down the
long gallery, launching wave after wave at them, sustaining
the belief that the next one must surely make the breakthrough. Chakaja roared out his weather-magic, blasting
apart the thickest concentrations of uncanny presences; Yiman
roused his fighters to yet more feats of endurance; the tank
commanders dug deep and drove their units hard at appar-
itions of living nightmares; the squad sergeants, newblood
and veteran alike, got up time and again to brave the bursts
of phosphex and nerve gas and chem-laced flamers.

Shiban raced ahead of the swiftest of them all, darting
around the slamming choreography of impacts, knowing
that he had to be *seen*, to be *witnessed*, because if he could
somehow break the defences here, then those he commanded
would keep believing. No fighting he had ever done before had
mattered as much as this – not on the bridge of the *Swordstorm*
when the entire Legion's fate was in the balance, nor against
the debauched artisans of Fulgrim's entourage – because this
was no longer for himself, but for those who carried the flame,
for those who would lead in the future.

You were the brothers of the Storm, he had told his warriors
on the eve of the first assault. *When victory is achieved here, they
shall call you its lords.*

First, though, they had to survive this. Even as Shiban cut
his next opponent apart, he heard more cries of agony as his

people died. He saw a Plague Marine dragged to the earth by two newbloods, only to rise up again, shake them both off and resume the fight. He saw Orgiz, a wild and beautiful fighter, laid low by the horror of acid-charges, his priceless armour eroded away like moth-eaten fabric. He saw Chakaja crunched off his feet by the malign power of the instantiating daemons, then struggle not to be eaten alive by them as they swarmed over him. He saw a Conqueror battle tank stall on its charge, only to be smashed apart by Death Guard heavy weapons, its crew burned alive inside the raging hull.

'*Khagan!*' Shiban roared, his throat throbbing with the pain of repeated injunctions. '*For the honour of the Khan!*'

And those who still survived answered the call, fighting through the pain, trudging up through the mire and the miasma and the sludge. Their armour was blackened and befouled, their blades blunted and doused, their bolters jammed and their ammo-chambers clattering empty. Yet still they came, heads low and dogged, guided by the memory of what had been, and what could still be. They were unable to turn back now, unable to do anything but advance into that sliding avalanche of hatred and madness, preserving, for a brief moment, what it was to be human, and greater than human.

Shiban caught sight of his next target – a grotesque mass of blistered ceramite with tripartite horns protruding from a scabrous helm – and forced himself up to the attack-sprint. When the monster turned to meet his charge, he saw just how scooped-out by the warp it was. Virtually nothing of the old human occupant could have been left in that mouldering assortment of rotting armour, fogged with crawling insects and glistening with exposed viscera. It was a *thing*, not a living soul – a vile jest at the expense of the entire species. No spark of mortal fire resided in that tortured psyche still, only emptiness, numbness, surrender to an insane torpor that took away the surface agony even as it chewed through what little remained of the human within.

They are killing us, because they have already lost everything, Shiban realised, leaping into contact, his glaive held tight and the disruptor snarling. *So what must we lose, before we can match this? What sacrifice, what pain, must we endure before we can hurt them back?*

TWENTY-ONE

Devil-boy
The empty road
Little names

She seemed able to endure them all, even in combination.

And she herself was tripartite. Erebus found himself almost laughing when he discovered it. *Of course* there was more than one of her; of course there were tricks she hadn't revealed yet. The discovery was startling, but also a little thrilling.

You couldn't see the effect, at first. The arrival of his companions tended to confuse things. They ripped base matter up as they emerged through it, tearing it apart and mixing it with whatever clots of the warp they had dragged through with them. They made the air ignite, kicked the sand up into burning clouds, shattered the earthenware into flying splinters. They were immense, too – huge creatures of bone and sinew that burst the stone-built lodge apart with every stretch and bellow. They shimmered, they jerked, their outlines initially struggling to solidify, showering the ruins of the woman's old home with falls of broken stone and rubble. As they unfurled up to their full stature, unroofing the hovel and tearing the awnings away, the naked sky was exposed again, blood-red from the sandstorms.

But she grew with them. She never cowered or tried to get away. She rose up in parallel with those unnatural companions, her body swelling and growing translucent to match their own impermanence. That was when you glimpsed it first– that she had more than one face, and more than a single pair of hands, and different veils of clothing that rippled and flapped in the racing gyre.

The unnatural companions roared right at her, lacing the night air with venomous spittle. The bird-creature was first to strike, lashing out with its snake-headed staff. Then the bull-headed beast launched itself at her, swinging an axe that caught fire as it struck the earth. The serpent slithered around her ankles, swaying upwards to coil itself around her waist, even as the empty-eyed cadaver slopped and staggered its ruinous path towards her. They were steeped in the ether, those creatures – some of the mightiest god-aspects ever to answer his call. Their hides glistened with the afterbirth of the empyrean, their slanted eyes blazed with the specialised hatred-for-life that only they truly possessed. Their fangs snapped shut, their talons flexed open; they weaved in and out of one another's embrace until they formed a kind of single enclosing organism, a beautiful expression of the Pantheon's rare unity of purpose.

But she struck back at them. The earth itself rose up around her, the stone breaking off and erupting into shattered columns. The sand flew and blinded, caustic as acid, stripping away flesh as it scoured and burned. The sky cracked with thunder, the packed earth shook, and above it all the red moon shone. The beasts surrounded her, smothering and raking, and she marshalled her craft against them, more than holding her own.

Erebus found himself redundant as that all unfolded, standing back as his creatures went to work, his only function to bring them in, to help them cross the threshold. He gazed up at the contest, held rapt by it, feeling the deep art

unleashed, the mastery of powers he had never even dreamed
of. The ether dragged hard at him, ripe to haul the whole place
into its impossible embrace, only held back by this strange
counter-magic, this discipline lodged in a single place, a single
time. Was this strange strength of the warp, too? Surely it had
to be – its no-place was the source of all potency – but it felt…
different, somehow, as if its origins went down into the foundations of the physical world itself, a well that never dried up,
one whose black waters fed something truly primordial and
rooted and unforgetting. Ah, but the heresy of that! All roads
led to the empyrean in the end, whatever comforting stories
you might tell yourself otherwise. That was the very first article
of the faith, the one from which all the rest sprung, so he had
better remember it.

It was at that point that he saw her many selves emerge,
cycling rapidly like overlaid frames of a confused vid-animation.
He saw a woman taking on the daemons, her dark skin as hard
as the staff she twisted around her in her impressive anger,
majestic at the apex of a long life. He saw a youth, vital as star-
light, fast as the racing waters, slender limbs wielding a sickle
that flashed under the blood moon. And he saw a crone, withered black like an olive, hard as twisted tree roots, freezing
everything she clutched with long knuckled fingers. All of them
were deadly, and all of them were *her*, switching rapidly from
image to image, never settling, as if an eternity of evolution
had been jumbled up and replayed over and over, provoked
into being by this violation of the desert sanctuary, the place
where past and present and future merged into a kind of arid
timelessness.

Erebus had thought she was wearing a dress – a cotton-spun
thob – but now saw that it was a single piece of twine, wound
and wound about her but coming apart to form a cocoon
of protection. It was impossibly long, going on and on as if

forever, like the names the Custodians inscribed on the inside of their armour; but whereas those names marked the end of many lives, this was the signifier of a single life, ancient and interwoven with everything of importance that had ever happened here.

He tried to intervene, to wade into that great clash of god-aspects, but the sandstorm pushed him back, burning his flesh with its howling pressure. The entire crater seemed to be coming apart around them all, its concentric rings cracking and tumbling, with the detritus caught up in the maelstrom and sent sailing around the epicentre. He was losing his footing, slipping down into a whirlpool of hissing grains.

She cried aloud, and Erebus heard three voices overlaid, all of them enraged and in pain. The beasts were shrieking in their turn, wounded to their hate-hot cores by the power she unloaded at them. He saw the cadaver staggering, its loose flesh ripped from exposed bone. He saw the serpent crushed under a disdainful heel, and the bull-creature sent reeling from the staff's tip. The vile bird, with translucent plumage in every hue of an outlandish spectrum, jabbed in close, only to have its feathers plucked from its hide and its eyes put out with a deft flick of the sickle.

Blood started to enter the vortex of whirling matter, gobbets of it, some truly human, some just a cheap copy. Erebus caught glimpses of real pain amid the fury – a wince from the woman, a gasp from the crone. The twine was unravelling, severed in many places now. The quicksand sucked at them all, bubbling under their bloodied feet.

She could have been magnificent, Erebus thought to himself. *She could have been the queen of the warp.* He smiled ruefully, capable of pride even as the world around him shook itself into oblivion. *But I have stamped on another scorpion, and now the desert is almost free of its sting. Praise be to me.*

She killed them all, in the end. Or, since they were not truly of that plane, she *banished* them. She undid their ties to the world of the senses, unpicking them like a seamstress at a torn cowl. They yammered and they squealed, but she was remorseless, countering their outlandishness with a kind of infinite maternal patience. Watching it all, Erebus realised then how she must have done it. The Great Deed. And a kind of awe took hold of him, for he understood at that moment that she had been nothing other than truthful with him – she had hoped the whole thing would just end there, with the Scheme of the Anathema perpetually unfinished. And now, in her own home, he had demonstrated to her just how wrong she had been about that, how foolish, and what her intervention had actually achieved.

That was the stiletto he needed to finish her.

'Fury,' he said, at last making some progress through the tempest. 'Obsession. Despair. Power. These were the things He set Himself up against. These are the things I brought with me. You see it now, do you? You see what He saw, all those centuries ago?'

She was crying out by then, from the agony of her wounds, or maybe even from the knowledge he had given her. If she could have done, she might have called out to her old conspirator, the one with whom she had both created and destroyed, the one she had both loved and hated. But He was far away now, fully occupied with troubles of His own. She was fighting still, defiant to the end, but her soul's storm was faltering.

'I can admire that,' Erebus said. 'He made a choice. The wrong one, but a choice all the same. You, though. *You.*' He chuckled, pulling a knapped blade from his belt. 'You wanted it all ways. Meddle here, meddle there, and then return to the desert with your statues.'

His boot crushed the figurine she had showed him, and he barely noticed. The last of the unnatural companions was sent screaming back into the hole in reality, tumbling back down the vortex they had brought with them. Erda fell to her knees, bruised and lacerated, her shifting visage now settled back to how she had been when he'd arrived. Her dress hung in tattered loops around her, the threads prised apart.

Erebus knelt down beside her, hauling her exhausted head up so she had to look at him.

'Devil-boy, you called me?' he hissed viciously, remembering every slight that had ever been aimed at him. 'Maybe so. Maybe that's what I've always been. But you see what I can do now, what I can summon when the need arises. So maybe being a devil-boy isn't so very shabby.'

He pressed the edge of the athame against her blood-blotched neck, making the skin stretch.

'But I, unlike Him, have no pretensions against the divine,' he whispered softly. 'I would have raised you up as a monarch, had you grasped the chance. Even now, I feel the unfamiliar tug of mercy on my hearts. So, on the acceptance of the one condition that He has always resisted, I still propose to let you live.'

Her dark eyes flickered up to meet his. Despite everything, she wanted to hear it.

'Worship me,' he told her, smiling softly.

The fire in her eyes went out. Her limbs went slack.

This was the moment he lived for. The instant of total defeat. He watched her swallow, trying to find the words with which to accept his terms, to articulate lips that were caked with her own blood.

She drew in a painful breath, and spat across his helm. Then she smiled crookedly.

'I said no to Him,' she rasped. 'And He might even have been worth it.'

Erebus looked down at her, too inured to serial rejection to be overly surprised. His fingers tightened on the knife-hilt.

'As you wish,' he said. 'Gods, though, what a waste.'

Sigismund saw Khârn come for him out of the fog bank.

The World Eater made no attempt to disguise his attack run. Neither did those who came with him. More than a hundred warriors of Angron's Legion, with the sounds of many more coming up behind them. They were raving now, with the last slivers of a rational consciousness stripped from them. They howled as they ran, more like beasts than men. For a moment, seeing that, you could imagine you had been suddenly transported to some wild world of eternal savagery, not the ancestral home of the species itself.

The warriors under Sigismund's command were already outnumbered. He had been preparing to fall back again, once the Sons of Horus had been sufficiently blooded. That was the only thing his primarch had commanded him to do – to make them cry out from pain. In truth, it was all he was ever going to be able to do, for he could see clearly enough that the war was already lost. This was an act of defiance, nothing more. He might slow them a little, but his objective was, and had always been, merely to do damage.

He could scarcely remember a time when that hadn't been at least partly true. For seven years, they had fought the steady defeat, standing up against the heretics more out of a desire to punish them than out of a true conviction that the thing could be won. He had resisted that in his conscious mind. He had always pressed for more, prompted most strongly by those who had believed in him, like Keeler.

No longer. Vengeance was the whole sum of the universe, now. Vengeance was the entire truth. Vengeance was all that remained, the final performance of duty, not done for some external motive, but for its own sake.

He wouldn't stop going at them. Not now. Not ever.

'We engage,' he voxed to Rann, who was deep in his own combat with a Sons of Horus warrior.

No answer came. Rann was clearly too busy to reply, neck-deep in his own world of fighting, but the message would have got home to those that needed the command. All those who still fought alongside him, those who he had dragged out of their slack despair and hurled straight into the open jaws of the enemy, would have to hold firm for a little longer. Thousands of them would die for this indulgence, but that mattered not. He had made them sanctified. He was the maker of martyrs.

Sigismund pushed the corpse of his last sacrificial victim away. The lifeless body hit the viaduct's deck hard before toppling off into oblivion. Freed up, the sword shivered keenly in his hands. Its spirit was aroused, its chorus of slaughter whipped up by the fire-torn winds around him. It knew an enemy worthy of its status when it saw one.

At Sigismund's back was the terminus tower – a monstrous pile of plasteel and ouslite, parapets crowned with a destroyed cat's cradle of comms equipment. On either side of him was a plunge into a smoke-filled abyss. Ahead of him stretched the old elevated transitway, the blast-rails at its sides ripped clean off, the deck littered with mortar-punched holes. The World Eaters rampaged along it, leaping across the voids, howling and screaming in a rolling scrum of frenzy.

Behind him, he could hear his Templar Brethren forming up for the defence – the heavy clunk of shields being planted, the smart smack of magazines being slid into place. None of those warriors would get in the way of the ritual to come.

None of the enemy would trouble him either. Despite the hundreds of warriors already contesting that high place, the two of them might as well have been entirely alone. This was about them. From the beginning of time, and to its ending, this would always be about them. The knight and the beast. The believer and the infidel.

Khârn swerved around a heap of charred metal railings, picking up more speed. Sigismund got a final look in, before finally raising his blade into guard. He didn't recognise much of the man he had once known. They had fought one another in the bowels of the *Conqueror* without armour, a test of prowess that stripped away all the advantages of technology and sorcery, giving each fight a human signature of its own. The juggernaut thundering towards him just then, though, looked more like some ruined war machine than a Space Marine, swathed in cracked battleplate and seething blood-slicks. Khârn was far greater in stature than he had been on the primarch's flagship, the very air around him boiling off his steam-wreathed armour. His power axe, absurdly large even in such immense hands, was already roaring, spinning out gobbets of hot oil and blood from its last kill. He stank, just as he had done on the Lion's Gate walls – a stench of burned brass and rotting flesh, so pungent now that it blotted out the hundred other aromas of battle.

Sigismund planted himself firmly, braced for impact, and the two of them crashed together. The power axe smashed into the longsword, screaming as its teeth skittered down its edge, before Sigismund sidestepped away from the momentum of the charge, letting Khârn skid around to come at him again.

After that, the world around them both became unimportant. Faint cries and clashes got through, but already those meant nothing – the totality of the duel consumed them both. Sigismund's concentration was complete, immersed in the world of the sword, the blade immersed in his. His limbs moved with unconscious immediacy, honed by a lifetime of constant combat. No thrust was made with thought – it was all automatic now, muscle memory, instinct. The visual images before him broke up, no longer solid figures but fragments, the edge of a helm, the glint of a mica-dragon tooth, the rusted sheen of a pauldron-stud.

'You,' grunted Khârn, his voice already strained almost beyond sense, a breathy bloody mess of ground-down teeth and split lips. *'Again.'*

How many times had they battled before? A dozen? More? It had all changed at the Lion's Gate ramparts. The rules had switched there, the game changed. Sigismund had engaged the physical body in front of him, but had felt the infinite power that now coiled up under its skin – the raw witchery of it, bursting out of every wound. Strike this one, blood him, and more of that world of madness was revealed.

So Sigismund said nothing. No words now, not for this monster. No remembrance of the way it had been between them.

I no longer fight for the Imperium as it was.

He turned, he slashed. He withdrew, he parried. He blocked, he pushed back. He crunched in hard, he let the blow pass him. Automatic. Faster and stronger. And he still had more. The emptiness within was almost complete – a total hollowness, erasure of brotherhood, of laughter or sport, until it was just this, movement, action, reaction, throttle it, choke it, drive out the life of your enemy, stamp him, burn him, *punish* him.

'I… *murdered* you on those walls,' Khârn slurred. 'I would have… *taken* you then.'

Why was he talking? Why was he trying to reach out now? Did he want to resume the debate they had started, before his primarch had intervened and ripped the conclusion away from them both?

Too late. The arguments had all been made. That was the difference – Sigismund had nothing to contribute any more, at least not in rhetoric.

Swipe, slam, jab, crunch, crack, swing. In the past, he might have had some notion of attack, some idea of defence. Now the two halves merged together. He saw the black smear of his blade pass in front of his eyes, as if propelled by hands other than his own. He felt dissociated from it all, as if he were witnessing the contest from the outside. He began to sense that this was simply the beginning of a road, one devoid of anything other than the need to move along it; an empty road, featureless, stretching away forever.

'What has… *changed* in you?' Khârn growled, slashing wildly, trying to break through the impassive screen of attack-defence, raging against it as if it were a physical wall. 'Are you… *dead* already?'

Yes, maybe he was. Jubal had told him, long ago, that he needed to free himself of the chains, to generate some kind of joy in what he did, and for a while, for a long while, he had tried to learn from that. But now he needed the chains. The chains bound him to this beautiful, horrific sword, the blade that had helped him learn the truth, the weapon which suited him so perfectly that he might even begin to wonder if it had been made for him alone, then held ready, locked in some dark oubliette, for the day when hope was revealed as a chimera and it was made clear that the road led nowhere, for it was only about the road, the path, the ritual.

He struck the first blood-blow, severing Khârn's armour and stripping out a long sliver of skin and muscle. The World Eater staggered back, his onslaught checked, briefly amazed.

That was the moment, Sigismund thought. That was the point at which he might have said something to his old sparring partner – a morsel of comfort, a recognition that they had all been made into monsters by this war. Or he might have raged at him instead, spilling out the anger he had held close for so long, railing at the waste and murder their treachery had unleashed, recalling what they had once jointly wished to construct.

It was the last temptation Sigismund ever had. His lips remained sealed.

I fight for the Imperium as it will become.

Khârn surged back into contact, his axe-teeth screaming, his limbs pumping, blood and sweat mingling in the steam-gouts that flared from his ravaged armour. And the Black Sword met him squarely, as silent, cold and passionless as the grave.

Bhab Bastion had once felt like the centre of the galaxy, the place where tidings from a thousand worlds would inevitably find their way. You could occupy one of its many sensor-thrones, integrate with the lattice of incoming transmissions, and feel like you were within touching distance of the entire empire.

Now it was an island of faltering sight amid a sea of blindness. You might stand at its very summit, staring out of the thin slit windows of its reinforced siege-walls, and witness nothing but an all-consuming blackness, rolling up out of trackless battlefields.

Rogal Dorn barely took in the surroundings of the command chamber any more. People came up to him, then went away, sometimes faces he recognised, sometimes complete strangers. Archamus had been with him, then had gone somewhere – to fight? – before coming back again. Sigismund had spoken to him at some length about something trivial, before Dorn had realised that Sigismund was long gone, sent out into the maw of darkness to slow it all down, and so he must have been hallucinating, slipping into a waking sleep as his mind finally began to shut down.

Reality and apparition had started to blend together a while back. He looked into one of the few working auspex lenses and saw nothing but a cowled face staring back at him, indistinct in the dark glass, waiting, just waiting.

He rubbed his eyes roughly, slapped his cheek, willing himself back into alertness. Others might take their rest, others might sleep, but not him. He was the Castellan, the master of the fortress, the only soul alive who knew all its ways, its remaining strengths, its many potential weaknesses. He had to resist the voices that murmured ever more persuasively in his exhausted mind.

Give up! Walk away now. No one would blame you. You have done enough. Give up.

Archamus was at his side again, back from wherever his duty had taken him. A Blood Angel was there too, as was Amon, the captain-general's representative. Those armoured giants were surrounded by a clutch of senior officials from other branches, their uniforms frayed and their skin pallid. He remembered some of their names; not all.

'News of Sanguinius?' Dorn asked wearily.

'Orchestrating extraction from the final Europa-sector bastion,' Archamus replied. 'Due to report within the hour.'

Dorn smiled grimly. When had the Angel last slept? When had he last stopped *moving*, even? Then again, fighting was better than this. The primarchs had been made to be physical, to be warriors, not to be cooped up inside prisons of their own devising.

'When he confirms completion, signal the final withdrawal,' Dorn said, bringing up the orders of battle from the ghost-images that forever cycled down his retinal feed. 'Everything we have left to the Sanctum and Palatine, all other zones to be surrendered.'

The visual augurs had long since ceased to be useful, but Dorn's mind could construct a remarkably rich image of what was going on from the constant stream of audex bulletins – the screaming demands for reinforcements, the panicked reports from observation towers, the breathless accounts of retreating command groups. Together with realviewer data, he could collate a schematic of the entire battleplane – the immense infantry forces, hundreds of thousands strong in the vanguards alone, millions more now streaming along cleared avenues in the wreckage. The mobile armour, the mechanised walkers, the grav-platforms, assembled in uncountable numbers now, all grinding closer to the core. The Titans and the Knights, free to enter the Inner Palace at will, striding their way across levelled fields of pulverised stone. No army had ever been greater. The scale of it, marching through once indomitable bulwarks, streaming over the shattered walls and redoubts, all of it accompanied by the scream of the Neverborn, those revenants he had refused for so long to even countenance existing. They would all be in visual range of the Sanctum soon, eye to eye, blade to blade.

Overwhelming. Unstoppable. Unforgiving.

'Where is your master now?' he asked Amon.

'At the Tower, his mission accomplished,' the Custodian replied, his voice courteous but impatient. He, too, was itching to get back to the fighting. Dorn didn't ask what mission that had been. The Legio Custodes had already killed more daemons than any other branch of the loyalist forces – without them, the lower levels of the Sanctum would have been crawling with madness already. The captain-general was his own master, and would be present at the final contest for the Sanctum – that was all that mattered.

As for his own errant brother, though – his gene-kin – it was still hard to accept the recklessness of it all.

'Any signals from the port yet?' he asked, already knowing the answer.

'Nothing definite,' said Archamus. 'The Skye plate is destroyed, broken over Anterior. Whether it was enough to get them inside... that remains uncertain.'

Dorn grunted. Jaghatai's honour-contest felt as remote to him now as the void, just as did the Dark Angels' unexpected occupation of the Astronomican. Two tiny points of resistance, cut off from any help. Thousands of priceless warriors squandered on defiant stands when they should have been here, at the Sanctum, for when the Red Angel came.

'Monitor it,' he commanded perfunctorily. 'If you get anything, if he somehow gets himself out alive, alert me instantly.'

Archamus bowed.

And that just left one element – the one part of the defensive line that had not yet imploded, holding its own across nine subsectors even as enemy forces flocked to take it down. At present, it was a salient, jutting into surrendered territory like an arrow shaft. If it was not withdrawn swiftly, though, it would be cut off entirely, just another encircled fragment of loyalist resilience to be picked off at will.

'And Sigismund,' Dorn said.

'The Emperor's Champion,' offered one of the officials.

He turned on her, and she froze. 'What was that you...' He collected himself. 'Who calls him that?'

The woman wore the uniform of a major-general. She commanded armies. For all that, she swallowed, nervously. 'I... just heard it said.'

Dorn stared at her a little longer. He processed it.

They had called him the same thing, once. In the days when he had still allowed himself to leave the confines of this damned bastion, its suffocating walls, its spirit-sucking emptiness, that had been his title. His gaze wandered a little, and he saw the cowled face in every armaglass reflection again, mocking now.

All over for you now, Rogal. It hasn't been enough, has it? No one will ever really know how hard you tried. Even your little names have been taken away.

He drew in a long, dry breath.

'Suits him,' he grunted curtly. 'Get him back, all the same. He's done what I ordered – anything more is suicide.'

The functionaries scurried off to try to get the message out. Their numb expressions told him everything about how likely they thought success was.

Archamus remained. Solid, reliable Archamus.

'Will there be anything else, lord?' he asked.

Dorn might even have smiled then, if he'd had the energy. Another time, and he would have suggested something to lighten the mood. An extra Titan Legion, perhaps. Or Russ turning up from around the corner, never having gone off into the void at all, roaring with energy and laughter and with his feral Legion ready to be unleashed. *All just a bad jest, brother! Of* course *I didn't leave Terra!*

But he didn't have the energy. He could barely lift his eyelids. He just stared into the ranks of sensor lenses, watching the cowled face watching him.

'Signal the Eternity Gate,' he said emptily. 'Tell them to…'

Any precise command was pointless. They were already no doubt doing all that they could. But something still needed to be passed on. Something needed to be said, now, to mark the moment, before he headed to the Dungeon himself, surrounded by the tatters of all his elaborate defensive plans.

'Tell them,' he said steadily, 'it won't be long now.'

TWENTY-TWO

Blood brothers
Listening carefully
Rise

No, not long now. It would not be at a time of his choosing, sure, nor in a place of his design, but that made little difference – the outcome would be much the same.

There had always been the chance Jaghatai would risk a strike. Everything Mortarion knew of him had made it possible, even likely. If anything, the surprise was that Rogal had kept him locked down for so long.

If Mortarion had cared about the Lion's Gate port itself, then it would have been made truly impregnable, stuffed with every possible avatar of the god and turned into a swamp of such infinite depth and malice that even his loathed father would have thought twice before attempting it. As it was, though, this place, the derelict halls he strode through right now, had only even been a stage on the path to power. To linger here too long was to risk the glory of ultimate conquest going to a lesser soul – Abaddon, perhaps, or maybe even agonised Angron – and so his mind had always been half-turned west, across the burning wastes and towards the Sanctum.

His brother's move had been well timed. You had to give Jaghatai credit for that – he'd acted just as things were pulling together, all attention diverted towards the great advance that would see the wayward sons of the Blood God shoved aside in favour of a more dependable Legion. The White Scars were dangerous – they had always been dangerous – and so the intervention was not something he could simply brush aside and leave to his lieutenants to address. It needed to be snuffed out, finished here, and then matters could be set back on their inevitable course.

But he would always have killed Jaghatai. Whether here or in the Sanctum, it didn't matter. As Mortarion walked down the long observation hall, striding past thirty-metre-high windows with all the glass in them long shattered, surrounded by the near-silent tread of his Deathshroud bodyguards, he reflected that perhaps here was better. The business could be concluded, the rest of the old barbarian Legion extermi-nated, and then, with that prestigious kill under his belt, he could enter the final arena with his claim to pre-eminence established.

He might have chosen to call back those of his command council who had already been sent on ahead to the core – Kargul, maybe, or even Vorx. Not Typhus, of course – always better to keep him out of the way, running down his old ven-detta with the First, believing all the while that he acted in his own interest. In the end, though, no summons had been made. All unfolded as it had to. Soon the entire Legion would come together again to fulfil its destiny, the one he had set in motion for it during the pain of the warp. This impedi-ment would be eliminated, just as every obstacle had been cleared, ready for the greater game to come – domination of the warp-realspace hybrid Horus' victory would create. That was the real prize, now – not the fading embers of this already crippled mortal empire, but the empyrean itself, the coming domain of gods and angels.

That was why he had allowed the suffering. That was why he had permitted the paradox of his sons' wilful infection, their descent into madness and their mutation into creatures of the god. It had needed to happen. It had needed to take place, to transform them into beings capable of breathing the air of the warp as well as the air of the real. When the horizons of experience were breached at last, when Horus plunged his talon into the Emperor's heart and the barriers between the planes were obliterated, all that suffering would bring its final reward. The Death Guard would stand astride the threshold, indomitable still, their veins pulsing with daemonic ichor, their timeless patron chuckling even as he showered even greater gifts than those already bestowed.

No more Overlords. No more impassable peaks. No more poisons they couldn't ingest. Not now, not for the eternity to come.

He strode down the wide stairs, their bare surfaces still strewn with the last leavings of Perturabo's clumsiness. He turned his gaze within, allowing the ether to show him the state of the fortress from its high summits to its bilge-filled foundations. The whole place was riddled with disease now, and that contagion acted as a weapon all of its own. The invaders were slowing down – running into that resistance, even being beaten back in places. This fortress, given time, would be their grave. If any records survived at all, the Lion's Gate would be listed as the site of their last defeat, a final note of ignominy to add to the failures of Prospero, Kalium and Catullus.

But then they struck.

The observation gallery was a long processional space flanked by two high, armoured walls. It ran along the external edge of the western-facing redoubt, and was mostly empty save for its piles of war-refuse. Its internal lumens were long gone and its functional surfaces replaced by creeping slicks of organic matter. The far end was masked by thick spore clouds, from where transit shafts dropped down to the assembly bays and lifter platforms of the space port's operational levels. His entourage – seven Terminator-clad warriors of the Death-shroud, plus forty-nine Unbroken picked from a variety of different formations – clunked and wheezed their way down the avenue, their cloven hooves splashing and crunch-ing through the filth.

He sensed the attack just before it occurred. That triggered a grudging admiration even as his thoughts were snatched back into the present – not easy, to mask intentions from him in this place. Some art must have been used – the kind of cheap, bone-rattling magicks their shamans indulged in, which could be effective enough when used at the right time.

'Ward the portals,' he rasped, gesturing towards a cracked wall section some three hundred metres further down, where the arches over the high windows were already failing. Even as he spoke, bright light flooded through the gaps, and a roar of Stormbird engines rose up from the night sky beyond.

The Deathshroud moved instantly, forming up between the portals and their master. The rest of the Unbroken charged straight for the impending breach, targeting their bolters at the storm of noise and whirling lumens. Mortarion himself simply came to a halt, planting his scythe-heel on the rock-crete, more intrigued than perturbed.

The external walls blew inward with the thunderous clap of krak charges, followed by a percussive blast of heavy bolters. V Legion warriors flung themselves through the rents in the wall, leaping inside even while the shattered masonry was still in the air. At the same time, the familiar ozone-tang of teleporters fizzed, followed by hard bangs as air pockets were displaced. Ivory-armoured Terminators rippled into being, instantly joining up with their battle-brothers and driving on into contact. The processional erupted into a riot of flying projectiles and blazing energy fields as the two forces engaged.

Mortarion nodded silently, and his Deathshroud set off, trudging down the avenue to bring their deadly Manreaper scythes to bear. Not one of the White Scars warriors got close to the primarch – they were steadily forced back down the avenue towards the miasma field as the fighting intensified. The strike-from-distance had been a bold move, but it wouldn't get much further.

He almost went after them himself. It might do him some good, to stretch his own cramped limbs before the true killing started. But then he felt it – just behind him, in the shadows. Not the warp technology of a teleporter, but a subtler disturbance, conjured from discipline rooted in wild lightning and twin moons over eternal grass.

He twisted around, his ragged cloak snapping around him, only to see emptiness. But he could *smell* the change – something was *there*, buried down in all that spore-drifting gloom. He took another stride, the fighting behind him forgotten, eyes narrowing against the murk.

And then a shadow moved. It shivered, before sliding up to join another one. A shred of stray light developed motion, wriggling like a serpent to join another pool of illumination. The shadows and the lights danced around one another, coalescing rapidly, before winding their ghostly way up a support column and fusing into something that began to emanate softly with gold and white. The glimmer-play slipped into and around the roil of the spore clouds, firming up into something both there and not-there.

Mortarion never saw the moment when the Khan emerged. One moment it was all indistinct, just a spectral distortion over the building's structure, and then he was present, solid, standing free of the column, his blade already drawn and the glamour's edge dying away.

His weather-workers had some skill, then. They had brought him here, sent him ahead of the advance to ensure that they met undisturbed. That couldn't have been easy.

Still, it had always been about the two of them, ever since that first encounter in the ruins of Tizca. All their respective armies, all their war machines and their allies and their over-worked psykers, those were really just the mechanisms by which they could be brought together again.

Mortarion regarded his brother. The Khan had changed since Prospero. He still carried himself with that old arro-gance, the aristocratic aloofness he had always worn as close to his flesh as the self-inflicted scar. Something about his aura was different now. Resigned, perhaps. Or maybe just ground down, finally hammered to the same level as the rest of them. You couldn't fly free all the time; sooner or later, gravity would drag you back into the slime.

'*You look quite terrible, my brother*,' Mortarion told him.

The Khan made no move. No sudden burst into motion with the sublime *White Tiger* dao, no breathtaking leap into strike-range. He just stood there, his grip on the hilt loose, his battle-scarred armour glinting softly in the greenish nimbus.

In the end, he only uttered a single word.

'Wings,' he said contemptuously.

Mortarion chuckled. '*A tremendous gift. I am still learning how they work.*'

'A mark of your corruption.'

'*Tell that to the Angel.*'

'He wears them better.'

And that was the strangest thing of all – to talk to him again, brother to brother, just for a moment before it had to end. For so long, his every thought had been of the kill that had been denied him, but now it was just the old fraternal one-upmanship again, the kind of relentless needle all of them had given one another since the start. Because you could forget, if you were not careful, how alone they were; that no one, not the gods, not even their own father, perceived the universe just as they did. They were unique, the primarchs, bespoke blends of the physical and the divine, irreplaceable one-offs amid a galaxy of dreary mass production. In a fundamental sense, Jaghatai knew more of Mortarion's essential character than most of the Death Guard, and he knew more of the Khan's than the peoples of Chogoris. That had always been the paradox of them – they had been strangers in their own homelands, cut off by fate from those who should have been their blood brothers. Now they were all back on Terra, the place of origin, and all that seemed to have been forgotten amid the heedless hurry to murder one another.

'*So you choose to end your war here, Jaghatai,*' he said. '*On a world you never much cared for.*'

'I remain its defender,' said the Khan, finally placing his dao into guard.

Mortarion kindled the corpse-light over *Silence*, and the great scythe's blade shimmered with reflections of the other realm.

'*For a little longer,*' he said.

It hadn't been four hours. Ilya woke with a start, and knew instantly that she had been out for a very long time.

'Damn him,' she spat, reaching for a swig of water before swinging her legs over the edge of the cot, straightening her uniform out, brushing her hair back.

She had been dreaming. It was always the same dream – Yesugei's voice, sent to her on the bridge of the *Swordstorm*.

Do not grieve. We were made to do this, szu. We were made to die.

She felt sick. She should have seen it earlier.

'Damn *them*,' she repeated, reaching the door, unlocking it, and veering unsteadily out into the corridors.

Sojuk found her soon afterwards. He was fully armoured, helm on, and looked as if he might have been making ready to break out somewhere at short notice.

'I told you to wake me,' Ilya said.

'My apologies.'

'Which I've had enough of.' She fixed him with as steady a glare as she could manage. 'I changed my mind. We're not staying here.'

Sojuk looked back at her.

'There are three Thunderhawks in the last hangar,' Ilya said. 'I'm taking one.'

'Those are reserved for–'

'Don't tell me the plans – I worked them up myself. You want to fly it, or just watch me go?'

He drew in a breath. 'Permit me to know why.'

'Because he's going to die, Sojuk.' She brushed a distracted hand over her hair again, wondering if she looked deranged. 'I should have known it, when he came to speak to me. He told me he was coming back. I believed it. Then again, he'd never lied to me before.'

'Szu, I do not think–'

'Shut up. It was you that got me onto this. And then my dreams did.' She shook her head. Exhaustion still clung to her, making her thoughts sluggish. 'He didn't want my advice. He was saying goodbye. And I'm not having that. Not again.'

'If the Khagan–'

'–ordains it, then you won't question it? That's what you're going to tell me?' She squared up to him – a fragile human woman, dishevelled from sleep, up against a towering, armoured killing machine. 'Horseshit. It's this blindness that's brought the house down about our ears. Are you coming with me or not?'

Sojuk thought for a moment, then nodded.

'Good,' Ilya said, starting to walk again. 'You're a better pilot. I'd have crashed the damn thing in anger.'

They made their way quickly up the levels, most of which were empty now. As they went, Ilya heard the nervous chatter from the comms rooms, the failing whine of air filters. The place was evidently still undiscovered, which was a good thing. The skeleton Legion staff would have to think about evacuation soon, whatever happened at the space port. Until then, they were manning the augurs for as long as possible, doing what they could to keep the fractious comms lines functional.

They reached the hangar, where the three prepped gunships rested on the apron, plus a brace of personnel transporters. The place wasn't even guarded, given how few troops remained, so they could just walk up to the nearest one, unlock the cockpit and activate the flight controls. Sojuk settled into the pilot seat, calmly initiating the preflight sequence.

'This will be dangerous,' he said.

'You don't say,' she replied, strapping herself in. 'Take us across the gap at full speed. Remain at altitude, do not engage hostiles unless you absolutely have to.'

Sojuk started the engines up. They growled into life, echoing in the confined space, and made the whole chassis tremble. He turned on the main lumens to light up their passage across the threshold, then started the outer door countdown.

For all Ilya knew, there was a Warlord Titan on the far side of those hangar doors, just waiting for them to emerge so it could pick them off. Or maybe there was nothing at all any more, just a radiation-scoured wasteland with no living souls at all.

All that mattered was getting across to the far side, staying alive long enough to reach their final destination.

'And when we get there?' asked Sojuk, applying pressure to the controls and ramping up the motive power. 'What is our precise destination?'

Ilya sat back in her overlarge seat, clutching the arm supports and tensing up for the lurch of movement. A flight in a Legion gunship was an uncomfortable experience at full speed even for someone in prime condition. In her state, it felt liable to shake her to pieces before they got halfway.

'It'll be visible,' she said confidently. 'He'll have made sure of that.'

The hangar doors completed their ascent, revealing a narrow strip of smoke-churned night. The fires were still burning across a vista of ruination. In the extreme distance, Ilya thought she even saw the place itself – the plague mountain, thrusting out against a horizon of greenish flame – though maybe that was just her imagination.

Sojuk prepared to fire the boosters. 'You are sure, szu?' he asked, just one more time.

Ilya set her jaw. She was sick. Her head was already pounding, her skin flushed. She was also scared. Very scared.

'Do it,' she said.

The Thunderhawk's thrusters boomed, and it rose from the apron. Sojuk killed the lumens, angled the controls, and sent them shooting out into the blood-curdled night.

He was failing now, becoming weaker, getting slower. Jangsai's armour over his right leg and side was cracked open where a charge had got too close, something that compromised his protection from the airborne toxins. He'd taken glancing bolt-hits across his breastplate, and a serrated dagger had perforated the cabling under his left armpit. The blade must have been laced with poisons – the wound wasn't healing, and blood now leaked steadily out of the joint between ceramite plates.

Would a true Chogorian have done better? Would Ajak, say, have lasted longer against the relentless onslaught, evading the worst hits and punching back harder?

Impossible to know. Plenty of veterans of the ordu had already died in this place, and plenty of newbloods had made kills of their own. After a while it had become hard to even tell the difference – everything was coated in slime and gunk, the brotherhood sigils obscured and the fighting style reduced to a soul-draining slog.

He had fought beyond himself just to reach this point – up out of the wastes, in through the broken gatehouses, then further into the port's yawning innards. At times he'd been completely alone, at times he'd managed to link up with the remains of other Legion formations. Everything was broken up, though: shattered against the unmoving object set against them. Qin Fai should have been pushing through these halls by now. Instead, his forces were still bogged down, more than eight kilometres away through the bewildering tangle of corridors and transit vents. The only comms he received now were hissing fragments – snatches of increasingly desperate injunctions from what remained of the Colossi command. It didn't sound like they knew much about what was going on. Jang-sai couldn't blame them – no one did, not in this vile murk.

Sooner or later, you had to take matters into your own hands. With no other commanders in range, he'd gathered together what he could, and fought on towards where he believed the Amber spearhead must still be fighting. His ragged collection now comprised twenty warriors of the ordu – from seven different brotherhoods – and fifteen battle tanks – all Leman Russ units of one variant or another. Together they had made some progress. It was all painfully slow – advance in the shadow of the tanks, let them smash up the established defences, then the infantry could sprint out of the shadows and assault what remained. Then repeat, again and again, trying to ignore the wounds you were taking, the strength you were expending, the damage being done to the armour.

Now they were into the truly massive internal spaces, the ones where the void craft could be lowered and raised on mighty grav plates, leading steadily up to the exposed landing stages of the atmospheric levels. Jangsai pushed on, keeping his body low, flanked on either side by the rumbling hulls of the tanks. Bodies lay everywhere, mangled and dismembered, face down in the sludge, twisted between the empty caskets of destroyed vehicles. He could hear the smash and echo of fighting up ahead, and ordered the pace picked up.

He almost missed Naranbaatar. The Stormseer was barely breathing, slumped up against a huge support column, his staff burned black and the light of his helm-lenses extinguished.

Jangsai raced over to him, crouching down in the greasy water and lifting his head up.

'Zadyin arga,' he said reverently. 'Where are your guards?'

Naranbaatar coughed weakly, reaching out to Jangsai as if blinded. 'Sent them... on.'

'You must come with us.'

'No. No... no time.' He tried to rise, and cascades of blood ran down from his helm-seal. 'The Khagan. He strikes ahead. At the Lord of Death.' More coughing, more slicks of unclotting blood. 'Ganzorig is held up. Qin Fai is held up. Too slow. All must get... to him. Must be... faster.'

The Stormseer was on the verge of death. He sounded delirious, driven over the edge by some colossal internal trauma.

Jangsai lowered his head, trying to catch the stilted, gasping words. 'Where is he? Where do they fight?'

'Landing stages.' Naranbaatar's helm fell back against the column. 'Somewhere… up there. Make haste. All must… get to him.'

The landing stages were both numerous and enormous. Half the space port was taken up by their sprawl, and it might take days to fight across them all.

But there was no question of asking more. The Stormseer was on the cusp of death now. In other times, the warriors would have paused there, offered the rites of *kal damarg* – the ritual of the dead, honouring his sacrifice and undertaking to avenge him. After that, his warrior-soul would be joined to theirs, giving them fresh zeal for the fight, even multiplying – so the teaching had it – their sword-arms' strength.

'It will be done,' was all he said, moving Naranbaatar's broken body so that it would not slide into the waters at least. 'I swear it now, honoured master of storms. It will be done.'

Then he stood. The tanks were grinding ahead, throwing up waves of sludge as their tracks churned. The lead unit, the one marked *Aika 73*, had made a move towards what looked like an intact enemy position a kilometre and a half away, off in the shadows. Jangsai's warriors loped along in its wake.

'All units, full stop,' he commanded, splashing through the slurry to join them. 'New tasking.'

He switched his helm-view to the tactical cartoliths, the ones imprinted back at Colossi. Making progress would be difficult – it might all have changed, or been rendered impassable, or blocked by thousands of enemy troops.

'Locate the nearest lifter shafts,' he ordered nonetheless. 'We *will* find him.'

TWENTY-THREE

Prophecy
Earthfall
Last blood

He didn't find her, in the end. He found those who followed her. And that proved to be significantly less difficult, because there were thousands of them.

Until then, Loken had been fighting an increasingly lonely, difficult battle. The war-fronts had been closing in ever tighter, filling up the few remaining empty spaces across the desecrated urban wastes. None of the advance warbands were cultist dross any more – those poor wretches had soaked up their last bullets a long time ago. These were Traitor Marines, hunting in packs, roving ahead of their great war-hosts like hungry wolves.

He'd had to be careful. He'd killed where he'd had to, but mostly remained hidden, racing down lightless alleys and across the broken crater-fields while larger explosions masked his presence. He reserved the most hatred, of course, for the Sons of Horus. When he spied them, when he judged the risk worth taking, he let them see who he was before he killed them. That made them fight all the harder, because they loathed him as much as he detested them. He shouldn't have done it, really. There was always the chance that one of them would end him, and their numbers were growing all the time, but the small pangs of satisfaction almost made it worth the danger.

So it was that he came across the believers. At first, he had thought they were just more crowds of refugees, fleeing towards the core in the hope that there might be room for them somewhere. Since the very start of hostilities, those crowds had been rampaging inwards, desperate and famished. They were cut down in their droves, of course, but there always seemed to be more of them out there, limping and shuffling with their rags clutched tight about them.

But these ones, they weren't retreating. They were formed up, they were organised. They were marching like soldiers, all carrying some kind of weapon – a lasgun, a shotgun, a power tool. Many of them had flamers, constructed by the look of things from vehicle parts and plastek canisters. He almost mistook their front ranks for the enemy at first, until he saw the skulls they carried with them – on chains, around necks, atop long poles – and remembered the catacombs.

He came out into the open, shaking off the dust and lowering his bolter. They prepared to charge straight at him. He heard cries of 'Kill it!', and saw many in the front ranks activate their crude promethium nozzles.

But they weren't complete fools. Several held up their hands, recognising that he was no traitor – those never came into the open without opening fire.

A man edged warily up to him. He wore the torn uniform of an Imperial Army trooper, and had a half-cloak draped over his shoulders. In one hand he carried a service-issue lasgun. In the other, incongruously, was a thick bundle of fabric. Just visible was a child's head, tucked under the curve of a protective arm.

'My lord,' the man said. 'Can we assist you?'

Loken found himself staring at the child. 'Who are you?'

'Katsuhiro, Kushtun Naganda, now in the service of the Church. Like everyone here.'

'And… this?'

'A survivor.' Katsuhiro's face was drawn and skinny. He didn't have the look of a seasoned trooper, but there was a hardness to him all the same. That made sense – anyone still alive in all this had to have something about them, however things had started. 'No one else was going to watch him. So I had to.'

Was that commendable? It would slow him down, hamper his aim. Still, it was a human gesture in this swamp of inhumanity. Hard to condemn it.

'I seek the lady,' Loken said. 'Can you take me to her?'

Katsuhiro hesitated. It was one thing for him to run the risk that Loken might not be what he appeared to be. It was another to risk *her*.

'We were… we *are* friends,' said Loken. 'I came to protect her. Can you assist me?'

Katsuhiro drew back, conferred with some of the others. Loken saw them gesturing towards the Imperial insignias still just about visible on his armour. The discussion became animated. He let them talk, despite his impatience to get moving – he could already hear the noises of combat drawing in closer from the east.

Eventually, they reached agreement. Katsuhiro came back to him. 'I argued for it,' he said. 'I'd be grateful if you don't make me a greater fool than I already am.'

The bulk of the ramshackle army started to move again, heading – with enthusiasm – in the direction of the coming enemy. Katsuhiro motioned for Loken to come with him the other way. The two of them started to clamber across the wreckage and mortar-impacts as the ranks marched off, breaking into poorly tuned singing.

'They will not succeed,' Loken said. 'Against what is coming.'

'No,' said Katsuhiro. 'We lose every battle we fight.' He looked up at the Space Marine with bleak, tired eyes. 'But we take some of them down with us. Better that, we think, than wait for them to come.'

'Is that why you carry the skulls? You celebrate death?'

Katsuhiro shrugged. 'I'm not a priest. They tell us to collect them. We do what they tell us.' He smiled thinly. 'You need a symbol, don't you? People need that.'

'But you were Army, once.'

'Still am. Served at Marmax.' He pulled his half-cloak aside to reveal regimental badges. 'If there were any commanders still alive, I'd be taking orders from them.' He pulled the fabric back over, and the half-asleep child clutched at him instinctively. 'You take the help you can get.'

'I could carry that,' said Loken awkwardly. 'For a while. If you wished.'

Katsuhiro shook his head. 'It's *him*. But no. Thanks. He's my responsibility.'

They walked for some distance after that, heading roughly north-west. The habs around them became a fraction more stable-looking – stark outposts amid a static sea of rubble. Katsuhiro led him into one of them, past sentries half-buried in the rubbish, then up hollow stairwells. They eventually emerged at the very top level, an open platform with a low perimeter wall. The view from it was good, and a wide vista opened up. Hollow spires jutted up into the night sky, avenues smouldered, and greater constructions still towered up beyond them all, hunched and ringed with fire.

A few dozen fighters clustered at the summit's western edge, peering into Army-issue magnoculars and conferring among themselves.

As for her, she looked thinner than she had done. Dirtier, her hair longer and greasier. Her clothes were stained and hung from her meagre frame. No one's idea of a saint, really. When she turned to face him, though, he recognised the old look – that defiant stare she'd always had, the disdain for untruth, that essential fierceness.

'I didn't preach,' she said. 'Not once. They came to me.'

'As did I, Euphrati,' said Loken. 'And it took a long time.'

The two of them drew together. Both had seen better days.

'So what is all this?' Loken asked her.

'What they wanted me to do.' Keeler shrugged. 'They were so precious about it all for so long. Now I guess they'll clutch at anything.'

Loken glanced at the others. They were wearing tattered scholar's robes, for the most part, or embellished Army uniforms. They, too, carried skulls. 'But… you,' he said. 'Is it what you wanted?'

'Does that matter?'

'Of course.'

Keeler smiled indulgently. 'So you think I'm the victim, here. The lost girl they sent into danger, against her will. You'd like to save me, I guess.'

'Yes. I would like that.'

'Garviel,' she said. 'Garviel.' She reached up to his cavernous chest, pressing a finger gently against it, as if checking he was still real. 'You can't save everyone. It's a blasphemy to try. That's where we've been going wrong. It's all about the numbers. Two platoons. That would do for you.'

'Your pardon?'

'Look. Come with me.'

She led him to the summit's edge. Her magnoculars were waiting. She gave him the coordinates, and he let his helm-lenses do the work.

'Over there,' she said.

Thirty kilometres away, on the far side of a deep depression, another battle was taking place. It was a big one, just one of thousands no doubt raging all across the sector. Space Marines were grappling with one another, locked in their own uniquely brutal style of up-close combat. As Loken homed in on the coordinates, he recognised the armour styles instantly. Templar Brethren, supported by regular Imperial Fists, Blood Angels and auxilia, up against World Eaters and Sons of Horus.

One duel dominated the entire scene. An Imperial Space Marine and a World Eater knocking chunks out of one another. The scale of destruction those two were capable of unleashing seemed of an order greater than those around them. Perhaps greater than any Loken had witnessed before, save for the primarchs themselves.

'Sigismund,' he said softly.

'Magnificent, isn't he?' said Keeler, with feeling. 'I brought them here to witness him. They all saw it, before they marched off to replicate the violence. It fuelled their sense of possibility.'

There was something uniquely chilling about the way the two warriors fought. They were polar opposites – one frantic, the other contained. All the same, it was strangely repulsive, that level of immersion, as if nothing mattered, or could ever matter, save the contest immediately before them.

'It was about something, before,' Loken found himself mumbling. 'Exploration. Rediscovery. The end of superstition.'

'Yes, it was. And now it's about something different.' Keeler's eyes were shining in the magnocular lenses. 'Something purer. Something more valuable.' She put them down, and turned to him. 'This is how it has to be. This, or destruction.

Look at him. We tried to build an empire on enlightenment, and failed. But we could build an empire on *that*. It would last for ten thousand years.'

Loken deactivated the zoom. 'It would not be enough.'

'You're sure?'

'Don't extrapolate. He's always been in his own category.'

'He's an inspiration.'

'Only to madmen.'

'Then we will all become mad. If that's what it takes.'

Loken shook his head. 'This has been a mistake. You should come back with me. To safety.'

'There's no safety. There is only service. I can perform that better out here.'

'You cannot be in earnest.'

She looked right back at him. Her body had been ravaged, worn away, but her expression hadn't. It was just as it had been on the *Vengeful Spirit*.

'I'm not going back. They need me. There are hundreds of thousands here, millions, in every basement and undercroft. It would be the work of a generation to kill them all, even for these monsters. But we can turn that time against them. Make the survivors forget their fear, teach them to hate. Teach them to venerate the god on the Throne, teach them that their life means nothing in isolation from it. Give them a symbol, give them a means to make fire.' She smiled. 'You see a single Sigismund, and your stomach revolts. I will give you a million Sigismunds. A billion. A universe full of them. If that scares you, imagine what it will do to the enemy.'

'I do not believe that, Euphrati,' Loken said carefully. 'I believe, from what I know now, that the enemy would rejoice at it.'

Keeler laughed. 'You saw what he was doing. I don't think his opponent was laughing.'

'I do not refer to the lackeys. I refer to the masters.'

Keeler wasn't deterred. When she got an idea in her head, it was damned hard to shift. That, too, was just as it had been.

'Whatever,' she said. 'I'm not going back. You can try to take me, and see just how potent my army has become, or you can stick around, and benefit from it.'

Loken doubted very much that her entourage posed much of a threat to him. He felt confident he could kill them all handily, disable her, take her under his arm just as that trooper had carried the child. He could bring her back to the Sanctum, to what remained of the prisons inside, and reset things to how they had been.

But what would that achieve? What victory would that be? Just another use of force to quash a rising threat, another iron fist to snuff out another spontaneous expression of defiance.

And this was *her*, the last link to that lost world of youth and endeavour. Some things you didn't touch, not even to save them.

'You're not going to make this easy, are you?' he said.

'I didn't ask for any of it,' she countered. 'They sent me out here.'

He turned away from the battles. Somewhere down there, a few kilometres away, the believers he had encountered were now, no doubt, being butchered.

'I will remain with you,' he said. 'Maybe you will see sense, before it becomes too late.'

'You know I won't.'

'I never lose hope,' he said wearily. 'That seems to have become *my* creed, at any rate.'

The run in was as hellish as it had always promised to be.

The lighter bucked and dived, sometimes as a result of John's flying, sometimes after being hit and sent slewing off course. The impacts felt like small-arms fire, for the most part – lasguns aimed up at them as they speared overhead. A lot of those shots missed, but even a few clean strikes would start to cause serious trouble, so John worked the control columns hard, making the old lighter jump around like a kicked dog.

He sat alone in the cockpit, with the others all back in the crew hold, locked down tight in their restraints, no doubt gritting their teeth and waiting for it to be over. Once inside the city proper, visibility quickly dropped to near zero, and the scopes just gave him empty screens of static. The tilting remnants of the old towers lurched out of the gloom, and he burned in close to them, hugging the carcass-edges. He left the lumens off, making the craft virtually invisible in that thick, foul grime, and even the engine noise was almost entirely drowned by the ambient thunder of the continual barrages ahead. Still, it wouldn't take much to be noticed by something capable of troubling them – a stray glance up into the smog, a functioning augur somewhere ahead – so John couldn't relax, expecting at any moment to be detected, then swiftly destroyed.

Just the one life left, he thought to himself bitterly. *Concentrates the mind.*

For a long time, even after crossing the perimeter, the desolate cityscape remained strangely empty, as if the carnage had been so exacting that the place had been stripped down to hot stone. He spied scattered warbands amid the ash-thick chasms below, racing furtively from cover to cover, but no big formations. The skies, as far as he could see, were largely clear of aircraft, though the rows of downed fuselages at ground level were testament to the battles that had already taken place.

The biggest immediate challenge was the environment,

which was punishing for the engines. Ash clogged everything, getting into the intakes, smearing over the external viewers, smacking hard all along the exposed armour plates. At times it felt like flying through solid matter, with the risk of blowing out the turbine-blades and sending the lighter spinning into the nearest intact spire-skeleton.

Just as John began to get used to that, he spied the first large detachments, filing down obscured pathways far below, thousands and thousands of them, moving fast. The soldiers veered like rats through the maze of ruins, some of them power-armoured monsters, many more just the mortal rabble caught up in the frenzy. He saw old banners, some probably dating back decades, all defaced, hoisted up at the head of endless ragged columns.

The further in the lighter went, the harder it became to avoid those concentrations. He was soon flying over sections where the ground was entirely obscured under a living carpet of bodies. Explosions lit up the surroundings intermittently, and then you could begin to gauge just how many there were down there – numbers beyond imagination, rammed up against the remains of walls and tower foundations, jostling with one another, fighting with one another, gasping for air even as they marched.

One tiny aircraft, flying erratically with its lights out, was not much of a target for any of them. From what John could tell, most of the troops looked to be in some kind of stupor, either stuffed full of combat drugs or just drunk on killing. The Traitor Marines among them carried bandoliers of skulls and empty helms around their shoulders, testament to how many they had already killed. In the distance, masked by the ever-present rolls of fog, he could see larger machines strid-ing through the rubble – Knights, Imperial Army walkers, even Scout Titans. Those things weren't even fighting yet, just trying to get to the front. The sheer volume of bodies in the increasingly confined spaces meant that it wasn't easy to push on. The frequent outbreaks of brawls he witnessed came from frustration – these were the laggards, and they were frothing at the bit.

'*Are you seeing this, John?*' came Oll's voice from back in the hold, where he was manning the secondary augurs.

'Surreal,' John replied grimly. 'Like they're queuing to get in.'

'*Any resistance yet?*'

'Nothing I've seen.'

He swerved around the still-burning bole of some kind of destroyed defence tower, then shot close under the lee of a semi-toppled habitation block. Targets kept flickering on his augur screens, disappearing as soon as they'd been picked up. He witnessed combat aircraft scoring their way northward a few times, far off, flying much higher, their bigger engines adding fresh tracks of night-black smog to the already filthy skies. Some were troop carriers; most were attack gunships, the last dregs of the gigantic forces that had opened the air assault, months back.

He began to feel strange, light-headed. He had been flying for a long time without rest, and the conditions demanded extreme concentration. The route ahead became harder and harder to pick out. It felt as if he were flying underground, lost in a borderless world of dust and flame.

The longer it went on, the more his heart beat faster and harder. All it would take would be a single serious piece of traitor armament to lock on to them, to spot the shadow-against-shadow of their slender profile and go after it. The ruins kept on growing larger and grander, magnificent even in their dishevelment, and the minuscule lighter kept on threading a perilous path between them. The cramped spaces between the walls started to glow – a bloody flare of munitions and plasma discharges, steadily intensifying as they neared the combat zones.

Then their luck ran out. Alert runes flashed across the console. John swore, dropping the lighter down a little, trying to peer through the smoke to find some kind of cover to bolt for.

Something ugly swooped onto the scopes, something misshapen, hunchbacked and trailing filth. It was a gunship of some kind, though not any profile he recognised. Oversized guns were suspended underneath a spiked superstructure, crowned with vanes and skull-topped pennants. It slewed broadly as it wallowed through the air, its gigantic engines shrieking as if they had human voices. Its cockpit, a bestial mess of beaten iron plates, bled crimson from the viewports. That thing had no business being in the air at all, let alone surviving the firestorm of Legion aerial combat, and yet here it was – a throwback, a remnant, a piece of insanity held aloft by a brace of overworked turbines and the fanaticism of the things that flew it.

'Company,' John warned, though he guessed that the viewers in the crew hold would already be showing the others most of what he could see.

He piled on the power, forcing the lighter to hare briskly through the narrowing chasms. The monster came right after them, thundering along on its smoggy thrusters. It looked in position to take a shot a few times, but just kept on devouring the gap between them, looming ever larger in the rear viewers. John dared to hope that it might have run low on ammunition. Only too late did he pick out the bronze-rimmed flamers jutting from its prow – that was why it was waiting.

He dropped down even lower, killing the power and sending the lighter into a short-lived stall before restarting the drives. The sudden plummet cost them momentum but kept them alive – two plumes of fire shot out just above them, singeing the upper control vanes.

'Shit,' John growled, battling with the controls to keep them aloft. The way ahead was a rapidly shrinking slit between two giant hab-spires. The gunship swaggered its way in closer, priming to fire again.

He prepared to jink away, scraping as close as he could to the metal cliff-face on the right, just as someone clambered up into the cockpit alongside him – not Oll, but Actae.

'This really isn't the–' John started.

'Shut up,' Actae snapped. 'Keep flying.'

There wasn't much else to do. He squeezed every last morsel of thrust from his flimsy engines, doing what he could to stay out of range of those damned flamers. Even as he tried every trick he knew, he saw it wouldn't be enough – he could almost feel the rush of heat up the back of his neck, bursting through the rear hatches before thundering up into the cockpit.

Actae, though, took a quick look at the rear scopes with eyes that should not have been able to see anything at all, calmly reached out with her open hand, fixed the image of the pursuing gunship with a meaningful stare, and clenched her fist.

The volume of air around them suddenly flexed, as if they'd run underwater. The spire-edges blew out plasteel fragments, and John had to yank both columns back to stop them smashing straight into the incoming shoulder of the nearest one.

It was worse for the gunship, though. Through a snatched glance at the rear viewers he saw the entire thing imploding, as if clutched by a giant unseen version of Actae's fist. It stopped smack dead in the air, tipping spine over nose, before its flamer tanks ignited and it blew up in a riotous orgy of tumbling armour and blown spikes.

'Holy hell,' John swore, still fighting to keep them from smearing along the edge of the spire-ruins.

Actae's intervention may have staved off the threat from the

air, but even stimm-crazed troopers marching below couldn't
ignore an explosion of that size. A thousand faces looked up,
and behind them a thousand more. Seeing a damaged and
vulnerable flyer shooting overhead was too much of a temptation, and las-bolts began to snap upwards.

John tried to gain more loft, but the turbulence in the
chasm, coupled with the amount of gunk now rolling around
in his engine intakes, didn't get him high enough. A dozen
las-bolts smacked into the lighter's underside, followed by
more pinging along the higher armour.

The enemy had their range now – their outline was lit up by
the corona of sparks, leading to ever more shots being fired
by the mob below.

'This'll bring us down,' John grunted, keeping their velocity
up in the hope they could somehow overshoot the worst of it.

'Nothing can prevent that now,' said Actae, irritatingly placid
throughout. 'Get us through that gap alive, then we can hit
the dirt.'

John laughed out loud, though not from humour. 'Fine.
Nothing to that.'

He blazed through the gauntlet-run of las-fire, feeling every
strike and crack as the impacts threatened to send them all
sailing at speed into one or the other of the speed-smeared
spire-faces brushing close by. A lucky shot hit one of the fuel
lines, knocking out one of his two engines and making them
tilt crazily over to the left. Another set of strikes raked right
along the undercarriage, shattering the hatches for the landing
gear and ripping off a rear stabiliser fin. More hits came in
after that, but somehow failed to do much damage.

'What's our hull status?' John snapped, knowing Oll would
have a better grip on the signals.

'Pretty bad,' came Oll's voice over the comm. 'But now we've
got some… extra protection.'

For a moment John had no idea what he meant. Then he felt it himself – the hot prickle of psychic energy, wreathing the entire craft.

'Katt,' he murmured, then shot a dry smile at Actae. 'You've got competition.'

What followed might have been the very best flying John had ever done, though it counted for little when so few people were around to witness it. He piloted the lighter the full length of the chasm, maintaining enough momentum to send them spearing clear and out over a deep gulf beyond. Three giant causeways extended out over the deep artificial valley towards massive conurbation banks on the far side, and it was over these broad avenues that the traitor armies surged. Flames rose up unchecked on the far side, outlining the furious tempests of full-scale warfare. John got a fleeting glimpse of immense bulwarks under concentrated fire, their battlements half-demolished and huge siege engines being hoisted up to the parapets, before the damaged lighter dropped like a stone.

He frantically gunned the engines a final time, but barely got enough response to prevent a full-on smash into the uprushing valley floor. He watched level after level fly by, until he was boosting straight towards the base of an immense trench. Complete darkness swallowed them up, drowning them in oily blackness, until it felt like they had tumbled down an unmarked shaft into the heart of the planet itself.

John slammed all remaining power to his air brakes and jammed the trajectory columns over to their full extent. The lighter's nose lifted at last, not enough to pull them clear, but sufficient to make the impending crash-landing painful rather than fatal.

'Brace!' John managed to shout, before the underside of the lighter crunched down hard. The whole craft bounced up again, then flung itself wildly to the right, before smashing once more into a jumble of wreckage and rubbish at the base of the trench. A bone-jarring skid took them more than five hundred metres along the horizontal, shedding more armour plates and shattering the armaglass in every viewer, before the flyer finally ground to a halt, half-buried and smoking profusely.

Once the worst of the shock had subsided, he lifted his head painfully. He'd been yanked hard in the first impact, and could feel blood on the inside of his helmet. All the instruments were out. He couldn't see anything through what remained of the cockpit viewscreens. Actae had been hurt, too – both her hands were covered in blood. He shakily reached for the comm activation.

'Oll?' he asked.

'*All still here,*' came the reply. '*Just.*'

'So where the hell is… this?' John muttered groggily, unsure whether he could stop his hands shaking long enough to unclip his restraint harness.

'Just where we need to be,' said the sorceress, deftly untangling herself from what remained of her seat. 'Come. Alpharius will show the way.'

He never said a word. Never. Throughout it all, the Black Sword didn't say a thing.

The monster. The ghost. The mere shell.

What could be worse than this? What death could be as profound as this? What disappointment, what despair, could ever be greater?

Khârn raged at it. He howled in fury, coming at him again and again, shrugging off the wounds. He wanted the old one back. The one with some fire in his veins. He wanted some *spirit.* Just a flicker of something – anything – other than this flint-edged, iron-deep hardness.

They had laughed together, the two of them. They had

fought in the roaring pits, and had sliced slabs out of one another, and at the end they had always slumped down in the straw and the blood and laughed. Even the Nails had not taken that away, for in combat the Nails had still always shown the truth of things.

'Be... *angry!*' he bellowed, thundering in close. 'Be... *alive!*'

Because you could only kill the things that lived. You couldn't kill a ghost, only swipe your axe straight through it. There was nothing here, just frustration, just the madness of going up against a wall, again and again.

The Nails spiked at him. He fought harder. He fought faster. His muscles ripped apart, and were instantly reknitted. His blood vessels burst, and were restored. He felt heat surge through his body, hotter and whiter than any heat he had ever endured.

The Black Sword resisted it all, silently, implacably, infuriatingly. It was like fighting the end of the universe. Nothing could shake the faith before him. It was blind to everything but itself, as selfish as a jewel-thief in a hoard.

His chainaxe whirred as wildly as he'd ever thrown it, igniting the promethium vapour in the air, sending the blood lashing out like whipcord. He scored hits with it. He wounded the ghost. He made him stagger, made him gasp. The heat roared within him, turbocharging his hearts. He heard the coarse whisper of the Great God in his bruised ears.

Do it. Do this thing. Do this thing for me.

The ghost came back at him, tall and dark, his brow crackling with lightning-flecks, his armour as light-devouring as the blade he wielded.

Khârn became sublime, in the face of that. The violence he unleashed was like a chorus of unending joy. The ground beneath the two of them was destroyed, sending them plummeting in clouds of debris. Even when they crashed to the earth, they fought on. They rocked and swayed around one another, obliterating everything within the arc of a sword or the ambit of an axe-length.

'I… am… not…' he blurted, feeling the tidal wave of exhaustion drag on even his god-infused limbs.

He realised what had been done, then. In the midst of his madness, even as the Great God poured himself into his brutalised body, he knew what transformation had occurred.

They had always told themselves, after Nuceria, that the Imperium had made the World Eaters. It had been *their fault*. The injustice, the violence, it had forged that lust for conflict, for the endless rehearsal of old gladiatorial games, like some kind of religious observance to long- and justifiably dead deities. That had given the excuse for every atrocity, every act of wanton bloodletting, for *they* had done this to *us*.

'I… am… not…'

But now Khârn saw the circle complete. He saw what seven years of total war had done to the Imperium. He saw what its warriors had been turned into. He had a vision, even then, in the midst of the most strenuous and lung-bursting fighting he had ever experienced, of thousands of warriors in this very mould, marching out from fortresses of unremitting bleakness, every one of them as unyielding and soul-dead and fanatical as this one, never giving up, not because of any positive cause in which they believed, but because they had literally forgotten how to cede ground. And he saw then how powerful that could be, and how long it could last, and what fresh miseries it would bring to a galaxy already reeling under the hammer of anguish without limits, and then he, even he, even Khârn the Faithful, shuddered to his core.

'I… am… not…'

He fought on, now out of wild desperation, because this could not be allowed to go unopposed, this could not be countenanced. There was still pleasure, there was still heat and honour and the relish of a kill well made, but it would all be drowned by this cold flood if not staunched here, on Terra, where their kind had first been made, where the great spectacle of hubris had been kicked off.

He had to stand. He had to resist, for humanity, for a life lived with passion, for the glorious pulse of pain, of sensation, of *something*.

'I... am... not...' he panted, his vision going now, his hands losing their grip, 'as... damaged...'

The Black Sword came at him, again, again. It was impossible, this way of fighting – too perfect, too uncompromising, without a thread of pity, without a kernel of remorse. He never even saw the killing strike, the sword-edge hurled at him with all the weight of emptiness, the speed of eternity, so magnificent in its nihilism that even the Great God within him could only watch it come.

Thus was Khârn cut down. He was despatched in silence, cast to the earth with a frigid disdain, hacked and stamped down into the ashes of a civilisation, his throat crushed, his skull broken and chest caved in. He was fighting even as his limbs were cut into bloody stumps, even as the reactor in his warp-thrumming armour died out, raging and thrashing to the very end, but by then that was not enough. The last thing he saw, on that world at least, was the great dark profile of his slayer, the black templar, turning his immaculate blade tip down and making ready to end the last bout the two of them would ever fight.

'Not... as... damaged,' gasped Khârn, in an agony greater than anything the Nails could ever have given him, but with more awareness of the ludic cruelty of the universe than he had ever possessed before, 'as... you.'

And then the sword fell, and the god left him, dead amid the ruins of his ancient home.

TWENTY-FOUR

Dream come true
Back to life
Warhawk

It had been amid ruins there, too – in Tizca, surrounded by the mirror-glare of the pyramids – where the two of them had first clashed. Impossible, just then, not to compare the present situation with that first encounter, the only time the Khan had fought a primarch, *truly* fought one, with the expectation of death for one or both of them. Impossible not to recall how indomitable Mortarion had been in that empty realm of broken glass, how he had just kept on going, dogged, unshakeable, cold, lethal.

But it was a mistake to think back, of course, because both of them had changed so much. The Lord of Death had burst free of his old bounds, becoming grotesque and monstrous. He wore a human form only in outline now – his skinny body inhabited a ramshackle armour of corrosion and decay, a gaggle of loosely held panels and mouldy fabric, seemingly liable to fall apart at any moment. The air around him was acrid, suffused with a foulness that turned the stomach and made it hard to breathe. He was ruined, and yet exalted; crippled, yet stronger than he had ever been.

So the old encounter meant little. Then, it had been a matter of speed against intractability, and either approach could have emerged victorious. Now, though, the parameters had changed. Mortarion's brute strength had grown obscenely. The warp coursed thickly through his veins, pulsing under heavily mutated skin. Whenever he moved, reality flexed around him, recoiling at the violation of natural law. His great blade displayed reflections of the hell-realm beyond – its rotting gardens, its tormented flesh, its fertile pain-fields.

What did he, the Khan, have to set against all of that? The old prowess with a blade, some fine armour, the residue of that famed quickness. Not enough.

He had his hatred, though. That was different from before. On Prospero, the discourse between them had been regretful as much as anything – both of them disappointed at what was being thrown away by the other. Now his hatred was as infinite as the void. Too many had died at Catullus for it to be any other way – his warriors, his ships, his counsellor, all swallowed up by the monster before him, all owing their deaths to this single soul.

The Khan had that. He had his rage, deep as the world's core, fuelling every strike and swipe of the great dao blade. He had the keen edge of vengeance to propel his limbs, to find the chink that could wound this horrific amalgam of posthuman and yaksha, to keep going against the impossible.

They crashed together, then, cracking the stone underfoot as they braced against it. The *White Tiger* snared itself on *Silence*, releasing an explosion of mingled forces, and they both pushed against the other, testing strength and poise, feeling the harmonics in their weapons and gauging what it meant for the strength of their bearers.

The Khan fell back first. They exchanged more blows, rapid, heavier and faster. All around them, the roar of broader combat filtered up from the decks below – a chorus of screams and explosions that could not be filtered out.

The strikes accelerated, ramping up swiftly until the blows were exceptional in their heft and precision. Mortarion had speeded up, his old stolidity replaced by a phase-shifting, daemonic velocity. The whistling arcs of his scythe hissed with unearthly voices, wounding the atmosphere itself even as the Khan ducked away from its lacerating edge. When that warp-forged steel connected, the impact was bone-breaking, mind-jarring, a collision of dimensions as much as solid matter.

'I expected you to dance,' the Deathlord grunted, hammering the Khan back further. *'Lost your footing, as well as your judgement?'*

The Khan was already breathing heavily. The going was as hard as expected; harder, maybe. There had never been any illusions. He worked his blade rapidly, its edge losing definition as the point whirled faster than thought. The scythe met it in explosions of plasma and ceramite shards, swinging heavily, crackling with hissed imprecations of its half-formed daemonic choir.

'You are already defeated,' the Khan told him breathily. 'You have become what you hated.'

Mortarion snorted. *'Some hatreds were never worth pursuing.'*

'Tell yourself that, if it helps.'

The acceleration continued. The blows became denser than true-mortal frames could ever have propelled. The combatants smashed in close, then reeled away into one of the gallery's columns. The masonry cracked apart, driven into disintegrating dust clouds as the primarchs crunched their way clean through it. The Khan's armour took its first transverse slash, ripping the finery from shoulder to waist. Blood followed the path of the strike, splattering against the deck in black pools.

They were alone now. They had entered a world of exclusivity, a level of combat that no other being, xenos or human, could hope to match. Just to witness it, to try to follow it, was to invite a kind of madness. The primarchs kept themselves tightly under control almost all the time, wearing the trappings of mortality over their true natures. When they cast that off, when they unlocked their inner selves, the result was difficult even to watch, let alone intervene in.

'Time has been cruel, Jaghatai,' Mortarion said, still calm, still fighting within himself, cracking the Khan away yet again, smacking the gold chasing from his helm and rocking his head back. *'You are not what you were.'*

'I am what I always was,' the Khan snarled, driving back expertly against the flurry of hideously perfect blows and raking plague-censers free of their chains.

'Weak.'

'Loyal.'

'Same thing.'

The two of them barrelled into the gallery's external wall, hammering at one another so fiercely that the entire section collapsed as if torpedoed. They swirled and duelled through the tumbling rubble, then out into the exposed night air, completely absorbed now in their own private contest. The rest of the planet – the rest of existence – might as well have slipped away, shamefaced at the volume of physical brutality unleashed on its surface.

But that violence only ratcheted up, every second, ticking over, more, more. Mortarion nearly took the Khan's head clean off with a vicious diagonal swipe. *Silence's* curved tip carved a three-foot-deep trench into the deck; when pulled out again, it ripped up a whole clump of static-wreathed rockcrete. The Khan shouldered through the barrage to land a spiteful cut on the Deathlord's leading thigh, stripping the pox-riddled armour clean from the flesh and taking his first blood, before being hammered back.

They were out in the open by then, lashing and swiping across one of the big landing stages – a kilometre across and twelve hundred metres up. Above them the storm raged, coruscating with green lightning that snapped down the high reaches of the space port. Below them, the bulk of the immense fortress spread out in a panoply of jumbled stages and terraces. Every inch of it was fought over now – a million points of light exposing White Scars and Death Guard at one another's throats. It was as if the entire battle had found its apex, its distilled expression, so that all those thousands and thousands of individual duels created their gestalt combination right at the summit of the decaying pile, something to gawp and wonder at even as the blood foamed busily into the gutters.

'*This isn't about revenge, for me,*' said Mortarion, his rasping voice still contained. '*You're just in the way now. You understand that?*'

The Khan laughed bloodily, spitting out shattered teeth. 'Not how I see it, brother,' he hissed. 'I'm here for you. Nothing else.'

Mortarion backhanded him, cracking a savage hit into the Khan's throat, before following up with a two-handed down-thrust of the scythe. '*Indulgent. But then you always were.*'

Another smack against the helm, a discharge of virulent nerve gas as the edge bit, the destruction of the Khan's right pauldron, making him stagger.

'I led my Legion as I saw fit,' the Khan snarled. 'You might have tried the same.'

The *White Tiger* flashed, going for the jangling cables at Mortarion's neck, but it was swatted aside.

'*I led the Death Guard before you were even found.*'

The Khan held his ground against the onslaught, muscles screaming as they propelled his blade into dazzling arcs. Sweat pooled across his burning skin, mingling with blood now.

'Not sure your First Captain would agree.'

That unleashed the flood. Mortarion roared back at him, his gossamer wings rearing up as his mighty arms flailed, furious and devastating. He crunched and bludgeoned the Khan out across the face of the landing stage, wreathing him with plumes of poison, smashing the metal of his gauntlets, cracking his flanks with the shaft of his ether-snarled staff before plunging the curved edge back round and up into his torso.

To endure that at all, not to be completely swept away and broken into a thousand pieces, took every scrap of skill and tenacity the Khan still possessed. By that point he was fighting beyond anything he had ever achieved before, scraping the boundaries of the possible, and still he was being battered, bruised, hammered, driven across the storm-wracked port's edge like a churl being beaten by his lord. His head rang from the blows, clouded with blood-puffs as his skull rattled in its helm. His right arm was fractured, his flank lacerated, his cheek shattered. *Silence* swung around him like the wheeling stars, its length crackling with vicious energies, both faster than the warp's snarl and heavier than a star's heart.

'*You know* **nothing**,' Mortarion snarled, rearing up again, his cloaks whipping about him as the storm surge howled. '*Nothing of sacrifice, nothing of denial – you were the spoiled child, whining about the need for structure as the rest of us built an empire.*'

Mortarion's eyes flared with a maddened green tinge, his visible face twisted into true rage now. He was elemental, he was apocalyptic, he was phenomenal. The tempest shrieked around him, hurled into a vortex that amplified every killer strike, tearing up the ground they scored across and sending its remnants slamming and blasting across the Khan's retreating form.

'*You were shown the nature of the galaxy, and you turned away,*' Mortarion raged, slamming the scythe down and nearly breaking the Khan's trailing leg in two. '*I embraced it. I embraced the pain. I looked the god in the eye.*'

The tempest of Horus' wrath swirled overhead. Explosions kindled far below, creating constellations of plasma across the port's ruins. Further out, visible only to a primarch's vision, the beleaguered Inner Palace burned, too far for any intervention now. Unholy voices whined in the superheated wind, goading, crowing, delighting.

'*And you ran,*' Mortarion spat. '*Always running, too far away to matter, principles unknown even to yourself.*'

The scythe swung again, even heavier now, unstoppably fast, critically heavy, driving over the Khan's desperate attempt to block it, connecting with armour-cracking force and sending the primarch skidding to his knees. More blows rained in, iron-hard, exploding with the soul-eating spoil of the ether, smashing him down, lower, until he was on his back against the rockcrete, prone, ready for slaughter.

'*No running now.*'

The Khan's head snapped back, and blood sloshed down his neck. He had a brief glimpse of the skies above – the mottled incarnadine clouds, hiding the monstrous fleets above – before Mortarion's profile loomed up to block it.

And then the dream came true, just as Yesugei had described it to him – the Lord of Death, rising in darkness over a world of shadow, arms raised for the killing strike.

Not everything is fated, the Khan had told him then.

'*It ends,*' Mortarion said, his face a rictus of anger. '*Here.*'

The Khan chuckled painfully under his shattered, lensless helm.

'See, but I'm laughing now, brother,' he rasped, the thick blood in his throat making his words gurgle. 'You should start to worry.'

Crosius was still in a world of delight. He had been badly wounded, his right arm nearly taken straight off by one of those damned White Scars, but he was still walking, still carrying his weapon in the other hand, and he'd taken his time over the one who'd wounded him.

He marched through the miasma with his brothers, trudging through the knee-deep sludge, drawing the thickening air deep into atrophied lungs. He didn't know exactly where he was. The fortress' guts were starting to dissolve entirely, their distinctive features sinking into a slough of featureless slime-caverns. He sought out the enemy wherever they dared to push in closer, and that worked very well – they didn't hide their presence, but whooped and shouted as if all that effort might somehow make them a bit less fragile.

You had to learn how to fight again, with this new body. In the past, before the great change, Crosius might have trusted a little more to evasion, hoping to limit the damage he was taking before he tried to dole any out himself. Now that seemed foolish. He was so much more ponderous now that trying to evade anything was almost impossible. On the other hand, he could absorb so many hits that his almost dreamlike pace of combat was still dazzlingly effective. It made things simpler. You just walked up to the enemy, trusting in the restorative powers of your innate decay. No tricks, no deceptions. It was an honest kind of warfare, for all the fact that it was underpinned by essential sorcery. The kind he could grow to love.

The enemy didn't see it that way, though. He had to hand it to them – their combined arms were troublesome. If you weren't careful, those tank barrels could obliterate everything around you, sending you crashing down into shafts you'd never be able to climb out of. And if you let those momentous blasts take your attention, then before you knew it the White Scars would be among you and spinning their blades in your face. They were brittle in comparison to him, but so fiendishly quick, and so drearily committed. They took the whole thing very seriously. They *never* responded to his amiable attempts to engage them in conversation.

He was preparing to climb up out of the trench he had been occupying alongside a few dozen of his fellow Unbroken, ready for the long slog across jumbled terrain towards more oncoming tanks. The little presence at his elbow was already excited, jiggling up and down in its hollow.

When the power-armoured body crashed into the bilge beside him, the first thing he thought was that it was just another warrior of the Legion, come to engage in the diversions. It took him a moment or two to recognise Morarg, because they were all so alike now – so caked in grime and the patina of decay, their old insignias more or less rubbed away.

'Brother!' he cried, clapping him hard on the back. 'Where in the hells have you been?'

Morarg stood silently for a moment, knee-deep in slurry, his helm-lenses peering over the lip of the trench. He had a big chainsword held in his bulky gauntlet, but hadn't activated it. He smelled different, too – something of the ether, maybe, a whiff of the daemonic.

'Where is the primarch?' he asked, sounding distracted.

Crosius laughed. 'You are the equerry! Have you lost him?'

Morarg didn't laugh in response. 'I was... waylaid. The Deathshroud were due to escort him to the west front. I see no sign of him.'

'Then he is indulging himself somewhere else. No doubt giving the bastards a hard time, eh?'

Morarg turned to him, and seemed to notice the daemon for the first time. The little lord bowed, then belched up something yellow and lumpy.

'What is that?' he asked.

Crosius looked down at it affectionately. 'One of the marvels of the age. It has a twin – did you know they had twins?'

He couldn't really tell what Morarg made of it. For a horrible moment, he thought the equerry might swat it away, as if it were some venomous insect that had crawled up out from the sludge.

But then, Morarg reached out, gently, and caressed its spines. The daemon snickered in pleasure, and wiggled its many bellies. 'Beautiful,' Morarg murmured. 'Very beautiful.'

'Agreed,' Crosius said, smiling broadly. 'You see it now, then? You see how much better things are?'

The enemy tanks were grinding closer. Soon they would unload those troublesome guns, turning the landscape around them into explosions of mud and broken metal. Then it would get interesting – dangerous, but interesting.

Morarg withdrew his gauntlet, then activated the gummed-up engines on his blade. The blunt blades started to whirr. He looked up, and made ready to climb up the slope, into the onslaught of unbelievers.

'So you say,' he said, though still with a slightly haunted air. 'Maybe you were right about that. Best to put the past behind us. It isn't coming back.'

He should have been dead. It should have been over a long time ago, with Jaghatai nothing more than a smear of torn skin and armour-fragments on the floor. And yet, impossibly, he was still alive, still fighting back. His arms must both have been broken, his fused ribcage cracked into ribbons, his sword notched and blunted, and still he came back, again and again.

It was becoming almost painful to watch. The primarch
of the V, on his knees again after being smashed halfway
across the open landing stage, struggling to get back up. The
blood trailing from every armour-seal was so profuse that you
wondered how much more of it there could still be inside him.
Entire sections of his ivory plate hung loosely on sinew like
straps, flapping as he staggered around.

And through it all, he kept *talking*. He kept up the torrent
of petty jibes and slights. Even when Mortarion rained blows
at his dented helm, smacked him deep into the broken-up
rockcrete, the barbs kept on coming, sometimes acid, sometimes brutal, sometimes merely juvenile.

'Just take the damned mask off. I want to see your expression when I kill you.'

'Your stench is worse than at Ullanor. And it was putrefying
then.'

And the one that cut deep, for all its obviousness.

'I should have taken on the Legion Master. I should have
fought Typhon.'

It was childish. It was beneath them both. Mortarion was
beyond anger by then, and had progressed into a kind of
contemptuous weariness. Greater things beckoned. This petty
brawl should not have mattered. It should not have still been
happening. Power still pulsed through his system like raw promethium, the warp still animated his every gesture, his armies
still held their ground against a faltering White Scars attack,
but this was becoming infuriating now, a maddening bump
in the road that just would not clear.

So he swung back into the fight – two great strides, a
gathering of momentum, and then a truly brutal backhand
slash with *Silence* that tore Jaghatai's helm clean from his
head and sent his body arcing high. The Khan crashed to
the deck again, flat on his back, somehow keeping a grip

on his fragile blade even as Mortarion surged over him, slamming his staff's heel into his enemy's exposed midriff. Jaghatai managed to twist away at the last moment, only for Mortarion to plant a vicious kick against his face, breaking both nose and cheekbone.

Half-blind and groggy, Jaghatai lashed out with his blade, connecting with *Silence* and wrenching it from Mortarion's grip. Letting the staff clatter away, Mortarion dropped down sharply, piling in wildly with his gauntlets, slamming in punches, at the Khan's throat, at his chest, at his ruined face. The clenched fists flew, one after another, barely warded by Jaghatai's flailing arms, tearing up the remains of that beautiful lacquered ceramite and splattering the two of them in more gouts of forge-hot blood.

The Khan never stopped fighting back, but it was becoming pitiful now. He caught one of Mortarion's fists on the full, only for the other one to plunge deep at his stomach, bursting something within. Jaghatai tried to rise, and Mortarion cast him down disdainfully, fracturing his spine. They were both roaring by then, Mortarion from frustrated fury, the Khan from undiluted agony. They had been reduced to *this* – brawling across a derelict space port like hive world gangers, gouging and tearing at the body before them, trying to rip it apart with their own fingers.

Scions of the Emperor, masters of the galaxy.

Panting hard, feeling like his heart was fit to burst, Mortarion finally ceased the barrage. The first ache of exhaustion rippled up his arms, his vision shivered a little. Still something mortal in him then, after all, something that could know fatigue. He got up painfully.

Jaghatai still breathed. Somehow, amid the swamp of gore that had once been a proud visage, the air was still being sucked in, bubbling feebly amid floating flecks of bone.

Mortarion limped over to his scythe, hauling it up again, making ready to end the grotesque spectacle.

'*I thought you'd dance,*' he said again, genuinely mystified. '*You just… took it. Did you lose your mind?*'

Jaghatai started to cough, sending more bloody spurts out over the ripped-apart ground. His shattered gauntlet still clutched the hilt of his blade, but the arm must have been broken in many places. Only slowly, as he trudged back, did Mortarion realise that the sound was bitter laughter.

'I… absorbed,' Jaghatai rasped, 'the… pain.'

Mortarion halted. '*What do you mean?*'

'I… *know,*' Jaghatai said, his voice a liquid slur. 'The *Terminus Est*. You… gave up. I… did not.' And then he grinned – his split lips, his flayed cheeks, his lone seeing eye, twisting into genuine, spiteful pleasure. 'My endurance is… *superior.*'

So that was what they all believed. Not that he had done what needed to be done. Not that he had sacrificed everything to make his Legion invincible, even suffering the ignominy of using Calas as his foil, even condemning himself to the permanent soul-anguish of daemonhood so that the change could never be undone by anyone, not even his father.

That he had been weak.

The dam of his fury broke. He hefted *Silence* two-handed, angling the point towards the laughing Khan, no longer thinking of anything but sending its tip spearing through his enemy's chest.

And so he missed the Khan's suddenly tightening grip, the flicker of white steel, the rapid push from the deck and the upthrust of the masterful blade. The *White Tiger* penetrated deep under the single segment of Mortarion's armour plate that the Khan had managed to dislodge, biting deep, sending a flare of pain straight up into his straining torso.

Silence's strike missed its aim as he jerked clear from the blade. Mortarion reeled away, blood leaking from the deep wound. And then, to his incredulity, the Khan was clambering back to his feet again, still bleeding, still damaged, but already coming towards him. Mortarion, suddenly doubting even the evidence of his senses, staggered back into contact, doing just what he had done before – charging straight in, trusting to his colossal strength – and only then realised how drained to the bone he was by what had gone before.

And then – *then* – the Khan started to dance. Not with any beauty – that had been ripped from him – but still with that unearthly slipperiness, that mesmerising power of appearing to be in one place, inviting the strike, only to be a hand's width away, just enough to drop under your guard and slice a piece of you away. He could still do it. He still had something left.

'When we do this with our ships,' the Khan growled, no longer laughing, now deadly serious, 'we call it *zao*. The chisel.'

Mortarion swung his scythe clumsily, and missed. The dao blade struck him again, carving a deep rent along his trailing arm.

The change was mesmerising. The Khan was still on the edge of death, just one good impact away from annihilation, but he was moving again, faster and faster as his primarch's physiology did what it had been designed to do: keep him alive, keep his blade working, keep him in the fight.

Mortarion snarled, worked his scythe harder again, feeling his fatigued muscles scream even as his mind reeled from the realisation. He should have seen through it. He should never have allowed himself to be goaded.

Their blades clashed again, snarling in an explosion of mingled warp detonations, and the two of them both reeled away from the blow, barely able to keep their feet.

He was *damaged*. That had *hurt him*.

And the Khan came back quicker, his smashed ankles somehow propelling him across the erupted ground faster than Mortarion could react. When the dao clanged against the scythe again the blood splattered freely, but it was no longer just Jaghatai's.

Mortarion swivelled on his heel and smashed the Khan away. That sent the primarch tumbling, but he came straight back *again*, lurching from his catastrophic injuries as if drunk, his devastated face etched with excruciation, but still fighting through the toll of fearful damage. It was as if some malevolent spirit animated him now, pushing his ravaged body onward until it achieved the absolution it needed.

The sword spun faster, blurring across Mortarion's double vision, getting difficult to stop. The two of them traded earth-breaking blows, tearing more of their priceless battleplate from its place, smashing phials, rupturing cables, severing chain-lengths. Their cloaks were ripped to shreds, their finery destroyed, their raw selves exposed in blood-mottled canvases of skin-stripped muscle, their pretensions scoured back to the primal truth – that they were savage weapons, the numbered blades of an unwilling god.

Mortarion was still the greater of them. He was still the stronger, the more steeped in preternatural gifts, but now all that he felt was doubt, rocked by the remorseless fury of one who had never been anything more than flighty, self-regarding and unreliable. All Mortarion could see just then was one who wished to kill him – who would do anything, sacrifice *anything*, fight himself beyond physical limits, destroy his own body, his own heart, his own soul, just for the satisfaction of the oaths he had made in the void.

'*If you know what I did,*' Mortarion cried out, fighting on now through that cold fog of indecision, '*then you know the truth of it, brother – I can no longer die.*'

It was as if a signal had been given. The Khan's bloodied head lifted, the remnants of his long hair hanging in matted clumps.

'Oh, I know that,' he murmured, with the most perfect contempt he had ever mustered. 'But *I* can.'

Then he leapt. His broken legs still propelled him, his
fractured arms still bore his blade, his blood-filled lungs and
perforated heart still gave him just enough power, and he
swept in close.

If he had been in the prime of condition, the move might
have been hard to counter, but he was already little more than
a corpse held together by force of will, and so *Silence* interposed itself, catching the Khan under his armour-stripped
shoulder and impaling him deep.

But that didn't stop him. The parry had been seen, planned
for, and so he just kept coming, dragging himself up the length
of the blade until the scythe jutted out of his ruptured back and
the *White Tiger* was in tight against Mortarion's neck. For an
instant, their two faces were right up against one another – both
cadaverous now, drained of blood, drained of life, existing only
as masks onto pure vengeance. All their majesty was stripped
away, scraped out across the utilitarian rockcrete, leaving just the
desire, the violence, the brute mechanics of despite.

It only took a split second. Mortarion's eyes went wide, real-
ising that he couldn't wrench his brother away in time. The
Khan's narrowed.

'And *that* makes the difference,' Jaghatai spat.

He snapped his dao across, severing Mortarion's neck cleanly
in an explosion of black bile, before collapsing down into
the warp explosion that turned the landing stage, briefly,
into the brightest object on the planet after the Emperor's
tormented soul itself.

TWENTY-FIVE

Death rites
Landslide
The quiet ones

He knew. Instantly, as soon as it happened, he knew.

Shiban was far away from the site of it, buried in fighting on the approaches to the orbital batteries. The guns towered over him now, their silent ranks stretching off into the distance, still fought hard over by White Scars and Death Guard alike. The bolt-shells flew, the blades flashed, both sides surged up against the other, but still he knew.

It was like some kind of vortex bomb going off, something that sucked everything out with it, leaving only dumb shock in its wake. Every warrior across that huge battlefield, from both sides, stumbled, hesitated, looked up, as if their primarch was apt to appear there, somehow, but of course couldn't, and could never do so again.

The traitors shambled to a complete halt. Silent resistance was replaced by a kind of bewilderment – a loss of momentum, for reasons that their sluggish minds had no power left to explain. They could feel their master's withdrawal – not his death, his *withdrawal* – as if he had just decided, on a whim, to leave them to it. The surge of concentrated energy they had been riding dissipated, echoing down the long halls before blowing emptily out of the space port's gigantic vents, a spent force, a busted flush.

On the physical front, nothing had changed. But the Unbroken were more than physical now. They were tied into the grand bargains of the warp, its alliances and its contracts, and something had gone badly amiss, something unforeseen, inexplicable and terminal.

For the White Scars, it was completely different. The first sensation was one of abject shock – a nerve-jolt that welled up from the base of every heart and stomach, a wrench of sudden absence that affected them all instantly. Seasoned warriors, inured to all privation, bent double on the battlefield, incapacitated by the scale of grief. They had no doubts what had happened – it was as plain to every soul as if it had taken place right in front of their eyes.

He is gone. They have taken his light from the universe. He is gone.

Shiban felt the earth beneath his feet sway, his moorings cut loose, his blade fall from his grip. He fell to his knees, crashing heavily into the corrupted swill. For a moment, he saw nothing at all – just an infinity of blackness, extending in all directions. It felt as if a cold claw had reached into his chest and wrenched both his hearts out, dragging all hope and ambition and life with it.

He heard cries ring out across the battlefield, unlocked howls of disbelief and horror, and dimly realised that every White Scar across every rotten chamber and miasmatic cavern was experiencing what he was experiencing. A warrior of the Legions was not just an inducted soldier, given the Emperor's coin and handed a bolter. He was connected through warp-craft and gene-tech to his primogenitor, indelibly linked both temperamentally and psychically to the archetype. The bond was more than loyalty, more than filial duty. It was *everything*.

He wanted to vomit. He wanted to scream. He wanted to throw his head back and empty that unbearable grief out up at the shrouded stars.

But he was also a khan of the ordu, the one the others looked to, the carrier of the flame.

You are Tachseer.

You are *the Restorer.*

It could not go on. He could not indulge himself. He forced himself to stand again, shakily, and opened his eyes, and it was as if the night around him had become as black as bloody pitch, more hateful than before, emptier and colder.

He took up his blade again, ramming it firmly aloft, just as he had done when the Khagan had breached the first wall, when his ecstasy had been as profound as his loss was now.

'*Damarg!*' he roared.

That word had only one meaning in Khorchin. It only had one sacred use. Death. Not the death of old age or sickness, but the death of the fighter, slain in battle against an enemy; the death that had to be avenged lest destruction overcome all things. That grief-curse had been heard on the grasslands of Chogoris since the time before memory, a paean of defiance and honour and fealty, one that every sword-bearer knew and understood and venerated. They had cried it aloud when Giyahun had died, when Qin Xa had died, when Yesugei had died, and now they cried it for the greatest of them all.

'*Damarg!*' Shiban thundered again, his powerful voice hurling the denunciation out through vox-emitters at full stretch, striding out fearlessly now, heedless of any danger, no longer with the exuberance of that first vivid attack, but with slow, terrible deliberation.

All around him, White Scars looked up, heard their home

world's ancient tongue ringing in the vaults, and reached for their blades again.

Damarg.

Now the curse echoed darkly from the cracked walls, issuing first from a dozen mouths, then a hundred mouths, then a thousand. It fell into a terrible rhythm. They mouthed it in unison, again and again, uttering nothing else now, no longer holding to cover, but coming out openly, fists clenched tighter than adamantium, hearts bursting with a loathing that went beyond expression.

Damarg.

The enemy never responded. They had always been silent in combat, almost oblivious to those they fought, but now they stared in a stupor at those coming towards them – the unified presentation of utter loathing, utter resolve, utter commitment. The warp, orchestrated so perfectly by their master, was draining away from every chamber like a flood surging out through shattered walls and spilling out over the plains beyond. Where their opponents were now suddenly animated with this terrible, cold-as-ice fury, their own resolve had been ripped away from them without warning.

The remaining Terran Armoured units began to operate again, their confused commanders knowing better than to ask what was going on, only that they still had their duty, and that something astonishing was happening to those they fought with. Targeting lumens flickered on, engines powered up, long barrels swung once more towards their targets.

Shiban barely noticed. Those he marched with barely noticed. Their only focus was ahead, to the ones who had done this thing and who now would be punished. They strode into the open, the sons of the Great Khan, exposed to the return fire that came sporadically now.

Shiban reached up to his helm, released the seals, twisted

it off, and locked it to his armour. All those with him did the same. As one, they reached up with their blades, placed them against the ridged tissue on their cheeks, and drew the edge down. Fresh blood ran freely across their exposed skin as the old scars opened. They breathed in the toxic air and relished its bitterness. They fixed their gaze at the ranks of the enemy, and each one of them, in a movement of such perfect coordination that it might have been ordained since the dawn of time, angled a bloody blade towards the chosen target.

When their final great roar came, it made the caverns themselves shake, the waters tremble, the iron crack and the glass shatter.

Damarg!

And then they were charging, driven only by their unbounded hatred, sweeping across the ruins in a tide of ivory and gold and crimson, unstoppable, unrestrained, the lords of the storm, the merited vengeance of heaven, the bringers of death.

She saw it from the air. They were still kilometres out, juddering through the storm, their forward viewers showing them almost nothing but flying grime and ash, but Ilya had calibrated the sensors to give her a forward scan, routed to the lenses in front of her. Sojuk was kept busy saving them from being slammed into the spire-tops around them, while she relentlessly peered ahead, desperate for some sign of what was taking place in the port.

Her first view of it was a jumpy, grainy image that slid around the poorly aligned scopes. Even from that she could see the extensive damage, the rampant explosions, the fires crackling out of control in broad swathes across the stacked levels. Like every part of the once glorious Palace, the Lion's Gate space port was a smoking wreck now, a scraped-out mountain riddled with both plague and structural damage.

And for a while, that was all she got. Sojuk powered the

gunship as fast as he could, angling at speed along the same route the Terran Armoured units had taken, evidenced by the hundreds of burned-out hulls littering the chasms below. The space port gradually loomed nearer, emerging through drifting skirts of smoke and smog, its coal-black profile lit up with both eerie green glows and the purer light of physical explosives detonating.

But then she saw it. You couldn't miss it – anything within a hundred kilometres of the space port would have seen it, whatever else was exploding or disintegrating around them at the time. A translucent sphere of pale green, blooming silently out of the western landing stages, swelling up with alarming speed, followed by a raging kaleidoscope of ghostly lightning. A second later, and the sound waves caught up – a colossal, ear-ripping boom, followed by a roar of rushing atmospheres, all laced with something like fractured screaming. And then the turbulence hit them, a buffeting, crashing wave of thruster-hot gales that nearly sent them spinning into the flanks of the nearest hab-tower.

Sojuk performed admirably amidst all that, keeping them alive through some remarkable flying. Much later, Ilya would discover just how horrendous that moment had been for him, and how he had almost lost control completely through a mixture of shock and horror, but just then all she knew was that something dreadful had happened, and that they were still too far away to do anything about it.

'Keep us on course!' she shouted, trying desperately to get a better visual fix on what had taken place.

She managed to zoom in on the west front – that great mass of stacked landing stages, many of them kilometres wide and suspended on giant piers that jutted hundreds of metres up into the sky. What she saw shook her to her core.

The stages were falling, sliding, cracking, collapsing into a vast landslide of rockcrete, all of it underlit with that foul green light. Secondary explosions rang out, promethium reservoirs going off. The entire face of the fortress was coming down, subsiding with what looked like stately slowness, but must have felt, up close, like the thundering end of all creation. The wind still tore past them, still screaming at them. Though it was hard to pick out amid all the movement and lens-shake, Ilya thought she saw something incredibly bright still burning amid all the wreckage, like a dwarf star at the centre of an accretion disc.

The collapse slowly ground to a halt, hurling more mountains of static-laced dust towering up across the entire site. What remained was a long gouge in the immense space port's western shoulder, nearly a kilometre across, sparking with residual detonations, slumped into total ruin.

For a while, she couldn't find any words. She knew, somehow, with total certainty, who had been at the centre of all that.

'Get us there,' she said eventually.

Sojuk never looked at her. Flying alone in that unnatural storm absorbed almost all his concentration. 'We will not be able to land in that.'

'Then as close as you can,' Ilya snapped, her own voice sounding to her like it came from far away. She felt tears beginning to spike in her eyes, and angrily blinked them away. She had to *concentrate*, stay focused.

Sojuk somehow managed to find just a scrap more speed, flying now with a cold and furious desperation. The tempest raged past them, pushed against them, but he powered on through it as if his fury alone could rip the pressure apart.

Ilya turned to the comm controls. After that colossal burst of static, much of the instrumentation had been blown beyond repair, but the aftermath seemed to have actually released

some of the crushing interference that had plagued them for
so many weeks. She managed to get some locator-signals, even
pick up fragments of squad comms.

Da–

–marg

Dam– rg

The word made her spine shiver. She knew what it meant.
She knew *just* what it meant.

You could lose yourself in that hate. It could do incredible
things, but you could unravel yourself forever in its depths.
Just then, she so desperately wanted to do that. She wanted
to order Sojuk to fly the Thunderhawk right into whatever
remained of those who had done this.

But she was not a child of Chogoris. She was not a member of
the Legion, no matter how many times they had told her she was.

She was their honoured guest. She was their venerated sage.
Above all, as Yesugei had told her in that final, terrible com-
munication from Dark Glass, she was their soul.

'Range to broadcast,' she said, her fingers now working the
comms controls again, determinedly, rapidly. 'I *have* to get
there.'

Kaska heard it while they were still ascending the levels. It was
like no noise he had ever heard before – a kind of snatched
wail, like a child ripped from its parent's arms, only greater
and deeper and scarcely human at all.

They had been working hard to make the climb for hours.
He was exhausted, as were the rest of the crew. In normal
campaigns they would have withdrawn from combat whenever
possible to open the hatch, get some air into the hull, try to
get out of the cramped confines when it was safe. But here, in
this place, it was never safe, not even to pop the cover open by
a crack, and so they had sweated and panted and crouched in

the heat and the stink without respite. It was enough to drive
you mad. At times you wanted just to lash out, to stretch your
legs, punch your way free of the nightmarish enclosure, and
it took all your willpower to stay at your station, endure the
engine roar and the fumes and the stench, and just keep going.

They had refuelled and taken on water a few times, always
with the assistance of the White Scars, who were able to operate
outside the hull, siphoning what they needed from captured
bunkers or other wrecks. So they were alive, and mobile, but
not much more than that. The lascannon's power packs were
down to critical levels, and Merck had just a handful of shells
left in the rack. Dresi had taken it all hardest, driving without a
break almost since the opening of the Colossi doors, and now
barely responded to orders at all, just stayed silently in position
as if she'd been fused to her seat and controls.

Vosch was subdued too, which wasn't like her at all, though
Jandev's taciturn character seemed relatively unaltered by anything that had happened. As for Kaska, he felt permanently
sick. More than the rest of them, he'd got a good view of what
they'd been fighting. He'd been the one to scan across those
crowded battlefields, to stare into the faces of the… *things* out
there, and give the order to advance. It hadn't mattered much
that the White Scars had been alongside him to keep things
from coming apart entirely, at least not to the way it had all
made him feel.

Infantry despised tankers, went the old saying, because they
never had to look their enemy in the face. That had always
been an unfair slur, but now it was doubly so. He'd looked
at faces that no sane man should ever have looked at. If he
ever got out of this alive, he'd be seeing those faces for the
rest of his life.

He had to carry on, though. The khan of the White Scars, the
one calling himself Jangsai, drove them hard. A Space Marine

could run far faster than a battle tank over most terrains, and keep going for longer. The Legion warriors no longer sheltered in the shadow of the rumbling hulls, but pushed ahead, seeking out routes upwards and westward. From the sporadic comms traffic, it became clear that hundreds of similar detachments were trying the same thing, but Kaska had no real idea why – he assumed that some important objective needed bolstering.

Many of the big vehicle lifts – the ones that had shunted void-ship sections around – were damaged or unsafe to use, but they discovered a few that Jangsai pronounced fit enough, and so they had trundled onto the ascender platforms in groups of four at a time. That move may have put them far ahead of the others, who were busy searching for unblocked ramps, all the while running into enemy formations or nests of those malefic not-xenos beasts.

The journey upwards was nerve-shredding – a blind ascent, huddled in the shaking hull of *Aika 73*, hearing the bone-deep resonance of a structure around them under immense stress. If those shafts had collapsed, they would all have been buried alive, condemned to a slow and choking demise in the dark.

But they all made it to the top, one group at a time, until Jangsai's full complement of twenty Legion warriors and fifteen hulls started moving again, heading up a long covered incline towards the first of the open landing stages on the west front.

Aika 73 was less than halfway up it when the wail started. The rumble of destructive noise had been building for a while already, but this was something else – like the shrieks the not-xenos made whenever they were torn apart. Kaska had to pull his earpiece out for a while so it didn't drive him mad. Right after that started, the world started to crumble around them. The walls started to bulge, with cracks cobwebbing across the bare stonework, and metal struts sheared away from their footings.

'It's coming down!' Vosch shouted.

'What's coming down?' Merck demanded, unable to get to the forward viewslit.

'Drive!' Kaska cried. 'Full speed! Get us out of this!'

Every commander in the squadron had made the same decision. The White Scars ran too, powering up the incline as masonry *thunked* down around them.

The ground under their treads started to break up, rippling like yanked fabric, throwing them around crazily. Kaska had his head slammed into the inner curve of the turret *again*, while Jandev took a sickening smack to his helmet as he bounced around in his seat. The engines stuttered as Dresi missed a gear, before she fought it home and powered them on and up.

Kaska threaded his earpiece back in, pressing his face back against the periscope sights, trying to sway with the buck of the tank-deck even though his thigh-muscles were as raw and pain-filled as he'd ever known.

'Coming through!' announced Vosch, whose gunsights gave her the most stable view ahead.

'Keep up speed, driver,' warned Kaska, worried that the aperture ahead looked very unstable. Clouds of masonry dust were billowing crazily on the far side, which meant that something very big indeed was coming down on top of them all.

'Holy Throne...' Merck muttered to himself, gripping the breech-hatch with sweaty fingers.

Then they were out, shooting clear of the low tunnel entrance, bouncing on a patch of fresh rubble, before finding themselves, for the first time since the assault began, under open skies.

'Ready, gunners,' Kaska ordered, scanning for targets. 'Fire on my command.'

But there were no targets. There was nothing at all. Even by the standards of what they had been fighting through now for weeks on end, this place was a thrown-about, torn-up mess. From his narrow vantage, all he could see were towering banks of semi-demolished rockcrete slabs, each thirty metres thick or more, stacked on top of one another like the sedimentary layers of an ancient cliff-face. Those stacks crackled with lightning, and were punctuated with scree-defiles and twisted forests of exposed rebar. The entire expanse was still moving too, grinding and cracking open like some wildly accelerated tectonic event, overhung with roiling dust banks and the deep rumble of a whole fortress section collapsing in on itself.

All the tanks got out of the tunnel in time, but had to power onward fast to avoid being caught up in secondary landslips. The White Scars never hesitated, either – they leapt up the teetering slopes and vaulted across the gaps between the disintegrating platforms. Making progress was harder for the armour, but not impossible. *Aika 73* led the way, swivelling and gunning and pitching up and across the ever-shifting landscapes. Not for the first time, Kaska marvelled that Dresi was able to do it at all. She was like a machine.

'Keep in sight of the khan,' he told her. 'I'll get a comm-line to him, if I can.'

The immense subsidence around them gradually settled down amid more gouts of kicked-out dust, although the maelstrom overhead continued to rage unabated, flooding the bare rockcrete plates with a greenish pallor that shifted and slid like tainted moonlight on water. The squadrons made tortuous progress through it all, always following the lead given by the infantry, forever at risk of skidding down some steeply angled slide and over what appeared to be drops of hundreds of metres to the terraces far below.

After a while, Kaska managed to fix on to the comm-line

being used by the White Scars. The feed was intermittent, and in a language he didn't understand, but he got something. The truly crushing levels of interference that had plagued them for so long seemed to have been lifted somewhat, despite all the devastation obviously still going on around them.

Listening to the signals wasn't easy. The White Scars didn't sound at all as they had done when addressing him in Gothic. They were… enraged? Maddened? Desperate? Kaska could have sworn that one of them was almost out of control, but that was surely impossible – these were Space Marines, not pressed line troops.

Eventually, after what became a punishingly hard trek across a windblown section of bare rockcrete, the White Scars coalesced again, gesturing frantically towards one another. Kaska led the rest of the armour towards them, feeling very uncertain as to what was going on.

Even once they caught up, even after he had ordered the full stop and given Dresi a much-needed break, he still had no idea what was happening. The periscope didn't give him enough of an angle to determine what the Legion warriors were clustered around. They remained agitated, strangely inde- cisive, which was incredible to him, since their very natures had always been about decisiveness and lack of agitation.

'We're right out in the open,' observed Jandev dryly, look- ing up from his sights. Kaska noticed that he was nursing a long gash over his right eye from the earlier collision. 'Maybe think about that?'

The lasgunner was right. All the tanks were idling now, exposed, and the ground was highly unstable, liable to frac- ture further or slide into complete dissolution.

'Bring us closer,' Kaska ordered. 'But slowly. Very slowly.'

Dresi edged the tank in, and Kaska took to the scopes again. Both Jandev and Vosch did the same. He thought he could make out something immobile on the deck, and long blood-stains, and many pieces of broken armour.

'It's one of them,' said Vosch.

'Dead,' said Jandev.

'Throne,' said Kaska, swivelling the periscope to gain a better angle. 'That's not one of them. It's too big. That's a–'

He broke off. Vosch turned to look at him too, her face going grey as soon as she realised. Even Jandev seemed lost for words.

'That's a *what*?' demanded Merck.

Kaska didn't reply. He couldn't say the word.

'It can't be,' said Vosch.

'Can't be *what*?' blurted Merck.

'How do you know?' retorted Jandev, replying to Vosch. 'Have you ever seen one?'

'Of course she hasn't,' said Kaska. Throne, this was a night-mare. Something had to be done, or they would all die out here. 'Dresi, get on the tracker and find us a way down. Gunners – keep your eyes on those sights. Merck – shut up.' Then he switched his comm-status from *listen* to *speak*. 'My lord khan,' he said, his voice trembling slightly no matter how much he tried to control it. 'Can we assist you?'

For a moment, he got no reply. No indication, even, that he'd been heard. Then, slowly, Jangsai turned to face the tank's hull.

'*A casualty,*' he replied, in Gothic. He sounded numb. '*The body cannot be left here.*'

Why couldn't they carry it? Kaska had seen Space Marines haul the bodies of injured comrades for considerable distances. But then again, from what little he could see, this 'body' almost didn't deserve the name – it looked in absolutely terrible shape. Perhaps it would even break apart if they tried.

Kaska switched away from the open channel. 'They have a casualty,' he told the crew.

'It can't come in here,' said Merck immediately.

Jandev snorted. 'It wouldn't fit. I'm telling you, it's a–'

'They're our allies,' said Vosch. 'They wish to extract it. We have to help them.'

'But what can we do?' Kaska said, exasperated now. They couldn't just *stay* here.

When Dresi spoke, it took them all by surprise. Kaska discovered that he barely knew what her voice sounded like. She had an Albian accent, it turned out.

'There is solid ground five hundred metres down,' she said. 'I have plotted a course, and we can follow it – for now.' She looked up at Kaska. 'They will not leave the body. They do not believe they can carry it any distance without causing greater harm. They are probably right. It will not fit inside any of our units, even if we were able to open the hatches, because it is not of baseline human dimensions. But it could be carried topside. It could be hoisted over the air filtration housings behind the turret, with the main gun angled away, then shielded by warriors mounted on either side of it. If we went carefully, we could carry it for them.'

Kaska just stared at her for a while. So did all the others.

It was hard to read Dresi's expression behind her driving goggles and fume-mask, but she certainly sounded like she'd worked it all out.

'You will have to make the suggestion to them, sergeant, because just now they are not in their right minds,' she added. 'They may not like it. But I do not see another option.'

Kaska stared at Vosch next, who shrugged. Jandev chuckled dryly to himself, and shook his head. Merck, for once, didn't have anything to say.

Kaska really should have asked where they had found Dresi. He really should have made the effort to talk to her earlier. These were basic things – you needed to know your crew. Hells, it was always the quiet ones.

But that was for another time. The enemy still controlled large chunks of the world around them, and could emerge at any moment. The structures they stood on could collapse imminently. Any number of catastrophes could erupt without warning, all while they stood in that place, unable to make a decision.

So, after thinking it through one more time, he reached for the comm.

'My lord khan,' he said gingerly. 'I have a proposal.'

TWENTY-SIX

Old blood
Handing over
The blade

'We fall back.' That was the proposal. That was – seriously, now – what Crosius was advocating.

Morarg couldn't respond. It was like the oxygen had been suddenly taken away, rendering him powerless – something you had unconsciously relied on, never thinking about, now gone, yanked beyond your grasp and leaving you to suffocate.

He reeled, falling to his knees. He had been so powerful. The dead of the V were around him, slain by his hand. He had begun to enjoy himself, just as Crosius had done for a while. He had started to stop obsessing, to relish the painful gifts he had been given.

Now he looked up, and barely saw a thing out of his smeared helm-lenses. He would have taken it off, except he wasn't sure he could. Through the murk, at distance, he saw more of those damned Chogorians advancing. They weren't running now. They weren't trying to force the pace, compensating for their fragility with elusive movement.

They had gone mad, seemingly.

Had *they* done this to them? Had the Unbroken delivered so much pain that they had changed, just as the Death Guard had on the *Terminus Est*? Was such a transition possible? Had the White Scars discovered some new and terrible god of their own?

He couldn't even begin to process that. His head was ringing. His stomach felt empty, his hearts were yammering. Crosius had ceased his chatter, and was now limping away, back through the mire. The daemon he carried in his arm was screaming, and that was a horrible sound.

Morarg lurched up onto his hooves, and started to stumble after him.

'Wait,' he tried, reaching out.

'Fall back,' Crosius slurred.

Morarg caught up, snatching his elbow, forcing him to stop. 'We *never* retreat.'

Just looking at the old Apothecary's ruined armour was unsettling. It disgusted him. He'd always *seen* those changes, to some degree, but now he was *really seeing* them, as they must look to an outsider. By the god, what had they become? Once you stripped away the haze of forgetfulness, once you turned the lights on, you could see right through it.

'He's *gone*,' Crosius spat back. 'You sense it? Typhus was right. He waited too long.'

Morarg tried to concentrate, though it was difficult even to make out his brother's words. Who was he talking about? Mortarion? Yes, yes, he must have been. The primarch *was* gone. But where? And how?

'I don't...' he started. 'I don't...'

'Believe it!' Crosius blurted, sounding on the edge of losing his mind completely. 'Something happened. He's gone. And if he isn't here, why are we still?' He looked over his shoulder. 'Stuck inside with those mad bastards.'

Morarg remembered what the Remnant had told him. *He is loved, in the empyrean, like few others.* Was that what had happened? Had the empyrean taken him early, leaving the rest of them behind?

Not possible. The primarch would not have done it. *I loved you all too much. That is the only error I will admit.* Yes, that had been true. So what was going on?

'I had started to believe,' Morarg said numbly. From a long way back, he could hear that damned chant – the dirge the Chogorians kept on at now. 'That it was all planned out.'

Or had it been a lie? The whole thing, everything the daemon had told him? Maybe Mortarion had been a dupe all along, just as he had always feared. Maybe Typhus had always been the real power. Maybe, maybe. How to tell? Who to ask?

'This will pass,' Crosius insisted, agitated, still wanting to get moving. 'This is just psychic shock. He's been holding it all up, all around us, you understand that? We're just having… withdrawal. We have to *get out*. It will pass.'

Maybe that was right. Clear his head. Stop the agonised, sluggish pain that made every muscle shriek. 'To where?' he said.

Crosius lifted the little daemon up. 'Remember this? Remember I told you it had a twin? The other one's with the First Captain. He must be in charge now. He'll know what to do.' A slightly manic laugh. 'I mean, he always has done, hasn't he?'

Morarg wanted to contradict that, but he had already forgotten the reason why.

'This was *his* strategy,' Crosius went on. 'The primarch's. But it's not the only one. There are warbands already over the walls. We could join them. Kadex Ilkarion has crossed the breach, they say. Vorx, too.'

'I… can't fight.'

'You can. Psychic shock. It'll pass.' Crosius held up the daemon. Its wild eyes stared right back at Morarg. By the god, it was a foul thing, ugly as a devil-toad, and it stank. '*He* knew this moment would come. I see that now. I can speak to him.'

Typhus. The one who had ushered in all this pain. Morarg remembered being so very angry at him, wanting him dead. He remembered wanting just as hard to believe in Mortarion, to believe that the liberator of Barbarus could not fail, not before, not now.

'The primarch...' he began.

'He's not dead. You understand that? Just... absent.'

'We were all... committed,' Morarg protested. 'We *never* retreat.'

Crosius hawked up a phlegmy laugh. He was disgusting. 'This isn't retreat. This is advance. To the core.' He shuffled closer, bringing his stench of ordure with him. 'What does this shit-heap matter, anyway? Did we come through all of that in the void, for this? No, my brother. We came for the Palace. We fall back, we regroup. We stay here, in this state, with them, and we will die.'

Morarg already felt like his grip on reality was slipping away. The shift had been so sudden, so profound. The environment around him never steadied – it shifted, it shook. His own odour repelled him. He could feel the putrefaction under his rotting armour, and it made his stomach – what remained of it – turn.

The Remnant's words were already fading from his mind. Would he remember them at all, if he escaped this place? *You cannot ignore him, you cannot pity him – he is your primarch.* But his primarch was gone – he felt the truth of that in his every agonised cell. Why had he gone? *Where* had he gone?

Crosius remained close. He wouldn't let this lie.

'You hear me, brother,' he urged. 'We stay here, we die.'

In the background, that damned chant was drawing nearer. They sounded utterly demented now, the White Scars, as if something vicious and life-eating had consumed them, turning them into an army of obsessive revenants.

'You can... speak to Typhus?' Morarg slurred, trying hard not to vomit.

Crosius stroked the daemon's spines again, and its agitation seemed to reduce a little. 'It needs to be done. He'll sort this out.'

Just like he already sorted us out, Morarg thought bitterly.

But what else remained? To fight on, here, for a prize they'd never wished to hold forever, and miss the chance of true glory? Or to get out, to let the sickness pass, to start over?

Morarg stared at the daemon. How could he ever have thought of it with affection? Its sacs pulsed, its gills leaked, its knuckles cracked. At that moment, though, it felt like there were daemons all around him – daemons that twisted the past and the future, daemons in ivory armour that came with curved and bloody blades, daemons made of flies that ushered in yet more anguish, daemons with gossamer wings who had the temerity, right when it mattered, to fail.

So many daemons. Which one to pick?

As ever, Morarg thought, the one in front of you.

'Fall back, then,' he said, loathing himself for even saying it out loud. 'Damn it all, we fall back.'

Crosius nodded frantically, and started to limp off. Morarg went after him, his heavy treads kicking the filth up around him.

'And use that little horror to tell Typhus we're coming,' he said. 'I feel sure he'll be just overjoyed to see us all again.'

Only when drawing close did Ilya see the full scale of the devastation. It wasn't just the demolished west front, but everything about the once majestic space port. The details were hard to pick out in the dark, but weeks of constant bombardment had taken their toll, smashing up fascias and collapsing terraces. The fact that anything was still standing at all was testament to just how gigantic the structure's core was. You could probably still hammer away at it for months, and something would remain in place at the heart of it, such was the hyper-durability of gargantuan-era Imperial architecture.

For all that, Sojuk had been right, of course – there was no way the gunship could make a landing at the site she'd identified from the air. It looked like a series of huge stages had crashed down on top of one another, creating a tiered massif of still-shifting hardcore, all interlaced with static lightning and secondary explosions.

Maybe the Khan had been at the top of that collapse. Maybe wherever he had been fighting had been spared, somehow emerging out of the dust relatively unscathed. Or maybe he was interred underneath it all, something excavators would discover years later – if, that was, any excavators were left at the end of all this madness.

She had to find out. She owed him that, at least – to do everything she could. Her mind instantly went back to Ullanor, to those exhaustively terraformed plateaus. She remembered climbing up the cliffs, searching for something elusive, only for Yesugei to haul her up to safety.

'Be careful,' he'd said.

Throne, if only she had been. No one had been careful enough, that was the problem. They had all just pressed on, rushing headlong into disaster, time after time. Probably unavoidable, of course, but you could still regret it. And she had even given him the advice herself, this time – *It is time now, my Khan. This is why we came back.* All very true. But she'd said it so carelessly, confident that he was looking for reassurance, when he had been giving her a warning, preparing her for what would come.

'I am getting something on the augurs,' Sojuk reported.

The instruments were indeed functioning a little better. It was as if some enormous cloud of interference had blown itself out, freeing up the machine-spirits to do their work

Ilya roused herself, and started to filter through the signals. They were striking. She got movement indicators everywhere, from all over the ravaged space port, and they were all going in the same direction.

'Those are our people,' she said, taken aback. 'They're... moving very fast.'

'They are angry, szu,' said Sojuk flatly. 'Angrier than they have ever been.'

Ilya nodded slowly, remembering what he had told her. *We would be angry, like no force of the heavens has ever been angry.* He had known, hadn't he? He had known just what he was doing. He always did. Damn him.

'There are intact fortifications just below the main collapse,' she said, forcing herself to concentrate on the task at hand. 'See if you can find a landing site.'

Sojuk did as ordered, powering through the ongoing turbulence expertly. It was still very hard to pick anything out through the realviewers, so Ilya relied on the scanners to make sense of what lay ahead. The ruined shoulder of the west front hove in closer, rising up above them and swallowing the sky with its bulk. Only when you got this close did you appreciate that it was a city in its own right, a micro-world of its own. Going up against it had always felt like recklessness; this close, it seemed like rank insanity.

And then she saw them. They had their lumens on, against protocol, but she couldn't blame them for that – the path they followed was treacherous, marked by rockfalls and wall collapse. The effect was striking – a single column of slow-moving tanks, lit up, picking their way down from the worst of the destruction and out towards the remains of intact battlements below. Warriors of the Legion came with them on foot, arranged on either side of the lead vehicle in a tight protective formation. The entourage was moving steadily, just at that moment, out from under the shadow of a high-arched gate, one with its capstone still intact, making the scene look for all the world like a grand sortie from some besieged and ancient barbican, except that this was no act of war – this was a cortège, conducted in terrible silence.

She knew what they were carrying before she was close enough to see it in detail. The way they moved – with that painful reverence, with that weary emptiness – told her all she needed to know.

'There,' she said, her voice cracking. 'Down where they're headed for.'

The Thunderhawk ducked lower, sinking through the smog banks until it hovered over a wide flat parapet, where it set down amid gouts of dirty exhaust fumes. Ilya was unbuckling before they had touched the apron, fastening her environment suit up, checking her rebreather fixings, scrambling for the exit doors, fumbling on the lock-catch. Going outside would be dangerous. She would not have permitted any of her own staff to do it. But she had to see for herself, with her own eyes, not through some relayed vid-feed.

The lead tank of the procession growled its way to meet them even as she ran across the parapet deck. It was a Leman Russ, Ryza-pattern, no sponsons, heavily damaged. Two White Scars rode just behind the turret, which was swung at an angle to create more space on the narrow shelf behind it. As she approached, one of them jumped down to intercept her. When the warrior saw who she was, he bowed low.

'Szu-Ilya,' he said hoarsely.

She did not know him immediately. Like all those fighting now, his armour was caked so heavily that it was virtually black. She did spy what looked like the sigil of the Iron Axe under the dirt, so deduced that he was Jangsai, the Rijan newblood Naranbaatar had spoken highly of, the one who had been at the kurultai.

'Show me,' she said.

Jangsai hesitated. 'It is... very bad.'

As if that would have dissuaded her. She ran up to the tank's flank, climbed up the tracks herself, shrugging off Jangsai's attempt to help her.

Once in place, she could only bear to look for a few moments. In orbit over Ullanor, she had glimpsed a primarch up close for the first time, this one, and the splendour had been so overwhelming that it had been almost too much to bear. Now her first instinct was to clap her hand over her rebreather's intake to stop herself from crying out aloud. For a moment or two, she wasn't even sure what she was looking at. Then, amid the drifting ash and engine fumes, she caught the remnants of a noble face, the shattered remains of a hawkish nose, the hollows where cheeks had been. She saw a knife-sharp landscape of armour fragments, buried into a bloody patchwork of torn muscle beneath. She saw a broken blade laid lengthways along the body, its lustre gone, its perfect curve twisted.

She drew closer, only dimly aware of the hot tears running down her cheeks. She reached out, guiltily, awkwardly, and no White Scar attempted to prevent her. She touched the one fragment of intact skin she could see – the neck, just below the jawline, a single spot that remained unsullied. And as she did so, just a graze of shaking fingers, she felt it.

She jerked back, as if electrocuted.

'You have scanned him?' she demanded, turning to Jang-sai. 'You have checked?'

'Many times, szu. But our instruments…'

Ilya stared hard at the ruins of the body. It seemed inconceivable, impossible. No movement, no pulse, no breath. And yet…

Because I plan to come back.

'Malcador,' Ilya snapped, her whole being switching straight back into the old currents of command. 'We have to get him to Malcador.'

The change was instantaneous. Sojuk swivelled on his heel and sprinted back to the Thunderhawk. Jangsai's warriors roused themselves. Two of them raced to the gunship to retrieve stretchers, others formed up to lower the body from the hull. Even as she jumped down herself, Ilya's mind began to race – could they get back? How could they avoid being shot down? Did the Sanctum even stand, still?

They would have to find a way. They would *have* to – if there was any chance, any chance at all, then it was there, in the birthplace of the primarchs, at the hands of the ones who had made them.

'I will come with you,' said Jangsai.

Ilya nodded, before suddenly looking back, over at the space port summit towering above them. It was still contested. Thousands of Jaghatai's people were still fighting and dying within its depths, driven now by a hatred so intense that nothing would stop them destroying themselves upon its fearful altar.

Kal damarg. The Chogorian ritual of the dead, enacted across an entire Legion.

'No,' she said, even as the stretchers were hurried back from the gunship and the engines whined up for the lift. 'No, I need you here.' She came up to him. 'He wanted the space port taken. You understand that? That was the important thing. Not destroyed. *Taken.*'

Jangsai understood immediately. 'Then they must be halted.'

'When they reach the outer edge, when their madness carries them too far. It must be stopped *there*.'

Jangsai didn't reply immediately. Ilya could see that he agreed. 'But I am not...' he started. 'I am not someone...'

She smiled at him. 'Of Chogoris? Someone they'll listen to?' she asked. 'Neither was I, but that changed quickly.' She took both his gauntlets, reaching up to clasp them in her still-shaking hands. 'Find Shiban. He will do what must be done.'

It was only then that she saw the sword scabbard hanging at his belt. It was a famous one, guarding one of the great blades of Ong-Hashin. More importantly, she knew the name of its first bearer, a name known to all warriors of the ordu. Had Naranbaatar given that to him? Had he had a reason for that?

'Tell him I sent you, that the Khagan is with me now,' said Ilya, making ready to run back for the powering-up gunship. 'And, if that doesn't work, just show him the sword.'

It ended under stone.

It ended under the great sarcophagus of the Lion's Gate space port, which had once proudly scraped the troposphere with its high platforms, its manufactoria and observation domes, and had now been reduced by three separate sons of the Emperor into a semi-derelict haunt of daemons.

Jangsai ran deep within it, going as fast as he could, fighting his way through the narrow corridors and the booming halls. Dangers still resided everywhere, despite the fighting withdrawal of the Death Guard. Many of the yaksha hung around in the seeping depths, ready to crackle into instantiation. The interior itself was still an enemy, clogged with the knee-deep quagmires and sumps, much of it semi-sentient and seething with an almost conscious malice.

For all that, Jangsai was able to make rapid progress now that the White Scars' charge had driven the enemy so deeply back. The switch was astonishing. All three V Legion spearheads, as far as anyone had been able to tell him during the height of the fighting, had been locked in vicious stalemates against an enemy who lived for such warfare. The departure of both primarchs had produced radically different effects. Jangsai had no idea precisely why – the ways of daemons and their banishments meant little to him – but that didn't much matter. It had happened. The death-fury had done its work – united all three battlefronts into a single vast, obsessional push that had swept all resistance before it even as it consumed its own warriors from the inside out.

Jangsai was following in the wake of that, now. He ran past the corpses of both V and XIV Legion warriors, slumped in the mire, piled on top of one another. The corpse-tally was almost as astonishing as the reversal. A toll had been reaped, here. Perhaps neither Legion would ever be able to claim completely unqualified victory or defeat, so comprehensively had each side mauled the other. The place was a charnel house, just as the whole planet was.

And yet it was being shriven. It was being purged, exorcised, eviscerated, and the warriors of the ordu were doing the slaying now. The one task was to prevent that great surge of vital energy from becoming uncontrollable. The Sage had not underestimated the dangers – tales of warriors in a state of kal damarg destroying themselves were rife on Chogoris, so much so that even a newblood like Jangsai knew of them.

The one advantage he had was that his tactical sensors were operating again, at least partially. He could see false-colour cartoliths spidering away from him, each populated by clusters of light – heat signatures, movement vectors, locator idents. The closer he got to the port's eastern edge, the clearer the signals became. The White Scars had fought the Death Guard across the entire breadth of the enormous fortress, and were now threatening to fight them clean out of the far gates. They wouldn't stop there. Lost in their world of blood-tinged vengeance, they would just keep going, killing without reason, until the measureless armies of the Warmaster finally caught up with them all and burned their zeal from the universe forever.

He had to find Shiban. He had to reach the one voice who might be able to call them back before it was too late. And that was hard, as hard as anything he had ever had to do. His body was drained, his mind exhausted. Every instinct within him pulled his focus back to the gunship, to the tiny speck of metal now hurtling west, carrying with it the last faint hope for the Legion. Millions of warriors clashed across the fields it had to compass, surging up against millions more, and yet that one ship, fragile as glass, now meant everything.

The great halls passed by in a blur, empty now, stinking of blood and corruption. He vaulted along the shell-pocked stairways, clambered up the treacherous elevator shafts, skirted the dregs of ongoing fighting and sprinted across teetering gantries. Soon he could hear serious engagements again – the roar of the mobile armour, the massed disruptor-snarl of Legion weapons being brought to bear.

He broke into what had once been a major receiving hangar, one that opened out from the eastern flank of the port's extreme edge. Its apron must have been eight hundred metres across, its heavy roof a hundred metres high. The air was less clotted and foul than within the interior – ash-flakes driven in from outside gusted across the spoil of battle. Hundreds of warriors fought in that location alone, supported by the ever-present squadrons of the Terran Armoured.

Jangsai locked on to Shiban's signal, and raced to find him. As he closed in, he caught sight of the telltale glint of

augmetics amid all the gloom and grime. The Restorer was
fighting a larger Traitor Marine, and the encounter was already
impressively brutal. Jangsai had never seen a guan dao whirled
with such vindictive control before. The plague-ridden monster
fought back determinedly, but there was something missing in
all of the enemy troops now – the withdrawal of their old certainty, their old implacability. Shiban, on the other hand, was
simply electrifying. He just kept pressing, pressing, pressing,
taking hits but never so much as flinching away from them.
When the killing strike came – a leap, a transverse decapi-
tation – it felt almost merciful.

Jangsai caught up just as Shiban was about to stride out for
more prey. All the White Scars around him were the same –
grave-silent now, grinding their way towards the enemy,
pushing them back, stride by stride, out to where the gaping
hangar maws overlooked the demolished wastes beyond.

'Tachseer!' Jangsai shouted.

Shiban ignored him. He barely seemed aware of anything
around him, only the enemy.

Jangsai shouted again, with the same result, then raced
ahead, drawing his blade, just as Ilya had told him to. The
bloodstained tulwar flashed out in the dark, its disruptor
stilled but the naked steel vivid enough.

Only when Shiban halted, staring at it, did Jangsai remember
Naranbaatar's words to him, back at Colossi, when the weapon
had first been delivered.

*Morbun Xa is famed, not just for his prowess, but also for his
restraint. He is a model of the Path of Heaven, they say.*

Jangsai had never known him. Shiban would have done.
So this was the moment.

'I come from the Sage,' Jangsai said. 'The Khagan is with
her. She seeks a path to the Sanctum. She told me to tell you
that the port must be taken. Not destroyed, but taken.' He

looked into Shiban's unreadable helm-mask the whole time. 'That goes for the Legion, too.'

Shiban remained immobile for a long time. His stance radiated the urge for violence. It was so seductive, that state. Jangsai understood it fully. Given the right impetus, you could always imagine yourself sinking into it and never emerging again. A part of him, a part that every Space Marine possessed, was only truly at peace when killing. The World Eaters were just the most rarefied example, but all of them had the capacity, to one degree or another. The lesson of the entire war, you might say.

Then Shiban looked away, over to the lip of the hangar's edge. The White Scars had taken the ground leading up to it by then, harrying the remaining traitors beyond the perimeter. They were now preparing to follow them out, to drive spears of energised hatred into the fiery dark beyond.

For a terrible moment, Jangsai thought Shiban would still sanction that, joining them all in that charge into oblivion. There was nothing more to say, though – nothing he could add to Ilya's injunction. He couldn't know that the Restorer's only thought at that moment was not of the Khan at all, nor of Ilya, nor of the Legion's ultimate fate, but of the Terran khan he had once fought alongside on the White World, whom he had not forgiven, not until it was too late.

No backward step.

'Cease,' Shiban said softly. Then, more strongly, 'Cease!'

He was speaking over the open vox-grid. His Stormseer, who had been fighting alongside him, heard the command, and worked to ensure that it was heard more widely. Comms relays picked it up, and soon it was being propagated to units far out of visual range.

Next, Shiban started to walk – slowly, purposively, trudging up to the wind-torn window onto the outside world. Sensing that something fundamental had changed, Jangsai came with him. Under their feet were the mighty foundations of the space port. Over their heads was the colossal overhang of the hangar's roof. Directly ahead was the sky, that most sacred element for a Chogorian, even when it was poisoned and scored with flame and masked with unnatural clouds.

Shiban reached the fortress' edge, and rested the heel of his glaive against the rockcrete parapet. Those who had come with him, all those who had made it to the perimeter, stood alongside, waiting. Jangsai's helm-data told him that thousands more were doing the same thing – holding position, stirred out of madness by the word of the Restorer, just as they had been on the bridge of the *Swordstorm* over the similarly destroyed skies of Prospero.

Shiban took his time. He gazed out at the kilometres of pure devastation, the bitter fruit of Horus' rebellion. He watched the Death Guard make their way through the broken outworks in the dark, tens of thousands of them, bereft of leadership for now, but still intact and dangerous and capable of recovering their resolve. He observed the encampments of the lost and the damned in the hinterland beyond, those millions upon millions of low-grade soldiers that haunted every Terran ruin. He perceived the distant profiles of Titans, of Knights, of greater Legion formations even further out.

'This is where he fell,' he said softly.

The hangar echoed into silence. Jangsai listened. Every member of the Legion within transmit range listened.

'This is *our* place now.' Shiban's voice was still harsh from the augmetics in his throat, but no longer distorted with that elemental fury. 'This is holy ground. This is Chogoris on Earth. This is where he fell.'

The White Scars were responding. Jangsai's tactical read-out told him that they were *all* coming to a halt – all across the wide fortress perimeter, out on the causeways, up in the towers, down in the shadowed foundations. Wherever they had cleansed the taint of the enemy, they were standing watchfully now, heeding the words of the Tachseer.

'Yesugei taught us this,' Shiban told them. 'Do not become what is hateful. Do not become the thing you fight.'

Jangsai kept his blade unsheathed. They all had their weapons held ready now. More fighting would come, soon, just as fearsome, just as deadly, but this was the edge, the liminal place, the line of blood in the grime.

'So we set our mark *here*,' Shiban said. 'The rite of grief ends where this place ends.'

The remaining tanks came to a halt also, taking up positions overlooking the plains. Jangsai didn't know if any of the crew were hearing this, or if they understood it, but they had come this far, and fought superbly, and deserved to be present.

'They shall *never* have it. They may take all other worlds, they may master the warp, they may despoil the very arch of heaven, but they shall never have this place. It has our mark upon it. It is sacred.'

One by one, the khans were doing as Shiban did – planting their feet squarely, mastering their hate, returning to their right mind, restoring equilibrium.

'When we fight again, it will not be for conquest, nor for vengeance, but to preserve this.'

Above them, the green tinge on the bare stone was fading away. Lumens were coming on, flickering, then solidifying, then burning through the filth. The Lion's Gate space port had been ravaged, twice, but it had not been razed. Its surviving landing stages, its soaring walls, its colossal reactors and – most of all – its mighty guns, were theirs.

'We stand, here, now,' Shiban told them. In his voice there was just a hint of what had been there a long time ago on Chondax – the belief, the faint reflection of an inner joy. 'We cede no ground, we suffer no enemy to cross the threshold. It is our place, from this day, until the end of time.'

Then Shiban raised his glaive high. Chakaja raised his staff. Jangsai raised his blade. Every warrior of the White Scars in that place of sorrow and suffering raised their weapon, not in the cause of a curse as before, but as the khans of old had done under the twin moons, in salute, to mark what had changed, and what had died, but also what remained, and what was eternal.

'For the Emperor!' Shiban cried.

And all across the Lion's Gate, from the scoured depths to the cleansed heights, the throats of Jaghatai's people were opened in the timeless answer, the one that justified all their suffering and sanctified their victory.

For the Khan.

TWENTY-SEVEN

Aftermaths

He raised his head.

Rogal Dorn lifted his eyes from the battery of lenses that surrounded him, and looked out over the command chamber. Had he been sleeping? Or just immersed in some calculation again, running over the schedules of deployment one more time?

Something had changed. The crushing weight that had lain on his shoulders for so long – it wasn't gone, entirely. But changed. Merely physical, now; the product of weeks without rest. The malice of it had gone. The voices in his mind – gone.

He saw people working around him. They must have been there the whole time, but now he remembered their names, when they had arrived, who they had replaced. Acuity was coming back. The fog was lifting.

He shifted in his command throne, daring to hope for news from the east. A few depressions on control valves, insertions in the channels that he had reserved for this very purpose. And then news, encoded in the ciphers that only he could unpick, sent from the sources that only he had access to.

Archamus came up to him. Even he looked subtly altered, a little less stooped. 'Word from the port,' he announced.

'I know,' said Dorn, already working out what it could mean. Maybe little – just a strike back for pride. But maybe everything. It all depended what had been salvaged.

Archamus didn't ask how he had known. 'From what we can tell, the main structure has been taken. No solid communications yet, and little chance of getting them. Reports of major Fourteenth Legion formations moving north and west.'

Dorn took that all in. If Mortarion's forces had been expelled, and if they decided not to attempt the port again, then it could only mean they were heading for the centre now. That would be another factor for him to consider, along with everything else.

But still. *Still.*

He found himself cracking a weary smile. *Jaghatai, you insufferable, infuriating… prodigy.*

'Does it alter anything?' Archamus asked him.

Dorn knew what he meant – the withdrawals, the pull-backs, the fighting retreats. No, it didn't alter any of that. The Palatine was all that remained under his direct control now – that narrow ring of bastions surrounding the Sanctum itself, little more than a single urban zone, now about to be engulfed by the combined mass of Horus' many vanguards.

'All standing orders remain,' he replied. 'The final act comes next.' He shot a dry smile at his deputy. 'I almost find myself looking forward to it. Too long since I carried my blade to the front, eh?'

Archamus looked startled. It had been weeks since Dorn had so much as flickered a smile, let alone offered him anything other than fatigue-curt orders. 'Sigismund returns to the bastions,' he reported. 'His force is the last – then all is inside.'

Dorn nodded. That cheered him. The Emperor's Champion. And he found that now he couldn't begrudge the title at all – the grim old Templar had more than earned it.

'Try to discover what strength the Fifth retains, if any,' Dorn said. 'But do not expend much time on it – we cannot help them, and they cannot help us. I would have spoken to my brother before the end, if I could have done. A shame.'

Archamus nodded, and made to leave.

'But that end comes now, Huscarl,' Dorn said, holding him back for just a moment. 'Listen. Know that you have served me with perfect distinction. Perfect. It will be an honour, for me, to have my sons at my side.'

Archamus didn't look like he knew how to respond to that either. While he struggled awkwardly for an appropriate response, another aide raced up to the dais bearing a data-slate and a collection of message-tubes.

'Word from the Palatine, my lord,' she blurted. 'A Fifth Legion Thunderhawk has made it through the cordon, escorted in to dock, cargo now being unloaded.'

'What cargo?' Dorn asked.

The aide swallowed nervously. 'I think you should... well, I think you will want to see this for yourself.'

'The Fifth is back.'

Valdor digested that information. Diocletian, Tribune of the Ten Thousand, stood before him, his armour covered in the vivid scorch marks that gave away recent fighting against the daemonic.

'Alive?' he asked.

'Unknown.'

'Then find out.'

'I mean, captain-general, that his state – life, death – is currently unknown, to anyone. The Sigillite is doing what he can, but I am told that even his art is so far proving insufficient. *On the edge.* That is how it was described to me.'

On the edge. Weren't they all?

'Then we must hope he recovers,' he said. 'If he is here, if he can stand again before the end, then that is one more blade, and a rare one at that.'

Diocletian nodded. Since Valdor had returned to the Tower, he had never so much as hinted at the question. *Where have you been?*

Amon knew. The guards Valdor had placed over the bio-criminal as he worked, now in the depths of the Tower's own hyper-secret laboratoria, must have had some inkling. None of them would say anything. The Legio Custodes were so used to guarding their secrets that concealment was now an essential part of their nature – the default position, whenever matters of state arose within their ranks.

That didn't prevent the issue from preying on Valdor's mind. He still heard the whispers of all the creatures he had killed on Terra. The Emperor remained silent, and in that absence, all he had were those voices, teasing, tempting, reproaching, over and over again.

He could end this. If Fo was right, if he was even partly right, then the great experiment Valdor had watched unfold over centuries, the catastrophic creation of those quarrelsome warmongers, it could all be eradicated. To destroy them now, before they unravelled creation entirely, that might well have been the Emperor's will. It might be what needed to happen. Surely the day would have come, sooner or later, in any case. Surely there would have been an Ararat for the Legions, too.

So if Horus, greatest of them all, should make landfall here, if he should break down the gates and seek to enter the Sanctum itself, would that be the moment? And if so, would there still be an opportunity to look up at the Throne, to seek confirmation before all its great work was destroyed? Or would he have to make the decision before that hour came, alone, trusting in a faculty of judgement that had only ever been created to serve, not to lead?

And what if that judgement were wrong? What if the Emperor still had intentions, yet to be disclosed? What if *this* had been His plan all along, and only time, and patient loyalty, would yet reveal its perfection? Would he, Valdor, then be a greater betrayer even than Lupercal, led into error by those who had proven themselves over and again to be without scruple or wholesome emotion? Would he, as incorruptible as the stars themselves, be the heretic?

Or would he merely stumble at the appointed hour, too frozen by doubt to act? Or was this why he had been given the spear in the first place, to lead him to enlightenment?

Would it even work?

Should it work?

He had almost forgotten Diocletian was still standing there. Valdor collected himself and took up his spear once more. As he did so, he felt the static spike of transference, the abrasive reminder of the blood drunk greedily by this thing.

'Thank you for the briefing, tribune,' he said, rising from his seat.

'Then you will take to the tunnels again?' A sliver of reproach, there? Or was Valdor seeing phantoms everywhere now?

'I will,' Valdor said, preparing himself. It would only be worse from this point onward. More of them would be getting in, squirming up from the floors, out from the walls, rising in both stature and malevolence. 'I feel the need to make them suffer greatly. Perhaps you will join me on the hunt – two blades together.'

Diocletian bowed. 'It will be the highest honour.'

And then they were moving down the stone corridor, heading lower, to where the realms of experience mingled and the Neverborn were starting to breed.

And all Valdor heard were the voices, over and over.

Can it be done?

It had been done.

Erebus surveyed his work. The lodge was destroyed, the depression was burning. Erda's trinkets had been smashed. When the sandstorms came, the entire site would be erased, not even a wound in the world's skin to mark her sanctuary.

And he felt empty.

It would have been better to have come away with more. Even if he couldn't have talked her into alliance, he had at least hoped for enlightenment on how it had been done. Fewer maudlin regrets from her, a little more relish. Why were so many of those around him so obsessed with regrets, in any case? They had never bothered him. Sometimes he thought he might be the single most contented creature in the entire galaxy, never troubled by doubt or conscience, just doing the most exciting, the most rewarding, thing anyone had ever conceived of. Lucky him.

The residual danger she posed had been eradicated. The select fellowship of those who had walked with the Emperor in His youth had diminished a little further, just one more step on the road to total oblivion for their aberrant strain. If they could not be suborned, they would have to be purged, an evolutionary wrong turn to be culled from experience, and that was work he was temperamentally suited for.

All the same, it had been frustrated effort. He had worked very hard to find her, bewitched by the slender hope she might have been some kind of kindred spirit. As for now, he had no clear idea where he would go next, since he had no official function any longer at Horus' court. Maybe he would linger on Terra, maybe not. It felt as if his part in the proceedings was already becoming redundant, just a sideshow now, something greater players could choose to ignore.

He walked morosely back towards the path leading up the cliffs. As he trudged, his boot crunched through more of that woman's pathetic collection of toys. He stooped to pick one up – another fearsomely ugly statue, as fragile as all the rest of them.

He remembered how eager she had been to talk about those things. She must have known he'd come to recruit her or to kill her, and yet the prattle had all been about pottery. If he'd been her, he'd have wanted it all over quickly – get it settled, one way or the other.

Over quickly.

He stood still for a moment, pondering that. She'd had art. Art on a scale he'd encountered very rarely. If she'd been at all concerned with survival, could she not have tried to escape? This was her place, after all, one she knew better than anyone else. She'd never so much as hinted at the chance. Instead, she'd talked. Made him angry. Given him nothing.

He stared down at the broken figurine. She'd tried to persuade him these things were symbolic of something important. Perhaps they were. Or maybe she just liked the way they looked, and all that verbiage had served nothing but its own purpose.

As he had hunted her, he had been shown glimpses of other souls too – always just ahead of him, caught up in that whirl of warp worlds, slipping from one time and place to another. He'd thought they were a kind of phantom, some random fore-echo that he could safely ignore while he caught up with his real target.

But what if they had been something to do with her? What if the warp had been showing him soul-relationships, fate-skeins, chained destinies, just as it so often did? Had she guessed that too? Had she known much more than she'd ever given away?

It was so basic, and yet so suggestive. Had she *kept him talking*? Was that it? Were these people, these half-glimpsed ether-refugees, somehow valuable to her? Were they her kindred? Her emissaries, even?

He had accused her of doing nothing. But the great powers always acted through their agents – the Emperor had done, Horus did too. Perhaps this, then, was her very last play, launched in the knowledge that she would never see it accomplished.

He let Erda's figurine fall to the dirt, crushed it beneath his heel. Then he drew the athame from his armour, the little sliver of sorcery that helped him get around.

'Not over yet,' Erebus said, making ready for the ritual. 'One last leap into the dark.'

They were there already. All that remained was to limp through it.

Alpharius led them, of course. He claimed to know exactly where the tunnels led, and how to negotiate them towards the catacombs under the Dungeon itself. Actae trusted that confidence implicitly, and strode along beside him. Oll doubted it all. Surely someone would have sealed up all the ways in, even those deep underground? He kept close to the mysterious Space Marine, with John marching by his side. Zybes, Krank, Graft and Katt were next. Leetu brought up the rear.

Mother of God, he was tired. He was thirsty, and he was hungry. They had a few supplies left, but not many, and this place was gigantic. They might be days away from the promised insertion point, or even weeks. Who knew, in this inky underground world of twisting passages and blind drops into nothingness.

Getting out of the damaged lighter had been difficult enough. Then they'd had to tramp along the deep base of that hateful trench, which had carried its fair share of stragglers from the main battlefronts. Both Leetu and Alpharius had been invaluable then, as neither Actae nor Katt had wanted to risk using their particular gifts in such close proximity to those who might detect them. A Space Marine in action was an alarming thing, witnessed close up. Thinking about that killing potential multiplied by all the Legions in action around them, well that was just ludicrous. No wonder it had all gone wrong.

But they had made it, somehow, worming their way into the culvert that Alpharius had claimed to be expecting, and then down, always down, burrowing further into the sedimentary layers of forgetfulness, threading a path through the tiny filigree of tunnels that had been left behind when other worlds had died and been buried.

Soon they could hear the rumble of combat from both above and below, as if they traced their delicate path between two parallel apocalypses. It became hot, very hot. Oll's handheld lumen was already failing, but its weak light illuminated some very strange shapes carved into the dripping rock around him.

He looked at John. The logokine didn't look well. Maybe this last stage had been too much for him. Maybe it had been too much for all of them.

'You all right?' Oll asked.

John nodded. 'Keeping it together,' he said dryly. 'You?'

Oll thought about that for a moment. 'Don't know. I mean, this is it now, isn't it? We're here.'

'Not quite. Not till that Space Marine stops moving.'

Oll smiled, but he didn't like to think of that. He didn't like to think about what was at the end of the tunnels. The Emperor? Would Oll even recognise Him now? Or maybe the Warmaster, arrived well ahead of them and already ensconced on the Golden Throne? Or maybe neither of them, just more armies, more vile creatures, all milling about and trying to get to the same place, the singularity, the centre of the universe.

Enough. The decision had been made. They had to see it out, now.

'You had religion, once,' John said, looking over at him in the dark. 'Before they banned it. I'm curious. Do you still have it?'

Of course he did. That was the whole point of it.

'Why do you ask?'

John shrugged. 'Just wondering. How anyone could. Now we've seen all this. Done all this. Not to disparage it, or anything. Only curious.'

Oll walked on in silence. This probably wasn't the time to get into a theological discussion, not while a very plausible rendition of hell itself was on the very edge of bursting into existence right on top of them. But it was a decent question. Then again, it had always been a decent question, all through every war he had ever fought in. Pain had always existed, as had suffering. Those had never been sufficient, by themselves, to invalidate his certainties.

'Possibly,' he said. 'That might be the way to look at it. On the other hand, the flip side might be true, too, just like before.'

There was no light, save for that they brought with them. Just then, it felt like being lost in the void, alone, cut off, buried under an empire's worth of futility and self-inflicted carnage.

'That maybe it'll be the thing that gets us out the other side,' said Oll, still walking, one step in front of the other, eyes ahead into the dark. 'Maybe, once this is over, faith might be the only thing we have left.'

Yes, that was it. Make any other allegiance into nothing. Destroy it, forget it. And after that, only faith remains.

Sigismund stared into the face of his sword. It remained unsheathed even after the fighting was long finished. Now he rocked as the troop carrier rocked, its engines dragging him away from the combat he had perfected at last. His surviving Templar Brethren sat around him. The casualty rates had been higher than most of the engagements he'd fought in. But the numbers they had killed in turn, well… those had been astounding. He himself had always taken out the figureheads – the captains, the praetors – more than he could easily count, one after the other. More champions would come for him, now. They would race to meet their end at the edge of his blade.

He didn't make much of a distinction between the kills. He did remember Khârn, of course, because that one had been properly hard. Even then, though, he felt little else about it, other than that it was over now, that he had won, and another threat to the Throne had been taken out. He didn't feel pride in overcoming an enemy, even one who had beaten him before, because pride was in the past. Shame, yes – he could still feel shame. But pride felt somehow anachronistic, something belonging to a world of secular achievement, not of moral certainty.

'I didn't even know if you'd obey the command,' Rann said, sitting opposite him. 'To fall back.'

Sigismund didn't look up. He was all eyes for the sword, now.

'It was an order,' he said flatly.

That still meant something – the word of his primarch. In

the past, the sacredness of that would have derived from the
bond between the two of them: genesire and vassal. Now
it was something deeper. Dorn was less of a father to him
now, more a son of the Emperor – a living embodiment of
the Throne's will. There could be no question of not obey-
ing orders, not just because of the chain of command within
the Legion, but because the primarchs were only one step
removed from the fount of all righteousness. They were an
example, a model, created by Him on Earth to guide the
weak into resolution.

Finally, Sigismund slipped the blade back into its scabbard,
and looked up at Rann. The assault captain had taken some
heavy wounds. His helm was off now, revealing a patchwork of scabs and scars, all underlaid with a lurid smear of
deep-bruised tissue.

'But you were having so much fun,' said Rann.

Would that have provoked a terse smile, in the past? Maybe.
Not now. Sigismund was already thinking of the next operation. They would have to resupply inside the Palatine zone,
assuming there were any supplies left to draw on. They would
have to take direction from Bhab on what was coming for
them, then draw up plans to disrupt it as much as possible.

'It means… nothing,' he said, murmuring out loud without
really meaning to.

'What does?'

'These… animals.' Sigismund was thinking of Khârn again,
the way he had slavered and roared. He was thinking of the
other mutated horrors he had cut down, even the daemons.

'Then what do you *want?*' asked Rann, looking like even
his extensive patience was wearing thin with all this icy
moodiness.

Sigismund thought on that. What did he want? Now that he
had achieved the transformation, had cast off his self-imposed

restraints, there still needed to be growth, a way to hone things further.

He wanted an opponent who was worthy of his time. He wanted a Space Marine, not a chewed-through warp monster. He wanted one of the old guard, not a jumped-up lieutenant in captain's armour. He wanted a meaningful trophy to place at the foot of the Throne itself, so that he could say that the architects of this galactic heresy had been handed their due reward.

'Abaddon,' he said darkly, interlocking the fingers of his bloody gauntlets. 'That's who I want.'

The transport began to slow down. They were nearing the bastion gates. After they were through those, they would disembark, tool up, then head out to fight again.

'No peace now,' Sigismund said, calmly enough, but with that eerie sense of certainty that could chill even those who fought on his side. 'No peace, not on this world, not in the void beyond, until I find the First Captain.'

They found the First Captain easily enough, in the end. It turned out he had paid very little attention to his master's orders, and had maintained formidable forces just out of range of the space port. Those might even have been used to shore up the fortress' defences, had he been so inclined. But he hadn't been, of course. He was a bitter old soul, was Typhus.

It made the great muster easier. All those XIV Legion assets expelled from the space port soon picked up locator signals, and began to coalesce again across a range of sites to the north and west of the port's extreme edge. The numbers were enormous. Despite all the losses to the White Scars, this was still a Legion capable of causing tremendous damage.

Once the surviving leaders assembled atop the designated command location – a high ridge commanding views both

west and east, overhung by the corpse of a downed Imperial Warlord Titan – matters could be weighed up, decisions
could be made.

Kalgaro had not made it out. The Deathshroud had not
made it out. A large number of battalion commanders had
not made it out. Morarg had, though. Crosius had, as had a
few dozen company captains, a large number of Dreadnoughts
and some useful squadrons of armour.

Typhus stood among them all again, flanked by his own
bodyguards, the Grave Wardens. Out in the open, the volume
of his profile-distorting flies seemed to have grown. In fact,
he seemed to have grown in many ways, some of them physical, some of them not.

'We could still take it back,' Morarg told him.

The shock of Mortarion's withdrawal had faded, just as
Crosius had promised. Morarg's disorientation had ebbed.
He no longer found himself, nor those he fought alongside,
repulsive. All that was replaced now with a deep sense of
shame – for buckling under pressure, for letting the fortress
slip away. With Typhus back, with all his forces joining those
that had retreated out of the space port's many orifices, that
wrong could be set right.

'*Why?*' asked Typhus scornfully. '*What do we want in there?
In truth, what did we ever want in there?*'

'Revenge,' said Morarg, though without much conviction.

Typhus spat something from his helm-grille, making the
flies wobble. '*That was* his *business. I care nothing for a few
savages on jetbikes.*' He lifted a heavy gauntlet, and curled it
into a fist. '*We have time, despite all this wasted effort. We can
be there before the close of the drama. And I want to be there.*'

A murmur of assent ran around the assembled warriors.
Crosius, still with his pet daemon in tow, seemed especially
enthusiastic.

'So are you with me, equerry?' Typhus asked Morarg directly. *'You could exorcise his failure against a better target, if you chose to.'* The First Captain stared directly at him, as if in accusation, as if daring him to articulate the truth.

You were our betrayer. You brought this on us. The better part of us is gone, now, and we are only left with you — the snake that curled around his ankles.

Morarg said none of that. He remembered the Remnant, that shadow of a shadow.

We adore him.

What a tragedy. Whatever happened here now, whatever honour the Death Guard still earned, the chance for greater glory was gone. That had been Mortarion's vision, snatched away on the cusp of being realised.

The primarch was still the liberator. He had dared to carve out a future for them, one that fulfilled all their limitless potential. Another war was coming, one without end, an endless rivalry between factions that would weaken the Legion for all eternity.

What could he say, though? What would prevent that now? Nothing.

'I am with you, First Captain,' Morarg said, the lie slipping so plausibly from his lips.

And now he would be marching again under the banner of that lie. It wouldn't be the last one either, for they had become a Legion of liars, where once they had only ever told the unpalatable truth.

Lying would get easier. That was the way of these things – the first one was difficult, the next one would be less so.

'Good,' said Typhus. *'Then we march together.'*

It tasted bitter on his lips.

But it would get easier.

* * *

It did. It got much easier. The air was still too toxic to permit total relaxation of the protocols, but as long as they weren't required to venture back into the space port interior, Kaska allowed the crew a brief period outside the hull – wearing full rebreathers and sealed environment suits, of course.

It made all the difference. Just to be able to extend a leg properly, to stretch an arm. Everything ached. Kaska was covered in bruises from where he'd repeatedly collided with the turret interior. They were running low on potable water again, so would have to set off soon to see if a non-fouled cistern could be located. And then they had to think about fuel, and more ammunition, because none of them was foolish enough to think that their war was over.

But, for the moment, he stood on the same parapet where they'd halted, and looked over at his tank.

Aika 73. Not much of a name. Not much of a vehicle, either. It looked even worse now than it had in the depot. Something had made a fearful mess of its forward armour plates, and one track looked halfway to rupturing. He hadn't dared to inspect topside yet. He could see the lines of dry blood running down the side armour. Could that be cleaned off? *Should* it be? He had a feeling he would have to leave it there, at least if the Legion escorts had any say about it. They were strange people. Fine people, he thought, but strange, and with customs that he didn't pretend to understand.

His crew had all come through it, if not unscathed, then alive. Merck was busy explaining some longstanding issue he had about battalion regulations to Vosch, who was trying to ignore him while she saw to Jandev's nasty-looking gash.

That left Dresi. She was standing next to Kaska, waiting for him, he thought, to say something.

'So, you're not Army,' he offered at last.

She shook her head.

'Legion command staff?' he tried. 'White Scars?'

'Seventh Legion,' she said. 'Imperial Fists.'

Kaska exhaled. 'So. I didn't know your… lord was even aware.'

Dresi smiled behind her breathing apparatus. 'Oh, he was aware. Not much escapes him. Not on Terra.'

'So, I guess, there's the question…'

'Why?' Dresi shrugged. 'Do not be alarmed. Standard procedure.'

'There were others, then? In other units?'

'Seventy-three of us, at the outset.'

Kaska thought on that. 'Just so he knew what was going on.'

'To the extent possible.'

He looked away from her, and out over the parapet's edge. On the western horizon, far beyond the tract of land he was already beginning to think of as the Colossi Run, the storm clouds were gathering in intensity, angrier and darker.

'You can't go back,' he said.

'I know.'

'Then, I mean…' He turned back to her. 'I could still use a driver.'

'Absolutely. I intend to continue.'

That was good news. It explained, in hindsight, why she had been so damned good. Legion-trained. The very best.

'And afterwards?'

Dresi laughed. As far as he could remember, that was the very first time. 'Afterwards? You think we will see an *afterwards*?' She shook her head. 'Throne, I do not know. A Leman Russ is much the same as a Land Raider on the inside. Maybe there will be a way to continue.'

She looked over at *Aika 73*.

'Not a bad thing to drive, despite the reputation,' she said, almost affectionately. 'What more can you ask? It kept us alive.'

* * *

As did the machine. Maybe. Or maybe all that was left of him was a collection of physical remnants, just preserved inside a vile contraption that looked more like a torture device than a medicae unit.

Ilya hadn't left his side. Her general's uniform by itself didn't guarantee her access to the very heart of the Sanctum, but her face was familiar from the time she'd spent cultivating contacts in the run-up to Horus' arrival. And having Sojuk there had been an advantage too – the White Scar had shed his equanimity for something more menacing, and that had opened doors.

She didn't remember much of the journey in. Sojuk hadn't spoken about it. By rights it should have been impossible, but then again the air-lanes had been almost cleared by the wholesale slaughter in the weeks beforehand, giving them the slender chance they had needed. And Sojuk was an exceptional pilot. And maybe, for once, the fates had been on their side.

From the receiving stations in the Palatine Ring, they had been hurried into the heart of the Sanctum, and then down, down a long way. They had passed through chambers Ilya had never got close to before. If she had not been so preoccupied with the cargo she escorted, she might have taken a closer look at them, and observed how old they were, and how different they looked to any Imperial structures she'd seen elsewhere.

Now they were in the care of the Sigillite's people. Those all wore robes of deep green, and ghosted through the shadows with a lifetime's habituation to the dark. Their skin, where exposed, was drained of colour, threaded with augmetics of strange design. They had an unsettling way of looking at you, as if they were focusing on a spot just off to one side, a fraction too deep behind your eyes.

She had been grateful when one of the senior officials, a man named Khalid Hassan, had come to speak to them. He, at least, had looked relatively normal.

'The Sigillite has been summoned,' Hassan had told them. 'He will be here as soon as he can. Please, wait here – I shall see you are looked after.'

That wait had felt like hours. It was during then that the great machinery had been wheeled out, with its serpentine cabling and its frosted glass panes, hissing with vapours and hauled on long segmented tracks. Forests of instruments had been hoisted overhead on cantilevered arms, all of it gnarled and ancient-looking. What remained of the primarch had disappeared into the heart of all that, and after that Ilya had only caught glimpses of him, lost behind a clicking menagerie of arcana.

Malcador himself had come eventually, bustling through the outer portals, his cowl thrown back, his age-creased face lined with concern.

'You delivered him?' he had demanded brusquely.

'I did, lord,' she had said.

He had grasped her hand, squeezing it hard with his own desiccated claws. 'Thank you. *Thank you.*'

Then he'd disappeared too, clambering into the tangled core of the ever-expanding nexus of instrumentation, followed by cadres of esoteric assistants in full-length environment suits and reflective face masks.

Ilya and Sojuk were permitted to remain as promised, out of the way, but only by a door's width. It was left partially open, so she could see just a corner of the great device. One of its many panels was embossed with the numeral V, which made her wonder just how old it was, and what its origin had been.

After that, the real wait began. Ilya slumped against the bare rock wall, sitting on a shelf cut into it. Sojuk stood next to her.

All her infirmities rushed back in that moment. She suddenly felt her age. She felt her frailty, the footsteps of the impending demise that she had been stalling for so long that it had become almost comical.

'He knew,' she said. Her thin voice echoed oddly in those eerie catacombs.

Sojuk turned to her. 'If he did it, then it was necessary.'

Shiban had told her that too, a long time ago. *Killing is nothing without beauty, and it may only be beautiful if it is necessary.* But this hadn't been beautiful. Nothing about it was beautiful – it had been ugly, horrific, without any of the art that she knew he venerated.

'You felt it,' she said. 'You all did. He died, Sojuk.'

Sojuk didn't look like he wanted to speculate. 'The arch of heaven hides many mysteries. Let them do their work. This was where they were made.'

Easy to say, harder to do. She had to sit back, and wait. A lifetime of *doing*, of making choices and giving orders. In the chamber beyond, she heard drills going in. She heard lines being clicked into place. She heard the murmur of quiet, competent voices.

She let her head fall back against the stone. She was exhausted, but she wouldn't sleep.

There is always a Great Khan.

She clenched her fists. She had to stay awake.

Let them do their work.

For the labour had only just begun. The survivors of the Legion, already driven to the extremes of endurance, were now tasked with securing what they had won. The space port remained dangerous – the White Scars controlled its borders, had mastery of its major systems now, but many areas were still too foul to enter or remained teeming with nightmares. The long lines of battlements had yet to be compassed, the collapsed areas shored up, the power fully restored and fresh sources of untainted supplies located.

So Shiban never stopped working. Jangsai worked alongside

him, and slowly what remained of the Legion command joined them. Ganzorig was among those, though Qin Fai had been killed in action, as had Naranbaatar and the greater part of the zadyin arga. The attempt to count the full tally of the dead and extract surviving gene-seed had only just started, hampered by the need to burn the enemy corpses lest plague begin to spread again.

For all that, the port was theirs for as long as they had the power to defend it. The great palls of psychic despondency had lifted, replaced by a more prosaic weariness that could be fought through. As a result, once the raw business of survival had been attended to, once the reconstruction and defensive work was fully underway, thoughts swiftly turned to what came next. What could be done. What *must* be done.

'Any news from the core?' asked Ganzorig, standing awkwardly amid the ruins on a shattered and roughly splinted leg.

Jangsai shook his head. 'They would not risk the transmission, even if there was.'

'It matters not,' said Shiban. 'It must be now as he always wished for – not to defend, but to attack.'

To repress that urge for so long had been the greatest challenge, for it was just as he had told Torghun, all the way back on Chondax, before any awareness of heresy had even reached them. *We must fight in the way we were born to fight.*

'We can barely man the walls,' said Ganzorig sceptically. 'Do we have the strength?'

'Not over land,' said Shiban. 'Our war there is done, unless they dare to come at us themselves.' He gestured upward, and cracked a grin under his battered helm. 'But we have the guns. We get them working, we power them up.'

They all started to visualise it. It wouldn't be easy. But then, nothing worth doing ever was.

'Then we do what we came here for,' said Shiban fiercely. 'Target the fleet.'

ACKNOWLEDGEMENTS

Many thanks to the entire BL team for their guidance on getting this project over the finish line. Special mention to Nick Kyme and Jacob Youngs for guiding this series from the start. From expert editorial advice to the alchemical transmutation of authors' confused and confusing verbiage into indispensable research material, they have made it all possible. Rachel Harrison has overseen, as usual, absolutely incredible artwork and design. And then there's my fellow Siege authors – Dan Abnett, Aaron Dembski-Bowden, John French, Guy Haley and Gav Thorpe – all of whom went above and beyond in helping to create this story. Working on a Siege of Terra novel with such incredible creative people has been without doubt the highlight of my professional career – I feel very lucky to have been a part of it.

ABOUT THE AUTHOR

Chris Wraight is the author of the Horus Heresy novels *Warhawk*, *Scars* and *The Path of Heaven*, the Primarchs novels *Leman Russ: The Great Wolf* and *Jaghatai Khan: Warhawk of Chogoris*, the novellas *Brotherhood of the Storm*, *Wolf King* and *Valdor: Birth of the Imperium*, and the audio drama *The Sigillite*. For Warhammer 40,000 he has written the Space Wolves books *Blood of Asaheim*, *Stormcaller* and *The Helwinter Gate*, as well as the Vaults of Terra trilogy, *The Lords of Silence* and many more. Additionally, he has many Warhammer novels to his name, and the Warhammer Crime novel *Bloodlines*. Chris lives and works in Bradford-on-Avon, in south-west England.

YOUR
NEXT READ

AVENGING SON
by Guy Haley

As the Indomitus Crusade spreads out across the galaxy, one battlefleet must face a dread Slaughter Host of Chaos. Their success or failure may define the very future of the crusade – and the Imperium.